David Zeisberger, Eugene Frederick Bliss

Diary of David Zeisberger

A Moravian Missionary Among the Indians of Ohio: Volume I

David Zeisberger, Eugene Frederick Bliss

Diary of David Zeisberger
A Moravian Missionary Among the Indians of Ohio: Volume I

ISBN/EAN: 9783337016951

Printed in Europe, USA, Canada, Australia, Japan

Cover: Foto ©Raphael Reischuk / pixelio.de

More available books at **www.hansebooks.com**

storical and Philosophical
Society of Ohio.

— — —

Zeisberger's Diary,
1781-1798.

NEW SERIES—VOL. II.

DAVID ZEISBERGER

A MORAVIAN MISSIONARY

AMONG THE INDIANS OF OHIO

TRANSLATED FROM THE ORIGINAL GERMAN MANUSCRIPT
AND EDITED

BY

EUGENE F. BLISS

VOLUME I

CINCINNATI
ROBERT CLARKE & CO
FOR THE HISTORICAL AND PHILOSOPHICAL SOCIETY OF OHIO
1885

PREFACE.

The chief object of publishing Zeisberger's Diary is of course the furtherance of the study of American history, and certainly the work will be found to contain much in regard to the relations existing between the English and Indians in the fifteen years preceding the cession of the Western Posts to the United States in 1796. If I am not mistaken, however, the work will be equally interesting from a psychological point of view. The action of white men upon Indians, Christians upon heathen, the civilized upon savages, can well be studied in these pages. Here and there also can be observed the reaction of the Indian upon the white.

My ambition as translator has been simply to render the German manuscript as nearly like the original as the differing idioms of the German and the English would permit. Where Zeisberger has left a sentence without logical conclusion, I have done likewise, nor have I thought it needful to call the reader's attention to the fact; in the same way, if he has repeated a word, generally I have done the same. My failure, however, has been in reproducing the easy and lucid style of the original.

The German word which I have rendered brethren, in the original includes both sexes, and in my translation it will sometimes occur with sisters in apposition; it seemed better thus to use the word than to depart too far from the text. It should perhaps be said that where *brothers* is used without qualification, the word refers usually to the missionaries, or to the whole body of clergy of the Moravian Church. All words or phrases marked with parentheses, thus ( ), are my explanations or interpolations, Zeisberger's parenthetical expressions being otherwise denoted.

The collects, or verses from hymns, often given after the Scripture-verse or text, have seldom been translated literally, but in

(v)

preference I have selected corresponding verses from the Moravian hymn-book now in use, or from the earlier editions of 1832, and a few from the English edition of " Daily Words" for 1785.

In conclusion, I have to thank many friends for advice and suggestions and the loan of books. To several gentleman, who were perfect strangers to me, I am indebted for information about various matters, acknowledgment of which is made in the proper places.

Above all I must express my gratitude to the Right Reverend Edmund de Schweinitz, Bishop of the Moravian Church at Bethlehem, Pa. His "Life and Times of David Zeisberger" has been my guide in the whole course of· my labor; it is a book which leaves nothing to be desired in the ground it goes over, and its Geographical Glossary has been invaluable to me. My brief sketch of Zeisberger's life, given in the introduction, is almost entirely taken from this book. I have to thank Bishop de Schweinitz also for the loan of parallel manuscripts, for personal advice and assistance, and for many letters.   E. F. B.

Cincinnati, May 20, 1885.

INTRODUCTION.

I. The Manuscript.

The "Zeisberger Manuscript," as it has commonly been called, was presented to the Historical and Philosophical Society of Ohio, probably in 1854, by Judge Ebenezer Lane.[1] January 10th of that year he lectured before the Young Men's Mercantile Library Association of Cincinnati, and the records of that Association show that at the same time there was presented to them by the

[1] "Ebenezer Lane was born at Northampton, Massachusetts, September 17th, 1793. He studied at Leicester, and at the age of fourteen entered Harvard College, graduating with high honors in 1811. He then entered the office of Judge Matthew Griswold at Lyme, Connecticut, where he studied law, and was admitted to practice in 1814. In September of that year he located at Norwich and practiced there and (in) other small places, until his removal to Ohio in 1817. In 1818 Mr. Lane married Frances Ann, daughter of Governor Roger Griswold, of Connecticut. The same year he located at Elyria. In 1819 he removed to Norwalk, and was almost immediately chosen Prosecuting Attorney for Huron County. In 1824 Mr. Lane was chosen Judge of the Court of Common Pleas of the Second Judicial Circuit. Six years later he was chosen Judge of the Supreme Court, occupying a seat upon the bench of that Court until his resignation in February, 1845. In 1842 he changed his residence to Sandusky. Judge Lane was a remarkable man. He was a diligent student, not only of the law, but of history and science. His opinions have given him a national reputation. He died of cancer in the throat at Sandusky, June 12th, 1866." Alfred T. Goodman in Western Reserve Hist. Soc. Hist. and Arch. Tracts, No. 2, p. 5.

(vii)

Gnadenhütten Monument Association, through the Hon.
Jacob Blickensderfer, another manuscript of Zeisberger's,
a Delaware translation of liturgies and hymns.

The following inscription is written on the first page of
the manuscript:

> The Diary of David Zeisberger,
>   A Moravian Missionary,
>   whose last 60 years
>   were devoted ·
>   to preaching
>   To the Indians at Gnadenhütten,
>   Ohio.
>   His Biography may be found
>   in Loskiel, Heckewelder, etc.

The journal commences while on the journey from
Gnadenhütten to Upper Sandusky, a few days after he
and his companions were forced from their mission station.
The last entries are 1797.   He died, 1808, and lies interred
at the Moravian burial-place, in Tuscarawas County.

The members of the Moravian Society have placed this
volume at my disposal, and in their name I deposit it in
the Archives of the Historical Society of Ohio.

E. LANE.

The trifling error of expression in the sixth line, and the
mistake of using 1797 for 1798 will be noted.

The manuscript makes a stout volume of eight hundred
and sixty-nine pages, each page being nine inches by six
and one-half nearly.   Generally, the writing is easily read,
the chief difficulty arising from interlineations and marginal notes.   A few pages give trouble from the fading of
the ink, and others from its spreading, evidently from
dampness.   Only one page has suffered essential loss,

and, fortunately, this could be supplied from the Bethlehem MSS.[1]

From the Bethlehem manuscripts I have seen, it is my
impression that a copy of this Diary was not sent to Bethlehem, but merely extracts from it, and that this might be
called Zeisberger's private journal.   There are frequently
expressions of hope and fear, and pious ejaculations, which
I do not remember to have seen in the parallel Bethlehem
manuscripts.

The first thirty pages of this Diary—the first twenty-
eight in this translation—as far as Oct. 25, 1781, were published in German in the Deutsche Pioneer of Cincinnati
(November, '73–April, '74), but with many inaccuracies
and omissions.

II.   ZEISBERGER.

DAVID ZEISBERGER was born at the little village of Zauch-
tenthal, in the eastern part of Moravia, on Good Friday,
April 11th, 1721.   His father and mother, David and
Rosina Zeisberger, when young David was five years old,
fled their native country and went to Saxony, urged to this
flight by the desire for freedom in their worship of God.
Here for a few years they remained at Herrnhut, upon an
estate of Count Zinzendorf, so well known in the history
of the Moravian church, but in the year 1736 they emigrated to America and established themselves in Georgia,
in Oglethorpe's new colony, with other Moravians, to
whom had been given a tract of five hundred acres upon
the Ogeechee River.   Their son, however, was left in
school at Herrnhut, but soon he was taken to Holland to
a Moravian colony near Utrecht.   He was now fifteen
years old, and found the rigid discipline of the place too

---

[1] See Vol. I., p. 285.

severe; besides, he was falsely accused of theft. With a
companion of his own age he ran away, and landed in
England, having no wish to leave the church, but simply
to escape what were to him the persecutions of the Holland colony. In London he made the acquaintance of
General Oglethorpe, enlisted his sympathy, and by him
was aided to reach Georgia. Before he sailed he con-
scientiously wrote to Heckewelder, a clergyman among
the Utrecht Moravians, the father of John Heckewelder,
so often to be mentioned in this Diary, and set forth to
him the reasons for his conduct.

Zeisberger could have found no better place of appren-
ticeship for his future life of Indian missionary than in
the infant colony of Georgia. Probably his early years in
Europe had not been years of luxury, but his life in the
Georgia wilderness strengthened his feeling of self-re-
liance, a quality of which he certainly had shown no
lack when he fled to England. The life of a pioneer gave
vigor to his body, while his mind and heart were kindly
influenced by his intimacy with Peter Boehler, the German clergyman, by whom John Wesley was converted.

In the year 1740 Zeisberger was one of the little company of eleven persons who formed a settlement in Northampton County, Pa., at the "Forks of the Delaware,"
having been driven from Georgia by a threatened invasion
of Spaniards from Florida. Nor could the exiles long remain here, but the next year they found an abiding-place
at Bethlehem, which has ever since remained the centre of
Moravian influence in this country. Zeisberger was now
twenty years old, fond of out-door sports, strong and
active. He was attached to his mode of life and to the
country, and was filled with sorrow when he was chosen
as one of those who were to return to Europe. Bishop

Nitschmann noticed his despondency and inquired its cause. To him Zeisberger confessed: "I long to be truly converted to God, and to serve him in this country." Both these longings were satisfied, and his visit to Europe was delayed for seven years.

In the year 1744 Zeisberger became a member of a class of young men formed in Bethlehem to study Indian languages, under the instruction of Christopher Pyrlaeus, and early the next year he set out for the Mohawk country to perfect himself in the Mohawk language. With him was the celebrated Frederick Post. They were regarded by the English colonial government as spies in the French interest, arrested, and thrown into prison in Albany. They were shamefully treated, but released after imprisonment of nearly two months. Not at all discouraged by this unfortunate beginning, Zeisberger was ready to make another attempt to reach the Indian country. His companion was Schebosh, so often to be mentioned in this Diary, and the two were the assistants of Bishop Spangenberg. Late in May they left Bethlehem, passed a week in what is now Berks County, Pa., preaching the Gospel to the Indians, and about the middle of June, after a weary journey through the wilderness, reached Onondaga, the capital of the Iroquois Confederacy.[1] The Moravians accomplished their object in this journey, and obtained permission from the Iroquois to begin an Indian mission at Wyoming. Zeisberger's life thus far may be regarded as an education for his future vocation. The stern discipline of his boyhood, his hardy, but self-reliant life in Oglethorpe's colony, his persecution by the civil authorities, and this last journey to the lakes of Western

---

[1] Here Zeisberger was adopted into the tribe of the Onondagas, receiving the name, Ganousseracheri, or, On the Pumpkin.

New York, taught him to what he must look forward and how to bear his trials.

From 1745 to 1750 Zeisberger was employed in several ways. He kept up his study of Indian languages; with Mack he explored the River Susquehanna in a region where the Indians were perishing from hunger and pestilence; he served as interpreter to John de Watteville in his visitation of the Lehigh Valley, and was ordained by him to the ministry in February, 1749; he was sent to Shamokin, near Sunbury, in Northumberland Co., Pa., a post of difficulty and danger, where the Iroquois combined the vices of civilization and of barbarism; from this place he was summoned to a conference, and as a result of this was sent as interpreter for Cammerhoff upon a mission to Onondaga, again to make arrangements for a mission among the Iroquois. They found the Indians in no condition for receiving an embassy, and to pass the time until the Onondaga council should become sober, they resolved to visit the Senecas. Cammerhoff was seized with violent fever, the Senecas were as dissolute and drunken as the Indians they had left behind them in Onondaga, and Zeisberger had occasion to make use of all his powers of body and mind. Upon their return to Onondaga they got permission from the Council for two Moravians to live among the Iroquois. They went back to Bethlehem, after an absence of over three months, having travelled in all upwards of sixteen hundred miles.

In the year 1750, Zeisberger and Nathaniel Seidel were commissioned to visit Europe in order to report to the mother-church the condition and hopes of the Indian mission. They sailed Sept. 2d, met with tremendous gales in their voyage, and landed in England after a passage of seventy-eight days. Zeisberger was in Europe six months,

passing much of the time in Herrnhut, in the society of
Count Zinzendorf, by whom he was appointed perpetual
missionary among the Indians. In June, 1751, he and
Seidel sailed for New York, where they arrived late in
September, and four days later he was in Bethlehem.
The rest of this year and half of the next, Zeisberger was
busy in many places preaching the Gospel to the Indians,
especially in the Susquehanna Valley.

In July, 1752, Zeisberger again visited Onondaga, one
of the two Moravians who, in accordance with permission
given at his last visit, were to reside with the Iroquois.
He had already been adopted among them, and now he
took up his abode with them, studied their ways of life
and manner of thought, their superstitions, their conduct
of war, their methods of speech, and hereby acquired a
knowledge of Indian character which in after years were
to be invaluable to him. Several times he returned to
Bethlehem, but at last, in June, 1755, the mission among
the Iroquois had to be given up, owing to the difficulties
between the English and the French. Now began all the
horrors of Indian border warfare. Villages were plundered
and burnt, men were scalped, women and children carried
away in captivity. In vain the missionaries tried to
pursue an even way. Among the colonists they were accused of having a secret understanding with the French,
and in a time of great excitement the distinction between Indians and Indians was lost. On the other hand,
the savages often regarded the converted Indians as
whites. The awful massacre upon the Mahony occurred
November 24, 1755, where ten persons perished at the
hands of French Indians. Zeisberger came near losing
his life there. He was on his way to the Mahony settlement, just crossing the river, when he heard cries of dis-

tress; he turned back barely in time to save his life, rode at once to Bethlehem, where he announced the dreadful news at three o'clock in the morning of the 25th. So great was the disturbance caused by war that no attempt was made for the next six years to preach the Gospel to the Western Indians; the Moravians had to be content with keeping up their missions in the east. In this service Zeisberger was for the greater part of this time employed. Twice as messenger of the Mission Board he visited North Carolina, once he went to New England and for several months labored at Pachgatgoch, near the present town of Kent, in Connecticut. He was also interpreter for the government in treaties with Indians. The most quiet time in his whole life was the fifteen months he passed at Litiz, Pa., as superintendent of the brethren's house there. In the intervals of this active life he was at work upon an Iroquois grammar and an Iroquois-German dictionary.

Peace was made between France and England, Nov. 3, 1762, and the latter country became undisputed owner of vast inland territories of the present United States. The Moravians were at once ready to continue their efforts for the conversion and civilization of the Indians. Before the conclusion of peace in 1762, Zeisberger made two journeys to Wyoming, once as envoy from Sir Wm. Johnson to the chief of the Delaware nation. He came back the second time, because of a petition to the Mission Board that a teacher should be sent to Wyoming to live there permanently. The following year he repeated his visit to the valley of the Susquehanna, and was for a short time missionary at the Indian town, Machiwihilusing, on the Susquehanna, opposite Sugar Run, but the massacres in the Pontiac War induced the Mission Board to recall him

to Bethlehem.   Now for two years, 1763, 1764, was a time
of trial for the Moravian Church.   The whites could not
distinguish between the converted and the savage Indians.
Not only were the western missions abandoned, but those in
the east were almost blotted out.   One hundred and twenty-
five Christian Indians were carried away to Philadelphia,
and after shameful treatment from the hands of the mob
were finally quartered at Province Island.   Zeisberger and
Grube were with them, but from the illness of the latter
Zeisberger's burdens were doubled.   He must serve not
only as minister, but as superintendent.   His energy was
equal to the task, and he saw that his flock was provided
for, to use a frequent expression of his own, " outwardly
and inwardly."

In the year 1765, the survivors of this little band journeyed to the proposed station at Machiwihilusing   Led by
Zeisberger, early in April, they set out.   There were no
roads, and the journey was of inconceivable hardship.
They could hardly go five miles a day, they suffered from
hunger, they encountered the danger of a forest in flames.
This journey of perhaps one hundred and thirty miles
used up five weeks.   The town was laid out and built.
Some opposition on the part of the Iroquois was overcome by the eloquence of Zeisberger, who spoke as an
Iroquois by adoption.   The town doubled its population
in less than two years.   There was a great religious
awakening among the Indians.   " Upon wild Indians in
particular descended the power of the Holy Ghost.   They
came from far and near, and represented different nations." [1]

In the year 1767 Zeisberger visited the Delaware Indians
living at Goschgoschünk on the Alleghany River, by

[1] De Schweinitz' Life of Zeisberger, p. 312.

whom he was kindly received, and who sent by him to the
Mission Board a request that a resident missionary should
be sent them. Toward the middle of June of the following year, Zeisberger and Sensemann appeared among them,
accompanied by three families of Christian Indians. What
especial troubles they met with from lack of food, from
illness, from the hostility of Indian sorcerers, from the
hatred of backsliders, need not here be recounted. They
are the same which are to be found in the Diary herewith
published. The most distinguished convert was Glikkikan,
though he was not baptized till over a year later. In the
year 1770 this mission was transferred to the Beaver River,
on the banks of which Friedensstadt was founded. In
July Zeisberger was formally adopted among the Monsey
tribe of the Delawares, an event to which reference is several times made in the Diary. In October Jungmann became a member of the mission. Zeisberger, accompanied
by several Indian brethren, made his first visit to Ohio
in March, 1771, going to the capital of the Delawares,
Gekelemukpechünk, in the present Oxford Township,
Tuscarawas Co., where he was the guest of the chief,
Netawatwes. The next year we find Zeisberger at Bethlehem urging upon the church authorities there the importance of establishing a mission in Ohio. They agreed
with him, and gave him John Heckewelder as assistant.
With five families of Indians the two Brothers founded
Schönbrunn,[1] or Thuppekünk, as Zeisberger is apt to call
the place. This mission flourished, and soon Gnadenhütten
was founded. Chapels were erected in both places. Comfortable houses were built, orchards planted, fields cultivated.
Nor was the Gospel preached to the Delawares alone. The
Shawanese, Nanticokes, Mohicans, and two or three

---

[1] See note p. 2.

other Indian tribes were represented; even the Cherokees contributed one member, who was a captive among the Delawares. Zeisberger continued his literary labors also, and Easter morning, 1774, his Delaware version of the Litany for that day was used.

There now followed two years of great prosperity, in spite of troubles from "Lord Dunmore's War," and consequent hostilities among the Indians. The chiefs of the Delawares furthered the progress of the Gospel, doubtless with a view on the part of some of them of worldly prosperity. The Christian Indians were held to be a constituent part of the Delaware nation. Schönbrunn grew into a thriving village, with well cultivated fields, the Indians becoming husbandmen as well as hunters. Gnadenhütten was hardly less prosperous. Lichtenau was founded not far from the Delaware town of Goschachgünk [Coshocton], in order that the word of God might be immediately preached to the Indians.[1] One chief, however, was adverse,

---

[1] The reader may be interested by the Rev. Mr. Jones' account of what he saw at Schönbrunn in Feb., 1773. He was a Baptist minister from Freehold, N. J., and at the time of his visit to the Moravian town he was making a missionary tour on the "west side of the Ohio River." This extract is taken from Sabin's Reprint of 1865, p. 92: "These Indians moved here about August, 1772, and have used such frugality that they have built neat log houses to dwell in and a good house for divine worship, about twenty-two feet by eighteen, well seated, and a good floor and chimney. Their conduct in time of worship is praiseworthy. Their minister, the Reverend David Siezberger, seems an honest man, a native of Moravia, nor has he been many years in this country. He has been successful among these poor heathens, condescending for their sake to endure hardship. While I was present he used no form of prayer, which was not pleasing to me, therefore asked him if that was their uniform practice. He replied that sometimes prayer was used. Their worship began and ended with singing a hymn in the Indian language, which was performed melodiously.

B

Capt. Pipe, who, with a number of his followers, left the
men of his tribe and returned to the country about Lake
Erie. He alleged that he feared the hostility of the
Iroquois would be excited by their new plans, not that he
was opposed to the preaching of the Gospel.

After this period of prosperity came the troubles of the
War of the Revolution. The Christian Indians were
placed between the rival influences of Detroit and of Ft.
Pitt, the English and her rebellious colonists. These were
times of alternate hope and despair, made worse by discord among the missionaries themselves. Zeisberger for
the greater part of the time, 1776–1781, was at the new
town, Lichtenau, whither all the converts were at one
time called. They returned, however, to the Tuscarawas
in the year 1779, and New Schönbrunn[1] was built, and

In the evening they met again for worship, but their minister, inad-
vertently or by design, spoke in the German language, so that by me
nothing was understood. Mr. Siezberger told me that near eighty
families belong to their two towns, and there were two ministers
besides himself. I was informed that one of them, whose name is
Youngmann, is a person of good abilities. In the evening informed
Mr. Siezberger that it would gratify me to preach to his Indians. He
replied with some appearance of indifference that an opportunity
might be had in the morning. 'Tis probable he was a little afraid to
countenance me, lest some disciples might be made, than which nothing was more foreign from my intention. Or his reservedness may be
ascribed to his natural disposition." The next morning, however, Mr.
Jones' journal shows us that his desire to preach to our Indians was
gratified. The curious reader will be entertained by Mr. Jones' re-
marks upon following pages about Easter and Christmas and his horror that " Mr. Siezberger " should teach the Indians the observance of
these days.

[1] In the note given on p. 2, Vol. 1, by inadvertence the situation of
Schönbrunn, and not of New Schönbrunn, was given. The latter place
was on the other side of the river, somewhat over a mile from Old
Schönbrunn.

Salem the next year. The Delawares were generally well disposed to the Americans, and for this reason the English urged the other Indians to a campaign against them. The means of getting accurate information were few, and war often hung upon the chances of a false rumor. How much the Delawares were influenced for neutrality by the intervention of the missionaries cannot be overestimated. At one time the opportune arrival of Heckewelder with news of Burgoyne's surrender turned the scales for peace.

Zeisberger had passed a part of the summer of 1775 in Bethlehem, and now, 1781, he returned there, making his last visit "to the church." He was at this time sixty years old, and had been too busily occupied with the affairs of the missions to think much of promoting his own personal comfort and happiness. No thought of marriage seems to have come to him, and now, in taking a wife, he rather yielded to the advice of his friends than to his own impulse. He married, June 4th, 1781, Susan Lecron, at Litiz, Pa. She had been a Lutheran in religion, but in Litiz had joined the Moravian church. She had reached the age of thirty-five, her husband's junior by twenty-five years. She is now and then mentioned in this Diary, and generally called "Sister Susanna." She could not but have known to what a life of privation, self-sacrifice, and danger she was giving herself, and is deserving of the greater praise that she could have been deceived by no intensity of passion.[1] A week after their marriage, Zeis-

---

[1] Hildreth, in his Contributions to the History of the North-west, p. 115, says: "Whom he (Zeisberger) married does not appear, but females who could venture so far in the wilderness among hostile savages must have possessed the spirit of a Deborah, and the courage of a Miriam." After the death of her husband, 1808, Mrs. Zeisberger remained nearly a year in Goshen, Ohio, when she retired to Bethlehem and died there in Sept., 1824, eighty years old.

berger and his wife set out upon their westward journey, and reached Schönbrunn in the middle of July. At this time the Diary which follows begins.

We are met at the outset by the question how far the English and their Indian allies were right in their assertion that the missionaries gave notice to the American settlers of intended inroads. It will be noticed that at the very beginning of the Diary, Zeisberger expresses his satfaction that his diaries, letters, and other writings fell into the flames and not into strange hands.[1] Why this satisfaction if they contained nothing offensive to English eyes? In Vol. II of the Olden Times, p. 396, is published a letter of Daniel Brodhead, then in command of the Western Department, in which he speaks of letters he has received, that have convinced him the enemy is approaching in force. At the end we find " P. S. the letters received are from the Rev. Mr. Zeisberger, an honest man and faithful correspondent, but his name must remain a secret, lest his usefulness may be destroyed." It is hard to conceive how a humane man could have done less than give notice of these savage incursions, but the fact seems indisputable.

There is no need to set forth here the captivity, the tedious journeyings, the troubles of war and of famine, the founding of the various Indian towns, and the petty details of daily life of the next seventeen years—these will all be found in the following pages.

The last entry in the Diary, is made Sunday, May 27, 1798, in the town of Fairfield, on the Thames. Zeisberger remained there until the middle of August, when accompanied by thirty-three brethren, he departed for the Tus-

---

[1] pp. 1, 2.

carawas Valley, where he founded Goshen, within the
limits of the present Goshen Township. Here he passed
the remaining ten years of his life. Though an old man he
kept up as far as possible his former manner of life. He
performed the daily duties of a missionary. Besides, he
was a teacher of Indian languages to young missionaries,
and continued his labors in translating various religious
works into the Indian language. It is sad to record that
his latter years were made weary by the vices of the Indians about him. He longed for rest. He died Nov. 17,
1808, in his eighty-eighth year.

Zeisberger's literary labors have occasionally been mentioned in this brief sketch of his life. Besides his volu-
minous diaries, of which this herewith published is but
one, he wrote a history of the Indians, which, unfortun-
ately, has never been printed ; lexicons and grammars
of the Onondaga language ; a dictionary in German and
Delaware, various glossaries and vocabularies, and many
translations into Delaware of hymn-books, liturgies, and
sermons. Brinton[1] calls him, " The principal authority on
the Delaware language, whose long and devoted labors
may be accepted as fixing the standard of the tongue."
De Schweinitz devotes Chap. XLVII of his Life of Zeisberger to an enumeration of his published and manuscript
works.

In person his biographer[2] tells us that Zeisberger was
of small ·stature, but well porportioned ; that his face,
though marked by the exposure of hardy life, was cheerful and pleasing; that his dress was plain and neat. He
had acquired the Indian habit of taciturnity, and when he

---

[1] Brinton's The Lenâpé and their Legends, p. 76.
[2] Bishop de Schweinitz in his Life of Zeisberger, p. 680.

spoke his address was often such as he might have given
at an Indian council.

His life seems a sad one. It was his fate to labor among
a hopeless race. In his last years he could see no lasting
monument of his long labor. Even the Indian converts
immediately about him were a cause of sorrow to him.
Nor could the prospect have seemed better at any of the
time covered by this Diary. The greater praise then to
his activity, his cheerfulness, his patience with his erring
converts, his contempt of danger, his forethought for
others, and his perfect sacrifice of self.

III. ZEISBERGER'S FELLOW-LABORERS.

At the time this Diary begins there were in the Muskingum Valley six missionaries, Zeisberger, Heckewelder,
Sensemann, Edwards, Jung, and Jungmann. Jung and
Edwards were unmarried, the others had their wives with
them, and two of them had young children. Jungmann
was the oldest, being sixty-one years old, Zeisberger one
year his junior, and Edwards four, Heckewelder and
Jung were of the same age, each thirty-eight, and Sensemann two years younger. In spite of the hardships of
their missionary life, with the exception of Sensemann,
they all lived to extreme old age, Edwards dying at the
age of seventy-seven, Heckewelder in his eightieth year,
and the others several years older.

As regards the character of his associates, Zeisberger
gives us so little color that I find it hard to form any defin-
ite idea of these self-sacrificing men, or to distinguish one
from another, except in the case of Heckewelder, where
many other lights are thrown upon the picture than are
afforded by this Diary. For the very reason, however, that

so much is said of him, I have felt less need of saying any thing.

GOTTLOB SENSEMANN was born Oct. 9, 1745. His father, Joachim Sensemann, had also been a missionary among the Indians, and his mother, Anna Catharine, was one of the victims of the massacre on the Mahony, in November, 1755, when his father narrowly escaped sharing the same fate. Gottlob had been Zeisberger's companion in several journeys among the Indians of the Susquehanna Valley and in Western New York. With Zeisberger he went also to Goschgoschünk, 1768, and shared with him the perils and the success of his sojourn there. In the year 1780 he came to the Muskingum, and was stationed at Schönbrunn. From this place, with the others, he was carried away to the Sandusky, 1781. While our Indians were settled on Clinton River in Michigan, Sensemann returned to Bethlehem, but rejoined the mission at New Salem, Ohio, having been away from May 17, 1785, to Nov. 9th, 1790. During the rest of the time included in this Diary, he remained with the Indian church, though, in the year 1793, he made a journey to Niagara upon business of the mission. He often preached to the whites in Canada, who were settled near Fairfield, and had to decline their proposition of being elected to the Assembly. At Fairfield also he died, Jan. 4th, 1800, while yet in the prime of life. He was often the school-master of the station, and perhaps the progress of the pupils was as much due to the excellence of their teacher as to their own application, though Zeisberger attributes it to the latter. He was eloquent in speech and energetic in action.

JOHN GEORGE JUNGMANN came to America with his father in the year 1731, being then a boy of eleven years. At Oley, Berks Co., Pa., where his parents settled, he be-

came a convert to the Moravians against the opposition of
his family. 1745 he married the widow of Gottlob Büttner,
who had died in February of the same year. He served
the church in many ways and in various places, until in
the year 1770 he became Zeisberger's assistant on the
Beaver, and when Zeisberger went to Ohio to] found the
first Christian-Indian town, Jungmann was left in charge
of this mission. The next year we find him at Schönbrunn, and there he remained for five years, until during
the trouble of 1777 it was thought best, especially on his
wife's account, that he should return to Bethlehem. In
the year 1781 he and his wife were Zeisberger's companions, when the latter, after his marriage, went back to his
Indian mission. He shared all the sorrows and hardships
of the Indian church recorded in this Diary up to the
time of his final return "to the church." This occurred
May 17, 1785, Sensemann going to Bethlehem at the same
time. Jungmann was now sixty-five years old, and was
retired from active service. He lived in Bethlehem the
remaining eleven years of his life, and died July 17, 1808,
being over eighty-eight years old.

MICHAEL JUNG was sent to the Muskingum mission
just a year before this Diary begins. He was born Jan.
5, 1743, came to America, 1751, with his parents, who set-
tled in Maine, where he became a Moravian. He went to
Bethlehem, 1767, and stayed there till he went to the
Muskingum. He was absent from the mission nearly
four years, leaving it when it was at New Gnadenhütten,
Michigan, and rejoining it when it was already on the way
to Pettquotting. He then remained with the Christian
Indians until the year 1813, when, after the battle of the
Thames, Fairfield was overrun by the Americans, and our
Indians fled from fear. Jung then retired to Litiz, quite

broken by his many labors, and in Litiz he died, near the end of the year 1826.

WILLIAM EDWARDS was by birth an Englishman, a native of Wiltshire, where he was born April 24, 1724. Bred in the English church, he became a convert of the Moravians when he was twenty-five years old, and soon afterwards emigrated to America. He became Zeisberger's associate at Lichtenau, in November, 1776, and he remained with him during all the course of this Diary. With Hecke-welder he led in 1798 a portion of the Fairfield congrega-tion back to the valley of the Muskingum, whither Zeis-berger followed in less than three months. Here at the town they founded, Goshen, he passed the rest of his life. Though worn out by the infirmities of age, he was unwilling to return to the States; he preferred to die among his dear Indians. Like Zeisberger himself, if he had given much to the Indians, he had also received much in return. He died Oct. 8, 1801.

JOHN GOTTLIEB ERNESTUS HECKEWELDER was born at Bed-ford, England, March 12, 1743. His father was a German exile, and we have already had occasion to mention him in speaking of Zeisberger's life in Holland. In the year 1754 the family came to America, father, mother, and four children. In 1758 he was apprenticed to a cedar-cooper, with whom he remained four years, and then became Fred-erick Christian Post's companion in his second visit to the Muskingum in the year 1762. He was Zeisberger's assistant in the Susquehauna Valley in 1765, and to him for a time was given charge of the Machiwihilusing mission. During the following nineteen years he was much of the time a fellow-laborer with Zeisberger. Heckewelder was the founder of Salem, on the Tuscarawas, and in the chapel there, July 4, 1780, he married Sara Ohneberg, the ven-

erable Adam Grube officiating, probably the first wedding
of a white couple within the limits of the present State of
Ohio. He was with the Indian church during all the
early troubles recorded in this Diary, but finally, owing to
the illness of his wife when upon the Cuyahoga, he returned to the church at Bethlehem, Oct. 9, 1786.[1] Hence-
forward he was not immediately connected with our mission, though he made it two or three visits, being employed in other duties, especially as agent of the Society
for Propagating the Gospel among the Heathen and as
one of the Peace Commissioners sent to treat with the Indians. In the year 1798, however, he came to Fairfield,
on the Thames, to assist in conducting a portion of the
the church to Goshen, staying there only nine days. In
the valley of the Muskingum he labored until 1810, when
he went home to the church, being now nearly seventy
years old, and having well earned repose. He died Jan.
31, 1823.

Heckewelder is the best known of all the Moravian
missionaries who labored among the American Indians.
For this he is much indebted to his books, but also to his
social qualities, which made him more a man of the world
than were his coadjutors.[2] He had the strength of character to resist the insidious tendencies of the solitary life
among savages, the effects of which can be seen in Edwards
and Zeisberger.

IV. THE INDIANS.[3]

At the time of the beginning of this Diary the present

---

[1] See pp. 299, 300.

[2] " In disposition," says Hildreth, " he was like the Apostle John ;
while his companion, Zeisberger, partook of the spirit of St. Paul."

[3] See Lossing's Pictorial Description of Ohio, p. 129; Mag. of Western History, Vol. 1, p. 41, and Bouquet's Expedition, passim.

State of Ohio was divided among the Indians in somewhat
this manner: In the eastern part in the Valley of the Muskingum were the Delawares; along the upper Ohio, the
Mingoes, emigrant Iroquois; in the Scioto Valley, the
Shawanese; along the two Miamis, the tribes from which
the rivers are named, the Miamis, or Twightwees, as Zeisberger always calls them; the Wyandots, or Hurons, were
in the north-western part of the State; near them were the
Tawas, or Ottawas; a few Chippewas wandered along the
shores of Lake Erie. In Michigan were the Chippewas
and Potawatomies. In the present Ontario, opposite
Detroit, was the principal seat of the Wyandots, or Hurons,
and when the mission was at Fairfield, on the Thames,
many Mohawks visited the Christian Indians.

A surprising circumstance is the frequent communica-
tion and commingling of all these tribes. The presence of
the white man seems often to have made them forget or
postpone ancient hostilities, and for a time to have united
men who were hardly more capable of lasting union than
the wild beasts of their forests.

The greater part of the Indian church were Delawares
of the Monsey tribe, a tribe into which Zeisberger had
been adopted. Schönbrunn was inhabited at first by Delaware Indians, Gnadenhütten by Mohicans, originally from
New England, but after the return from Lichtenau and
the founding of Salem and New Schönbrunn (1780), this
distinction of tribes seems in great part to have been lost.
The Nanticokes, who had been adopted by the Delawares,
and were originally from the coast of Maryland, are mentioned occasionally, but generally as a patronymic. During
the St. Clair and Wayne campaigns Southern tribes are
spoken of, and there were already one or two converts
from the Cherokees, captured in war by the Delawares,

and then adopted. Most singular is the presence of the Carib woman, a brief account of whom is given in Vol. II., p. 522.

V. The Mission.

It was the rule in the Indian mission towns that none but Indians should live there, except, of course, the missionaries and their families. There are a few apparent exceptions to this regulation; Schebosh, for instance, but he was an assistant missionary, and had married an Indian woman; Richard Conner had for a wife a woman who had been for many years a captive among the Shawanese; John Leeth was taken captive when a boy of seventeen, and his wife, when less than two years old.

The inhabitants of an Indian mission-village were divided into *choirs* or *classes*, and each choir had its festival-day, as will often be observed in the Diary. " The younger girls, the elder girls, the sisters, the married brethren and sisters, the widows, widowers, the younger boys, the elder boys, the single brethren, all constituted distinct choirs, and had their stated and special meetings." [1] In the census which Zeisberger gives at the end of nearly every year this division into classes can be noticed.

Laborers and *Teachers* are the modest names by which the missionaries speak of themselves.

Assistants, or Helpers, were selected from the converts. Their duties were to visit the brethren from house to house, to comfort and care for the sick, to settle quarrels among the brethren, between husband and wife or among members of the same family, and generally to see that the

---

[1] Sketches of Moravian Life and Character, p. 41.

ordinances for civil and religious life were observed.[1] These assistants were chosen from either sex, and their fields of labor correspondingly divided. Frequently husband and wife were selected.

An *Assistants' Conference* was occasionally called, when matters of importance in discipline or in regard to Indian tribes were brought before them, or when, as a body, they needed admonition.

Chapel-servants, or simply servants, were those to whose charge the meeting-house was given. There were also *Servants* whose duty it was to provide for the entertainment of visitors.

New People are those whose attention has been aroused. If they show themselves earnest they become *candidates for baptism*, and later are *baptized*. If their conduct continues satisfactory they are *candidates for the communion*, and are admitted as *lookers-on* at the Lord's supper, and finally themselves become *communicants*.

Such expressions as the *home-church*, the *church of the baptized*, etc., explain themselves.

A *Service* was held every day, usually early in the morning, but, at times, for convenience, in the evening, when a short discourse was frequently delivered, suggested by the Scripture-verse or text of the day.

The *Lord's Supper* was generally administered once a month, and also upon certain festival-days. Notice of it was given the Sunday preceding; between this time and the day of the celebration the brethren were addressed and admonished, as each one had need, by the missionaries and their wives, and by the assistants, and especially was this done on the two days preceding the

---

[1] See Vol. 1., pp. 171, 230; Vol. II., pp. 236, 342.

Saturday when it was administered. The next day, Sunday, the communion liturgy was read.

There has been prepared by the Moravian church, since 1731, a selection of short passages from the Old and the New Testaments for each day in the year, and each passage is followed by a stanza of a hymn. These selections from the Old Testament are in this translation called *Scripture-verses*, and those from the New Testament, *Texts;* the stanza which follows is called the *Collect*.

In matters of great difficulty the Saviour's advice was asked by *lot*. This is somewhat obscurely mentioned by Zeisberger. By consulting the references given under " Lot," in the Index, it will be seen that resort to it was not made infrequently.

Love-feasts were held upon many occasions; birthdays, anniversaries of baptisms, the arrival or departure of brethren, were thus observed. Besides there were love-feasts for all the inhabitants, and contributions were made to defray the expenses of these simple feasts.

The missionaries sent to Bethlehem their Diary, and in return received the *Bethlehem Diary*, also in manuscript. They had sent them also the proceedings of the synods and the reports of the meetings of the *U. A. C.*, or Unity Elders' Conference—the initial A from the German for elder. By this interchange of journals and reports the whole church, home and mission, on both sides of the sea, was knit together into a great whole.

VI. The Calendar.

Besides the ordinary festivals of the Christian church, there were others to which the Moravians gave especial prominence.

The *New Year* was entered upon with a service, which began shortly before midnight.

The Sunday following Epiphany was the *Children's Sunday.*

On Maundy-Thursday was the ceremony of the *Washing-of-feet.*

April 3 (1785) is mentioned as a memorial day for those *baptized* during the year.

May 4th. *Unmarried Sisters'* day.

Aug. 13th was carefully observed in remembrance of what happened at Herrnhut on that day, in the year 1727 : "The baptism of the spirit upon the infant church by occasion of the celebration of the Lord's supper." This day was regarded as the spiritual birthday of the renewed church, and the community was moved to work for Christ generally and to carry the Gospel to distant heathen lands.

Aug. 29th. *Unmarried Brothers'* day.

Aug. 31st. *Widows'* and *Widowers'* day.

Sept. 7th. Festival for the *Married.*

Sept. 29th. The *Angels* were praised.

Nov. 13th. The church calls to mind that the Lord Jesus is the Chief *Shepherd* and *Head* of the church.

VII. Subsequent History of the Mission.

When Zeisberger, in the year 1798, returned to the Valley of the Muskingum, he brought with him to Goshen' only a part of the Indian congregation. This station steadily declined, and was at last abandoned, the few remaining Indians finally settling in New Westfield, Kansas.

The Fairfield mission was broken up by the war of 1812. Three years later it was revived under the name of New

Fairfield, not far from old Fairfield, but on the other side of the Thames, where it still exists.

There is also a Cherokee mission at New Spring Place, Indian Territory.

The total number of converts in all these three stations was only two hundred and seventy-six in the year 1883, hardly half the number to be found, 1781, in the Valley of the Muskingum.

DIARY

OF

THE INDIAN CHURCH

IN THE

WESTERN PART OF NORTH AMERICA, 1781.

CHAPTER I.

REMOVAL FROM THE MUSKINGUM—ACROSS THE WILDERNESS TO UPPER
SANDUSKY—JOURNEY TO DETROIT—RETURN TO SANDUSKY.

Beloved Brethren : We begin now in God's name again
to give you news of our health and conduct and of what
has happened to us, for a great change has occurred with
us. You[1] will also have wondered how it happens that
you have heard nothing more from us since we are come
to New Shore.[2] We were not in condition, and it was
not and is not yet in our power to give you news of us,
nor yet do we know whether and when this will come to
your hands, but will write it in hope of better times. Our
diaries from the Muskingum and letters which lay ready
to be sent off with Br. Schebosh,[3] as likewise all other

---

[1] It is hard to decide where in this diary Zeisberger makes his record
day by day, certainly by September 18th. Possibly he made notes
from time to time, and put them into their present form upon his return from Detroit in November.

[2] I have been unable to find what place this is.

[3] John Joseph Schebosh, now sixty years old, was born of Quaker
parents, his real name being Joseph Bull. He was named Schebosh
by the Indians and John at his baptism in 1742. He married an Indian woman. He was devoted to the Indian missions. Neither the
death of his son, the first victim in the massacre at Gnadenhütten in
1782, nor his own captivity, could quench his zeal. He will often be
mentioned in this diary. Under September 5, 1788, Zeisberger gives
his biography.

writings, were lost, and· yet were we glad that they fell
into the flames and not into strange hands. We have,
since our captivity, on the 3d of September until now,
when we are come back from Detroit [November 22] had
no pen in our hands, and have strictly kept our promise;
therefore we can give you no very exact diary, but will only
mention the most noteworthy things which remain in our
memory.

Brothers D. Zeisberger¹ and Jungmann, with their wives,
came to Schönbrunn July 15th [the Scripture-verse being:
Yet will I gather others to him beside those that are
gathered unto him], with a large company of Indian
brethren, who already had waited for them in Pittsburg
over two weeks, on which account the brethren at home
were already much distressed, and had consequently sent
messengers to the Fort to learn where they remained, who
met us more than a day's journey from Schönbrunn. On
all sides there was great joy over the arrival of this company. Thereupon the laborers from the three places came
together in Schönbrunn, rejoiced with one another, and
thanked the Saviour for all the goodness he had done us in
time, and read Br. Reichel's² letter, which he had written
to them; whereupon we learned how we had to distribute
ourselves for the time, namely: Br. Jungmann and his
wife went with Br. Zeisberger and his wife to Schönbrunn
to live; Br. and Sister Sensemann to Gnadenhütten, and
Br. Edwards with them; Br. Mich. Jung, on the contrary,
with Br. Heckewelder and his wife, to Salem.³ Br. David,
with his wife, visited thereupon in Gnadenhütten and

¹ Zeisberger returning from his last visit to Bethlehem, Pa. During
his absence he married Miss Susan Lecron, at Litiz, Pa. He was now
sixty years of age, and Sister Susanna, as she is called in this diary,
thirty-seven.

² John Frederick Reichel, Bishop, from Germany, now passing two
years in the United States on an official visit.

³ Schönbrunn, settled in 1772, Gnadenhütten 1772, and Salem 1780,
were all in the present Tuscarawas county, Ohio. Schönbrunn was
two miles south-east of New Philadelphia, Gnadenhütten near the
town at present so called, and Salem one and a half miles south-west
of Port Washington.

Salem, spoke everywhere to the brethren, and administered the Lord's Supper. The brethren from all these places were then in undisturbed quiet, knew and heard nothing about the hostile Indians, except that several times warriors went through our towns with prisoners and scalps, who, however, gave us no trouble, but were glad if we gave them any thing to eat. One of the prisoners, an old but vigorous man, offered Br. David $200 in cash if he would work him his freedom, which, however, was for us an impossibility. The Indian church already, in April, had been visited by warriors, who wished to carry them away, but by the entreaties of our Indians had been prevailed on not to use force. We had, however, to expect that they would not put off carrying out their plan, but would execute it.

Somewhere about August 13th we heard that a strong party of warriors was on the march for our towns, on which account also we could not have the Lord's Supper, although we had prepared ourselves therefor, for on their account we could no longer be easy, they having already begun to assemble in Salem and Gnadenhütten. Up to the 16th and 17th about 300 warriors had assembled. Their chief men were, first, an English captain (Elliot), with several others, among whom were also Frenchmen, the Wyandot Half-King (Pomoacan), from Sandusky, with his warriors, Pipe,[1] with the Delawares, some Shawanese, Chippewas, and Tawas. The Half-King, in his usual pretended friendly way, sent out messengers announcing his approach, and let it be told our Indians they should not be afraid, not the least harm would happen to them, for on this account was he himself come to protect us, so that no one should do us wrong; that he had something to say to us, and we should therefore let him know at which of our three places this should occur. Since Salem was but a new place, and they could not support the warriors from want of corn, Gnadenhütten was appointed for them, for

---

[1] Captain Pipe, whose Indian name was Kogiesch quanoheel, a Delaware captain of the Wolf (Monsey) tribe.

we could come also from Schönbrunn to the help of our brethren, so that it might not go too hard with them. We thought also that they would not remain long with us, for the whites who were with them, informed us that they had a great undertaking in hand, either against Wiliink (Wheeling), McIntosh (Beaver, Pa.), or Pittsburg, or against all three places, but they said this only to make us easy. We entertained the Eng. captain and his company[1] the best we could, and showed them all kindness so far as lay in our power; they likewise behaved in a friendly way toward us, but had secret guile, and we could trust them not in the least.

Aug. 20. After the warriors had taken quarters, and at the west end of Gnadenhütten had put up huts and tents, Pomoacan, the Wyandot Half-King, spoke to us and to our Indians as follows: My cousins, ye believing Indians, in Gnadenhütten, Schönbrunn, and Salem, I am no little troubled about you, for I see you live in a dangerous place. Two powerful and mighty spirits or gods are standing and opening wide their jaws toward each other to swallow, and between the two angry spirits, who thus open their jaws, are you placed; you are in danger, from one or from the other, or even from both, of being bruised and mangled by their teeth; therefore it is not advisable for you to remain here longer, but bethink ye to keep alive your wives, and children and young people, for here must you all die. Therefore I take you by the hand, raise you up and settle you there where I dwell, or at least near by me, where you will be safe and will live in quiet. Make not here your plantations and settlements, but arise and come with me, take with you also your teachers, and hold there, whither you shall come, your worship of God forever, as has been your wont. Ye will at once find food there, and will suffer no want, for on this account am I come to say this to you, and to bring you to safety [whereupon he gave a string of wampum]. The Scripture-verse of the day read: Take coun-

---

[1] McCormick is here written in the margin.

sel together, and it shall come to nought; speak the word, and it shall not stand: for God is with us; for here is Immanuel.

Is God for me, what is it—That man can do for me?

This word of the Lord gave us consolation and hope that all would go well. Brs. David (Zeisberger) and Heckewelder had come together from their respective stations to Gnadenhütten, where we with the national assistants considered about this, and on the 21st answered the Half-King, as follows:

"Uncle, and you, Captains of the Delawares and Monseys, who are our friends and one nation with us, we have heard your words in which you say to us that we are placed between two evil, mighty spirits who open their jaws toward each other, and you admonish us that we should think of our young and old people, our wives and children, seek to keep them alive, and about them we are most concerned. Your words and exhortations are therefore pleasant for us to hear, and we wish to do as you have pointed out to us, bear the same in mind, and consider them, and we wish, Uncle, even before next spring to send you an answer, thereupon can you depend."

We gave this answer without a string of wampum, since this should follow after a time, and it appeared to us as if the Half-King were content therewith: we believed also that he would have been satisfied with it, had not the English captain concealed himself behind Pipe and other Delawares, and urged them on to excite Pomoacan to carry on the matter farther with us. Then we soon heard that our given answer was not satisfactory to them. On the 25th again, Pomoacan made an address to our Indian brethren in Gnadenhütten that our answer was not yet enough, we had appointed too remote a time, and he wished to have something in his hands to show the nations from whom we had orders about this, that he had really made negotiations with us. Br. David went therefore again to Gnadenhütten, and, Aug. 27 [when the beautiful fitting Scripture-verse was: Thou shalt know that I am the Lord: for they shall not be ashamed that wait for me.

My times are in thy hand—I'll always trust in thee], we gave to them through a string of wampum the following answer, and said to them that it was impossible for us to do for them what they required. We could not by any means bring our wives and children into such need that they must suffer hunger and perish, while hitherto they had had plenty, and in nothing felt any want. We bade them leave us time enough to harvest our fields, so that we, with our wives and children, might have something to live on; for we saw that we put ourselves in extreme need and misery, if so blindly, without consideration, we went away from our towns where we had enough to live upon, into the bush, where there was nothing to be found; they should at least leave us time enough to prepare for our departure. The Half-King seemed to be well content with the answer, for he said he had now in his hands something from us, namely a string of wampum, which he could show to the nations, and by which they could see that we were willing to gratify their wishes. Thus the matter passed by, and we hoped always that the Saviour would bring about our release. We prayed earnestly day and night to him that he would help us also out of this need, and not suffer that his Indian church should come to harm and be dispersed, since once they had tasted of his blood. Opinions and thoughts over the matter among our Indian brethren were also various, as likewise among the assistants. Some thought we should at once arise and go with the warriors without considering the results therefrom. On the contrary, others were against this, and said they would rather die on the spot, for in the bush must they all perish. It was impossible to convince all of the propriety of what we held it best to do. Herein, also, we had ourselves taught[1] by the Saviour what we should do, and he let us know that we should do nothing farther than we had done, and that the answer we had given was enough. We wished to do nothing to the harm of our churches in the land. We were also unwilling to take

---

[1] This consulting the Saviour by lot will often be mentioned.

upon our necks the charge of having brought our Indian
brethren into such need as they afterward felt, since they
would have reproached us with being guilty therein because we had acceded thereto. We wished rather to let
it come to the worst, so that we might be without fault.
Meanwhile, the daily services were held, and we ceased
not to exhort the brethren, to encourage them, to comfort
them, and to point out to them the Saviour. Among other
things, especially were they reminded that the Saviour had
intrusted to them his word of atonement, which they
should look upon as a great treasure, and which should
be their daily food. If they became indifferent thereto,
and should be disobedient to God's word, he would again
take it away from them. In Gnadenhütten there were
many disorders among our people; not only of late, but
already for some time, many had begun to take up again
the old heathenish customs and usages, and when they
were reminded of this and talked to, not only did they
not suffer this, but they waxed wicked and stubborn, and
especially by these circumstances bad people made the occasion useful, since the town was full of warriors and
rough, wild men, who became the worse the longer they
were there, who at first indeed were quiet and modest,
but afterward began to dance, to play, and to carry out
their own devices. Yes, it went so far that some wicked
people spoke and gave us to understand that while there
was now war, they could prescribe us rules, and that our remaining and our getting through, in short, our life and
maintenance, depended upon them, and that we had reason to be silent, and they would let us do only what they
wished. In Schönbrunn and Salem the brethren were
reasonably quiet, and if warriors visited them now and
then, yet there was little disturbance. From both places
we had to give them provisions, slaughter swine and cattle for them, so long as they were there, and this we did
still cheerfully, if only they had left us longer in peace.
Meanwhile, parties of warriors made excursions, and they
brought some captives to Gnadenhütten, and the place
became a theatre of war. [Elliott's camp displayed the

English flag, which at last the Wyandots took possession
of, and it was then thrown into the fire.] In this matter
they were themselves not without fear of being fallen
upon, and upon every side they sent out spies.

Aug. 30. Sister Anna Sensemann was delivered of a
son, who was baptized into Jesus' death in Schönbrunn,
Sept. 1st, by the name, Christian David. Eight days before she had been brought here from Gnadenhütten, since
there, on account of the warriors, who committed many
excesses, it was very unquiet, and here it was yet tolerable,
for the warriors came here in no great number. Meanwhile, we well saw that our hard circumstances were not
over; we had tokens enough that the worst was still before us. We could do nothing, however, but give ourselves up to the will of the Saviour as he should find it
good and permit. We might think, as we would, upon
ways and means to escape our calamity; on every side we
were fastened in, and there was no outcome to be seen.
We had indeed reason to believe that the Half-King and the
captains had already as good as given up their purpose to
use force against us; it was said even that they would withdraw and give us time first to harvest our fields so that
we could prepare for our departure. But the English,
who were with them, left nothing undone to excite the
captains and warriors, and to spur them on to drive us
out by force. In addition, the warriors found out that
our Indians were not of one mind, for had they been so,
had they held together, and sustained one another, the
warriors would have accomplished nothing; but there were
faithless, wretched men among us, who gave them information, and proposed schemes to them for reaching their
ends. They gave them plainly to understand, that if they
would only take us white brethren prisoners away with
them, then the Indians would all follow them. To our
pain and mortification, we had to hear and see this on the
part of our own people, and be silent about it, at least, for
the time. We had also to see harlotry openly carried on,
and could not prevent it. Since we afterward found out
every thing in detail, I will here introduce what we learned

from trustworthy sources. The captains had a plan to kill us whites, and when this was not thought enough, to kill the assistants also.[1]

Sept. 1. We had a message that all the white brethren from Schönbrunn and Salem, with the assistants, should come to Gnadenhütten. Br. David, with some helpers, went there from the first place, but left Br. Jungmann with the other two brethren there, and Br. Heckewelder came from Salem, where he left his wife and Br. Mich. Jung. We soon heard here all sorts of rumors of what awaited us, for there were among the warriors some people who rather wished us well than ill, and who said to us what they heard. Thus we awaited our fate in great perplexity and tribulation until, Sept. 3d, it came to an outbreak. The warrior folk became steadily more wanton, and gave free play to their wildness. We felt the power of darkness, as if the air were filled with evil spirits. When they first came here they were starving, and were glad to get something to eat, and herein we let them suffer no want. After they were sated and become wanton, each one acted after the bent of his own wildness. They shot dead our cattle and swine, although we refused them nothing, and if they demanded swine or cattle for slaughter, gave them. This they did not only from hunger, but from caprice, for they left the swine lying dead round about in such numbers that the place stunk with them; still the daily services were held as usually.

On the above-named day, Sept. 3d, the Half-King and the warrior captains again beset us, among whom the Delawares made themselves the most forward, and urged upon us we should once more plainly declare ourselves, whether we would give in to their wish and at once go with them or not. We answered them briefly that we stood by what

---

[1] Here ends this note abruptly, but the Bethlehem manuscript says that the warriors imparted their plan to a leading chief, who advised them against it, seeing therein no advantage for them. They then held another council, with the same result; but there the chief spoke more plainly, threatening vengeance if the missionaries were harmed, and thus their schemes came to naught.

we had already answered them, and we could give them no
other answer. Then we heard a murmur among our Indians that they had heard we white brethren should be
taken captive, but in all this we were quite comforted,
though we could not say in contradiction it might not happen. In the afternoon we went together a little back of
the town, where a Monsey captain spoke with Br. David,
and asked him whether he had heard what he had said in
Schönbrunn to Br. Luke, and what Br. David thought
about it, for he would like to know at once his opinion
about it. This captain had already some days before in
Schönbrunn said to Luke, since probably he knew what
was going on, that the Monsey nation had adopted Br.
David, and looked upon him as their own flesh and blood,
he knew that this was accomplished in his nation. If Br.
David would accede to this and appeal to it, he would
bring it about that no one should lay hand upon him;
they, the Monseys, wished to own him as one of their
nation, but he would have to go with them where they
dwelt. This was also well considered,[1] for thus they
thought to get our Monsey brethren, who were the greater
part.

The Monsey captain probably meant well; his people,
the warriors, had also before all others shown themselves
good to us, and had done us no harm ; they often showed
their discontent with the conduct of the Wyandots towards
us, and said they had experience how they had done with
them, and so would they do with us if we went with them.
But Br. David had purposely taken little notice of the
proposition, for he saw that it only had to do with his own
person, and perhaps with Br. Jungmann, who lived with
him, but that the other brethren in Gnadenhütten and
Salem would be shut out; therefore he gave no positive
answer, but did not altogether decline the proposition, and
would have been glad of further information about it.

But while he was still speaking with him, there came three
Wyandots to us, laid hands on Brs. David, Heckewelder,

---

[1] This word is conjectured.

and Sensemann, led them away captive, and brought them first to the Delaware camp, and yelled out over us the Death Hallow. They stripped us and took away all our clothes, hastily loaded their guns, for in all this they were not without fear they would find opposition on the part of our Indians. While this was going on, the whole swarm of the other warriors rushed into the Brothers' house and plundered it, each man taking what he could lay hands on and snatching it away. Some of our young men had stationed themselves in front of the house-door with tomahawks, and would not let them in, but they had to give way to the stronger party.

They showed no desire to touch Br. Edwards, who was in the house, for they were too much set on plundering, and each wished to have the most booty. Finally he went out to the house and to Br. John Martin,[1] where an Englishman met him and brought him into camp to us, where he saw we were all yet living, for as they were bringing us into camp, he heard several muskets fired one after the other, from which he concluded that already we were all dead, and so it would have happened, for they had it in mind, as we afterwards heard, unless a higher hand had ruled over us. The Delaware chiefs and captains, while this was going on, had drawn aside, probably from fear it might not come out well: but they were the same who had allowed themselves to be used to take us prisoners, for the Wyandots would not have dared to do it. Our Scripture-verse was wonderful, it read: Though thou wast angry with me, thine anger is turned away and thou comfortedst me; and the day after it was: God will come and save you.

After they had stripped us we were brought into the Englishman's tent, who, indeed, as he gave out, wished to show us compassion, and said it had not been intended that we should be thus treated, although there were express orders from the commandant in Detroit to bring us away by force, could it not be done by gentler means.

---

[1] National assistant, afterward killed in the massacre at Gnadenhütten, in 1782.

And this was the first mention that they relied upon the
governor in Detroit, hitherto they had not said so, and yet
they had no such orders. But we well knew that he was
the originator and prime mover of the whole business.
He brought it about, however, with the Indians, that they
gave us back some old clothes, so that we were not quite
naked, and Br. David got an old night-gown to put on,
which had belonged to Sister Sensemann; after this we
were brought into the huts of the Wyandots for safe-
keeping, but we were not put in bonds, as were the other
captives. We had now neither blanket nor any thing else
to lie upon save the bare ground, unless our Indian brethren
had lent us some blankets.

After this one party of warriors went to Salem, another
to Schönbrunn. To the first place went thirty warriors;
they arrived there in the night, took prisoners Br. Michael
Jung and Br. Heckewelder and his wife with her child,
led them out of the house and placed them in the street:
they plundered the house, took away with them every
thing they fancied, likewise also Br. Michael Jung, and
came early in the night to Gnadenhütten crying the
Death Hallow. Sister Heckewelder, however, with her
child, got leave to remain till the next day, whom the Indian brethren then brought in. In Schönbrunn, to which
place only two Wyandots with a couple of women came,
they took prisoners Br. Jungmann and Sisters Susanna
(Zeisberger) and Sensemann: then they said many warriors would come afterward and undo them; that they
should put themselves in their hands, so that they might
remain alive, they would bring them to Gnadenhütten
with all their things, which they would pack up, and all
of which they would give back to them. The sisters
helped them pack until they saw that the beds were cut
open and the feathers thrown about the street, and found
themselves deceived in their intentions, just as had also
happened in Gnadenhütten and Salem. But some Indian brethren, as well in Salem as here, who were more
kindly disposed, took away secretly from the hands of

the warriors some of our things and gave them to us afterward, so that we again got some little.

The Indian brethren stood quite amazed, wept aloud, and knew not what to do; some wished to make defense, others deemed this inadvisable and prevented them. They plundered not only our things, but also what belonged to the church, as for instance, the love-feast and the communion utensils were all taken away, and they brought the brethren together with their plunder in a canoe to Gnadenhütten. Sister Anna Sensemann, who had been delivered of a child only three days before, had to go by night and in the mist, so that it would have been no wonder had mother and child perished, but the Saviour, to whom all is possible, let not the least harm happen either to her or to her child.

They were brought into Gnadenhütten early before daylight, likewise with the Death Hallow. From our camp we saw their reception, and how we felt thereby can not be described. But when it became day we got leave to see them, and then we bade one another welcome in our captivity, and comforted one another, and each party had hearty compassion upon the other. What in these sad circumstances was comforting to us and cheered us up, was the fact that the sisters were so resigned and cheerful and bore all with patience. Br. Jungmann and the sisters were set free when it was day, but remained awhile by Br. Schebosh and his wife, for in the brethren's house every thing was wasted and scattered, and there we visited them also often and they us. We saw the warriors going about in our clothes and making a display, while we had nothing upon our bodies, except perhaps some old rags, and though we were again and again promised we should have some of our clothes again, yet this did not happen, for those who had them were unwilling to give them up.

Our Indian brethren who came to visit us in camp bought some trifles from the warriors, and gave them to us again. Out of our own linen, of which they had been robbed, the sisters had to make shirts for them. Also we had nothing to eat except what our Indian brethren and the warriors gave us. Among these there were many not at all content with our treatment, in particular among the Delawares and Monseys, and they said that certainly they never would have gone upon this expedition, had they known it was aimed at us. Many of them came immediately after we were taken prisoners and gave us their hands and showed their compassion. After the five brethren, David, Edwards, Heckewelder, Sensemann, and Michael Jung had been captives three days in the Wyandot camp, and the captains saw very well that so long as they held us fast, nothing would be done about our departure, and if they wished to have all our Indians with them, they must first let us go, they let us go, and this happened Sept. 6th. Before this, however, a singular thing occurred the second day after we were made captive. An Indian woman, who had come with the warriors, and had nothing further to do with us, had seen with the others how we fared, and said to an Indian sister she could not forget how we had been handled; she could not sleep the whole night on this account, and this gave her much to think about. She took Capt. Pipe's horse, the best in the whole company, and hurried away to Pittsburg. This was straightway made known, and she was followed and overtaken, but she got away again and brought news of our captivity to the Fort. The warriors were angry at this, and laid the blame upon us and our Indians, and gave out we had sent letters by her to the Fort, and called upon the Americans to free us from their hands, and since this woman was a friend of our Isaac Glikkikan,[1] to whom besides they were very hostile, they seized the occasion to wreak their vengeance on him, saying he had sent her. On this account they sent a war party to Salem, brought him bound to Gnadenhütten, yelled out over him the Death Hallow, and there was great uproar among the warriors, and it was a common saying among them that he ought to be tomahawked. The Delawares, who were the

---

[1] A famous Monsey warrior and orator, baptized in 1771, a frequent companion of Zeisberger, and devoted to the interests of the Indian missions, killed at Gnadenhütten in March, 1782.

movers of this, would have struck him dead if the Half-King had not interfered and warded them off. They examined him, beset him with many reproaches and threats, but then let him go. It is worthy of note that this Indian brother, who formerly had been a captain of warriors and counsellor of chiefs and a very prominent man among the Indians, as soon as he came to the Lord, had to suffer ignominy and persecutions almost to the end for the Saviour's sake.

After they had again set us free, that we might be among our Indian brethren, they, at the same time, ordered us to encourage our Indian brethren to make ready for departure, and promised us also that upon the journey we should always be with our Indian brethren, and that they, the warriors, would always encamp behind us, in order that, if we were attacked, they might fight for us. The first was agreeable to us for this reason, that the warriors might not overpower our sisters and separate us from them, which we had reason enough to fear.

It is also to be observed that the Half-King, as soon as he came, made quite another speech than he had made to us at Lichtenau,[1] in August, 1777, when he established with us, as it were, a bond of friendship, and had declared us, white brethren, his fathers, of which he now made no mention, but named us cousins, and our Indian brethren likewise. We made ready for departure, ordering our Indian brethren from Schönbrunn to come hither. Thus, on the 8th we made a beginning, and we white brethren went by water, and in the evening got to Salem, where we waited two days for our brethren until they all followed, and since we could be alone there and in quiet, we white brethren strengthened ourselves with the body and blood of our Saviour in the holy sacrament, and realized our Scripture-verse of to-day (Is. lxv. 13, 14), of which, in our present circumstances, we stood in pressing need. The Saviour comforted us also in our trouble, and let his friendly face shine over us.

On the 9th, the sermon was upon the Scripture-verse of

---

[1] A Christian Indian town below Coshocton, O., abandoned by the converts in 1780.

the day, and the little son of Brother Abel and Sister
Johanette, born on the 8d Inst., in the night when we
were captured, was baptized into the death of Jesus by the
name of Jonas. We were thankful to the Saviour, and it
did us much good that we could be among our people, for
it is a hellish life to be among murderers and robbers, and
in their power.

On the 10th, early service was from the Scripture-verse:
Behold, the Lord's hand is not shortened, etc. Especially
at this time we had beautiful, comforting, and hopeful
Scripture-verses, only we wished them to be at once fulfilled; thus we should have been helped at once, yet we
must still content ourselves in hope and faith.

Now came also 100 warriors here from Gnadenhütten,
and the wild life went on with them as before. Our
brethren from Schönbrunn and Salem came together, and
encamped by the river. One can easily imagine that all
the brethren were bewildered, and, as it were, in a dream,
so that they could hardly trust their senses. We knew
now that the warriors would not be got rid of until we
should be forth with them, and they had left our towns
to go to war; there was thus nothing better than to go.

On the 11th, we broke up, and thus turned our backs
upon our homesteads and places where we had enjoyed so
much that was good and blessed from the hands of the
Saviour, and where he had really been among us and with
us. Before us we saw indeed nothing wherein to rejoice,
yes, we could imagine nothing but need, misery, and danger, and otherwise had we nothing to look forward to.
We must possess our souls in patience, and go where certainly we were unwilling to go, for we saw no other result from our actions, but we went towards more misery
and hardship; thus also were our Indian brethren minded,
but they must go against their will. Could they have
acted according to their inclination, or secretly brought it
about, many of them would have got away, and we should
have been scattered, but it could not be, for the warriors
not only did not let us whites out of their sight, but also
not the Indian brethren either, and had such careful over-

sight of us that none could escape; they dared not remain behind, they must go forth with us. Indeed, many of our Indian brethren, who always had an inclination for the savages, and were of the opinion we should all go off to them, felt now they had nothing good to expect, and began to perceive that they had wished and sought what was bad for themselves, and began now to regret it, but too late.

We came on September 14th, to Goschachgünk (Coshocton), encamping on the Walhonding, from which place we broke up on the 16th, and followed up this creek northwards. Many brethren went by land, others again by water, just as they could get on. It was a good thing for our sisters with the children that they could go by water, for by land it would have been hard indeed for them to travel such a long, bad, unbroken way, for here one must expect no such travelled and good road as to Pittsburg. We continued our services, and had them nearly every evening, even if the brethren could not always come together for night-quarters, and the warriors, who went with us, commonly lay a little distance from us.

The 18th. Since it rained very hard last night, and the creek was swollen, we had to go, huts and all, away from the creek to higher ground, since we were in danger of overflow. Two canoes with their whole lading were swept away by the stream, and the brethren lost all they had, for they sank to the bottom. This concerned us too, for in one of the canoes were many of our things, all of which we lost, and before this not much was left us. A child, two years old, that died yesterday, was here buried.

On the 19th, came to us the Half-King with the Wyandots from Salem, where they had passed the time, and not only completed the plundering of our towns, but had also seized upon the things which our brethren had buried or hidden in the woods, as many as they could find.

The same day a war-party came back from the settlements with two prisoners, from whom we heard that when the news of our being taken captives reached Pittsburg, they wished at first to follow after us and rescue us from

2

the hands of the warriors, but that they afterwards gave this up. This had hitherto been our greatest concern, that if this should happen, we should be placed in the greatest danger, and with our Indian brethren come between two fires, for the first thing would have been to kill us whites. This also the Saviour turned away from us.

On the 20th, a sister was brought to bed with a daughter, and on the 21st was another born. Then a couple of our young people took away from the Wyandots one of our horses, which they had in their hands, together with the saddle. And two of our sisters took away from them a great kettle which they had appropriated and which belonged to us, and gave it to us again.

After we had lain quiet four days, on account of high water, on the 21st we moved on, and encamped on the 22d at the second fork of this creek where is an old Indian town, and a pleasant beautiful country, as indeed all along the creek so far as we have come.

The 23d we lay still. Pomoacan came to us with his council, and told us to hasten on to Sandusky and to leave behind those who could not go forward. Some women were brought in prisoners. The Monseys, who had thus far journeyed with us, left us and went home another way. Their captain spoke with us, and showed his displeasure at the conduct of the Wyandots towards us.

On the 24th we went on both by land and by water. The creek forked here, and our Indians wished to go up the greatest and strongest fork, which would have been easier and better to follow, but the Wyandots would not permit it, and we must go up the other creek, which was hard to follow it was so small.

We passed Memekasink, an old Indian town, and several such places, and they who went by land always took their course as nearly as possible towards those who went by water, so that we might have night-quarters together. Brs. Michael Jung and Edwards, who went by water with the Indians, found wild honey. On the 26th we came to Gokhosing, the last old town on this creek, and here our

journeying by water ended, and from there on we had to go
by land. We had hard work to come so far with canoes,
for very often they had to be dragged over shallow places.
Here we stayed till the 28th, until all those came up who
were behind. The Wyandots, who always urged us on,
had to borrow some horses for us, since we had not
enough and our Indian brethren found all theirs needful
for their own use. The Delawares left us here also,
and went home, as the Shawanese had already done the
day before yesterday, and the Wyandots, whose number
was now small, remained with us. With these then we
set out, and while our Indian brethren were still packing
up when we went away, we white brethren were quite
alone with the warriors, who drove us on like cattle,
without having the least compassion for the children and
sisters, for they left them no time to give the children
drink once. Besides the way was very bad, for it went
through a swamp and many marshes, where at times the
horses stuck fast. Susanna (Zeisberger's wife) fell twice
in quick succession from her horse, and it was a wonder
she got off with little harm. Some Indian brethren hurried after us with all their might, as they could easily conjecture that the Wyandots would hurry us on, heels over
head: they overtook us as we were about to get our night-
quarters ready, which we should have done near the warriors, had not our brethren come, but now we encamped
somewhat away from them.

The 29th. Early before we broke up, several brethren
came to us, which gave us joy, and took us again out of
the hands of the warriors, and told them, if they were in
such haste, they could go their way and would not find
it necessary to wait for us. We came at noon of the 30th
through the swamp at the head of the Scioto, and into a
country altogether different from what we had thus far
passed through. We went through a perfect plain, where
there is nothing but grass, which is so high and long that
on horseback a man can hardly see over it, only here and
there a little clump of bushes. No hill, much less a moun-

tain, in sight, but all the land is flat, consequently it is a
moist soil, since the rain-water can not run off.

Oct. 1. At noon we came to the Sandusky, where we
encamped. Here the Wyandots left us and went on ten
miles towards their home, after they had abandoned us in
the wilderness, where there was no food to be found and
no game to hunt, and many among our brethren had
nothing left to eat, but lived only upon what those, who
yet had something, divided with them. In the evening we
considered our beautiful Scripture-verse of to-day: My
people shall dwell in a peaceable habitation, etc., which we
applied to ourselves, and comforted us with its beautiful
promise.

On the 2d we went a couple of miles down the creek
and encamped on a height in the plain, in a little thicket,
near an old Wyandot town, on the creek. But the neighborhood did not please us, for upon the plain there is no
timber, and where there is wood and timber-land, it is
a perfect swamp and morass. But for the time being we
built our huts, until we could find a better place.

The 3d. Yesterday and to-day the brethren arrived,
who had remained behind. Pomoacan with his counsellors
visited us and made a speech to our Indians. He said he
was much rejoiced that we were now with them, and that
all who had the same color, were together, a thing they
had already long wished; we should now only look to him,
guide ourselves by him, and if the Virginians should
come, do as he would do. But about our holding our
religious services as we had been wont, which he had
always promised us in Gnadenhütten, he made not the
least mention, but now began to go on with his speech, and
summoned our Indians to fight. Further, he said we
should see the neighborhood and settle where it best pleased
us, as far as where the Sandusky falls into the lake, but if
it pleased us here in the old town, since there was good
pasturage, it was all the same to him. There yet stood in
the old town many houses which he offered for our use, if
we wished. But, in the first place, on account of wood, it
was hard for us, for none could be had far or near. Sec-

ondly, it was a pit of murdered men, where only a year
before many prisoners had been tortured to death and
burnt alive, evidences of which were plainly to be seen.
When we were still on the Muskingum, they had proposed
to us a place on Lake Erie, which they had destined for
us, and the Monseys would have been pleased if we had
gone there, but no one of our brethren was acquainted
with it. We considered together what to do, and resolved
rather to be quiet and not to give ourselves useless trouble,
for we and the brethren had nothing to live on.

Since we knew not what was best for us, and had the
choice, yet would be glad to know the Saviour's mind, we
took advice of him, and he let us know that the best
thing for us was to winter at Upper Sandusky, and
that was also our heart's desire.

4. After we had better examined the country around
us, and had passed a place[1] a mile up the creek, where
there was good timber for building, although it was
not beautiful to the sight, but there was none better to be
found, we began at once to build houses, and on the 7th
we moved to the place, only we had lack of sustenance,
and it would have been a much wished-for thing had
manna rained from heaven. Br. Schebosh, with his wife
and sister Rachel, arrived with their families, who had remained behind. Conner,[2] who stayed with his family in
the old town, and was about to go to Lower Sandusky,
came here and said to us that he had heard a rumor
among the Indians that we white brethren would be
brought to Detroit, which indeed we had already heard,

[1] In regard to the site of this place, see Butterfield's Crawford's
Campaign against Sandusky, pp. 162, 163, 180. Robert Clarke & Co.,
Cincinnati, 1873.

[2] Richard Conner, from Maryland, married a white girl, a captive
of the Shawanese. At the close of Dunmore's war they settled at
Pittsburg, but later came to Schönbrunn in search of their son, who
was still among the savages. Here, contrary to Moravian usage,
they were permitted to dwell and were "consistent and worthy members" of the church. When our Indians left New Gnadenhütten, on
Huron (Clinton) river in Michigan, Conner remained behind.

but taken little notice of, for besides, we were disposed that at least two of us should make a journey there as soon as we should have got our houses built and show ourselves to the governor there in person.

Oct. 10. Came many Delawares and Monseys to visit us from the neighborhood, but alas! almost none is willing to hear about the salvation of his soul, but they joke and laugh about it, when it is spoken of to them. News came in also that the Half-King's two sons, who between here and the Muskingum had gone away from us back to the settlements, had fallen in the war there, on which account in the Wyandot towns there was great lamenting, outcrying and weeping among men and women, and after this the Half-King always blamed us that we were the cause of the death of his sons, and he could not be persuaded to the contrary.

11. The brethren, who are all busy in building and have much to do, fenced in a place in the middle of the town and made it ready for holding our meetings, since at present, on account of our much labor, we could not think of building a house, and while the daily services were held in the evening, we made two fires in the midst, which served us in place of lights. We white brethren got our houses under roof. They were small and slightly built, but we were yet joyful that we could have a place to hide ourselves in from the cold this winter, so long as the dear Lord shall permit us to dwell in the same in peace and quiet, at least until the coming spring.

12. Came really all of our Indian brethren who had to remain behind in Gokhosing, from which place we went by land, so that we were now again all together. Two widows, however, had gone to their friends among the Shawanese, because they thought they could better live there. Since we white brethren had nothing more to eat, those brethren who yet had something, got together some Indian corn for us, many giving a handful, others somewhat more, according to their means, and thus something like a bushel and a half was collected for us. We sent word to Pomoacan that our brethren wanted to go to their

towns and harvest their maize, so that if he wished to send with them any of his people, they might make themselves ready. This we did because they always had a suspicion against us that we were still in correspondence with those in Pittsburg. At the evening meeting Br. Heckewelder baptized into Jesus' death a child born on the third of this month with the name Samuel.

13. A Frenchman from the Shawano towns came here to buy cattle; from the same place also came one of our Indians, who had heard much concerning us there, that the Shawanese were much displeased with the Delawares and Wyandots, that they had brought us away from our towns and placed us in such want, when we, where we used to be, not only would have had every thing in abundance, but could have given also to others who were in need; they had always comforted themselves with the thought, that if they suffered want, they could yet from us get or buy something, and we were the only hope of all the Indians, that we could keep them alive with wife and children, but now they had no more hope left; they, the Wyandots and Delawares, were thus the cause of ruin to so many Indians.

14. During the sermon from the text, Thou shalt love the Lord, thy God, with all thy heart and with all thy soul and with all thy mind, two children were baptized into Jesus' death. The first, the daughter of Br. Adam and Sister Sabina, born on the journey, Sept. 20th, by the name of Mary; the other, the daughter of Br. Adolph and Sister Susanna, born Sept. 21st, by the name of Martha. In the afternoon Wenginund came with Pipe's brother, who made known to us a message from Mr. McKee (English Indian agent) to the Delawares and Wyandots, which was as follows: "My children, your father over the lake has been much pleased at the news that you have brought in the believing Indians with their teachers, so that now all nations may be one and that the hinderances are out of the way; that the birds will no longer sing in the woods and tell you many lies. And now the Virginians will be in darkness and light will shine for them no more.

It is left to you where you shall be pleased to establish
them and where they can dwell. In a few days a boat is
expected for you from Detroit at the Miami (Maumee)
river with goods. You must all go there to receive them.
Your father over the lake requests also that Capt. Pipe
and Wenginund should bring to him the ministers with
some of the principal believing Indians, for he would like
to see them and talk with them, and he says: ' I know better how to talk with them than you do, for I know them ;
I can also better take care of them and entertain them than
you can, since I have means therefor.' " We answered him,
this was pleasant for us to hear; we would hold ourselves
ready so soon as they found it good. Moreover, we should
have gone to Detroit, even if we had not been asked. And
as we learned from him that the sisters were not summoned,
we said to him we should be forced to leave two brothers with them, for we could not leave them alone, and this
he did not oppose.

15. Many of our brethren went to the neighboring towns
to get corn, but it is enormously dear, and there is little to
be had, although it is just harvested, for the Indians did
not plant enough for themselves.

On the 17th Israel[1] came to visit us from the Shawanese.
In the spring, when Goschachgünk was destroyed, he, with
the other Delawares who remained behind, on their way
to Pittsburg, had been overpowered in Gnadenhütten, and
carried off there, where he had since been. He complained
to us of his outer and inner need, the unrest of his heart,
and wished to be again with us. He showed great sympathy with us white brethren in our tribulations, and we
had sympathy with him, for he loved us.

18. The assistant brethren considered together and settled, who of them should go with us to Detroit, who should
go with the brethren to the Muskingum to get corn, and
who of them should remain as guards, that the town might
not be quite deserted, all of which was regulated and es-

---

[1] Delaware chief of the Unalachtgos ('Turkey) tribe, converted at
Lichtenau, 1776, called Captain Johnny.

tablished. On the 19th Israel spoke again with us. After
he had again gone home and said that he was resolved to
make himself quite free, to give up his rank as chief and
to come back to us, for he was weary with his restless
heart, so to go about, and he believed it would be well with
him if he should again be with us. He wished only to go
home, to put his affairs in order, and yet during the winter
to come again, and this afterwards so happened. There
came also back to us two families, who over a year before,
had left the church, and through all sorts of circumstances,
relapsed into error. We now learned the real connection
of events and reason for our captivity from trustworthy
hands and who were the peculiar causes of our whole fate.
We had already heard something thereof in Gnadenhütten, but we reflected little upon it, because we were not
certain about it. What the occasion must have been and
what sort of reason was brought forward for such a plan,
all this is unknown to us. The Six Nations who have
woven the whole plot and have sought to bring about the
destruction of the Indian church, although they would not
themselves undertake to do it, in their usual crafty way
and manner, sent a messenger to the Chippewas and Ottawas, and made them a gift of the whole Indian church to
cook a broth of, which is an Indian war-term, and means,
"We give them to you to slay." The Chippewas and Ottawas declined this offer, saying they would not undertake
this, that they had no motives thereto. Hereupon the Six
Nations made the offer to the Wyandots in the same words,
and they undertook it. Now the Half-King said he did it
to rescue the believing Indians from ruin and to save their
lives. Probably he did it from political motives, thinking
that his nation, which was very weak, would thereby become strong, for he is hardly in condition to raise over a
hundred men, so very much has his people melted away in
the last war, and yet more in the present one, for as regards
the Wyandots over the lake, they are nothing to him, but
only those who live in Sandusky. This was the occasion
of his undertaking the expeditions against our towns, only
he wanted the consent and orders of the governor in Detroit,

and so soon as he had them, he set to work. He did
not imagine that he was able to do this alone, and therefore took to himself reinforcements. He took with him
all the Delawares and Monseys who live in Sandusky, and
first they went to the Shawanese, where they held a secret
council, but got only a few of them. The warriors did
not know, when they were marching from the Shawanese
to our towns, what the scheme was, except some of the
captains; and the two Englishmen, M(cKee) and E(lliot),[1]
who kept with the Shawanese, left nothing undone to encourage the Half-King and the captains. Capt. M. made
a great feast for the warriors, for which an ox was roasted
whole, and he bade them bring us away, and should it
cost us our lives, it was of no consequence; that they expected good success from this expedition, was to be seen
from this, that they sent men, namely, whites, who should
either buy our cattle from us, which they thought to do
very cheaply, or else otherwise get possession of them,
and steal them, but in this last plan they had no success.
The Wyandots, who hitherto had pretended to be friends

---

[1] "McKee was an Indian agent of the British government, a prisoner
released on parole, hurrying, in flagrant violation thereof, to Detroit,
in order to give all the information he had gathered while among the
Americans. Elliot, a trader, but secretly holding the commission of
a British captain, had been at Pittsburg as a spy."—De Schweinitz,
Life of Zeisberger, p. 462, in recounting events of 1778.

Matthew Elliot was by birth an Irishman. At the breaking out
of the Revolutionary war, he lived in Pennsylvania, and was a tory.
He was ever afterwards with the British, and held, as will be seen
later in this diary, large estates in Canada, and with him was asso-
ciated Alexander McKee.—Crawford's Campaign, Butterfield, pp. 176–
178.

So many and so just reproaches have been cast upon these two men
that I can not forbear giving a few words I have found in commenda-
tion of McKee. They occur in an extract from a letter written Jan.
17, 1799, quoted in "Sketches of the City of Detroit," p. 62, and are:
"The old, virtuous Col. McKee died at his seat on the river Thames,
the day before yesterday. His remains have been interred this afternoon with great pomp at the seat of his son, Tom, at Petitte Cote.
. . . Great Britain has lost a great support, the Indians a tender
parent, and the United States the most inveterate and unnatural
enemy."

[but this lasted only until they had a good chance to show us their treachery], would never have undertaken to do this, had they not been supported by the Delawares, and these two have carried out the thing, for the Monseys and the few Shawanese, who were indeed in the camp, after a fashion kept themselves aloof, and often absented themselves, giving it to be understood that they had no satis-. faction in the conduct towards us, and they showed their discontent with it. The Monseys, who had the most friends with us, for by far the greatest part of our church was Monseys, may well have thought on this occasion, to get their friends away from the church, and to control them, which may, perhaps, have induced them to take part in the plan. But since they afterwards failed in this, they were vexed at the whole expedition, which in some way also may have been the case with the Delawares, for many of them were much discontented after the affair was over. The Delawares—I mean, in particular, the Unamis— about whom the brethren had already concerned themselves, and taken much trouble to bring them to recognition of their salvation and of their Redeemer, to whom the gospel had already many years been preached—the Delawares, I say, had not received it, but always opposed it, and shown themselves enemies of the gospel. These let themselves be used as tools to break up the Indian church, for they had put themselves foremost in the matter, and taken upon them to accomplish it. This was from the very beginning, when the brethren came to the Ohio, their common saying: "This must have an end, that in the land of the Indians the gospel is preached, it must cease, and it would yet come to this." So long as we lived on the Muskingum, they used all sorts of devices to involve us with themselves, especially in their chief things and councils, for they thought hereby best to have access to our Indians, if they made something of them, and looked upon them as wise and intelligent men, and this they did under good pretense and excuse, in so subtle a way that they could not always be shaken off and withstood; hereby they sought to confound us little by little with themselves, and when they could not bring this about, they tried in another way to do us ill, to pervert our people in all sorts of ways, and to turn them away from the church, and this succeeded with some, though they were but few.

Many of their head-men and chiefs tried year after year to force themselves into the church under the finest pretenses and the best representations, which they made to us, what great advantages would accrue to us, how it would introduce the Indian church into the Indian country, and what strong increase it would get hereby, and all the time they were pretending to do so much good, they were plotting the ruin of the Indian church, which, besides, they could not altogether conceal, for when they could get at one of our weak people, they left nothing undone to lead him astray. Had their chiefs who worked so hard to get into the church succeeded in so doing, in a shorter or a longer time they would have become masters of it. They would have acted as chiefs of it, and have wished to lay down rules for us, and to assert their own authority. When at the outset we tried to be rid of them by good means, and this was of no use, we made several statements why it was not for them to dwell in the church, and when they saw that they could not attain their end, they became angry with us, and sought to harm us when they could. By all this I do not wish to deny that many of them were our good friends, and convinced we taught the Indians nothing but good.

20. We moved again into houses, which we had built us for the winter, after passing fully two months in huts and tents in the bush, where we had all sorts of night-quarters and lodges. Thanks be to the good Saviour who gave us health and generally good and dry weather, for both were necessary and precious to us.

21. In the Assistants' Conference we resolved to take no share in the presents given to the warriors, which they were to receive on the Miami (Maumee), from the governor in Detroit, if indeed they should be offered us, so that none of our Indians might find it needful to go there. It

would be said, in case we took presents, that the captains got thereby the right to make us go out to war with them, and we should take upon ourselves a load of trouble. They could reproach us and say: " You have taken gifts, now you must do service therefor as we do."

22. To-day, and the following days, many brethren went to our towns on the Muskingum to get corn, for they had nothing to eat and here could get nothing. Warriors came in with two prisoners, who had been six days in Schönbrunn, and said it was perfectly quiet there, and no danger to be feared from white people. This gave our brethren greater courage to go thither.

1781, Oct. 25. After several days had gone by, it was told us by the chiefs, Pipe and Wenginund, that all of us white brethren, together with some of our Indian brethren, from our head-men, must go to Detroit, where the commandant wished to see us in person. For this we showed ourselves willing and ready, and prepared for the journey; only we obtained one thing by entreaty, that two brothers might stay with the sisters, whom we could not leave alone, and the chiefs could not make the least objection to this, since they saw themselves it could not well be otherwise. Thus we four brethren, David, Heckewelder, Sensemann, and Edwards, with the Indian brethren, William, Isaac Eschicanahund, Tobias, and Joshua, went our way in the name of the Lord, took tender leave of our friends and departed, committed to the mercy of God. [N. B.—Isaac Glikkikan, however, did not go with us.] Truly we did not know whether we should all meet again and whether we should not be separated from one another. On this account the leave-taking was somewhat doleful; at the same time, too, that we must leave the brothers who remained at home, namely, Brs. Jungmann and Michael Jung, with the sisters, in wretched circumstances, that we knew not and saw not on what they could live even two days, on which account we recommended them, the best we could, to the care of the Indian brethren, who, however, were themselves in just as desperate circumstances and had nothing. We came in the afternoon to

Pipe and Wenginund's town. To them had been intrusted by the commandant to bring us to Detroit, but the
first had already gone on before and the last could not go.
Thus we journeyed with our Indian brethren our way
alone and got some corn on the way, although very little.
All the Indians we saw in this neighborhood were Delawares, who had helped take us prisoners in Gnadenhütten, and were therefore not strangers to us. From here
we soon came to a camp, where by a creek we found a
hut, in which we passed the night, for it rained very hard.

26. We went through deep swamps and troublesome
marshes, in the afternoon came upon Indians out hunting,
from whom we got some meat, and with whom we passed
the night. On the afternoon of the 27th we came out of
the camp and met on a creek Indians again out hunting,
and here we stayed. Here our Isaac, who went out hunting a little, shot a deer.

Sunday, 28. After we had come many miles over plains
where there was nothing but water, so that nowhere a
dry spot was to be found, where we could dismount from
our horses, and afterward through a long swamp of several miles, where also no bit of dry land was to be seen,
and the horses at every step must wade in the marsh up
to their knees, we came in the afternoon to the Miami
river, where we met Pipe, who advised us to remain there
over night, and so we did.

Monday, 29. We still remained here, for we were waiting for Mr. Elliot, who also came in from the Shawanese, to
divide among the Indians of the whole neighborhood the
presents which a sloop from Detroit had brought here. We
were offered the opportunity of going in her by water, but
we resolved rather to continue our journey by land, since
the voyage is very uncertain, for often they have to wait
several days before getting over the lake, when the wind is
contrary. The Indians had many prisoners with them here,
whom they were taking to Detroit; a part of them seemed
very miserable, and were half starved; many of them came
and begged for something to eat, and though we were ourselves in want, yet we gave them some meat. This they

eat forthwith on the spot, raw and bloody too, and did not take time to cook it. Towards evening there arrived an express for Pipe with the news that some of our Indian brethren who had gone to Schönbrunn and our towns to get corn from the plantations, had been taken prisoners by white people, and also some of them put to death, which was for us disagreeable and grievous news, and caused us much anxiety.

Tuesday, 30. We went a piece farther to Elliot's camp, to speak with him again before we set out for Detroit, but did not meet with him, for this morning he went down the river to where the sloop lay; so we followed after, but missed him, he having gone back another way before we arrived. Meanwhile, we spoke with the master of the sloop, who advised us to go back to the camp before we went farther, so that on our journey we might not meet with inconveniences, and this we then did, although we had not intended it, and we came late in the evening again to the camp and stayed over night. Here was our Isaac, who had remained behind in our last night-quarters and intended to overtake us, but never came in, and brought us news of the capture of some of our brethren, and also that three or four had been killed; likewise, that the white people in large numbers were under full headway for Sandusky, and by this time according to their reckoning had already accomplished their purpose. If now we wished to believe this news true, we could believe nothing else than that we should never again see our brethren, and this placed us in great perplexity, and we thought much about this, what was best for us to do, but we saw no outcome, we must push on to Detroit. Our only hope was still this, that if the news was true, a second and third messenger would follow after and bring us greater certainty about the matter.

Wednesday, 31. After we had arranged what was necessary with Elliot, and had been informed by him what we had to do after we came to Detroit, since Pipe, who was to take us there remained here, and Elliot had given us some provision for the journey, we set out early on our

way to Detroit, not without much trouble and perplexity
over the news and the danger in which we saw and considered our brethren at home. Here we left the Tawa
(Ottawa) river, so called because the Tawas dwell here,
some of whose towns we passed through. This neighborhood was much commended to us and praised, that it was
a fine place for us and our Indians to settle in, because it
had also the advantage that the vessels from Detroit came
there, to which one could sell every thing, be it what it
would, and so get subsistence, at the same time, since our
Indians had many cattle and busied themselves with ag-
riculture. But we saw very plainly it was no pleasant
place for us, although the forest is a fine open forest, yet
it has no other cultivable land along its borders than
plains on which nothing but high, long grass grows, so
that a man on horseback can hardly see over it. The
land in itself is good enough, but so tough and grassy
that our Indians could not work it or plant it; granted
that it could be plowed, yet the open land is good for
nothing for cultivation since it is too wet and is merely
swamp and marsh; yet more about this hereafter. We
met to-day, as indeed every day as far as Detroit, a multitude of Indians of various nations, who were all bringing
from Detroit horse-loads of wares and gifts, and in such
number that one would think they must have emptied all
Detroit. We came, Thursday, Nov. 1st, to the lake along
the shore or strand, where we went some distance and we
looked up the open lake without seeing any land on the
other side. Many Indians whom we met, pitied us, and
several said they hoped we should be well treated: it
would distress them if the people in Detroit should treat
us ill.

Friday 2. We came partly through great swamps and
marshes, and partly over great plains, through much water,
to the strait between Lakes Erie and Huron, along which
we went up as far as Detroit. Since we could not get over the
river Rush (Rouge) from want of a boat, we had to pass the
night, three miles from the city, under the open heaven,
but had nothing more to eat. · We could see very plainly

the city and the whole country round about on both sides the river, which is about a mile wide. We passed to-day various towns and settlements of the Wyandots, but nowhere can it be seen that they have planted much, but they support themselves by hunting and fishing, besides they contrive to get something out of the white people of the neighborhood.

Saturday, 3. We had indeed asked some Indians on the other side of the river to go to the commissioner in the city and tell him to send us a boat and take us over, but this morning we managed to borrow from Indians, who live across the strait, a canoe, in which we crossed, and came at once to Detroit, after we had first passed through the settlement this side of the city, which is thickly settled, and is built like a village along the river. When we came to the first guard and asked for the commandant,[1] they let us pass and showed us the way there. Thus we went through the city straight before his house, and had ourselves announced by the sentinel: in a little while he admitted us : we made him our compliments, and he asked us if we were the Moravian Ministers from the Muskingum. We answered, " Yes." Whether we had all come, for he had heard there were six of us. Where then were the others? Answer: " We had left two of our number behind us in Sandusky with our wives and children, for we could not leave them alone, since they needed help, and could not rightly be left with the Indians." He asked us then why we had not brought our women with us, which he had plainly ordered, for he had it in mind to send us back to Philadelphia. Answer: " We had expressly inquired of the chiefs whether our women also were summoned, and they had said to us, no." He said farther, the

---

[1] The commandant of Detroit at this time was Major Arent Schuyler de Peyster, who served for several years in America with the 8th Regiment. He was second cousin of Gen'l. Philip Schuyler, of Albany. He was born in New York in 1736, and died in 1832.

In the year 1813 he published, at Dumfries, Scotland, a volume of poems, entitled, Miscellanies by an Officer. In the appendix to this book are given several letters relating to his service in America, and a short vocabulary of Ottawa and Chippewa words. This rare book is in the Society's Library.

reason why he had had us removed from our settlements on the Muskingum was this, that he heard we corresponded with the rebels to the harm of the government here, for many complaints against us came in. Answer: "We did not doubt at all that much must have come to his ears about us, for this we could infer from the treatment we had to endure. but that he must have been wrongly and ill informed about us, and we accused of things of which, were they investigated, we should be found innocent." He asked farther, who had come with us, where our Indians were, and how many of them there were, likewise, how many men, and whether we thought of again returning to them.

We answered him that four of our Indians had come with us, that our Indians now in Sandusky were altogether between three and four hundred, that we indeed gladly would go back there so soon as we were set free, for we could not look upon it as a trifling matter to be apart and separated from our mission, which had been intrusted to us, and if this should happen, would of itself go to destruction, and all our labor of forty years would have been in vain. He said, "Think you so?" and replied, "But if your Indians were harmful to the government?" Answer, "They would not be harmful, but useful, that would he learn, if he were better acquainted with us, for they were an industrious, laborious people." He asked whether our Indians had ever gone to the war. Answer, "No." He was very attentive, and took notice of what we said to him, but broke off the conference because he had no time, and gave the commissioner, whom he had summoned, orders about our lodging and entertainment, and about our horses, whereof we were relieved. He told us that tomorrow or the day after he would call us again and then speak farther with us. We were then quartered with a Frenchman (Mr. Tybout), together with our Indians, and some provisions were sent to us for our entertainment, which also was so done as long as we were there, not merely something, as is usual with prisoners, but when that was gone, we could get more for ourselves and our Indians.

Our verse of Scripture, with which we came, was very consoling to us. It read: He said, surely they are my people, children that will not lie; so he was their Saviour. Jesus my shepherd is—'Twas he that loved my soul, to him in his mercy we committed ourselves and our affairs to conduct in this place, where it seems dark indeed, and where as yet no brother has been.

Sunday, 4. We remained quiet in our lodgings. People went in the street to mass, but since we had come in very wretched clothes, torn and ragged, we held it best not to go out much, for we had been robbed by the warriors of all our clothes, and Br. Sensemann got here again a waistcoat, which a white man had bought of the Indians, and cheerfully given up to him for nothing; likewise, also, a white woman, who had bought a white apron, gave it back again for nothing, well understanding that it belonged to us. Many officers, English and German, and also many Frenchmen, came to visit us, had compassion with us that we had been so ill-treated, and promised to help us, so far as lay in their power. The French priest[1] also called upon us, quite an old man, with whom, however, we could not speak, for he knew not English. Several officers, after speaking with us, said they had become of quite another mind about us, and if the commandant had thus heard us, as they had, he would be so too.

Monday, 5. We sought to get an audience with the commandant, but he did not admit us. When now we saw we could not come before him, we wished to prepare a memorial to send him, and went therefore to the commissioner to ask for paper and ink. He asked us what we wanted them for, whether we wished to send letters round about the country. We answered, no, but to the commandant. He said it was not necessary, for he was waiting for Pipe, and would determine nothing until he had heard him. In the evening we had visits from officers, also prisoners, on parole, among them a major from Vir-

---

[1] "There was a Roman Catholic church. The priest was then Peter Simple, an aged and infirm man."—Sketches of Detroit, p. 6.

ginia, who often came to see us, knowing us from having
seen us on the Muskingum.

Tuesday, 6. Our Indians tried to get an audience with
the commandant, but also were not admitted. This evening, however, we heard that Pipe was near, encamped a
few miles from the city. Since now we saw that our trial
rested upon Pipe, that Indians and warriors were to pronounce our sentence, we prepared this evening a speech
to him with entreaty that he would speak for us before
the commandant, and be helpful to us to get back again
to our friends. With this the next morning quite early
the brethren went out to meet him before the city, and he
gave them a good reception. So we had to stand among
heathen, who were our enemies and were opposed to the
preaching of the gospel, who must be our witnesses and
pronounce judgment upon us, although we were among
men who wished to be called Christians. Br. David had
already on the way and also here arranged with the Indian
brethren what was to be done in case we could not go
back again. In this way we must rely upon no man, but
upon God alone, who will also conduct our affairs and
bring them about, according to our Scripture-verses of day
before yesterday, yesterday, and to-day.[1] Nothing else is
in our power than to observe what the Saviour will do
and bring to pass, to whom we commend ourselves. We
learned now exactly how it is with our brethren at home,
that Schebosh with others has been captured, but that none
has perished, and that all is quiet at home.

Wednesday, 7. We heard here and there that we
should be brought to Montreal. The last two ships of this
autumn had departed ten days ago for Niagara; so we could
not think that the governor had any such plan in view,
but it was reported that they were awaiting orders still in
the river below. Therefore we were anxious to hear the
conclusion about us.

Thursday, 8. Pipe came into Detroit with the warriors, as is usual, with the Death-Hallow, which they

---

[1] Is. xl, 10; xxv, 8; xxviii, 5.

repeat as often as they have scalps and captives; the former they bore aloft on stakes, the latter they drove among themselves through the city, just as is the custom in the Indian towns.

Friday, 9. We were at last called to the council. When we came in we saw the warriors assembled, and Captain Pipe, with several other captains with him. The commandant, Major de Peyster, with several officers, sat in front of them, and a place apart was pointed out to us. After they were all assembled Pipe began his discourse, giving to the commandant his scalps, which he had brought with him, and said to him among other things: he did not know whether the deeds he had done were praiseworthy, and whether he had done right; perhaps it was wrong that he had ruined these men, for they were his friends, not the Indians theirs, they were his flesh and blood, his nation, and his color. The commandant himself took the scalps from him, and had them put aside. In the same way the other captains acted and delivered their scalps, for which they at the same time demanded their pay, all of which he took from them. Thereupon the prisoners also were given over to him. We had our own thoughts about this, that we should be heard judicially in a war-council, and our sentence spoken. After the ceremonies were over, Pipe arose and addressed the commandant, as follows:

"Thou hast ordered us to bring the believing Indians with their teachers from the Muskingum.· We have done so, and it has been done as thou hast ordered us. When we had brought them to Sandusky, thou didst send word to us to bring to thee here the ministers and some of the head-men of their Indians, thou didst wish to see them and to speak to them, for thou didst know better than we how to speak with them, and thou couldst also better entertain them since thou hadst no lack of any thing. They are now here before thine eyes, thou canst now thyself speak with them as thou hast desired, but thou wilt speak good words to them, and I say to thee, speak kindly to them, for they are our friends, and I hold them dear and should

• not like to see harm befall them." This last he repeated again, and then sat down. The commandant addressed him and the Indians, saying to them he had had us brought on this account, because he had heard complaints against us, especially that we had corresponded with the rebels and from time to time given them news when the warriors wished to make attacks on their settlements, whereby many warriors came to harm, that many lost their lives, and since the warriors had always said they could have done more had we not been there. If this were so, we were harmful to this government, as the warriors had always repeated to him; that he had also strictly given orders in writing that we should not remain there, but come hither, which, however, had not been done; that that was the reason why he had us brought in, and he said to Pipe, since they were now altogether to tell him the exact truth, whether this were so, whether the complaints against us had foundation and whether we had corresponded with the rebels. Pipe answered, there might be some truth about the thing, for he could not say that it was all lies, but it would now not again happen since we were away from there and now here, where it could no longer happen. But this answer was not yet satisfactory to him, on which account he asked him again : " So they have then corresponded with the rebels and sent leters to Fort Pitt; for from thine answer I must conclude that it is true." Pipe became somewhat angry, arose, and said . " I have told thee that there is something in the matter, and now I tell thee straight out, they who are ministers, are innocent, they have not done it of themselves, they had to do it." He struck himself on the breast, and said : " I am guilty of it and the chiefs who were with me in Goschachgünk; we compelled them to it and forced them; thou must hold us responsible for this, but since we are now here it will not happen again, as I have already told thee." The commandant said further to Pipe : " You have probably at home not only thought about the ministers, but also conferred with one another what was best to be done with them ; he should now tell

him whether the Indians would like to see them go back
to their Indians or whether they would rather see that
they did not go back." The interpreter did not rightly
understand this question, and translated it wrongly to Pipe.
We soon observed this, but kept perfect silence, since thus
far we had been questioned about nothing. Since we had
beforehand conjectured that in regard to our abode something would occur, we had considered with one another
whether we should do any thing in the affair, as we were
here, and should make representations. The Saviour, however, did not approve of it, and so we kept silent. We
saw also that the governor left it to us and the Indians
where we should settle, and this was satisfactory to us, for
in this whole country, so far as we had come, we have
found no place which in any way is suitable for us, and
we have observed that every step we have made towards
the north, has increased our wretchedness. The commandant heard then from the answer that they had not
understood and repeated his question, when Pipe answered him : They had promised the believing Indians,
when they were themselves brought away, that their
teachers should remain with them as hitherto, and that
they should have their religious services unhindered; it
was not their thought that they should be robbed of their
teachers; it would be pleasing to them if they were again
suffered to return to them, for they looked upon the ministers as their friends, their flesh and blood. All was
written down.

Thereupon, the commandant turned to us, and asked
whether all of us there were ordained ministers? Answer:
"Yes." Whether one of us was superior over the others?
Answer: "Yes, namely, Br. David." Whereupon, he
turned to him and asked: "How long already we had
been with the Indians?" Br. David replied: "Already
more than thirteen years ago he had come to the Ohio; the
others first after him, one earlier, another later." "Whether
we had gone among the Indians of our own accord, to
teach them, or whether we had been sent?" Answer:
"We were sent to the Indians to preach them the gospel."

"By whom?"   Answer: "By our church, which is an old
Episcopal Church."   Question: "Where are your bishops?"   Answer: "Here in this country and in Europe."
Question: "Where have the bishops come from, who are
in this country?"   Answer: "From Europe."   Question:
"Are you ordained by those bishops, and sent to preach to
the Indians?"   Answer: "Yes."   Question: "Have you
not got your instruction from Congress when you went to
the Indians?"   Answer: "No; but from our bishops."
Question: "Did Congress know about this, or did you
have permission from the same to go?"   Answer: "We
have not been with our Indians, without the knowledge
and permission of Congress; it has put nothing in the
way of our labor among the Indians, but also it has pre-
scribed us no rules and given us no instructions in what
way we should conduct ourselves."   He then said he not
only was not opposed to the Indians being civilized and
instructed in Christianity, but it was pleasing to him; in
this matter he would not hinder us, nor interfere in religious matters, but we should be on our guard, and not interfere in war-matters; for, if we did so, he would be
forced to interfere in our affairs and make us halt, for he
was a soldier; but so long as we did not interfere in his
affairs, he was unwilling to interfere in ours; and since he
now saw that we had been wrongly accused, and things
were not as they had been represented to him, we could
in God's name go back to our families and to our Indians,
as soon as we pleased; he would in our behalf write to
the general in Quebec, and learn his disposition in regard
to us until spring.

Question: "Whether we would take the oath."   Answer: "No; it had never been required of us."   "So,"
said he, "I will not burden you with it."   This was also
interpreted to the captains and warriors who were present.
We repeated also what he had before said to us, that he
had sent out in writing an order in our behalf that we
should come nearer to him and answer him; that we had
never seen the same, nor had it come to our hands; it
was then needless to treat us with such harshness, to plun-

der us, and to behave so ill towards us. He spoke also to
our Indians: that he was pleased to see them, for he
liked to see Indians who loved goodness and sought for
it; they should go back home again with their teachers, obey them and abide by that which was preached
them and not meddle in the war. He said: "There are
Indians, Chippewas, for instance, who may not take part
in the war, not from religious principles, but they are
lazy, and to them I give no gifts, for they could go if they
would. They shall get nothing from me, but to you, although you do not yet take part in the war, will I give
something from my store, which you may use for your necessities [namely, you who are here], and if hereafter your
people come to me they shall be welcome and never go
away empty. Thereupon he arose, shook hands with
them and the captains, and said to us he wished to speak
further with us. We could now come to him whenever
we would; that his house was open to us, and now that
our innocence had come to light, he would give orders
that clothing and what besides we needed should be given
us out of the king's store, as far as could be done, for ourselves, our wives, and our children, since we had been
plundered. Thereupon he went away, and we returned
home, happy and thankful that the Saviour had conducted
our affairs according to the verse of Scripture for to-day:
Cast ye up, cast ye up, prepare the way, take up the
stumbling-block out of the way of my people. 'Tis thine
alone to change the heart—Thou only canst good gifts
impart. Many English and French, with whom we had
before become acquainted, rejoiced with us that our affairs
had come out so well and happily. The majority of the
inhabitants here are French; therefore the usual language
is French, though there are many English, but of Germans
only very few.

Saturday, 10. Brothers David and Heckewelder went
to the governor, as he had told us; now he admitted us to
his apartment, a thing he had not done before, nor asked
us to sit down, as he now did. He was now quite different towards us, in every way friendly; asked all sorts of

questions, how we had lived on the Muskingum, what
kind of houses, or whether we had had houses, and wondered much at hearing we had lived so pleasantly and reg-
ularly. He said to us now, since it was found we were innocent, he wished in some way to make good the losses
we had suffered. Since now we know that a trader in the
city had bought from the Indians four of our watches, we
told him so, and he promised to get the same for us at
once. He summoned the trader, demanded the watches,
and promised to pay him again what he had given for
them, and gave them all back to us. Then he gave us an
order upon the commissary of the king's store, who gave
us blankets, some clothing, and house-utensils, for us and
our sisters at home; wherefore we were joyful and thankful, although our loss was far from replaced, for we had
lost beds, clothes, furniture, and every thing, and what we
now got was only to relieve our greatest necessities, and
if nothing more should be given us, we could not get
along. But now that we were ready and could go home
if we wished, and we wanted to be off, the sooner the better, we found that our horses, which had been given to a
Frenchman to take care of, had either been stolen or had
run away, and although our Indian brethren sought for
them, they could not find them. We went, therefore, to
the commandant and complained before him of our needs.
He indeed gave orders that the Frenchman should and
must get our horses for us, but they were not found. The
man must, however, lend us other horses in their stead
until ours were found, and the commandant promised us
we should either get our own horses again or be paid for
them, but we have never got them.

After we were ready for our departure and had been provided with provisions for the way, for we had ourselves
not a penny of money to buy any thing with, except what
was given us, we went again to the governor, asked him
for a pass, which he gave us, in which he gave notice that
we had permission to go back to our Indians and to remain
with them, in order to instruct them in Christianity; that
no one should put any thing in our way or injure us. He

again repeated, as he had already said in the council, that
he had written to the governor (in Quebec) and expected
his answer and advice about us in the spring, and added
that he then still could do something in our favor, since
he had heard us and investigated our case. He made us
many excuses, saying to us that we must not be too much
vexed with him, that he had had us removed from our settlements, for he had seen himself compelled so to do, since
so many complaints against us had come to him, that, in
duty bound, he could not have acted otherwise, although he
now saw that all the accusations against us were groundless
and false. It had also been entirely against his orders to
plunder us and handle us in such a harsh manner, and he
said, in conclusion, that for his part, he wished peace
might soon be restored. But those who were the
cause of this war were to be blamed, and were the
origin of so much misfortune, which then the innocent must suffer. We also asked of him, since now
we were going back to Sandusky, if any future complaints
against us came to him, not to believe every thing, but to
be so good as to send us a few words, and thus we would
inform him at all times about the affair, how it was in regard to truth, for among the Indians we had many
enemies, who were opposed to the preaching of the Gospel,
and on this account made up all sorts of lies about us, and
spread them abroad. We thanked him for all the kindness he had done us, and showed him our gratitude, since
we very plainly saw, inasmuch as every thing was enormously dear, that our expenses must have run up to at
least £100, and took leave of him. Still, he said to us, if
we had letters to send to our church, we should only send
them to him; he would then, at once, give orders for them.
For the present, however, it was too late, for all the vessels
and ships for this autumn were already gone, and until
spring no more would depart. We then took leave also of
Commissioner Bawbee, who was also well disposed towards
us, and had shown us much kindness, and then departed
Nov. 14 with our Indian brethren, but since it was late we
came only a few miles and encamped in the bush. The

Scripture-verse read: For a small moment have I forsaken thee; but with great mercies will I gather thee. Does it seem for a time as if God forsook His own? Surely I know and believe this: He helps at last, yes, certainly.

We came the 18th to the Tawa river, where we met many Indian acquaintances, who were very joyful at our return. We met here also Alexander McKee, agent of Indian affairs in this department, who showed himself friendly to us. But we knew from trustworthy sources that he had been the head-instrument of our calamity, and after our captivity had labored for this that we should be separated from our Indians and driven altogether from the Indian country. We showed to him the pass we had received in Detroit. We learned here how it fared with our people and brethren at home, and were glad to hear that they, after Br. Schebosh, with five of our brethren, had been captured in Schönbrunn, had remained in perfect peace, and that no one of them had lost his life. We complained to him of the wants of ourselves and of our Indians, that we had nothing at all to live on, nor could we see when we could earn or buy any thing, since among the Indians, who themselves had nothing, nothing could be had. He saw our need very plainly, but could give us no advice.

The 19th we journeyed on and came upon Israel, with a large body of Indians on their way to Tawa river, where McKee distributed presents to them. Many came and greeted us in a friendly way. We saw that many had real joy that we had freedom to go back to our people, for most of them had believed we would remain in Detroit in prison; thus we found it everywhere among the Indians where we came; all were glad to see us again, and welcomed us. If we had been held prisoners, things would not have gone on well among the Indians; on our account they would have come to blows among themselves, and the ringleaders of the whole affair would not have come off well; of this we had proof enough before we went to Detroit. Pipe also was well aware of this, and therefore did his best to be helpful for our release from Detroit. Now must I say something about this whole stretch of land we have

come through. The whole country is so flat and level that
no hill at all is in sight, for it has great plains, many miles •
in length and breadth, on which nothing grows except long
grass. These for the most part are, so to speak, flooded
with water, which circumstance comes from this, since it
is so flat and level that the water can not run off, and even
when it does not rain for a long time, it is still full of water,
and seldom becomes dry land; a little rain can put such a
plain under water, and often our horses had to wade
through water up to the saddle, and at times even swim; in
short, it is like land near the sea shore, which is flooded and
never becomes dry. These plains are full of crawfish, which
have their holes in the ground; therefore the game, raccoons, foxes, etc., which are here in large numbers, get
their food in abundance, live on the crawfish and wax fat.
No practicable road can be kept there, for it would soon
become a deep marsh, so that there would be no getting
through, but nearly every one makes a new track through
the long grass, so that at last it becomes a broad road. The
woody land, on the contrary, is not so much flooded, yet it
is wet and swampy and likewise full of water, so that here,
too, little dry land is to be found. The land is especially
clayey, which is one reason why the water remains standing and does not sink away. The bush is either beech-
swamp or ash, linden, elm, and other trees, such as grow
in wet places, yet it has many oak groves, and all around
Detroit it has white-cedar swamps. Here and there also
are to be found white and black walnut trees. Since now
the country is so flat the creeks rise at once very high,
even from a little rain, so that it is hard to get through.
The Indians use the whole district for nothing else than
hunting, and the game is not very plentiful on account of
the wet.

We came then on the 22d November, happy and in good
condition, to our brethren in Sandusky, who, as well as we,
heartily rejoiced together, and could not thank the Saviour
enough that he had been with us, had stood by us, and
brought us back again, especially also that he had given
us good weather on the journey, which had much eased

for us this so difficult way, for in rainy weather in this country it is impossible to get through.

Many tears of gratitude and of joy could be seen running down the cheeks of our brethren, for they had just heard news of us from an Indian who came from Detroit that we, either all of us, or at least the greater part, would remain captive; and this story was still told and worked over as we came into town, and hence their joy was so much the greater, and they were quite overcome.

Nov. 22. Returned the Brothers David, Heckewelder, Edwards, and Sensemann, with the Indian brethren Isaac, of Gnadenhütten, Tobias and William, from Detroit. At the same time also some brethren came back from our towns on the Muskingum, where they had got corn from the plantations, in which, however, they were much hindered by their fear of the whites, and what they brought they must, so to say, almost have stolen. On every side joy and gratitude over our return were to be seen on the faces of the brethren, for in our absence many lies were put abroad about us, which were circulated about the town, and when we arrived were even then repeated, that we would be kept in prison in Detroit, and be brought to Quebec, that two of us at least, namely, David and Heckewelder, would not return, and that the sisters with the two brothers, Jungmann and Michael, would also be carried away. This was related as the real truth by a white, who said he had seen us in Detroit, spoken to us, and knew how it was with us. The greater then was now the joy, so that many wept for joy, but others were ashamed. The white brethren had especial pleasure in seeing one another again, and we thanked the Saviour who had again brought us together. We told one another what the Saviour had done for us in the time, as well at home as on our journey, how he had been with us and conducted our affairs according to the promise in the verse of Scripture when we were taken prisoners: Though thou wast angry with me, thine anger is turned away, and thou comfortedst me; and of the day after: God will come and save you.

At home services were held by Brothers Jungmann and M. Jung as usually. Two children, one Salome's and the other Johanna's, were born in the time. Five children and Sister Johanette died meanwhile, and were buried.

24. McCormick and Dawson arrived, the former from the Wyandots, the other from Lower Sandusky: they were glad we were again here, and offered us their services if we in any way were in need. We asked them, inasmuch as they carried on business with the Indians, to buy corn for us, since we had nothing to eat, and this they promised to do. Several brethren came back from the Muskingum with corn. It is a hard, dangerous, and long way on which to bring corn; we saw, however, no better and easier way for us to get any thing, for from the Indians in this neighborhood little is to be had, and that little enormously dear, so that we and our brethren are not in circumstances to buy any thing.

25. During the sermon upon to-day's Scripture-verse, in the open air, since we have as yet no chapel, the little daughter of Jonas and Amelia, born on the 18th Inst., was baptized with the name Benigna.

Tuesday, 27. There was a conference of assistants, they were told, since for the greater part they were at home, what occurred upon our journey and in Detroit, how the Saviour had directed and conducted our affairs, that unimpeded we could preach the gospel, since many of our brethren had been of little faith and thought never to see us again, and had already given us up, many lies having been told them about us, that we should be taken to Montreal. What occurred in the council with the Indians in Detroit about us, and what was concluded, was told to all the brethren around a great fire under open heaven, since we have neither chapel nor any other house large enough for this purpose: thereby all were very attentive, joyful, and thankful for all the Saviour had done for us.

At last they were reminded, and it was given them for consideration to build a chapel or house of the Lord, since now nearly all of us had dwellings. To this all gave their consent at once, and went briskly to work, although they had little time left, but must devote all their time to caring for themselves and their families and to getting the means of life, and thus have they therefore, as likewise we also, lived only from day to day, and very often the day before have not known what we should eat the next, but have yet come through with the Saviour's help.

Wednesday, 28. Fell a good deal of snow, on which account the brethren went out to get meat for use while building. For us the brethren collected corn, for we had no more, and each gave according to his means, a handful or even somewhat more. The poor widows are the worst off, who have neither horses nor otherwise opportunity to get any thing.

Thursday, 29. The meeting-house was blocked out. Several brethren went to the neighboring towns to get corn, but little can be had. The want of necessaries of life is all the time already great. What will it yet become? For the longer we are here the greater will be the pressing need.

Saturday, Dec. 1. John Williams came back from Lower Sandusky, where he has been since we are here, to earn corn, which he got too. Br. Conner and his wife are also there, and will probably remain there the whole winter, for here there is for them no outcome.

Sunday, 2. Because we have yet no chapel, we could have no service, the snow remaining. Among our brethren a rumor began that there are some people among us who are guilty, and have thereby contributed that we were carried away captive and placed in such misery.

Tuesday, 4. Our chapel was roofed. Since we learned that several wished to go to the Fort (Pitt) to look after their friends, we forbade them, lest we might have trouble.

Friday, 7. We laborers, the brethren apart and the sisters by themselves, held an open-hearted and intimate conversation with one another. The Saviour gave us grace and his blessing thereto, that we stood together in love and unity, one with the other, and all was accom-

plished, for in this time much that was unpleasant had occurred among us, and we had thereupon—

Saturday, 8, the blessed supper of our Lord. We held
to-day the first service in our newly-built chapel, which,
with prayer and entreaty to the Saviour, was dedicated,
that he would be with us, dwell among us, and go with
us, and that he would bless his sweet Gospel also in this
place, as well as in our hearts and in the hearts of all
those who should hear it. See the Scripture-verse of to-day
(Is. xlix. 2).

Sunday, 9. Br. Edwards preached. In the afternoon
service upon the text: The Lord shall comfort Zion, and
he will make her wilderness like Eden, was baptized
with the name Anton the little son of Br. Christian and
Sister Cathrine, born the 29th of last month. Thereupon
was a service for all the inhabitants of our place, with
whom in a very direct and open-hearted manner he discoursed and held before them the shortcomings which
many of them had been guilty of towards the Saviour and
their teachers, and also pointed out to them that they had
put themselves in such misery through their disobedience
and sins before the Saviour.

Monday, 10. Heckewelder held the morning service.
The assistant brethren spoke with Joshua on account of
his bad conduct and with some others here. Then the
brethren resolved to send a petition for corn to the Shawanese.

Wednesday, 12. Sensemann held the early service. In
the afternoon was the burial of the widow, Priscilla, who
yesterday departed in blessedness. She was baptized in Old
Schönbrunn, Aug. 20, 1775, by Br. Jungmann, and there
also came to the enjoyment of the Lord's supper, Feb. 15,
1777, and led a godly life, so that there was hearty rejoicing over the grace the Saviour showed in her. In the
autumn of 1778, however, she was led by her friends through
fear to leave the church, and she remained away a whole
winter. But it was too hard for her. She had no peace
and a discontented life, on which account she again asked

4

for forgiveness and begged again for reception, which she received also, and came again to the enjoyment of the Lord's supper, since which time she knew better how to value the church and the grace which the Saviour had shown her in the church; passed her time contentedly and in intercourse with the Saviour. She let herself be moved by nothing further nor induced to leave the church during all the unrest of the war and all the hardship and affliction which we had to endure. Thus she came with us here to Sandusky, where she had to live through a most grievous time, whereby her heart, however, blessed in the Saviour, was undisturbed. At last she became ill, and the Saviour wished to take her away from all want and trouble. She longed for this too, and so departed with the blessing of the church.

Thursday, 13. Br. Michael Jung held the early service. Afterwards he and Br. Heckewelder went to the Wyandot town to the trader, Mr. McCormick, to get the corn he had bought for us; they came back the 14th.

Saturday, 15. The brothers, Samuel Nanticoke, Isaac and John Martin, went away to the Shawanese with a petition to ask them for aid and to help us with some corn, as we had likewise helped them in Lichtenau when they were equally in need.

Sunday, 16. John preached and Br. David held the congregation meeting over the Scripture-verse.

Tuesday, 18. Two whites came to visit us, Mr. McCormick, from the nearest Wyandot town, and Mr. Robinson, from Lower Sandusky. The former told us that he had again bought some corn for us, and both promised to come and help us, that we might not suffer from want, while we thankfully acknowledge and praise the care of our Heavenly Father and glorify him therefor, for the whole time since our coming here we have been able to see no outcome, how we should get through, and we have lived from day to day from grace upon what our brethren have given us from their own poverty, for they themselves had nothing.

Wednesday, 19. Abraham went to visit a sick woman,

Ann Charity's mother, who is sick and had asked for a visit from the brethren. The two white men returned home. They are troubled about us, and it presses hard upon them that we may suffer no want, and therefore they seek to help us as far as it is in their power. A couple of Indians, Weschnat and another, came to report about Josy and Abraham, who had secretly gone to the Fort, how it was with them. They went away without saying any thing to us, though we had warned them and forbidden them to go, but they wanted much to know whether their friends are in life, who were taken prisoners, and how they are.

Thursday, 20. Heckewelder held the morning service over the Scripture-verse: Rejoice ye with Jerusalem, and be glad with her, etc. When now it had been cold weather more than three weeks, and most days had snowed, rainy weather came on, so that the snow quite went off, which happened very luckily for our beasts, for they had to get their food in the woods, and if it should be a hard winter, must still go out, especially our cattle.

Friday, 21. Br. Michael held morning service. Abraham, who went to visit a sick woman in the Wyandot town, but found her no longer alive, came back. Several brothers came home from hunting.

Sunday, 23. Br. David preached upon the Epistle: Rejoice in the Lord alway, about the joy of the children of God in the Saviour's incarnation, sufferings, and death. Sensemann held the children's service and Edwards the congregation meeting over the Scripture-verse. The brothers Samuel, John Martin, and Isaac, came back from the Shawanose, where they had good success, and their petition was very well received. They had then forthwith, for one hundred string, brought together corn for our town, and promised them, so soon as their people should be at home, for only a few men were there, since they were all off hunting or otherwise scattered, that they would collect it all and then send us word to come and get it. The chief, who was at home, received them in a very friendly way, and said to them they had long waited for us to ask them for help, and if we had not done it they would yet have

1

thought of us and helped us, but that it was so much
the more agreeable to them that we had come to them.
They well knew that neither we nor our laziness was the
cause of our coming to such want; they also were not
the cause of it, but we were torn away from our towns by
force where we had the means of life in overabundance,
therefore were they willing to help us. [The Mingoes who
live there said the same.] They pitied us much for our
losses and for what we had endured, and now, especially,
that we lived near the Wyandots in such a wretched district of land, which was quite unsuitable for us, that we
could not plant enough for ourselves, as we had been used
to do; they said we could seek out a better place which no
one could prevent; they looked only to our good, and if
they should see that we supported ourselves and wished to
move to a better place, they wished to come to our aid at
once with as many horses as they could get together. It
troubled them, as it did also the Delawares in the same
neighborhood, that Pipe herewith grew and boasted that
he had taken prisoners the believing Indians and their
teachers, and they were therefore his prisoners and slaves,
and they say, "Are not the believing Indians his friends?
It was a shame to regard his own friends as slaves." The
chief and some others who were at home talked almost all
night with the brethren, and asked them, among other
things, this also, where their teachers and ministers came
from and got here, for all white people, English, French,
Spanish, and so many as they had seen, had their ministers
and their worship of God, but they all went to war, but
we not. The brethren answered: They were originally
from over the sea, and finally came to us and brought us
the word of God, and we have received it, since we found
and felt in our hearts that it is truth, eternal life, and glory;
among all white people there are indeed ministers, all have
their worship of God, have the Scriptures, and can read
them, but since they are unbelievers, they become no better
therefrom; they are thus unbelievers, as are the Indians,
and so no better. The chief bade them greet us, their

teachers, and said he would like to see us, perhaps he would come sometime to visit us.

This afternoon the Half-King came with his interpreter, partly on business, partly for a visit. The brethren took occasion to speak with him about the two who had gone to the Fort, of whom we have already heard so much from other places, and told him as much as we knew about them. But we soon heard that he had more news of them than we, for they sent word to him by Indians, and let him know what they intended, so that it can cause us no prejudice or harm.

Monday, 24. We begin Christmas week with praise and thanks that God, our Creator, himself became man, and that we, through him, have peace with God, since he has blotted out our sins through his blood. We asked him also forgiveness of all our transgressions, not to be mindful of them, and to be merciful to us, again to bless us, to be with us in this place, and to recognize us as his peculiar people, and to send us his peace, which he also did, and we had comfort and assurance therefrom. Love-feasts we could not have, for we were too poor and could not afford so much. The history was read, and over the Scripture-text was a discourse. The chapel was quite filled.

Tuesday, 25. The morning sermon by Br. Hecke-welder, the children's service by David. These rejoiced, and sang: The Infant Jesus in his manger lies, right prettily, and all who were present let tears of joy run down their cheeks. Br. Jungmann held the congregation meeting over the Scripture-verse. The brethren encouraged one another, and rejoiced together in God, our Saviour, who in all circumstances had shown himself gracious to them, and filled their hearts with comfort and joy.

Wednesday, 26. Br. Edwards held early service; thereupon we had a conference with the assistants. A woman, a widow, obtained, upon her request and prayer, permission to dwell with the church. Nicodemus, who in the spring, from fear, allowed himself to be moved and went from the church, and now came again, was likewise received. Israel was told we could not yet allow him to be

in the church. It was told to the church that we could
not suffer Jacob's family to be in the church, seeing the
manner they had conducted themselves in Gnadenhütten
and up to the present time, on account of the children, and
other reasons too. At last also Nathaniel and A. Salome
were earnestly spoken with about their daughter, and they
were advised what they had to do.

Friday, 28. There was a conference with the assistants
about maintaining order among the people and putting
disorder out of the way. Many of our brethren suffer
hunger, and as no corn can be had, they must subsist upon
wild potatoes (Ipomœa Pandurata), which they have to dig
up laboriously and bring from a distance.

Saturday, 29. Since the creek is so high from rains that
it can not be crossed the brethren made two canoes.

Sunday, 30. Br. David preached about the foundation
and corner-stone, Jesus Christ, whereon his church and
each member thereof is built. In the afternoon was a conference of assistants, who spoke with Gideon about his conduct and unrighteous behavior in Gnadenhütten with the
warriors, for which he defended himself. Br. Edwards
conducted the congregation meeting.

Monday, 31. Jungmann held the morning service, and
exhorted the brethren for Jesus' sake to bury every thing
in his death, and to take nothing over into the new
year. In the afternoon was the burial of Br. Nathaniel,
who died yesterday in blessedness. He was baptized in
Bethlehem, Aug. 30, 1749, by Br. Nathaniel Seidel,[1] and
July 8, 1775, in Gnadenhütten, on the Muskingum, was
admitted to the enjoyment of the Lord's supper. He remained steadfast by the Saviour whom he loved and by
the church, and had a lovely and blessed intercourse with

---

[1] He was born in Saxony, in 1718, in Laubau, a short distance from
Herrnhut. He came to America in 1742, where he labored in various
stations until 1750, when, in company with Zeisberger, he returned to
Europe for a visit. He came back the next year. As " Elder of the
Pilgrims " his visits extended as far as Surinam. He was made
bishop in 1758, and died in 1782, overwhelmed with sorrow at the news
of the massacre of the believing Indians at Gnadenhütten. De Schweinitz'. Some of the Fathers of the Am. Mor. Church.

the Saviour. By nature he was somewhat simple, but if he spoke with his laborers from his heart, it could be seen that he well knew what he wanted, and what he had from the Saviour, for this he had understanding enough, and he was not wanting to him, but for other matters, especially bad things, he was indiscreet, yet it was never observed that he frequented and gave himself up to bad company. That his mother, who died in peace in Lichtenau, told him, shortly before her death, he should abide by the Saviour and the church his life long, that forgot he not, and he repeated it often. The occasion of his death was a broken leg, and thereupon gangrene, so that in a few days he departed with the blessing of the church. He was forty-two years old. To-day was the conference of assistants: they investigated the old matters about the children of Jacob and Philippa.

At the usual time we assembled at the end of the year, thanked the Saviour for all the mercy and kindness he had shown us, but confessed to him also our faults and shortcomings, and begged the forgiveness of all our transgressions and the consolation of his grace, to be merciful to us, and to acknowledge himself to us as our Helper and Saviour.

CHAPTER II.

1782.

UPPER SANDUSKY—MISSIONARIES CALLED TO DETROIT—SETTLEMENT ON CLINTON RIVER, MICHIGAN.

Tuesday, Jan. 1. Br. Edwards preached from the Gospel about Jesus' name, who is our Saviour and Redeemer. The baptized brethren renewed their covenant with him, to be and to remain his own. They were exhorted to give their hearts entirely to him; to desire nothing in the world except to live for him. Sensemann held the congregation meeting from the Scripture-verse: I will not contend forever, neither will I be always wroth. Meekness, humility, and love—Through all thy conduct shine. We took the texts from last year for use, since we have now indeed no hope left of getting any. In regard to other matters, we had to hear from without many bad and unplesant stories over the fact that two of our Indians had secretly gone to the Fort, without our knowledge, on which account many lies were spread around that we had sent letters by them, and they said we should again be made prisoners and altogether brought away from the Indians. Satan rages and it is as if we were given over to devils to plague us utterly, to torment us and to make trial of fortune with us, while we are here, more than ever before, not only from without, but also from within. For in the church there were people who upheld them in their false dispositions and applauded them, who wished to establish by force that wicked life of his and heathenism. If we oppose them they become angry and set on the wild Indians against us, wish to stop our mouths, bearing witness thereagainst, and to bind our hands, so that we may do nothing to dispense the powers of darkness and root them out from among us. But we did not let ourselves be turned aside, but courageously bore witness against them. Such a change has now come in the Indian church that the bad,

wicked people can not be cast out, but they wish to be
there and to cause harm in the church, for they in the
wild towns have occasion enough therefor and no one
would say any thing to them about their sinful life. If
we discipline them, therefore, or only say it were better if
they remained away from us, they go into the towns and
accuse us of sending people away, urge on the savages
against us, who then tell them they should not regard us,
that we are prisoners, and that it is their business to command us.

We are not, however, cast down nor disheartened, but
oppose with might and with all our strength, to destroy and
cast out of the church the works of Satan.

Wednesday, 2. There was a conference of assistants.
Br. Michael Jung held the early service. Rainy weather
came on, and the snow melted, which is a mercy for our
cattle. On the other hand, the brethren had their houses
full of water, as is the case hereabouts in thawing weather
usually.

Thursday, 3. John held early service. The brothers,
Mark, William, and Christian, went in the name of
the conference to Pipe, some ten miles from here, to
speak with him and his chiefs about the evil reports circulated concerning us, and to get information about them.
They came back on the 4th and had good success; they
were well received by Capt. Pipe, who told them he had
indeed heard many chance rumors, but had not troubled
himself about them. That ten of our people had gone to
the Fort, even that they had stolen away, he could not
take ill, for he well knew how it was among Indians—
if one of them had his father and sister carried away captive, he ventured his life merely to find out whether they
were alive or dead, and how it was with them; there were
ill-disposed persons among the Indians, who had pleasure
in spreading abroad lies about us; but we should not be
troubled about it, they did no better with him and told lies
about him; it should remain fast, he would remain fast,
we should remain fast by what had been fixed and concluded about us in Detroit. Thereupon he told them

what had happened in Detroit in regard to us after our own departure. There came in some Delaware captains while Pipe was still there; they held a council with the governor, and said to him : " We have removed the believing Indians with their teachers at your command from their abode, and have brought them to thee in the hope that thou wouldst again send them home whence they came here. We thought that had ceased, and that from this time on there would be no ministers among the Indians. To our great wonder and astonishment, however, hast thou set them free and sent them back to their Indians. Surely, thou knowest not how injurious they are to us, for theirs is the guilt that so many of our friends perished at Goschachgünk ;[1] they have always made our friends there feel secure by saying to them they had nothing to fear from the Virginians, until they were suddenly attacked. The ministers have always written letters to them and given them information when our warriors have gone to their settlements, by which means many are come to overthrow and harm, and have lost their lives through their betrayal." The governor answered them that only a few days before, in the presence of the chiefs and warriors, he had investigated the matter and the charges brought against the ministers, but he had found them innocent, and that all the charges against them were groundless; what he had thus arranged and concluded with Capt. Pipe should remain until he had well-founded reasons for calling us away. He said further, why then did they now first bring these charges against us; already a long time had gone by, why had they not done it at once? After this he should receive no further complaints, but would abide by what he had agreed with Pipe in the council. After this, the captains could say nothing further. Thus it goes among the heathen when they get a little power over us. We have many foes, but still also many always who are our friends, yet often meet those who are not well-disposed to us, and who are opposed

---

[1] Where Col. Broadhead, the April preceding, had killed fifteen warriors and taken twenty captives.

to the preaching of the Gospel, fight for us and do us good
service, as now Pipe, although they have always their own
object in view, and this will not cease. McCormick visited
us to-day and went back again. We heard that our things
are come to the lake.

Thursday, 3. Nicholas and Joh. Sabina's child born. ·

Saturday, 5. The assistants had a labor-day with young
married people to reconcile them. We laborers had a
conference about our staying here, and found it best not
to waste our time in moving about, but to remain here.

Sunday, 6. We celebrated Epiphany. The Saviour of
the heathen allowed himself to be felt comfortingly among
us, acknowledged himself to us in all our services,
blessed us, and let us feel his peace. An adult was baptized with the name Phœbe, and a child, the little son of
Nicholas and Joh. Sabina, born on the 3d Inst., with the
name Timothy, and two sisters, Rebecca and Juliana, were
absolved and prepared for return to Gnadenhütten, where
they remain.

Monday, 7. After the early service, which Br. Edwards
held, we spoke with the assistant brethren about getting
corn from our towns from the plantations, and exhorted
them to neglect nothing, since now was the best time and
the least danger to fear from white people. Likewise we
told them our opinion in regard to our dwelling here ; that
we held it best to stay here, not to waste our time in moving about, whereby we might still incur the extremest
need and poverty, since we well saw we should not better
our circumstances, but make them worse, if we went far
away from here, for thus we should again have the warriors constantly in our town, which here, however, we had
not so much to fear. Moreover and besides, we could draw
upon ourselves the discontent and dissatisfaction of the
chiefs if we went away, who would then leave us in the
lurch if we had any thing to complain of, since now indeed they were our friends. Thus here we should have to
bear one thing patiently, and to seek out the nearest, best
place for planting, and our greatest care and labor would
be to get the necessities of life. This was also in accord-

ance with the hearts of the brethren, to cause us no unnecessary labor and uneasiness, but to enjoy quiet as far as possible.

Tuesday, 8. Sensemann held morning service. Israel, who came here a short time ago and asked to be taken back, but received no permission to live here, repeated his wish, and gave us to understand that he had not acted with a view for the salvation of his soul, but that he had acted with other objects in wishing to be in the church, and he confessed that he had not known his heart, but thought he had indeed done nothing wrong when he left the church; that he had done no sin, and that it was not so bad with him; but this he now saw, and found quite otherwise; that he was a sinful man, who had no Saviour, but he would indeed like to be blessed, to turn again to the Saviour and to the church, and to remain with them his lifelong.

Wednesday, 9. Brother Michael held early service. We went out to-day to inspect a little the neighborhood and the land on the creek, and where towards spring we could make our fields, and indeed found places where there was good fine land, but it was somewhat too wild and much overgrown with wood. We heard that a whole party of Goschachgünk Indians, who the year before had fled from there and had lived thus far with the Shawanese, wished to move near us; but they had nothing to eat, and already there was constantly famine with them, on which account they also went to our towns and wished to get corn from the fields, as we hear.

Thursday 10. Jungmann held the early service. Nearly all the brethren went out to dig wild potatoes, on which, for the most part, they now live, especially those who are not able to buy or earn any thing, and among the savages corn costs already from three to four dollars, and daily becomes dearer, yes, many have already had to give eight and more. We have sold some of our cattle to a trader for corn, and on this we thought to live for a while, and yet it was little to get. Sara Nanticoke was brought to bed with a son: likewise in the night Anna Paulina with a dead daughter.

Friday, 11. David held early service. John went to McCormick to get corn for us, and came back home in the evening.

Sunday, 13. In the sermon it was especially urged upon the boys and young people to ask more obedient hearts from the Saviour, who had been a boy and learned obedience. In the next service the little daughter of Zachary and A. Elizabeth, born on the 8th Inst., was baptized with the name Dorothy, and in the service for the baptized, Sister Johanna Sabina was absolved. Thus the Saviour and the Holy Ghost bring the erring back again, one after the other, and into the right fold.

Wednesday, 16. Many of the brethern went to the Shawanese towns to seek for corn, for here in this neighborhood no more is to be had, and what there is, is enormously dear, and so some went also to the Muskingum to harvest yet something from our plantations. Br. Jungmann, with Brs. Michael, John, William, and Adam went to Lower Sandusky to get some provisions, which had come for us by water from Detroit.

Thursday, 17. Heckewelder held early service. We heard that warriors had again gone out to our towns.

Saturday, 19. To-day and yesterday yet more brethren have gone, partly to the Shawanese, and partly to the Muskingum, to get corn. To the Shawanese it is a good day's journey, to the Muskingum five or six. Two of our brethren would cheerfully have gone with them there, to get corn for ourselves, but we dared not venture it, for we had no permission.

Sunday, 20. During the sermon the little son of Br. Samuel Nanticoke and his wife Sara, born on the 10th Inst., was baptized with the name Jeremy. Our brethren are almost all scattered, partly to the Muskingum, partly to the Shawanese, to get the means of life. Our need grows greater daily. Our brethren become disheartened and listless, and have no hope of rescue, for always it gets worse and worse, this we can see before our eyes. Our

Saviour and our dear heavenly Father must know better
than we how to bring us through, and how to devise. It
is a great comfort to us that we have no reproach, and
have given no occasion for the famine in which we are
found, for although many brethren said to us, when we were
still on the Muskingum, that we should at once promise
the warriors to break up and go with them, and were discontented with us that we did not at once give our consent, yet we could not do that, for we foresaw all that
which now meets us, but we preferred to be taken captive. We said to them even then that we were not so very
much troubled about ourselves where we should get the
means of life, as about them; for we should first be helped
but not they, and therefore we were much more troubled
for them than for ourselves. Those, now, who so much
wished themselves here, and entertained so sweet antici-
pation of what great advantages they would have here,
that they would have cattle and could sell milk and butter
at a high price, these find themselves deceived, their cattle,
one after the other, die off, so that there is no hope of
their bringing any through the winter. They begin now
to see that they have desired ʹand worked for their
misery and ruin. In this we pity the upright and good
hearts who mean well, and are sorry that the innocent
must suffer with the guilty.

Monday, 21.   Heckewelder held the early service from
the text : Fear not, for thou shalt not be ashamed, about
the consolation and foresight of a child of God who recog-
nizes the Saviour as his Redeemer. Again many of the
brethren went to the Shawanese town for corn.

Tuesday, 22. Br. Edwards held early service. It snowed
hard, and we were troubled about the brethren getting
through, who had gone to Lower Sandusky, for we know
it is a bad road, for in this country there is no good road
to be found, mere marsh and water; therefore when it is
frozen it is easiest to get over.

Wednesday, 23. David held early service. We heard
that the Delawares in this neighborhood held their war-
dance in the Delaware towns, and again go to war in good

numbers. A wicked Indian, who was our enemy, and did
us much harm, has filled his measure, has gone from time,
and is gathered to his fathers. McCormick, who is much
concerned about our welfare and seeks to help us, came
here to visit us, and remained over night. Our cattle generally suffer the greatest want, many die, and it appears
that few will live through the winter, so our need increases
everywhere.

Thursday, 24. Brothers Jungmann and Michael returned
from Lower Sandusky with some provisions, which we had
ordered brought there from Detroit by water when we were
there, and which the commandant had given. To Lower Sandusky sloops and vessels came up the river eighteen miles
from the lake. With them came also a white man, Mr.
Robinson, who visited us, and the next day went back
again.

Saturday, 26. We made the beginning and preparations
for sugar-making a good rifle-shot from town, over the
creek. Sybilla bore a daughter.

Sunday, 27. Michael preached from the gospel about
the cure which the Saviour through his blood makes on
poor, lost sinners, and that he blesses them.

Tuesday, 29. Early before day the Saviour took to
himself Cornelia, the four-year old child of Leonard and
Rahel, and he was

Wednesday, 30, buried. For three days we have very
hard, cold weather, so that at night we can hardly keep
warm. Our cattle fare worse every day, for we have ourselves hardly any thing to eat, and they really nothing.
We have no sheds for them, and could make none, it was
so late; thus every day some die, and it is as if the Saviour
were angry with us. Ah! may he yet have mercy upon us,
and help us out of our need.

· Friday, Feb. 1. John and Michael went to McCormick
to get corn for us, and came home at night. The sisters,
Sensemann and Jungmann, have taken something to sew
for him, that they may earn something in their great need.
Now for some days it has been extraordinarily cold, so that
some people in this neighborhood say that for ten years no

winter has been so cold. The hunger among our people
here at home is so great that for some time already
they have had to live upon dead cattle, cows, and horses;
never in their lives have they felt such want; we pity these
people, but we can not, we know not, how to help them.
Why then does the Saviour let all this come upon us? We
have thus far in our want got some corn from a trader,
wherefor we give him cattle in payment.

Saturday, 2. We had the pleasure of again seeing
young Jos. Schebosh, who, in the autumn, went to the
Fort to search for his father and sister, carried away prisoners. With him came his sister and the son and daughter of Rachel; but two others have remained behind in
Gnadenhütten, whom we formerly expected, so that all
the prisoners are now again with us, except Br. Schebosh,
and he, we now hear, has gone to the church (i. e. Bethlehem). We are pleased at this, that the brethren should
have a chance to hear something circumstantially about
us, and we look upon it as a providence from our Saviour
that it should so have happened, and that these brethren
must have been taken prisoners so as to give news of us.
By them, to our great joy, we received letters from Litiz
(Lancaster Co., Pa.) of the end of August and beginning
of September. The last was written when we were already
prisoners. We got also some weekly journals, but we had
to keep all this secret, and dared not once give a greeting
to the brethren. We learned also that a brother, Daniel-
son, from Bethlehem, had been in Pittsburg. Likewise,
also, we could hope that we should now be set loose from
our captivity.

Sunday, 3. David preached in the forenoon and Jungmann held the congregation meeting in the evening.

Monday, 4. Pomoacan came with a following of Indians and some whites, to hear the news from us, whom
we referred to Jos. Schebosh, who politely disposed of
them. Isaac, however, who had been sent around the
town to find something for them to eat, came back and
said to them, and especially to Pomoacan, that he could
find nothing for them to eat, for our own people had them-

selves nothing but dead cattle to live upon, and he said to
him : "When thou wast in Gnadenhütten, thou didst ask
of us tea, bread and butter, milk, pork and beef, and whatever pleased thee, and we gave thee all thou desiredst.
Then thou didst say to us we should not regard our plantations, but arise and go with thee; we should find'everything again and yet more than we had left behind. Whoever takes a bird or duck, he strives at once to get it
something to eat. Thou hast brought us here, but hast
not given us a grain of corn. Thus hast thou cooled thy
wrath on us." He and those with him were quite still at
this and could say nothing.

Tuesday, 5. David held the early service over the Scripture-verse: Israel, thou shalt not be forgotten of me.
Adam, who came home from the towns, had likewise heard
that we white brethren in the spring would all be brought
to Detroit, and said thereupon : "There are so few brethren
at home, they are all scattered in the bush and in the
towns, among the Shawanese and on the Muskingum, so
can it happen if we again come home, that we shall not
again meet and you will be carried away. If this shall
happen we shall all be in pitiable circumstances. I wish
then no longer to be alive, for I could not look upon the
misery. You would have no want and would be better off
than you are now, but with us things would be bad indeed." Br. David comforted him, saying, the Saviour
would ever help us and not permit us to be separated
from them, and should he permit it, he would give them
advice what they were to do.

Wednesday, 6. Joshua and Jacob, who went to the trader,
must there hear much about this, that the former had gone
to the Fort to get back his sister and the others who were
made prisoners, and they accused him of taking letters
there and bringing letters back, which is yet quite false.
He had brought a newspaper which Br. David sent with a
letter to the governor in Detroit. It is true, we could
have written by him, and he begged us to send letters by
him, but we dared not on account of our unfaithful people.

5

We saw from this that they who pretended to be our friends are still secretly our enemies, that in our presence they appear friendly for their own gain, to make profit from us still, and behind our backs they are our foes and would like to hasten our ruin and utter destruction.

Thursday, 7. Several brethren returned from the Shawanese towns, where they had bought corn, and for about a bushel they must pay five dollars, thus still dearer than among the Wyandots, though they had expected to get it cheaper. Again some have gone to the Muskingum, and we are left at last here alone. Sugar began to run.

Saturday, 9. Came again seven brethren with corn from the Shawanese towns, and several from here went to the Muskingum, for they have now heard from those who have come from the Fort, that they have nothing to fear there. Thus all wish to go there, and this is also their only hope of getting the means of life, and although the corn still stands in the fields unharvested, yet it is still good and unhurt.

Sunday, 10. Heckewelder preached and David held the congregation meeting. There were, however, very few brethren at home.

Tuesday, 12. Susanna, Sophia's daughter, wife of Mark, bore a son.

Wednesday, 13. To-day and several days preceding, yet more brethren have gone to the Muskingum. Indeed they would prefer to move there than here to suffer want and hunger, if they had permission, for of this place they have had quite enough, even they who came here willingly.

Friday, 15. The little daughter of Sybilla, born Jan. 26, was baptized with the-name Sara.

Sunday, 17. Heckewelder preached. At a love-feast we congratulated Sister Susanna upon her thirty-ninth birthday, and wished her many blessings from the Saviour. We white brethren are quite alone at home, since most of those still remaining here are sugar-making.

Wednesday, 20. Warriors came in who went to the war, and they staid over night. They went about, and when they saw so many cattle lying dead, they laughed and scoffed about it. The savages are pleased now that things go hard with us, that we suffer famine and anxiety, and our cattle all perish, and they say we have now become like them, we should be no better off than they, and so it was. They envied us our quiet and that we should have no want in the means of life.

Sunday, 24. Many brethren came from the sugar-camp home for the sermon, which Br. David preached from the text: God so loved the world, but there was no translator there. A party of Wyandots in the last few days has gone to the war.

Monday, 25. It was again winter-like, and it snowed after we had had for some time fine spring-weather. Up to this time during this winter we have remained so far quiet and undisturbed, although we have always heard as well from the Shawanese towns as also from those near us, the Wyandot, Monsey, and Delaware towns, that we, the missionaries, would be taken this spring by lake to Detroit and separated from our Indians. This was especially incredible to us, because the commandant in Detroit had given us such good assurances and a pass, wherein it was expressly announced, and all our names were named, that we should be unmolested, remain with the Indians, and teach them. Yet when we saw the hostility of the wild Indians to the preaching of the Gospel, and that they thought only to ruin and destroy the Indian church, for that was their end and object from the beginning of our captivity, we were often not without trouble and anxiety.

When they saw that we again were building a meeting-house, they said, "What is that? We thought preaching would stop, and now again shall it first make a good beginning?" Thus we thought this would finally be the end of our pain, and so resigned ourselves to God's will as he would let it happen, since now in this matter we could neither do nor alter any thing, if it should happen. We had already some time ago arranged with the national assistants, when we were still together, to remain here, since we have not yet seen a place where we could better

and quieter be than here, though we knew and saw that
as long as we are here we should have nothing but hardship
and trouble from the Indians, especially from the Wyandots,
who were resolved to do us all the injury they could, which
we always heard from a trustworthy source. Our Indian
brethren were now partly in the Shawanese towns, partly
on the Muskingum, and in the bush, scattered about to get
the necessaries of life, and only some few old brothers and
sisters at home; so it came about that we,

Friday, March 1, through a messenger, were summoned
to Pomoacan, who sent word he had something to tell us.
Br. David, who was especially summoned, went there Saturday, the 2d, with Br. Heckewelder and two Indian
brethren, where also a council of Wyandots and Delawares
was assembled; there it was told us by the Half-King that
a letter had come from the commandant in Detroit, which
a white man, Simon Girty[1] by name, had given him to read,
and indeed it was not written to us, but to him, and to our
great amazement it contained the following sentence re-
garding us missionaries:

"You[2] will please present the strings I send you to the
Half-King and tell him I have listened to his demand.
I therefore hope he will give you such assistance as you
may think necessary to enable you to bring the teachers
and their families to this place. I will by no means allow
you to suffer them to be plundered or any way ill-treated."

So far his order. It is easy to conjecture what heart-
rending news this was to us, and here nothing was to be
done but to resign ourselves willingly to our fate, for the
most common objections we could have made would have
been utterly useless, and only have given the Wyandots opportunity to take us in hand, and misuse their power by ill-

---

[1] The historians of the Border Wars of the Revolutionary period can
find no words strong enough to express their detestation of Simon
Girty, the worst of the trio, Elliot and McKee being the others. His
life may be found in detail in Butterfield's Crawford's Campaign, p. 182.
He is said to have perished in battle at Proctor's defeat, on the River
Thames, Oct., 1813. Howe's Hist. Collections, p. 246.

[2] This quoted passage is in English in the original.

treating us; this we could conjecture from the order, though
it may not have been so intended. We gave then to the
Englishman a written acknowledgment that we had received the commandant's order, would conduct ourselves
accordingly, and obey his command, that in fifteen days
we would be in Lower Sandusky, when we begged that
we might be brought over the lake by water, for our sisters, with the little children, could not possibly make the
toilsome journey by land; and this also was granted us.

In the evening we came back home to our brethren, who
at this news were with ourselves amazed and saddened,
and all the Indian brethren who heard it passed a sleepless
night. Yes, we could not contentedly resign ourselves to
leaving our Indian church, and thought it impossible that
the Saviour could permit it. If we were all destroyed, then
once for all we were freed from all need; thus, however,
were we upheld to endure more deaths. But so it was,
and we saw no other plan wherever we cast our thoughts,
and meanwhile we had to comfort ourselves with to-day's
Scripture-verse, which read: My thoughts are not your
thoughts, neither are your ways my ways, saith the Lord,
and with the collect[1] therein say to the Saviour: We will
put our trust in thee.

Sunday, 3. To-day we sent at once a messenger to
the Shawanese towns, where some of our brethren were,
likewise an express to the Muskingum, to call in some
brethren with horses, to take us to Lower Sandusky, and
also once more to take counsel with them.

The brethren in the neighborhood, who were making
sugar in the bush, of whom there were only a few, all came
home at this sad news, and to them, in a meeting, a discourse
was delivered over to-day's Scripture-verse: Since thou
wast precious in my sight, thou hast been honorable, and I
have loved thee. Jesus! thou art all compassion—Pure,
unbounded love thou art. It was told them that in a
short time we should be taken away from them, and they
were exhorted to cling the closer to the Saviour, to keep

---

[1] The collect is the stanza of a hymn, placed after the Scripture-verse.

together in love and unity, and not to give Satan the satisfaction of seeing the church destroyed. They could now
perceive clearly and plainly enough that from the outset
it had been their object and aim to hinder the Saviour's
work and to destroy it utterly. There was such weeping
in the room that our hearts broke. A stone might feel
pity to see and hear the distress of the brethren; should
not God feel pity for his elect, who wept and cried aloud
to him? All the brethren who came home wept their fill
with us, and we comforted them the best we could,
though we ourselves needed comfort. Advice we could
not and dared not give them, save a little, for good reasons,
but only say to them to look to their old, sensible brethren,
to obey them and do as they did.

We could now see, from all the information we had
heard for some time back, that already in the autumn,
soon after our departure from Detroit, or while we were
still there, it had been then resolved to have us all come
there in the spring. Capt. Pipe had indeed said, in the
council there about us brethren, that we should get permission to return to our Indian brethren; but we heard
after we were come home, that other Delaware captains
had come in after our departure who were not pleased that
the commandant had let us go, and since Pomoacan had
again sent him a message about the matter, this order followed. We have also afterwards heard what he had had
written the commandant about us, namely, he required that
he should remove the ministers, for his heart did not feel
right so long as he saw us there, and feared a mishap
would come over him, and if he did not take us away, he
would take counsel with himself, for go we must. Thus
it seems probable to us that the commandant would
have given orders in the autumn, had we all been together. Capt. Pipe also said to us himself, he had had a
great contest with the other captains about this, who had
not been content with him, and had said he had done
every thing by himself, without their consent, he had
therefore nothing more to say, and should be of no further
account, whereupon, from vexation, he went away a

long distance into the bush hunting. And it is true that
Pipe had acted in our favor as far as he could, but the
captains opposed him, and have now brought the matter
so far that the Indian church is robbed of its teachers.
Our intelligent Indian brethren would often have liked
to open their mouths against the savages in regard to us,
but have refrained, since we white brethren were in the
power of the warriors, from fear we should suffer for it,
or even lose our lives; thus they preferred to be silent and
let all manner of hardships come upon them. They now
see very well what sort of friends they have, who made
them many fine promises, how good they would have things
here if they would come here. Instead of this they have
suffered hunger and anxiety, their friends have not provided for them, nor in any way helped them, their cattle
have, for the most part, perished, and they are utterly
poor, for they who had something had to give it up for
corn. A brother came and said: "I am guilty of your
misfortunes, for I have betrayed you as Judas betrayed the
Saviour, and must now be lost unless you forgive me."

Monday, 4. Few as are the brethren now at home, we
spent the whole day in listening to them, comforting
them, encouraging them, and exhorting them to stay fast
by the Saviour and his death on the cross. We heard and
saw now the condition of our brethren's hearts and minds,
how disinclined they are to the heathen's life, and how
dead to those friends who have brought them to such want
and wretchedness. They are prepared and hardened for
these circumstances, and their eyes have been opened.
These events have conduced more to bring them to a
proper state than we have been able to accomplish the
whole time we have been with them; for they always inclined towards their friends, who did them harm. Many
now said to us: "I care nothing for outward loss; that I
am stripped of every thing I had, and am become poor;
that I have to suffer hunger and want; that all my cattle
have perished: all this will I cheerfully endure and not
be concerned, but that they at last rob us of our teachers
and wish to destroy our souls' weal and food, that cuts

me deep to the heart, and is above every thing. They
shall not see, however, that I associate with them, and
take up again their heathenish life ; rather will I go into
the bush, separate myself from all human society, and
pass the rest of my life piteously. They shall not get me
into their power nor force me to any thing for which I
have no pleasure or inclination." [Others again had other
plans, many of them, however, to go to Pittsburg.] Some
said this from whom we had not expected it, and it was to
us a great comfort to see them in such disposition of soul,
but as often as they thought that in a short time they
would see us no more, the tears immediately ran down
their cheeks.

Tuesday, 5. Br. Heckewelder held the early service
over the Scripture-verse of the day : Thus saith the Lord
God, Behold I will lift up mine hand to the Gentiles, and
set up my standard to the people, and they shall bring thy
sons in their arms and thy daughters shall be carried upon
their shoulders. Outstretched see his arms of love—Haste
his tender heart to prove—Haste, ye sinners, ye will find—
Jesus casteth none behind.

Wednesday, 6. We had a laborers' conference, and consulted with the Saviour, among other things, what we
could advise our brethren in these circumstances, now that
we must leave them. We asked then, after we had declared our opinions one to another, whether, in these circumstances, we should advise our assistants what to do
after we were gone? Answer, "No."

Thursday, 7. We received some news of our brethren
on the Muskingum that all was well, and that they were
just about to come back again, that they were not without
alarm for us white brethren, that something was happening
to us and that we must be taken far away from them. The
brethren at home came and wept over us, that in a short
time they would be forsaken and would be like sheep
without a shepherd, and many said: "O, could we only
keep our teachers with us, I would certainly obey them
better than I have hitherto done." Others again would
take up arms and fight the matter out by force.

Friday, 8. The son of Br. Mark and his wife, Susanna, born in the bush Feb. 12, was baptized with the name Jonathan. For several days we have rainy weather and at last severe thunder-storms; the Sandusky has risen very much, so that the high water will delay our journey.

Saturday, 9. Michael held the early service over the Scripture-verse: The chastisement of our peace was upon him. Joachim came back from the Shawanese, and brought news that the others still there would follow in a day or two. The high water keeps them back very much. From our brethren on the Muskingum we hear strange things, especially from the young people, in regard to us, since as yet they knew nothing about our forced departure. It begins to be clear to us why we neither should nor could advise our brethren.

Sunday, 10. At last came some from the Shawanese towns, namely, Abraham, after we have some time awaited them. We long very much for our brethren on the Muskingum, for we can not get away until we have horses, and we must be prepared for the Wyandots taking us and carrying us on, into whose hands we have no wish to come, for we have already learned what it is to be in their power.

Wednesday, 13. We sent out a messenger to meet those brethren who are on their way from the Muskingum, to bring them on, for we already feared some accident had befallen them, they were gone so long.

Thursday, 14. Very early the Indian, George, came with the frightful news that all our brethren who went to Schönbrunn, Gnadenhütten, and Salem had been captured by the Americans and taken to Pittsburg; the messenger related many unpleasant things that occurred, for example, that they were bound and some killed, but all of this we could not believe. But that our Indian brethren are taken to Pittsburg is the more pleasing to us, were it only all of them there, and had they again a brother with them. We shall be glad to bear our captivity if only our brethren are rescued.

Friday, 15. We went away from Sandusky in company with some Indian brethren.

Departure from Sandusky, 1782.

Friday, March 15, was the day appointed for our separation from our Indian brethren and our departure, on which account a Frenchman[1] came yesterday, who was to lead us safely and go with us to Detroit. The Half-King also came to-day to look on and be present at our departure. Early in the morning we assembled for the last time in our room here with our brethren, who in accordance with our Scripture-verse of to-day: Therefore with joy shall ye draw water out of the wells of salvation, were exhorted, now that we must leave them, to hold fast to the Saviour, who is the fount of all weal and blessedness, and to his wounds from which flow to us all that is good and blessed. They should always earnestly bear in mind that they have been cleansed of their sins by his blood and baptized into his death. In prayer upon our knees we thanked the Saviour for all the goodness and comfort we had enjoyed from him in all our unhappinesses and burdens, in all our need and danger from without, recommended as well ourselves, who were going away, as especially our Indian church to his mercy, to the care and oversight of the Holy Ghost, and to the guard and protection of our dear heavenly Father, to hold them together until we should see each other again. We thought also of our brethren on the Muskingum in our prayer. Many hot tears were shed, which he will not leave unnumbered and disregarded. At the end was baptized into Jesus' death a well-grown child, the youngest daughter of Rachel, with the name Maria. The brethren then took leave of us one after the other, which to us on both sides was very grievous. Thereupon we went away, accompanied by some Indian brethren and two sisters, to Lower Sandusky, in order to go on further to Detroit by some chance ship or by boats. Several brethren besides went some distance with us, and then turned back again. Since we did not all have horses, for we had lost all our own horses, and our

---

[1] Mr. Lavallie, Heck. Nar., p. 329.

Indians could not get enough for us, most of them being on the Muskingum, some of us had to go afoot through water and swamps, yet we were glad that the sisters all had horses; but our things we had to leave behind. How woeful and grievous it was to leave our Indian church, can easily be imagined; could we have taken this with us we might go where we would, but now that we must be separated from them, we have neither joy nor comfort. We came to-day about ten miles, to McCormick, near a Wyandot town, where we encamped under the open heaven. Here we sent back a messenger, and told our Indian brethren to bring our things after us by water.

Saturday, 16. Here we were promised more horses, but our leader, the Frenchman, could buy none; therefore many of us had to go by water in a canoe we had brought with us to pass a deep creek, as far as the falls, and thus far, to-wit, some twenty miles from Lower Sandusky, the creek is very fine for a canoe, but then we had to go altogether afoot, for our canoe was quite small, and we did not dare to go down the falls in it. Our safeguard, the Frenchman, lent meanwhile Br. David his horse to ride. He was very pleasant with us, and had patience with the sisters. There were two days of very cold weather, so that we all caught bad colds, and it was a great wonder that the children,[1] whom the Indian sisters generally carry in their blankets on their backs, bore it so well. Br. Edwards, who had to go all day afoot, through water and marsh, was quite cheerful, but came off with a lame leg, from which, after the journey was over, he suffered a week before he could again walk.

March 19. We came to Lower Sandusky, and encamped at first in the bush, pitching our tents there. This morning, before we had broken up camp, one of our Indians came as messenger to us, who brought us the news that our baggage was coming down by water, and that they had heard nothing further from our brethren, who had

---

[1] A daughter of Heckewelder, about a year old, and a son of Sensemann, still younger. De Schweinitz' Life of Zeisberger, p. 535.

gone to the Muskingum, whom we believed taken captive.
Here were several white people, traders from Detroit, who
trade here with the Indians, who received us and treated
us well, for we had no food except what we had brought
for the journey, and had also nothing else in our possession, and took with us all we had, and that was now exhausted. But these people saw that we suffered no want,
and not that alone, but they took us into their houses and
did not permit us to encamp in the open air.

Here is a small Wyandot town, from which the Indian
men had all gone out to fight with the Americans, and the
whites were for the most part making sugar in the bush.
To this point ships and vessels from Detroit can come up
the Sandusky, but this seldom happens, unless troops are
sent over, for the traders bring their wares over in the
boats. Also Frenchmen are here with the English traders,
and many white prisoners from the Americans among the
Wyandots, who do not give up their prisoners to the English. They prefer, by keeping them, to strengthen their
own nation. We met here Br. Conner and his wife, who
moved here last autumn, when we went to Upper Sandusky, for they could maintain themselves better here.

March 21. The Indian brethren, William, Abel, Adam
and Joseph, the Delaware, and Sisters Martha, Augustine and Petty turned back again home to their
friends. They had come with us thus far with horses.
It was a renewed sorrow, for we thought never again
to see any of our brethren. To them also we could give
no advice, for we knew not ourselves what would be best
for them. Therefore we merely told them always to hold
together as far as possible, wherever they might be, and
not to be mingled and lost among the Indians.

We learned now what had really been the occasion of
our again being called to Detroit. We had indeed in the
first place looked upon it as done by the commandant for
our safety, and so indeed it was. But especially the Wyandots, and in particular the Half-king, at the instigation
of some white people, had complained to the commandant
that so long as we were in Sandusky we corresponded

with the Pittsburgers, and would certainly yet bring them
here to blot them out, on which account they besought
the commandant to take us away, and send us back home
again. The Half-king said : His affairs would not be well
so long as we were there, and he feared still another misfortune to fall upon him. Yes, besides this, we heard,
that if he had not quickly summoned us, they would have
put us all to death. During the winter we had indeed
forebodings of this, and an especial feeling that our se-
curity was not too well assured, yet we did not know that
our lives stood in such continued danger, as we now
heard from people who knew it very well from having
always heard it from the ringleaders themselves. Thus
we could look upon it as a providence from the Saviour,
which he had thus prepared for our rescue since he will
yet still uphold us. It had seemed to us, when we were
taken from our place in Upper Sandusky, and driven out,
so to speak heels over head, as if we went out of Sodom,
only we pitied our Indian brethren, whom we now looked
upon, and ever had upon our hearts and in our minds, as
lost sheep that have no shepherd. The Wyandots, who
have always appeared so especially friendly towards us,
and we have believed it too that they were our good
friends, they are now our greatest foes; for they have
brought us and our Indians into the greatest misery, and
have us, so to speak, in their power; they would like to
extirpate us and our Indians, had they nothing to fear afterward from other nations. And since they are angry
with us, they are fearful about us, for their conscience ac-
cuses them of having treated us so ill, and they fear that
our Indians will take revenge on them, and make them
some return for what they have done to us. The Half-
King's brother, who came with us here, and who is to go
with us to Detroit, probably that he may get a good present, but this in the end could not happen, and was unnecessary, he borrowed from a trader here the first night
a pistol, and being asked what he wanted to do with it,
answered, he was afraid of us, that we should undo him;
from which is to be seen that they have no good con-

science. That the Half-King's two sons last autumn died in the war, of that no one is accused except us, and he can not be persuaded otherwise.

March 23. The Frenchman who is commissioned to take us to Detroit sent an express to the commandant there that he should send boats or a ship over to transport us, till that event we must remain here, meanwhile also the weather will become more tolerable, for it is yet too cold to go upon the lake, and at present, as we hear, it is not yet free from ice. By Joshua and Jacob, Rachel's son, who brought our baggage by water as far as the falls, we have to-day the first trustworthy and very affecting news of the horrible murder,[1] March 7th, of our Indian brethren in Gnadenhütten, and March 8th, of our brethren in Salem.

See our Scripture-verse for March 7th and 8th, which are worthy of note.[2] Our brethren at home numbered 86 missing, but they could not certainly say whether all were killed or some taken prisoners: we hoped the latter, and that some few, though not the greater part, are yet alive. Our Indian brethren during the whole winter had to make shift to live and suffered great hunger, for among the Wyandots and Delawares, living in this neighborhood, nothing was to be had, for they themselves not only now, but every year, suffer want, for they are lazy and plant little, and although they got some corn from the Shawanese, yet it was not enough. Since now they heard from those who in the autumn had been taken to Pittsburg and had again come back, that in our towns there was corn enough and that they had nothing to fear in going there to get it, they made ready and went away, for they saw nothing else before them if they remained, than that they and their children must starve. We advised them at Christmas and on New Year's day to go there, for as long as the snow remained there was least danger, but they did not

[1] Read also Heckewelder's account of this massacre in his narrative, and see W. H. Howell's account in the Atlantic Monthly, Vol. 23, p. 95.

[2] Is. lxvi., 19, and x., 22.

go until the snow melted and then it was too late and
dangerous: when they were there they used not the least
forethought, for they believed themselves quite secure.
Instead of hastening to get away again, they stayed several weeks in the towns and fields, having then enough to
eat. The most wonderful thing is that while hitherto
our Indians had always been careful and distrustful and
fearful, and if they thought themselves at all insecure,
had fled into the bush, and at least would not pass the
night in the towns, now when they really saw the danger and the white people before their eyes, they were not
at all suspicious and went straight into danger.

The militia, some 200 in number, as we hear, came first
to Gnadenhütten. A mile from town they met young
Schebosh in the bush, whom they at once killed and scalped,
and near by the houses, two friendly Indians, not belong-
to us, but who had gone there with our people from Sandusky, among whom there were several other friends who
perished likewise. Our Indians were mostly on the plantations and saw the militia come, but no one thought
of fleeing, for they suspected no ill. The militia came to
them and bade them come into town, telling them no harm
should befall them. They trusted and went, but were all
bound, the men being put into one house, the women into
another. The Mohican, Abraham, who for some time had
been bad in heart, when he saw that his end was near,
made an open confession before his brethren, and said :
" Dear brethren, according to appearances we shall all very
soon come to the Saviour, for as it seems they have so resolved about us. You know I am a bad man, that I have
much troubled the Saviour and the brethren, and have not
behaved as becomes a believer, yet to him I belong, bad
as I am; he will forgive us all and not reject me ; to the
end I shall hold fast to him and not leave him." Then
they began to sing hymns and spoke words of encouragement and consolation one to another until they were
all slain, and the above mentioned Abraham was the first
to be led out, but the others were killed in the house.
The sisters also afterwards met the same fate, who also

sang hymns together. Christina,[1] the Mohican, who well
understood German and English, fell upon her knees before the captain, begging for life, but got for answer that
he could not help her. Two well-grown boys, who saw
the whole thing and escaped, gave this information. One
of these lay under the heaps of slain and was scalped, but
finally came to himself and found opportunity to escape·
The same did Jacob, Rachel's son, who was wonderfully
rescued. For they came close upon him suddenly outside
the town, so that he thought they must have seen him,
but he crept into a thicket and escaped their hands. They
knew his horses, which in the autumn they had seen at
his home, and inquired for him, for he was one of those
taken prisoners, probably therefore, by the very men who
were now there. He went a long way about, and observed
what went on.

John Martin went at once to Salem when the militia
came, and thus knew nothing about how the brethren in
Gnadenhütten fared. He told them there, the militia were
in Gnadenhütten, whereupon they all resolved not to flee,
but John Martin took with himself two brethren and
turned back to Gnadenhütten, and told them, there were
still more Indians in Salem, but he did not know how it
had gone with them in Gnadenhütten. A part of the
militia went there on the 8th with a couple of Indians,
who had come there to Salem and brought the brethren
away, after they had first taken away their arms, and when
they came to Gnadenhutten, before they led them over the
stream, they bound them, took even their knives from
them. The brethren and the sisters alike were bound, led
into town, and slain. They made our Indians bring all
their hidden goods out of the bush, and then they took
them away; they had to tell them where in the bush the

---

[1] " Christina, another widow, who had been an inmate of the Bethlehem 'Sisters' House' in her youth, spoke English and German fluently,
and was a woman of education and refinement, fell on her knees before Col. Williamson, and addressing him in English, besought him to
spare her life. 'I can not help you,' was his cold reply. " De
Schweinitz' Life of Zeisberger, p. 549.

bees were, help get the honey out; other things also they
had to do for them before they were killed. Prisoners said
that the militia themselves acknowledged and confessed
they had been good Indians. They prayed and sang until
the tomahawks struck into their heads. The boy who was
scalped and got away, said the blood flowed in streams in
the house. They burned the dead bodies, together with
the houses, which they set on fire.

In regard to the brethren in Schönbrunn, when we
learned we were to be taken to Detroit, we sent at once a
messenger to the Muskingum, for a very short time was
given us for getting away, that they should come with the
horses and help get us to Lower Sandusky. This messenger came to Schönbrunn on the very 7th of March when
the militia reached Gnadenhütten and delivered his message. They sent at once the same day a messenger to
Gnadenhütten to let them there and in Salem know what
was happening here. Before the messenger got quite to
Gnadenhütten, he found young Schebosh lying dead by
the wayside and scalped, and when he looked about he saw
that many white people had gone to Gnadenhütten. He
at once turned back to Schönbrunn and brought them this
news, whereupon they at once retired. The militia separated the next day, one part going to Salem, the other to
Schönbrunn, where, however, they found no one, although
our Indians saw them in the town; and of these, six perished
who were in Gnadenhütten and Salem, but no one of the
others perished, and they all came back to Sandusky after
we had already set out. This news sank deep in our
hearts, so that these our brethren, who, as martyrs, had all
at once gone to the Saviour, were always, day and night,
before our eyes, and in our thoughts, and we could not
forget them, but this in some measure comforted us, that
they had passed to the Saviour's arms and bosom in such
resigned disposition of heart, where they will forever rest,
protected from the sins and all the wants of the world.

The Wyandot and Delaware warriors, not only while
we still lived on the Muskingum, but also now, when press-

6

ing hunger drove our Indians there, have always labored
to bring upon us the whites, and whenever they came
back from murdering they came through our towns, in
order that, if they were pursued, the white people might
fall upon us, and so they now also did, for as soon as our
Indians went there, the warriors went too and did harm
to the settlements beyond the river. It happened then
that a war party came to Gnadenhütten with a prisoner,
whose wife and child they killed near Gnadenhütten, and
had impaled. The prisoner talked with our Indians and
warned them to be off, for the whites were already assembled, would follow up the warriors, and fall upon them if
they did not go away. When the warriors moved away
he perceived that two of them remained behind. In the
first night-camp afterwards, however, the prisoner escaped,
and had the good luck to get off, and soon after this the
militia came and made very sharp inquiries what they had
done with the wife and child, but this they could not answer them. From this it can be concluded that the prisoner had betrayed to them that our Indians were there.

March 25. Br. Sensemann went up the river with two
Frenchmen to the falls, to bring back our baggage with
horses—so far the two Indian brethren had brought it
down by water—and he came back the next day, but the
two Indian brethren, Joshua and Jacob, returned to
Sandusky.

27. Through Mr. Robbins, a merchant here and our
friend, who has come back from our Indians in Upper
Sandusky, where he bought cattle, we heard that our Indian brethren still kept up their meetings, and he told us
he had himself been present at them, and had seen with
his eyes how they sang together, exhorted and encouraged
one another, and with one accord lifted up their voices
and wept aloud together, which had made deep impression upon him, and he had great pity for their grievous
circumstances, and to us also was it agreeable and pleasing
that they kept up their meetings, as we bade them do at
our departure. He said our Indians did not blame the
white people that so many of them had lost their lives,

but the warriors, especially the Wyandots, who led us away captive, and had ruined the Indian church. These now rejoiced to have led and brought them into such misfortune and that so many are ruined.

28. On Maundy-Thursday we were heart and soul in the church, and silently begged a blessing from the Saviour, for here we were with only the world about us, and could not have the Lord's supper.

29. We read together to-day the story of the passion of our Saviour, who let himself be put to death for our sins, and by his death has brought back to us everlasting life, with humble and contrite hearts. So also on the 31st, Easter morning, we read the Easter litany, and at the proper place we prayed for eternal communion with our brethren, both on the Muskingum and in Sandusky; but, above all with them, who on the 7th and 8th of this month perished as martyrs in Gnadenhütten, the thought of whom goes always to our hearts.

April 2. The brethren, Samuel Nanticoke, Matthew and Thomas came to visit us. The first two were come back from Schönbrunn, and had been present at the calamity. But they knew no more than had already been told us, and of the brethren in Salem they knew thus much, that they had been brought to Gnadenhütten, where they were stripped and bound. We learned from them that the Half-King advised our Indians, after our departure, to go away from that neighborhood and seek out another place, where they could remain; that on this account they resolved to move to another place towards the Miami (Maumee.) In this matter we could not advise them, since we did not ourselves know where there was a quiet place for them to find, for the world is on all sides too narrow for us. We knew not how to help ourselves, and our Indian church has among the heathen nations not a friend left, much less we, for we white brethren have the bitterest enemies in the Wyandots, Shawanese, and Delawares, by whom we are surrounded, and if the hand of God had not worked a mighty miracle for us, we should already long ago have been wiped away from the earth,

for there has been no lack of will on their part and of
thirst for our blood, so long as we were with our Indians
in Sandusky. A good thing it was that we knew it not
then, as we afterwards heard enough about it, for we
should have had much unnecessary perplexity, and the
Saviour has spared us that.

We conversed with the assistant, Samuel, and we told
him our thoughts and disposition in regard to their difficult and dangerous circumstances, and the great want in
which our Indians now are; that all this hardship and
their troubles have not come upon them without cause;
they had sinned against the Lord, their God, had been
disobedient to their teachers, had heaped sin upon sin, and
if their teachers disciplined them therefor, and were strict
with them, they had become wicked and scornful towards
them, and when they got a chance, namely, when the warriors were strong enough in our towns, had as good as betrayed and sold their teachers, in order to show us we had
no power to punish them for their sinful lives, as if they
wished to show us that our life and position depended
upon them; they wished to close our mouths that we
might not bear witness against their wickedness and sinful
ways; we had great compassion with those who remained
true and upright, who had to suffer with the guilty; it
grieved us to the heart that in all our need and perplexity
there were yet ill-minded people among us, who were always heaping more sin upon themselves, and who, now
that we are away, always lay the blame upon their teachers that they fare so ill, and indeed even say we were the
cause of the death of the brethren in Gnadenhütten, and
had well known it beforehand; we looked upon all the
evil which was come upon them as a deserved punishment
from the Saviour upon them, and they would do well to
confess their sins, and to repent of them, and to ask forgiveness from the Saviour, that he would again let them
feel his mercy and pity; to this the assistant, Samuel, replied it was even so to him, and he had already long
so thought.

These three brethren returned home on the 4th, but

on the 5th came three families, namely, Adam, Ignatius, and Rachel, with their wives and children, so that we had always yet brethren with us. The poor people knew not where to turn, they are like sheep that have no shepherd, and it is a great comfort to them merely to see us once more, but we can not look upon them without great compassion.

7. Warriors came in, bringing a prisoner, from whom we now get the certain news that all our Indians in Guadenhütten and Salem were put to death, and that none were spared; he said the militia had 96 scalps, but our Indians numbered only 86, who went away from us. The rest then must have been friends, who did not belong to us. The prisoner said farther that two men alone had accomplished the whole murder after the Indians had been bound, and they had killed them one after the other with a wooden mallet.

8. A groundless alarm arose among the Indians in town, that our Indians now here had killed a Wyandot woman or several women. This thus came about. A woman was going home from her sugar-shed, and some miles from here heard a shout or playful outcry, and reported somebody must have been killed. When investigation was made, the story was found false. From this can be seen that they have no clear conscience, and are always afraid that our Indians may take vengeance upon them for having treated us so ill.

From Upper Sandusky an Indian came as express, bringing news that after the militia came back from their murderous work in Gnadenhütten, they killed also the Delawares, who had already lived a couple of years near the Fort; two from there escaped and came to Sandusky, one of whom is our Anton, who went away there from Salem to see his brother, but had spoken to no one about his plans. I have often thought during the time of our captivity, if we had retreated betimes to Fort Pitt with our Indians, as was several times proposed to us, we should have escaped all this want we have encountered. We have often thought about this and considered it in one way and another, but could never make up our minds to it, finding too much opposition and difficulty in the way, so that we had to give up the plan. But now we plainly see that if we had gone there with our Indians, we should, unwittingly, have gone into the greatest danger. Nowhere is a place to be found to which we can retire with our Indians and be secure. The world is already too narrow. From the white people, or so-called Christians, we can hope for no protection, and among heathen nations also we have no friends left, such outlaws are we! but praise be to God, the Lord, our God yet lives, who will not forsake us. He will punish us if we deserve punishment, that afterwards he may be the more merciful to us.

April 11. A war-party arrived with these prisoners and two scalps. The prisoners confirm the news that none of our Indians remain alive, but of those in Pittsburg most have escaped. An Englishman who lives among the Wyandots, who received the order to conduct us to Detroit, but, because, together with the Indians, he went to the war, had got another to take his place to go with us, came back from the war and showed himself a Satan towards us, swore at us, and threatened to bury the tomahawk in our heads. Through the whole night he drank his fill in the house where we were, and we were in danger of our life, not alone from him: a Wyandot squaw who robbed us in Schönbrunn, we heard say again and again, she would come and kill us all. We could not sleep the whole night, for he was like one mad, and worse than the drunken Indians, yet the Saviour shielded us from harm, and let the angels sing': They shall be uninjured.

13. Through the Indian brethren, Samuel Nanticoke and Thomas, who came last evening once more to see us, we learn that Mark, with half our Indians, has gone to the Shawanese. Abraham, William, Samuel and Cornelius, however, with the other half, have gone into the neighborhood of Pipe's town, near the Delawares, but not to remain, but to settle further on near the Miami. That our Indians should take refuge among the Shawanese, of whom we have always warned them, was not a pleasant

thing for us to hear, for there is the very theatre of war
in the Indian land. To-day two boats came from Detroit,
sent by the commandant to carry us, for which we had
long and eagerly waited, and with them came also a sergeant and fourteen rangers to take us thither. The commandant wrote to the merchant in whose house we are,
very favorably about us. He hoped that the English
traders would have received us, and entertained us well,
and if any one had done us harm or ill-treated us, he
should let him know it. The sergeant with his men had
strict orders to treat us well, and to place us in no unnecessary danger while upon the lake, should it be
stormy.

14. After we had taken leave of our brethren who are
here, and had recommended them to the mercy and protection of God, we departed, and towards evening, passed
through the little lake with a good wind; it was somewhat rough, and Sister Susanna became somewhat sea-
sick. At night we encamped on an island in the lake,
where, for a year or more, two Frenchmen have lived,
having come to-day somewhere about 30 miles.

15. In the morning we came at once into Lake
Erie and coasted along the west shore of the lake, but
could go on daily only a while in the forenoon and a
couple of hours before evening, for the wind blew so hard
that we had to run to land, and every night draw the
boats ashore, if we did not find a suitable harbor or creek
to run into, for otherwise the high waves would have
straightway struck the boats to pieces, and therefore they
had to be drawn ashore. On the 18th we came to Cedar
Point, where there is no wood but cedar to be found.
Not only here, but everywhere, so far as we came, were
many Indians, Chippewas, Potawatomies, Wyandots,
Tawas, etc.

19. We had to go over a bay, the wind was ahead and
pretty strong, so that the waves struck well into the boat.
This is the bay where the Miami falls into the lake. We
got over by good luck, and then with a good wind 40
miles and more into the straits, and in the afternoon of

the 20th to Detroit. Our boatmen, the rangers, who in other respects are like the Indians in manners and customs, have borne themselves towards us in a very friendly and modest way. The sergeant took every care of us upon the lake and exposed us to no danger, and thereby, too, lost no time. With ships and large vessels you can go directly over the lake, with a good wind, in four and twenty hours from shore to shore. But with boats they dare not venture it, but must keep close in shore, so that if the weather be stormy they can land, and there it is often dangerous, if the wind sets from the lake towards the shore.

We [1] were quartered here in the old fort in the barracks, where we were surrounded by soldiers alone, who daily had their drill in the fort at the parade place, and where all day long we heard nothing but drumming, fifing, and music. But we were glad and thankful to have a large, roomy chamber to ourselves, and no one disturbed us or put any obstacles in our way. The commandant, Major de Peyster, soon summoned Br. David. A sentinel, however, was placed before our quarters until he had spoken to us. He said to Br. David he had not expected to see us so soon again when he sent us away in the autumn, but so many complaints had come in against us, to which, however, he gave no credence and which he believed false, that he was compelled to call us away from Sandusky and to have us come here; he had done it against his will, but must needs do it for the sake of our own safety, to make us come here, for he could assure us that our lives were in the greatest danger if we remained longer in Sandusky. [He had received Br. David's letter.] Now that we were here, he wished to leave it to us to remain here or to go home, and if we chose the latter, to leave it entirely to us if we wished to go away, for in two days a ship would depart for Niagara in which we could go if we wished, but if we wanted to stay a week longer, that a ship went then, too, and we could do as we

---

[1] For a description of Detroit in 1778, see Sketches of Detroit, p. 5.

pleased; Br. David could come again to him after a while
and speak to him. He answered him that we had also so
regarded our removal from Sandusky as done for our
safety's sake; the charges brought against us were all
quite false and unfounded; as for our going home, we
asked time for consideration until the second ship went,
since this occasion was too soon for us. He was well
content with this, and added also that if we wished to go
now, we should gain nothing, it were just as well to wait
till August. He said he would give orders that care
should be taken for our maintenance, that we should suffer no want, and if we needed any thing we should say
so. Br. David gave him our thanks. Then the commandant came himself to our quarters, saw us all, and greeted
us most cordially.

22. Still another prisoner was added to our number,
whom the Indians brought in day before yesterday. He
was from North Carolina, acquainted in the Wachau:[1]
he was captured by the Indians with another man in Kentucky and would be sent to Canada in the next ship that
went.

25. Br. David went early to the commandant, who invited him to breakfast, and Br. David improved the occasion to speak to him about our mission, and asked him
whether there were no possibility that we and our Indians could settle somewhere in this neighborhood under
his protection; that he had heard a Gov. Sinclair lived at
Michilimackinac, who, if he were the same person, had
offered to our brethren in London several years before, a
place for a settlement on his land with the object of their
having an opportunity to convert the natives, who are numerous and strong there, to the Christian belief. He took
notice of what Br. David said, and answered: Gov. Sinclair was in Michilimackinac, his land lay not far off on
Lake Sinclair, but it was inhabited, and he did not think
it suitable and pleasant for our Indians; but seven or
eight miles down the river towards Lake Erie was an isl-

---

[1] A name given to the Moravian purchase in Stokes and Forsyth
counties, N. C.

and, where perhaps they could live, only it was very much
overgrown with wood, and would be hard for Indians to
clear. He had himself a stretch of land situated near Lake
Erie, and should its position be agreeable to us, we were welcome to settle on it. He said further: the Catholic priests
had taken great pains since this land was inhabited by
white people to bring the nations over to the Christian religion; they had found also among the Wyandots some
admission, but with the Chippewas could do nothing,
though they had taken pains with them. They did not
live steadily in towns, but moved from one place to another
on Lakes Huron and Superior, hunting and fishing, but
planted nothing, and thus their mode of life made it hard
to do any thing among them; there was said to be such a
number of them that where they began and how far they
extended, was not yet known, and some estimated them at
30,000 strong, which also the royal interpreters maintained, who were best acquainted with them. In conclusion, the commandant said to Br. David he would reflect upon his propositions, have him called again, and
give him further information. We were glad that yet one
chance showed itself of rescuing the remnant of our Indian church.

On the 27th he summoned Br. David again, who went
together with Br. Edwards, when he said to us he had
thought over what Br. David had proposed, and if we
made up our minds to remain here and get our Indians
here, there should be no lack of help on his part; we
should reflect upon it, and let him know our conclusion,
which we promised soon to do, and expressed to him our
thanks and gratitude for his help and good disposition towards us.

The brethren consulted together in the matter, and it
was especially called to our mind that here the Saviour
had given us occasion to assemble and rescue our mission,
or what was left of it, so that there could well be no question whether we should accept the commandant's offer,
for it was our duty and necessity to venture every thing
for our Indian church, and to receive such an offer with

a thousandfold joy. But to do away with every doubt
and to be able to act in the matter with greater assurance
and joy, we wished to know exactly our Saviour's will and
have his approbation. We asked him accordingly, and
begged him to advise us according to his heart, and he
gave us to understand his good pleasure that we should
call our Indians here and accept the commandant's proposition ; should take this with joy and regard our mission
as not altogether a thing of the past, but should regard it
as a token that he wished to get together again here in
this neighborhood his Indian church. And so we told the
commandant that since he had given us hope that our
mission could be saved from perfect ruin, we accepted his
proposition with joy, for we felt ourselves bound to ad-
venture body, life and all for it. We quite gave up the
idea of going home, but would remain here ; we asked,
however, from him that he would send word to our Indians, call them here, and at the same time let them know
that we awaited them here, and, if they came, had permission to live with them ; that this should be done as soon
as possible, that no time might be lost, and that the Indians might yet do some planting. He promised to do for
us all we thought necessary. He wished, however, first to
speak with the Chippewa chiefs, who were in town,
whether they would not let our Indians settle on their
land some twenty miles from here on Huron river (now
Clinton), and he did not doubt they would give their consent ; he would put this going this very day and make
preparations, and if this succeeded he would call us and
give us further information. What moved him to favor
this plan was this : he saw very well that if we lived below Detroit we should be much disturbed, not only by the
Wyandots, who live the other side of the river, but also
by warriors, since the road goes that way, but above the
city we should not have this to fear, for the Chippewas do
not go to war, and both he and many people in the city
said to us they were much more tractable and approach-
able than the Wyandots and many others.

May 2. We had a chance to speak to an Indian, who,

ten days before, had come from the Shawanese, from
whom we got some news of our Indians, who have moved
there, and because in the morning he was going back
there again, we spoke with the commandant about sending by this opportunity a message to our Indians. He was
at once willing, and asked whether one or two of us would
not like to go too. We considered this, and replied that it
did not seem advisable for us to go there; in the first
place, since certain white people among the Wyandots, who
are our avowed enemies, would set the Indians against us
with force, and would make every effort to get us altogether out of the way, and would say to the Indians:
"You see you are not rid of these people; you must bring
about their destruction." And secondly, if we came to our
Indians, and the Shawanese, Delawares, and Wyandots
hear we have come with such intentions, to take our Indians away, we should not only find great opposition, but
we should not be sure of our lives. He readily saw this,
and therefore sent a Frenchman with the Indians, with a
written message and a string of wampum, and summoned
them to come here to their teachers, and he let them know
that here we had freedom to remain; they should all come,
and if all would not or could not come, yet some, at least,
and if this could not be, that the three brethren who were
expressly named, Samuel, William, and Mark, should certainly come. He said also that if our Indians there were
well provided for, he had no objection to our going back
and living with them, but this we at once declined, saying
that this could not be in the Indian land while the war
lasted. He said farther, that he was sorry we had so
much trouble about our mission ; we must not think him
the cause of it. He was not guilty of our misfortunes,
but during this war had to let many a thing happen which
he did not approve, but yet could not prevent. He would
not, for all the world, have the reputation of having ruined
our mission, such a praiseworthy work among the Indians ; he wished to be helpful to us in every possible way,
that our Indians should again be got together and established in a secure place, and if they came there, he would

furnish some head of cattle for our use at the outset, since we had lost every thing; he would also give our Indians tools and whatever they needed to cultivate the ground again. He had spoken with the Chippewas and arranged with them that we and our Indians should settle on the Huron river, some twenty miles from here, which was said to be a fine place and good land. We expressed to him our gratitude and recognition of his kindness and goodwill. The messengers departed the next day, the 3d, and we spoke both with the Indian and also with the Frenchman about the message to our Indians.

6. By a ship, bound for Niagara, Br. David sent a letter to Bethlehem by way of Montreal and New York, the first letter since our captivity. The commandant in his own hand wrote the address, that it might go unhindered. In this ship we should have gone, when we first came, but this is now changed since we await our Indians here. The ship was filled full of prisoners, sent to Canada, and with Indians, with them also our fellow prisoner went away, Moore by name.

7. Since a boat went to Lower Sandusky, Br. David, with the consent of the commandant, sent a message to a trader there, to send an express to our Indians in Upper Sandusky, and tell them they should all come here together, the sooner the better, in case the message sent to our Indians among the Shawanese should be late in reaching them.

10. We heard from the interpreter of the Chippewas the description of the land on the Huron river, that it is a fine country, good land, and lies some ten miles up the river, and thus somewhat out of the way. This man, who was the intrepreter in the affair, and knew all about it, told us that the chiefs were asked whether they had any objection to the Christian Indians settling with their teachers on their land; they made only one objection, that perhaps the Delaware nation would not be pleased, and would look upon them as having drawn their friends away from them and alienated them. This notion was soon taken from them, for the commandant and Bawbee (the Indian

agent) said, since the Delawares had driven the ministers, their teachers, out of their land, and would no longer have them there, thereby they had also driven away the Christian Indians and hunted them off, and thus they must go where they would be received, and the Delawares had no right to say any thing against it. We learned now also that the land belonged to Mr. Bawbee, to whom the chiefs had given it.

12. The notorious McKee and Elliot came from the Shawanese; we hoped to hear something about our Indians there, but from such people no good news is to be expected.

13. But to-day we had the pleasure of seeing here our Gabriel, with an unbaptized Indian besides, who had just come here from there, and we heard that they were all well. They met the messengers to our Indians on the way, but knew nothing about the matter.

14. Br. David was summoned to the commandant, who wished to know the contents of the letter he had written to Bethlehem, since he wrote about this to the general in Canada, and recommended him to send on the letter, saying that he knew its contents. Br. David translated it into English to his satisfaction.

17. Since the commandant had a house vacant for us outside the town, where prisoners had lived who were now sent to Canada, we moved out of the barracks to-day into our lodgings near Yankee Hall, close by our house, which has its name from the fact that only prisoners who were brought in by the Indians live there.

19. We recommended ourselves in stillness to the care of God on this day of the Holy Ghost, and begged of him to make us mindful of all that our dear Lord will have done by us to fulfil with us his aim and end. We read the printed discourse of the sainted disciple (Count Zinzendorf) upon this festival, with a blessing for our hearts.

20. We saw that the Indian who had been sent as messenger to our Indians was come back. Br. David went to the commandant to learn how things looked, and found out that the Indian had turned about at the Miami,

since the Indians he met told him that our Indians were all scattered, that none would come, and it was in vain to call them, but that the Frenchman had continued his journey to them, and in accordance with his order would deliver his message; thus we have still some hope that some one of our Indians will come;

24, but we heard from an Indian acquaintance that the greater part of our Indians was still together near Sandusky, that as soon as Br. David's letter came to Lower Sandusky, one of our Indians who was there went away at once to them with the message. We wish they would soon come, so as yet to do some planting.

Sunday, 26. We read together the church litany.

Thursday, 30. To-day, as also through the whole week, a multitude of Chippewas has come in, who were summoned to go to the war. They are praised by all the other nations for being the best and most kindly Indians, but even such Indians are much corrupted by white people, and led to every offense.

Sunday, June 2. Br. David baptized in the city, upon request, a merchant's child, Elizabeth, and at the ceremony delivered a short discourse to those present, who were very attentive, and

Monday, 3, at the commandant's request, through a sergeant, he attended the burial of one dead, whereby likewise he spoke a word of exhortation to those present.

Tuesday, 4, was a great festival and holiday, the king's birthday, which was very solemnly celebrated.

Friday, 7. We learn from Wyandots who have come in from Sandusky that our Indians have received the commandant's message, and make ready to come, that they were already busy planting. This was uncommonly pleasant for us to hear, and gives us new hope of seeing again soon our people, as we have long heartily desired.

Saturday, 8. From Delaware Indians who came from Sandusky we heard the same about our Indians, with the addition that since there is great famine among them, as among all Indians, the like of which has never been, our Indians had gone to the Muskingum to get corn, on which

account they will not yet come. We desire nothing so
much as to see again our Indians, for we fear their perfect
ruin and destruction.

Monday, 10.   News'came in of a fight between the Virginians and English and Indians in Upper Sandusky, in which
the first had the worst (in Crawford's Campaign).   In this
affair we could think of nothing but our Indian brethren,
and recommend them to the Saviour's protection.   Had
we still been there, where we were last winter, it would
have been hard with us and dangerous, for we were just
under headway when we heard that they had gone back
to our town where we had been, but where no one was
left., The messenger told Br. David they had sought to
make such an expedition as in Gnadenhütten, but came off
worsted.

Friday, 14.   To-day and for several days all sorts of rumors have been flying about and many preparations made
for war.   In a ship from Sandusky the Conners came here
with their children ; they had to come on account of the
unrest caused by war.   Of our Indians we heard that they
were all with the Shawanese and had received the message,
both Br. David's letter, and the commandant's, and are yet
awaited here.

Sunday, 16.   We read together a discourse of the sainted
disciple from the extracts about Matthew's Gospel.

Tuesday, 18.   We again had some news of our Indians
from two prisoners, that they all lived by themselves together in one town, had built houses and planted, that as
soon as they could be ready they would come here.

Saturday, 22.   During the week we have heard on every
hand rumors that do not much concern us.   We daily saw
many Chippewas and Tawas, some of whom at times visited us.   Their speech has much likeness with the Delawares, and we wished our Indians might soon come.   Who
knows whether the Saviour may not gain some of these,
for among them the priests here have found no reception.

Sunday, 23.   Br. David preached to a number of prisoners, men and women, in English, and baptized a child,
Elias Schmidt.   Many were right glad to hear a sermon

again, and wished to do so oftener if only we had a place
or house suitable.

Wednesday, 26. Br. David spoke with the commandant, from whom he sought information, but he had not yet
heard from our Indians that they were coming; he had
learned nothing about them, and wondered at it. Br.
David told him his concern about the matter, namely, that
white people in the bush among the Indians held them
back and would make them cautious about coming here.
Whereupon he answered, he did not expect that, for he
had expressly written to them to send our Indians here.
Thus he believed they would come when first they had
planted. He said further, we should not think that he in
any way put us off with fine promises and wished to make
things appear other than they were; he was honorable and
upright towards us, and he had promised us in the first
place to do for us what was in his power, that we might
continue our work among the Indians. Br. David answered we had not the least doubt about him, but that
there were people who found pleasure in utterly ruining
our mission, and were not fully content with what they
had already done. He said he saw very well we had many
enemies among the Indians, and it was good luck for us
that we came here betimes, for he had good grounds for
believing that at this time we should not have been safe
among the Indian people, certainly we should all have perished had we remained in Sandusky; that he had also
heard that our Indians were reported to have said [but to
this he paid little regard] that if they knew their teachers
were sent home they would go to the war too, but since
we were yet here in Detroit, could not do so. Br. David
answered him: there could be some bad young men who
wished to go to the war; against that he would not contend, but from this no conclusion was to be drawn about
the whole, for among such a number of people there might
well be some bad people, and this could hardly be avoided.

Sunday, 30. We read together a discourse of the sainted
disciple, from the text: Immanuel, God with us. A Ger-

7

man soldier asked to borrow a book from us, to whom we gave one of the sainted disciple's printed discourses, as we have several times already lent to others. It is something wonderful here and pleasant, if any one is found who shows a desire for God's word, for the place here is like Sodom, where all sins are committed. The French have indeed a church here and a priest, who, however, is quite old, and never preaches, but merely reads mass. On the south side of the river are also a church and a priest, where both French and Indians go, there to be seen in their heathenish garb, with painted heads in full war-array. But the English and Protestants have neither church nor preacher, and wish for neither, although they could have them if they would. The Indians wonder at this, as is natural, for they see among the so-called Christians no good examples, but bad alone. The Wyandots, though already baptized, are not only heathen, but much worse than many heathen, much more savage and blood-thirsty, for the Chippewas, none of whom is baptized, are much more humane and kindly disposed towards their fellow-men, and are much easier to get along with.

Sunday, 7. Br. David preached in English in a Frenchman's house, who offered it to us from seeing that the place where preaching usually was, was too small, and a fine number came together, mostly prisoners.

Monday, 8. At last, after long waiting, we had the pleasure of welcoming here with us two families of our Indian brethren, namely, Samuel Nanticoke and Adam, with their wives and children. They left behind two or three families, namely, Abraham, Zachary, Thomas, who also are already on the way here. They came from the Shawanese towns, where most of the brethren live together, and have planted. Our Indians had received both Br. David's letter and the major's message, and were joyful over them, had likewise resolved to make ready at once and to come here. But since from the want of supplies for the journey [for they suffer great hunger], they could not at once put this in execution, they were made to hesitate by Indians who went there from here, who told them as a fact we were no longer in Detroit, but were sent down the country; this they had not merely heard, but with their own eyes had seen us go aboard ship and sail away. This caused their journey to be given up. But their brethren would not rest content with this, but wished to be certain, to come here and see for themselves whether we were yet here or not. They were not less rejoiced than we to meet us here. They said to us they could find no rest, and it had not been well with them since we left them; they were forty days on the journey, had suffered great hunger, so that a sister once nearly wasted away from hunger. We soon gave them enough to eat, and Br. David informed the major, and got an order for them to draw provisions. Now we wished to see here only our dear old Abraham.

Wednesday, 10. With our Indians who have built their huts near our house we had this evening some singing. This was to all people something extraordinary, which in the case of Indians they had never seen nor heard. Many came and were present. Others, since it was in the street outside the town, stood still as they were going by; others again got upon the palisades in the shipyard and listened, but no one made any disturbance.

Thursday, 11. There came another of our Indians, Joseph by name, who had arrived with warriors, but had known nothing about us, that we are here. He had left our Indian brethren nine days ago, and said most of them were rather listless and in doubt about ever seeing us again ; but if they should learn that we were here, and that they would again be with us, most of them would come here; he knew also many who had no thought of coming. He begged on his own account, saying : "You see well, my brethren, that I no longer look like a brother [for he was painted like a savage]. I had already quite given up the hope of ever again having the opportunity of hearing God's word, as most of us have, and so I thought I must get favor with the savages and make myself like them, so as not to be persecuted, but so soon as I saw that the Indian brethren came together again, and that the brothers are with them, I wished to beg you to receive me again."

We did not fail to give our Indian brethren news of us as often as we had a chance, and a week before, by some white prisoners who went there, we had again sent them word, and yesterday Conner also was dispatched there on business by the commandant, and him we ordered to give exact information, so that we expect most of them ; but it requires time and patience, for they, with their families, must get through with great trouble and accomplish it with the Indians, for they have nothing to live on. We did not doubt, however, that many of them were fallen into error, for many have already departed and are scattered. Besides they are in danger from these wolves, since the Shawanese and Delawares, whose neighbors they are, will not let them go, if they hear they wish to come again to us ; they will not permit the brothers to be again with them, to which they now think they have put an end.

By ships in from Fort Erie the cheerful news comes that an armistice has been concluded and that there is hope of speedy peace, wherein we had more interest and joy than the inhabitants here showed.

Saturday, 13. Since now two families of our Indians have come to us, who altogether make fourteen persons, and according to every appearance we can not soon expect more, for we understand that our Indians are very incredulous about finding us here and have let their courage fall, we considered together for and against, whether it were good and practicable to go with them, the two families of Indian brethren, to the place appointed for us, or whether we should not wait for them and delay until more came.

In order then to cause ourselves no unnecessary trouble and difficulty, not to build upon uncertainty, and not to do any thing in doubt, we asked the Saviour's advice therein, and he let us know that his good pleasure is that we, with the two families of Indian brethren, should betake ourselves to the appointed place as soon as possible. This, his gracious advice, was not only quite according to our own wish, but we were heartily thankful therefor, and now we could set to work with comfort and confidence, in case difficulties should arise, especially from the Chippewas, we are so few: thus we know the Saviour's will. [Evening service.]

Sunday, 14. There came, about half-past one, a hundred Chippewas from Michilimackinac, who were summoned here to go to the war. They were welcomed by the discharge of three cannon from the Fort. This is no token of an armistice with the Indians.

At the meeting with our Indians from to-day's Scripture-verse: The people that walked in darkness have seen a great light; this meeting we held daily in the open air from want of other place. Many white people came, and all were attentive.

Monday, 15. Br. David made an early visit to the commandant, to whom he announced our intention to move with our Indians into the bush, and to this end begged his aid. Since, however, he was getting off ships and also Indians, and had other pressing business to attend to, he bade us have patience until he had accomplished what was most necessary; he hoped in a couple of days to be able to see to us, and then he would undertake and despatch our affairs. We again sent a message to our Indians by Delawares, that we were going with those now here into the bush, and that we awaited them with longing hope. We learned by experience that either they did not give our message at all, or indeed gave quite the opposite of it, that our Indians might not come here. This evening unexpectedly, to the hearty joy of us all, came our old Indian brother, Abraham, to us with one more family. We had always wished this; if only he would come before our departure we should be comforted, and now, praise be to God, we begin our mission anew, with four families of Indian brethren, a plain and simple beginning, but we have no doubts, for the Saviour, whose own affair it is, the honor and the shame, he will bless and prosper us in accordance with the promise in our Scripture-verse of to-day: Yet will I gather others to him besides those that are gathered unto him. On this day, and with this Scripture-verse, a year ago Brs. David Zeisberger, and Jungmann, with their wives, arrived from Bethlehem at Schönbrunn on the Muskingum.

Thursday, 18. Br. David went again to the major to speak with him about our departure. He was exceedingly inclined to be helpful to us in every way with what was needful. He gave us at once a written order to draw from the king's store tools, provisions, and whatever we needed, and our Indians were not forgotten either; on their account he gave a separate written order for all that Br. David told him to be necessary for them, all which they took and provisions besides. When Br. David told him at the same time that two more families were come, and that we expected others soon, this was pleasant both for him and for his lady to hear. She provided us also with seeds of all sorts for planting, and the major was so good as to. lend us his own boat, with sails, to go away in, and gave us besides a large canoe to keep for our own use.

Br. David spoke particularly with him about the French priests, asking whether we were likely to have from them any care or trouble, and whether they could not put some difficulty in our way; it was not the business of the brethren to interfere in other people's work, and to labor for Indians who were already under the care of others, but we by far preferred to have to do with those who had not yet heard of the gospel, as, for instance, the Chippewas; since now they would be our neighbors, it might happen that some of them would receive the gospel, and the French priests would conceive suspicion and jealousy of the brethern, therefore Br. David wanted to tell him this beforehand to avoid all misunderstandings. The major answered that we should be easy about this; the priests should not be hard and troublesome to us, and should they put obstacles in our way, the thing would touch him and they must arrange it with him. At our evening meeting many French and English were present.

Friday, 19. We prepared for our journey. Our Scripture-verse read: Thy children shall make haste. We had

from the first resolved that Brs. Heckewelder and Senseman should stay here with the children, and at the same
time help forward such of our Indians as might arrive
from time to time.

Saturday, 20.   We set'out with four families of Indian
brethren, namely: Brs. Zeisberger and Jungmann, with
their wives, two unmarried brethren, Wm. Edwards and
Michael Young, with the Indian brethren, Abraham and
Anna, Samuel and Sara Nanticoke, Adam and Sabina,
Zachary, and Anna Elizabeth, and eleven children, among;
them two great girls, in all 19 Indian souls.   Our neighbors, prisoners from Kentucky, who during our stay here
had been with us daily, were sorry to lose our companion-
ship, even were so much affected as to weep for us.   Three
miles from the city we came to an island where we took
aboard our two pilots, who were to conduct us to the appointed place.   Towards noon, with a good wind, we came
into Lake St. Clair.   At the upper end of this lake Gov.
St. Clair, at present Governor in Michilimackinac, holds
lands and estates.   Since we sailed out in the lake far
from land, we fastened the two canoes in which most of the
Indians were, to our boat, in order to be able to protect
them in case a strong wind should arise, and so we reached
the land in the evening, when it was already dark.   But
we were in no condition to land, notwithstanding we tried
our best, on account of the marsh which stretches along
the shore far into the lake.   Besides, on account of the
mosquitoes, we could not stay in the marsh, and must consequently sail out into the lake and pass the night in the
boat.   Our pilots could not recognize the place because it
was night and were uncertain in their reckoning.   The
wind blew somewhat hard till midnight, and we were in
fear a gale would spring up, but afterwards it became more
calm, and we rested until morning.

Monday, 21.   When it was day the pilots recognized the
land, that we yet had the mouth of the Huron river before
us, and not behind us, as they had thought.   We ran up
there this forenoon, and after landing, cooking something,
and refreshing ourselves, we went all day up the river.

From Detroit our course was north-east as far as the Huron river, then north-west. The river is very deep, with hardly any current, so that oars have to be used. In the evening we came to the place appointed for us to settle in, and encamped, but were welcomed by mosquitoes and so badly treated that we had little rest, although we made a fire round about us, so that the air was filled with smoke and steam. Thus far we have found no place satisfactory to us, for all the land we have seen is too low, swampy, and exposed to overflow, though we landed several times and examined several places. Besides we did not dare to settle within a distance of eight miles from the lake, for the land both sides of the river belongs to some Detroit merchants. We did not wish so to do either, for it was no place for us. Since now the place of our encampment, which the pilots had assigned us, did not quite please us, though indeed it lies higher than all the land we have seen here, and is also good, rich soil, we examined, the 22d, further up the creek, and found on the south side of the river a fine place to lay out a town on a height, not inferior to that at Schönbrunn, and it has the same slope, according to the compass, and the course of the river, which Schönbrunn had.

On the north-east side of the town, between the river and the height, there are many springs along the height, which in separate little brooks flow into the river, and have exceedingly good water, which in this country is a rare and unusual thing. The land on the site of the town is sandy, which is a token [and therefore the more pleasant to us] that it is not wet and marshy, as is nearly all the land in this country. The bottoms or lowlands are very rich, but very thickly overgrown with heavy timber. The common kinds of trees are oak, poplar, linden, walnut, ash, hickory, elm, beech, and a great number of sugar-trees and wild-cherry trees, which have a fine red wood, of which in Detroit the most beautiful cabinet-work is made, and which is much finer than walnut. There are asps and sassafras, these last of such thickness as we had nowhere seen before, so that boards two feet wide could be cut from them. The uncommon height of the trees shows us that this is no cold climate. Hills there are none, but everywhere the land is flat. There are stones in the creek, but only a few, elsewhere none. The hunting is good, and our Indians shot their first deer to-day. Thus we chose this place before all others for our town-site, as the only one in this neighborhood, and we went there to-day, pitched our tents, for heavily-laden boats, too, can go even to the fork, a half mile higher up than we are, and canoes much farther. We were glad and thankful to have found so good and, according to all appearances, so healthy a spot, where for a town-site nothing was lacking, and we could lay out plantations both sides of the river, as we pleased.

In the evening services held near our fire, to-day's Scripture-verse was the subject of consideration : For ye shall go out with joy and be led forth with peace. With a mother's hand leads he his own. It is still another advantage that we live here so apart, where we hear nothing of what goes on in the world, and that we quite alone can be in communion with our unseen Friend, whom we love so much.

Tuesday, 23. Last night there was a heavy, severe thunder-storm, and a tree was struck hardly a stone's throw from our huts. Br. Heckewelder returned to Detroit in the boat with the two pilots who had shown us the way to this place. We at once made preparations to plant some vegetables, the plants we had brought with us. Thus we did the following days, and sowed turnips and lettuce, planted beans and some garden stuff, though it was somewhat late in the summer.

We found many traces that a long time ago an Indian town must have stood on this place, for we saw many holes in the ground, which were now indeed filled up, but quite recognizable, in which the Indians have even now the custom of keeping their corn and other property. We could also quite plainly see the little hills where corn had been planted, but where now is a dense wood of trees two to six feet in diameter. Another deer was shot.

26. We built a hut of bark to store our supplies in. We live in tents until we shall have built a house. Br.

Michael Jung caught a mess of fish, the first caught here.
In the evening was the service and consideration of our
Scripture-verse. The glory of the Lord shall be revealed.
May this soon happen here, where all is yet in darkness,
and where the name of the Lord is not known—this was
our hearty wish.

Saturday, 27. We marked out our town, in the first
place only where two rows of houses shall be built, and
the street four full rods wide, but each lot has three rods
front. Indian brethren who went hunting several miles up
the creek came upon a cedar-swamp and found many
traces of bears in the same neighborhood, but the bush in
the summer is so wild, overgrown with weeds and thick-
ets, that it is very hard to get through, and consequently
is not then good for hunting, for the game gets off before
a man has sight of it, and the mosquitoes are so bad as to
be almost intolerable. We are very much incommoded by
them here day and night, though we live on a height
where the wind can blow somewhat, and though the bush
is not so thick as elsewhere; and we have to sit in a thick
smoke if we wish relief from them. On this account we
have not so fully examined the country as we have wished.
In Detroit no one is acquainted with this region, and the
merchants who own the land along the river have never
seen it.

Monday, 29. We began to fell the woods on our town
site, so as to build our houses, and thereby also get a little
more air—a protection from insects. In regard to snakes
here, there are very few, though on our other plantations
usually we have had very many; we have nowhere seen
fewer of them than here, so that as far as regards them
one can wander about the bush unconcerned.

Tuesday, 30. With the help of our Indian brethren we
got together the timber for our first house, which to be
sure was quite near us, and yet we had to carry it.

Thursday, Aug. 1. Br. David wrote to our brethren in
Detroit by some Indian brethren, who went there to get
provisions in exchange for baskets they had made here.

Friday, 2. We began to block out the first house, but

as there were only four of us, this was rather hard. When
now all our hunters were away, so that we could expect
no fresh meat, a deer came by our camp to the creek,
which old Br. Abraham shot, but which our heavenly
Father sent. Br. Abraham expressed his thoughts, and
remarked about the troubles which have befallen us, saying, "The Delawares, Shawanese, Mingoes, and Wyandots, who live over the lake, have heard the word of God;
the brethren have lived with them and announced it to
them, but they have despised it, thrust it from them, and
driven away the brethren who have announced it; therefore the Saviour has taken it from them, and will give it
to others who will receive it."

Tuesday, 5. Brs. Samuel and Adam came from the
Fort and brought us letters from our brethren there, from
which we learned they were well. At the same time
we heard that an army was marching to the Shawanese
towns: this caused us to think much about our brethren
there and to be anxious about them, and to wish they were
with us out of danger.

Saturday, 10. This week both we and the Indian
brethren have been busy cultivating; they have now also
made the beginning, but they run short of provisions, for
the allowance they get is not enough for them, though we
manage to get along with ours; therefore they have to
exert themselves to get the means of life. This evening
we had our services around our fire, and considered our
Scripture-verse, praising and glorifying the name of the
Lord here in this wilderness, where probably it has never
been heard. Thus far we have seen no strange Indians
here, for we are placed quite out of the way.

By one of our Indians, who came from Detroit, we heard
that another attack had been made on the Shawanese
towns, and inasmuch as our Indians are in that quarter,
having planted there, we were very uneasy about them,
that they might have come to harm. Afterwards,
however, we heard they had fled and were scattered in
the bush, and thus none of them had been injured.
Though we live here so remote from all rumors of the

world, yet Satan can not rest and be content with us, but
must set on the ill-minded Indian people to say to our
people, since they have put themselves under the protection of the English people, they will all perish; had they
put themselves under their protection, they would have
been safe and free from every danger. What a satanic
and barefaced lie and what wickedness is this! Have
they not themselves driven us away? They have not
rested until they had us here. Have they not ruined us
and our Indians, house and barn, property and land, and
placed us in the greatest misery, so that we must have
starved and miserably perished unless also the dear heavenly
Father had again mercifully upheld us and helped us
through? One would think they would be content to
have wreaked their vengeance so far on us, but no, for
since they now see that they can not accomplish their aim
of putting us out of the way and of killing the name
of the Saviour in the Indian land, but that we shall yet
again settle down and assemble and moreover outside their
bounds too, and since they foresee already that our Indians
will follow us, they bring them wicked rumors, threats,
and lies, to make our Indians fearful and to frighten them
from coming here, though they are the causes of our being
here, and believed that here there would be an end of us;
therefore they are now scornful and angry that their
schemes have not only not succeeded, but since their eyes
begin to open and they see that they will indeed have
done themselves the greatest harm, and they know that
their nation will therefore yet come to nothing. O, what
great scorn has Satan! Perhaps, however, he knows he
has but little time.

Sunday, 11. Br. Jungmann preached, and in the evening
Br. David had an hour of song with the Indians.

Wednesday, 14. Several of our Indians went again to
the settlements to get food, by which opportunity we wrote
to our brethren in Detroit. When they came here, they
were so starved that their rations, already given to them,
did not half suffice, though they got the same quantity
as we. Br. Abraham and our family besides yet remained

at home, whom we for the most part have to maintain from our own allowance, and we do it willingly, if only we have enough.

Friday, 16. We roofed our first house, and we have the timber for a second building already on hand.

Tuesday, 20. The Indian brethren returned from Detroit. From Br. Heckewelder and Sensemann's letters we learn that they are well in Yankee Hall.

Wednesday, 21. Brs. David, Edwards, and Michael Jung, with some Indians, went to Detroit to get supplies, and also to bring here our brethren yet there, for now we have some food. With a good wind we got there in the evening, and had the joy of welcoming and speaking with the Indian brethren, Mark, William, Isaac Eschicanahund, and Stephen, who got there day before yesterday from the Shawanese towns to see and hear how it was with us. Mark told us he had been negotiating with the Twightwees, and they had given him a district to live on. He would like to have one or two brothers go there with him, and he believed all our scattered Indian brethren would then move there. We had to refuse him this utterly, since for the time no brother could be in the Indian ·land, for the Indians would not permit it, and no one could be sure of his life. Mark's wife died.

On the 22d, Br. David spoke with the commandant in their behalf. He had them come to him, and invited them to come here to us with all our Indians and to remain here until there was peace, for here they would have liberty to remain, or to move elsewhere if they knew a better place. He promised to provide them with supplies until they had planted and could supply themselves. Mark promised him that they would all come in the autumn, but we had our doubts about his promise, for we saw his position and intentions, which indeed he hid as far as possible, and sought merely to please the commandant and us in his words so as to get gifts. He had a speech from the Delawares, Shawanese, and Wyandots, who had dictated what he should say to him, but since we saw that the only aim of this was to create difficulties between our Indians and

him, for they saw the commandant to be our friend, and
to set them each against the other, we forbade him to deliver this speech, and this so remained.

Br. David spoke with the commandant about supplies
for our Indians and got a very favorable answer. He said
we must not think he had put us where we must suffer
want; he wished to supply both us and our Indians with
food until we ourselves had a harvest and could supply
ourselves, and that we might have no reason to doubt
about this he read to Br. David a letter from Gen'l Haldimand (the commander-in-chief), received two days before
from Quebec, that we might see that what he did was done
with his approbation. Since it was said that another governor would come here, Br. David made the necessary
arrangements in this regard, and he promised, should it be
necessary, to summon Br. David, in case he had to go
away.

In the evening, we had with our Indians, of whom a
fair number was present, a meeting in the open air, outside
the town, whither also many white people came, and the
singing of the Indians pleased them much.

Saturday, 24. We took leave of our Indians, who are
going back to the Shawanese towns to their friends, and·
we bade them greet all our brethren there, and tell them
we invited here all such as were troubled and in perplexity
about their salvation, and we should much rejoice to see
them here, the sooner the better; to tell them also what
good offers the major had made to them here, who had
besides given written orders that those of our Indians who
come here should have supplies given them on the Miami
for the journey, so that they could come here, and this
happened too, only many other Indians also made use of
it, and gave out they were our Indians that they might
get supplies. We set out then to-day, with Brs. Heckewelder and Sensemann with us—had at first a good wind,
but in the afternoon thunder-storms, with rain, and were
compelled to pass the night in a windmill we came to,
where the people received us very kindly.

Sunday, 25. In the evening, we came through Lake St.

Clair into the Huron river, and remained over night, but our two little children were so stung by mosquitoes that in the morning they were swollen all over. We arrived—

Monday, 26, home at Br. Jungmann's and sister Susanna's, who, in our absence, had the first visit from the Chippewas since we have been here.

Thursday, 29. Brs. Heckewelder and Sensemann felled timber to build them houses. Two Delaware women, who came here visiting, and were now again going home, gave Br. Abraham to understand that they should like to live with us after they had harvested their corn on the Miami. To them we said, not every one could live here, but only they who believed and wished to live for the Saviour. Our Indians were busy cultivating the land at this time. The unmarried brethren we blessed with our hearts at their feast-day, and we wished them the near presence of the Saviour.

Monday, Sept. 2. Brs. Heckewelder, Sensemann, Edwards and Michael Jung, went to Detroit to get a cargo of boards, which the major gave for our building.

Tuesday, 3. From the Scripture-verse, which we had just a year ago this day, we recalled our captivity, and this text (Is. lxiv, 5) has the Saviour fulfilled, for he has again placed our feet in a wide space after we have certainly been in very narrow and dangerous circumstances. Thus we could not do otherwise than filially thank the Saviour for his wondrous conduct of us, and not sufficiently wonder at his wise leadership. Although our brethren's calamity on the Muskingum, where so many perished, is always, alas, a stumbling block to us, so that we must think if only that had not happened, then in the end all had gone well and as we wished, but he knows best why he has allowed that also.

Friday, 6. By the brethren who came back from Detroit we had news that a new governor was about to come, who had already got as far as Niagara. We were sorry to lose our good friend and benefactor, Major de Peyster, for we could not know how his successor would be disposed towards us. About peace, however, nothing more was heard, but the contrary. In the States the rangers[1] and Indians do great damage, and a short time since have taken prisoners or killed over two hundred in Kentucky.

Saturday, 7. At the wedding-feast we had a service with the single Indian brethren. He made himself known to us and blessed us.

Saturday, 14. This week we have all been busy in the fields. On the 13th we congratulated Sister Jungmann upon her sixtieth birthday. We have had much rainy weather, and yesterday the first frost, which, however, had not much to say.

Sunday, 15. Inasmuch as we white brethren were alone, except old Abraham, we read a discourse of the sainted disciple upon the text: One is your master and all ye are brethren.

Friday, 20. The joyful announcement was made to the brethren that, since now we are so far along with our house, we would have the blessed holy communion, which we could not have since we came away from Sandusky, nor with the Indian brethren since we came away from the Muskingum. In Detroit we had no service, for we could not be alone, for as soon as they heard us singing all came running to us.

Saturday, 21. We had a love-feast, and afterwards the holy communion with the Saviour's near presence, the first time in this place. To the Indian brethren too, five of whom were present, was it an unspeakable blessing, which they had had to do without for more than a year. To-day also another family of our Indians, six in number, came from Sandusky, where they have been meantime. But the Indians, as we hear, took all conceivable pains to keep our Indians from coming here, and lied to them on every hand that they were no longer safer with the English than with the Americans.

Sunday, 22. The holy communion liturgy was read, afterwards a sermon, and in the evening an hour of song.

---

[1] Led by Simon Girty at Blue Licks.

Tuesday, 24. Chippewas came in who went through here hunting. All who have thus far come are friendly and very well-behaved.

Saturday, 28. Another house, Jungmann's, was roofed and preparations are already made for others.

Sunday, 29. Br. Jungmann preached in the morning, and the congregation meeting was from the Scripture-verse, and after the collect of the same we gave ourselves anew to the accomplishment of predestination in the care of the Father, in the bridegroom's leadership, and in the steady impulse of his spirit, to the protection of the angels of whom we especially thought, and we were heartily thankful to them, as also to the Saviour, for their service and protection.

Tuesday, Oct. 1. We remembered that a year ago to-day we arrived in Sandusky, and we thanked the Saviour and our dear heavenly Father for the gracious oversight which he has had over us. With Zachary in from the Fort, came also Stephen from the Shawanese towns, who brought us news that he, with yet another family of eleven persons, had come to Detroit, and was waiting for us to fetch them in a canoe. Adam, whose mother is still there, came there with him. As far as we learn, however, few of our Indians are coming here, for Mark, who has made himself head and chief, holds back all who would come here. His falseness and treachery come to light now. When he was lately in Detroit he spoke so beautifully with us and the major, and made fair promises that he would come here this autumn with all our Indians, but when our backs were turned he has changed his coat, for the land promised him by the Twightwees, as he said, blinds him, for I showed him plainly and clearly that the Indians had been false to them often enough, not only about property and goods, but about their salvation, had been their ruin, and now they were not content, but wished to betray them farther, so as to have them in their power, and, if possible, to ruin their salvation. To-day and yesterday Sensemann's house was blocked out.

8

Thursday, 3. The Saviour took home to himself Elizabeth, the daughter of Ignatius and Christina, two years,
ten months and one day old; she was buried on the 4th
and was placed the first seed in our God's acre, which
was thus dedicated, a beautiful even place on a height, the
finest we have anywhere had. To-day Chippewas came
again on their way hunting, from whom our Indians
bought some corn. They went about, looked at every
thing, and measured as well the height of the houses as
their size.

Sunday, 6. During the summer the little daughter of
Ignatius and Christina, born the 3d or 4th of June of this
year, in Sandusky, since we left there, was baptized with
the name Naomi; she was the first to be baptized here,
and this baptism was especially accompanied by the nearness and presence of the Saviour. In the afternoon Chippewas again went through, from whom our people bought
some supplies.

Wednesday, 9. Three families more came to us from
the Shawanese town by way of Detroit, namely, Stephen,
Joshua, with their families, Magdalena with her daughter
and the widow, Zipporah, with her grandchild, Phoebe, in all
eleven persons. We learned from them with sorrow that
Mark, who has made himself head-man among them, and
to whom, as he himself said, the Twightwees gave a tract
of land, holds back the brethren who wish to come to us,
and says to them: that he looks upon this invitation as a
perfect trap for them; if they come here they will live
north of Detroit, and permission ever to come back would
be quite cut off from them; for the major had expressly
said to them that this would last only so long as the war
lasted; if then they afterwards knew a situation or place
which pleased them better they could then go again
where they pleased, and the proposition was only to help
them for the present that they might live quietly and
out of the way of the war. These brethren have come
away from them in spite of all opposition and threats
and are come here, though they were often told that in a
short time they would all perish, for all who came here

had nothing else and better to expect. Mark informed the brethren that, if they would dwell in their land he wished to invite their teachers there. Those, however, who have made themselves chiefs among the Delawares said to him, he should not let himself fancy he could bring us there again, for as sure as we came again, an end would be made with us, and it should never again happen that the Gospel should be preached in the Indian land; that should now cease. They accused us white brethren of writing to Pittsburg, and of making the Virginians the proposition to bring them upon Gnadenhütten, and they slandered us with many more accusations, not at all that they really believed them, but from wickedness and hatred towards us. In spite of this, however, we heard of several more who wish to come here, if not also this autumn, and who will be bad, so let him be. In Detroit the commandant gave them provisions and took care of them fourteen days till we came down there. By them he sent word to Br. David that he wished to speak with him as soon as might be, and that he had received letters from London for us which he did not like to put into the hands of any body else, and that he had also more to say to him. Two Tutelee Indians, one from friendship for Shikellimy,[1] came with them here from Niagara. They said the believing Indians would all be summoned to Niagara.

Thursday, 10. Br. Heckewelder's house was blocked out so that we white brethren have now four houses standing, but the unmarried brethren have as yet no dwelling except that Michael Jung lives in a bark hut.

Sunday, 13. The sermon treated of the wedding garment, Christ's blood, and righteousness. Those who have put on Christianity will stand before God and enter the kingdom of heaven with joy.

Monday, 14. We set out in our boat for Detroit, and came with a moderately good wind over Lake St. Clair, and the day after, the 15th, in the forenoon, we arrived.

---

[1] The Iroquois sachem converted at Shamokin (Sunbury, Pa) 1748 See De Schweinitz' Life of Zeisberger, Chap. VII.

Br. David went at once to the major, who was glad to see
him, and said to him he had letters for us from London,
which he at once gave him, saying he had wished himself
to deliver them to him and put them into the hands of no
one else, for there were letters of credit from Mr. La
Trobe, about whom he asked, and Br. David told him he
was the brethren's bishop of London and of all England.
Sir John Johnson,[1] who some days before, by way of Michilimackinac, had come here and had also gone to Niagara,
brought them here. The major said to Br. David that
our circumstances and the calamity caused by the Americans had been judged in London in the severest way.
Although this was truly and not unjustly judged, Br.
David answered that much might have contributed
thereto, since they had yet no news by letter from us. In
the spring, to be sure, as he was aware, he had written to
Bethlehem, but he wondered at getting no answer from
them. The major replied that he had provided for Br.
David's letter in the best way, had sent it to Gen. Haldimand, and also written to him that he had himself seen
it, and had no scruples about forwarding it. There was
also with him an officer, Capt. Potts, who has been in
Bethlehem, and is not altogether unacquainted with the
institutions of the brethren, and talked much with Br.
David. At last the major asked Br. David what we
thought of doing now we were come. He replied that
we thought with our Indians of taking provisions with us
for the winter, while the weather was yet passable, not
too stormy upon the lakes, and before the cold came on
to freeze. He said that was quite right; in the morning
we should tell him the number, and, as regarded the Indians, what sort of supplies were most suitable, and he
would give orders about it. Br. David took leave, went
to our quarters, where we refreshed ourselves by reading
the letters we had received with unbroken seals. We
thanked the Saviour for the sympathy and remembrance
of our dear brethren, that he renewed for us correspond-

---

[1] General Superintendent of Indian affairs in Canada.

ence with them, for already it was more than a year since we had heard from them or they from us.

Wednesday, 16. Br. David went to a merchant, Mr. Askin, in the city, who is connected in business with Mr. Dobie, in Montreal, and whom the major had recommended to us; with him we spoke about the letter of credit we had received and showed it to him, and asked whether he had not already had advices from Mr. Dobie, in Montreal. Yes, he was willing to advance us at present what was necessary until he had written to the merchant and received from him an answer. When we came into the city we were welcomed everywhere, people were glad to see us, gave us good wishes, and showed themselves serviceable to us. There were some people who offered us on credit or upon payment to provide our Indians for fishing, with flour, corn, and all materials in the winter, when the lakes were frozen, an important matter for us, and one that had always interested us. Thus our heavenly Father cares for us and our people in all circumstances.

Thursday, 17. Br. David received an order from the major upon the commissary for six months' provisons for us, that is, until April of next spring, when the lakes will again be open. He had the commissary called, and gave him the order in Br. David's presence to give not only us, but our Indians, full rations of the best provisions. The boat which we have thus far had at our disposal he let us keep for further use. The major promised to visit us this winter when the lake is frozen. Br. David wrote to Br. Wollin,[1] in London, and the major undertook to forward the letter. By a white man, who is an Indian interpreter, just back from the Shawanese towns, where he had seen and spoken with our Indian brethren, we learned that most of them would come to us this autumn. William had charged the man to tell us this, and that they could no longer abide there on account of the wild Indians who steal all they have, and even take things away

---

[1] Mission Agent in London.

by force, and, as it seems, circumstances must make them glad and quite willing to come here, though most of them there would not have come, for which there may be many reasons, since they have grossly sinned, and this frightened them.

Friday, 18. When we were about to load our boat and examined our cargo, we found we were hardly able to take it in three trips, and the commissary so told the major. He thought of sending with us a second large ship as far as the mouth of the Huron river, but because the shipmen were too timid, and had never gone to this neighborhood, they did not like to venture to put the ship in danger; therefore the major ordered a small transport to carry our things there. We set out then with our boat, and left Br. Edwards in the transport that came after; we came, however, since we had windy weather only, on

Monday, 21, home to our brethren, who were glad enough to see us again, and sympathized in the joy we had in getting letters from our brethren in London. But hardly were we arrived, when came a little canoe, which had been with us, but could not keep up, and informed us that the transport already yesterday evening had got to the mouth of the river and was waiting for our boat. We sent then Br. Michael Jung, with the boat, some Indians, and all the canoes down there, to unload the transport and bring the things here, and with them they also,

Tuesday. 22, came, and we were glad that now the journey was successfully ended. One of our Indians, Joseph by name, who, since spring, had lapsed into error, came to us in Detroit and begged permission to live with us again. His wife had a short time before came here from the Shawanese towns. He was allowed to go to her again. So, as we hear, are others among our people situated that man and wife are separated and that disorder is among them. The Indians, of whom, together with children, there were 36 persons, got as supplies for six months 130 bushels of corn, 19 barrels of pork, and some little flour, so that they are as well provided for as we could expect.

Wednesday, 23. We again went to work upon our

houses to finish them, and the Indians did likewise and
built them huts for the winter to live in. Some days ago,
while we were in Detroit, the weather was cold and it
snowed, but now it is again fine and warm, so that frogs
are heard.

Sunday, 27. Br. Michael Jung preached. We must
still hold our daily services in the open air until we can
build a shed for them, and this can now soon be made.
The congregation meeting was held by Br. David, and he
bade the brethren think about a meeting-house as soon as
possible.

Monday, 28. We went again to work. The late cold
weather compelled us to bring all our houses soon under
roof; especially for the sisters and children is this quite
necessary.

Wednesday, 30. The holy communion was announced
to the brethren in a separate service. The Indian brethren worked during the week on a meeting-house for us,
which they,

Saturday, Nov. 2, finished, a pretty, and for the time
being, a spacious house, for which we were joyful and
thankful. The communion brethren received the holy
sacrament of the body and blood of our Lord. In a conference we had considered about the Indian brethren who
had lately come to us, and since we found all of us had
anxiety about admitting them to the holy communion,
we asked the Saviour about each one of them, but one only
had permission to go to it, namely, Stephen, who enjoyed
it with us after receiving absolution by the laying on of
hands. One among them, Ignatius, confessed to Br. David
his sins against the brethren, his teachers; that he was
among the guilty and had aided our being taken captive,
for he had complained about us to the chiefs of the warriors in Gnadenhütten, that we had always written letters to Pittsburg; since that time the matter had always
troubled him; his heart had accused him that he had behaved towards his teachers in a cruel and treacherous
way; he had had no rest until he again came to us, and

now that he was here, yet he had an uneasy heart, and could not be content until he got forgiveness.

Br. David answered him that indeed he told him nothing new, for he had known it well when we were still in Thuppekünk¹ and Gnadenhütten, what he did and planned. "But what good has all that now done thee, nor hast thou been able to do much harm to me and us white brethren, but thou hast thyself the greatest harm from it. Thou hast put thyself in misfortune and misery outwardly and inwardly. Thou and others like thyself gave up your teachers into the hands of murderers as though ye would say to them: do with them now what ye will, and had they struck us dead, it would have been quite right in your eyes, but the Saviour, whom alone we have to thank for our rescue, and not you at all, he has not wished a hair of our heads to be injured. Since now thou comest and speakest thy heart to me, I speak uprightly with thee, and say to thee—thou hast great guilt lying upon thee, and therefore reason to seek forgiveness from the Saviour. Thou seest now thyself, with the savages thou canst not remain, and to be with the brethren, hast thou no righteous and perfect heart; thus art thou a poor man whom I must pity, therefore give thyself entirely to the Saviour, and not by halves, thus art thou a blessed man."

Sunday, 3. Br. Jungmann preached after the communion liturgy, and David held the congregation meeting from the Scripture-verse: He said, surely they are my people, children that will not lie: so he was their Saviour.

Tuesday, 5. We had to-day the first service in our new chapel, now completed, from the Scripture-verse: The Lord God will come with strong hand, and his arms shall rule for him: behold, his reward is with him, and his work before him.

---

¹ Thuppekünk, the Indian name of Schönbrunn on the Muskingum, often used by Zeisberger. In his Delaware spelling-book Thuppeek= a well or spring. By adding the locative termination, ünk, we get Thuppekünk. I am indebted to the Hon. Wm. M. Darlington, of Pittsburg, for the substance of this note.

Wednesday, 6. We considered in our conference about Joseph, who came for the second time and asked permission to live here. Since he has been here, we have heard he was present at the horrible murder of Col. Crawford,[1] with which, in Detroit, all are much displeased. When reminded of this, he confessed, but begged us exceedingly much to let him live with us. Since we had great reluctance, at the very beginning of a new settlement, to admit such a man, and yet had compassion with him, for he said he knew no place where he could find rest except with the brethren, and if he went away would certainly rush to eternal damnation. Then we asked the Saviour, and he told us to let him go, and to advise him for the time being to remain elsewhere.

Friday, 8. The child of Ignatius and Naomi, six months old, which died yesterday, was buried. The weather up to date is still fine, pleasant weather. We have had, to be sure, some snow come already, but it has not remained a day. The wind varies here as elsewhere in all places, for on the Ohio and Muskingum we had south, west, and north winds, but seldom and almost no east wind. Otherwise the difference in the weather here and there is not great, but in Canada below it is said to be very cold and very different, yes, in Niagara it is said to be colder than here, and, considering its situation, it is not strange.

Sunday, 10. The sermon treated of the advent of the Saviour and the hope of believers. Br. Jungmann conducted the congregation meeting from the Scripture-verse.

Monday, 11. Br. Michael Jung held the morning service about the Scripture-verse: Of the increase of his government and peace there shall be no end.

Wednesday, 13. We went early before our Lord and the Elder of his church, begged for the aspect of his mercy and the forgiveness of all our sins and shortcomings which we had been guilty of towards him, which were first mentioned and brought to the remembrance of the brethren, especially their disobedience to him and his servants,

---

[1] See Butterfield's Crawford's Campaign.

whereby they had brought upon themselves great hardship and want, which they need not have had. They were incited to give themselves anew to him, to look upon him as our Lord and head, to vow obedience and fidelity, and to beg from him gracious absolution. This did Br. David, with the hearts of all the company and in the name of all. He heard our entreaty, comforted us about all we had not done according to his mind, and sent us recognizably his peace. With all this, however, there remained behind a certain pain about the past in our hearts, an unforgetable pain, which always urges us to draw nearer to him.

Thursday, 14. Br. Heckewelder held the early service, and on the 15th Br. Edwards.

Friday 15. Our Indian brethren went out hunting for a time; at home only old Br. Abraham and the sisters remained.

Sunday, 17. Instead of the sermon Br. David read to the brethren something out of the History of the Days of the Son of Man.[1] Three white people came here from the settlements on their way hunting, and could not wonder enough at all that has been done in the short time of our living here. They said they saw very well we were another people, that could be seen from our work and from what we purposed, namely, to make a regular settlement. Otherwise no road passes through here anywhere, but the place is quite out of the way, except that the Chippewas go through on their way hunting, and then very few.

Tuesday, 19. The brethren came home who had been hunting, since the place where they were did not please them. The three white people went back home, who will have enough to tell about us, for they have taken notes of every thing they have seen.

Wednesday, 20. The laborers had a conference together, and considered again about Joseph, who, in spite

---

[1] A Harmony of the Gospels, narrating the history of Christ's sufferings and death, and containing the lessons which are read every day in public service during Passion Week.

of our telling him he can not live here, for the time being, persistently begs and laments, asking to be allowed to stay here. This spring, in Upper Sandusky, after our departure, he took part in a horrible and awful murder (Col. Crawford's), whereto he was led by the savages. The Saviour showed us to put from us both him and his wife; this was done, and Joseph took leave of us all, and begged we should not altogether throw him aside, but meanwhile think of him, whether the Saviour might not yet have mercy upon him, and he hoped to see us again. We could not but have compassion with him, but we hoped all this would tend to his good.

Thursday, 21. Some went by water to the Fort and the settlement to make purchases. The Indian brethren went hunting, but thus far the weather has been bad for this, for in the bush it has been too dry. Snow or rainy weather is most serviceable for this.

Saturday, 23. The unmarried brethren's house was roofed, which is made only ad interim for the winter; now both they and each family has its own dwelling and lots, and indeed we live near the meeting-house or lot, on both sides of the street. Each lot, as well ours as the Indians', is forty-nine and one-half feet in front, but each can take as much land inward as he chooses. We are very thankful for the exceptionally fine, warm weather at this time of year, which we had not expected. It is pleasanter than we ever had at this time of year on the Muskingum.

Sunday, 24. In the forenoon was a sermon about the Saviour's sermon on the mount, Matthew, v.

Wednesday, 27. Chippewas came here on their way hunting. They take all their house utensils with them, and remain away the whole winter, boil sugar in the spring, and do not go home before planting-time.

Thursday, 28. We white brethren laid out plantations, that during the winter we might prepare and clear them, if the weather should be tolerable. We hear in this place too, on every hand, stories and threats about us, and, as it seems, the end is not yet. Many of the Delaware captains said, to our Indians who are come here, that they

had thought that in the Indian land the word of God
would cease to be preached, but they saw us brethren settling down again, instead of which we should have been
banished. They wished, therefore, instead of going by
way of Detroit, to seek us out straight through the bush,
and to kill us, in order that once for all they might be
done with us. They said to our Indians in the Shawanese
towns not to allow themselves to think they would ever
again bring their teachers there, for no word of God should
again be heard in the Indian land, they should resign
themselves to this, and accept heathenism and live as they
lived, and as sure as they brought their teachers there
they would be killed. Here can be seen their hostility to
God, his word, and his church.

Sunday, Dec. 1. On the first day of Advent, Br. David
preached, exhorting the brethren to give their hearts to
the coming of our Saviour, that they might rejoice in his
birth, to receive him, and with joy take him into their hearts,
for then they could expect many blessings from him.

To-day came back some Indian brethren who had been
to the settlements; they brought word that another attack[1] had been made upon the Shawanese towns, and
three of their towns wasted and ravaged, many Indians
thereby perishing. Since many of our Indian brethren
live near there, this news caused us anxiety about them,
that at least some of them might have been affected, but
we have no further news how it is with them, and we eagerly wish soon to hear about them. We heard, however,
that many of our Indians stayed there, and this makes us
uneasy about them.

Friday, 6. Chippewas came here; one of them, a captain, asked whether some one did not understand Shawanese. Abraham brought them to Samuel, and then he
said to our Indian brethren that their chief had pointed
out and given to us this country to live in, but we had selected a bad neighborhood, and had gone by the good
places at the mouth of the river, where there were old

---

[1] Probably the expedition under Gen'l Clark in the Miami Valley
is referred to.

towns and cleared land easy to plant; they did not see
here where we could plant, for all was bush; if in the
spring we wished to move down there, we should be welcome. Our Indians gave them no answer until they had
spoken with us. But the reason we came so far up is
that the major had pointed out to us the distance from
the mouth of the river to this place, for the Chippewas
had given that land to white people, who certainly would
not have objected to our settling and cultivating it, but
we must have been ready in a year or two to vacate it,
and thus all our labor would soon have been in vain, for
we must always have been pilgrims, and have had no
abiding home. Thus we wished to be sure of our affair,
and not build upon another's ground and land, since the
country is not yet surveyed. A second reason why this
place pleased us more than others is that it is high and
dry, for all the land further down the river is very low,
wet, and unhealthy, and often flooded. That there is no
open land here, but that all is bush, is indeed true; it is
thickly grown with trees, but good land, and not hard to
clear; we shall find a place where we can plant, and for
this during the winter we can prepare much.

Saturday, 7. The weather has hitherto been fine, but
lately it has been quite cold. The river ran thick with
ground ice and froze. It has snowed twice already, but
the snow remained not long, and we have thus far perceived no noteworthy difference in the climate between
this place and the Muskingum.

Sunday, 8. Br. David preached about the promises
made to the heathen, and Jungmann held the congregation meeting from the Scripture-verse: He hath made my
mouth like a sharp sword; in the shadow of his hand hath
he hid me.

Tuesday, 10. We heard from Chippewas, who came
from the Fort, that they had seen Delaware Indians there,
who seemed like our Indians, for they were not painted
nor hung about with wampum and silver. We thought it
possible that some of them were come there, and we con-

sidered about getting them here, or learning more certainly about the matter.

Thursday, 12. The brethren went hunting in a body
together, for they hunt in this way; they form a half
moon or circle, and go through a district where the deer
come within shot of one or another. Our Indians, however,
had to learn here hunting over again, for thus far they
have not been very lucky in it. In the first place, they
are not familiar with the bush, and, secondly, there is
nothing but level land, no hill, much less a mountain, to
be seen, and the bush very thick and wild, so that, if the
weather is not clear and the sun not shining, they very
easily get lost, and this has happened to them several
times, that in rainy weather, instead of going home as
they thought, they went straight away from home, but
by good luck came to the lake, where they again got their
bearings.

Saturday, 14. We had the Lord's supper, and tasted
his body and blood with hungry and thirsty souls. There
were this time six Indian brethren present, namely, four
brothers and two sisters. One sister, Zipporah, was admitted after receiving absolution.

Sunday, 15. First was the communion liturgy and then
the sermon by Br. Heckewelder. Br. David held the
evening service from the Scripture-verse.

Monday, 16. Samuel went with some brothers and sisters to the Fort to get some necessities. They went this
time, on account of the river being frozen, straight through
the bush, which way two Chippewas had come over two
days before. Some snow was on the ground, and they followed their tracks, for as yet they are not familiar with
the bush. They came,

Thursday, 17, back again, and brought us news that
William had come with his family from the Shawanese
towns to Detroit, and was again on the way to us. When
now we heard that he had chosen to come straight through
the bush, and was already three days on the way, we were
troubled about them that they might have gone astray;
we therefore resolved that our Indian brethren should

search for him the next day, but he came the next forenoon alone, and had left his family in his camp, seven
miles from here. He was full of joy when he came in
sight of our town. He remained through the day with
us, telling us much, and he gave us news of other Indian
brethren, and over some we must rejoice, but over óthers
be sad. We heard that the best among them had gone
apart and passed the winter some distance this side of the
others, wishing to hunt, that in the spring betimes they
might be on the way here. Mark, however, with the Mohicans, is determined not to come here, but to settle in
that neighborhood alone with the wild Mohicans, who
dwell separately thereabout. He, Mark, is already fired
with a chief's affairs and will be a great man, seeks honor
among men, and will harm many, for if any of the Mohicans wish to come here he does not let them come. This
he already had secretly in mind when he was in Detroit,
and spoke with us, though he then promised us he wished
to come certainly; and when he came home he said to the
brethren: "Our teachers wish no longer to be in the Indian land, and I say, I go not to the English land, for that
is a perfect trap for us, that we may all be ruined and
killed." In their towns it is said to be more wicked with
their dances and worse than with the savages, and those
who were assistants said to us, they dared not express
their mind; thus they are again become heathen. It may
be, however, that the calamity and the attack upon the
Shawanese make a change in their reckoning, in which
attack three of their towns were said to be destroyed and
848 killed or taken captive, and that they will be made
cautious. [A family of our people has remained there;
whether others, we know not yet.] The most painful and
saddest of all is that we must hear that some say, we
were the cause and reason of so many Indian brethren,
their friends, losing their lives in Gnadenhütten; we had
called the white people there, and had sent letters to them.

Sunday, 22. Br. David preached about the joy of believers in the incarnation and birth of our Saviour, and
Br. Sensemann held the congregation meeting from the

Scripture-verse: He hath sent me to proclaim the accept-
able year of the Lord.

Tuesday, 24. We began Christmas with a love-feast,
the first for two years, and we rejoiced in God our Saviour
for his birth, passion and death, brought him our filial
praise and thanks, and adored him in the manger. He
blessed us anew, and brought new life among the brethren, so that many tears were paid. him. There were
together fifty-three of us, white and brown.

Wednesday, 25. Br. Heckewelder preached from the
Gospel about the announcement of the angels to the shepherds and to all mankind that we should rejoice in the
birth of the Saviour. Thereupon was the children's hour;
to these was Jesus in his manger depicted, while they rev-
erently sang, many with tears in their eyes. Br. Jungmann
held the congregation-meeting from the Scripture-verse.

Saturday, 28. Chippewas came in, who are encamped
not far off, hunting. Among other things, they examined
our labor, where we wished to make and plant our fields,
with wonder at our clearing and planting such wild land
and so overgrown with wood. They, on the contrary, plant
very little, but live mostly from the bush, hunting, though
they like to eat corn and bread. If they can not have these,
then they fare very badly; they gather acorns and boil them
with their meat, though they use the worst sort of acorns.
Towards us they are very modest, not in the least troublesome, and behave in a very orderly way, though we are
in no position to give them any thing or share any thing
with them, for we have ourselves nothing, except what
was given us for our extreme needs. We wish that the
word of the Saviour's incarnation, death, and passion
might once find acceptance among them, that their hearts
and eyes might be open to recognize their Saviour and
Redeemer, who loved them even unto death.

We heard through William, who has lately come, that
the Delaware chiefs are still always wrangling, one with
another, about us, asking who is the cause that our Indian church has been so badly treated and ruined. Here
must Pipe have the blame. They are consulting about

the others, and are not yet done. In the autumn, at a
council, they said to Pipe and his people, when they were
advising how they should use the hatchet and press on the
war most advantageously: "Take and use the hatchet
against your foes, just as you have used it against your
friends, the believing Indians, who have done nothing to
you but good, and have not once raised a knife in their
own defence, when you used force against them." The same
chiefs who said this try to treat our Indians there in the
finest, best manner, and earnestly forbid the warriors to
do them harm, and wish the time may again come when
they may again have their teachers with them. This, however, is only from politic and not from worthy motives, for
they foresee the downfall of their nation, and, moreover,
that all our Indians who are here, one after the other, are
lost to them, and this, indeed, causes them much anxiety
and perplexity. They seek now, by kind conduct, to prevent
this, for by their cruelty towards us they have done themselves the greatest harm, but they are now well aware of
what they have done, for that is but the beginning.

Sunday, 29. Br. David preached about the sonship to
God, which the Saviour got for us, that we should be co-
heirs with Christ. During the sermon Chippewas came,
and inasmuch as no one was at home, but all were at
meeting, they gathered together some distance off till the
sermon was over. This the Delawares would not have
done. They go into houses when no one is at home and
steal.

Tuesday, 31. We closed the year with praise and thanks
to the Lord for all his goodness and for the kindnesses
the Saviour had done us in rescuing us from so many
dangers and in being so heartily interested for us, but
we confessed to him our transgressions and shortcomings and begged forgiveness of all our sins. The brethren
were reminded what through this year had happened to
us, and in what sort of ways the Saviour had gone with us,
and how he finally had cared for us and made a way for
our again settling and coming together. By the relation

9

of these, our affairs, which had come to pass, many tears were shed. We gave ourselves anew to the Saviour, to the blessed care of the Holy Ghost, to the protection of our dear heavenly Father, and he made us sensibly aware of his peace. In the consideration of the Scripture-verse: All flesh shall know that I, the Lord, am thy Saviour and thy Redeemer, the Mighty One of Jacob, among other things we said to the brethren: What in the end will the heathen have accomplished, who have made every exertion to destroy our church and in part have destroyed it? If only we be of true heart and mean to be upright with the Saviour, they will yet learn that we have a Saviour who will not forsake us and who knows how to bring his people through with a strong hand and outstretched arm. Upon our knees we begged for absolution, and with comforted hearts entered upon the new year.

NOTE.—The following letter, taken from De Peyster's "Miscellanies," p. 255, is not without interest, and refers to events of the year 1782.

"Copy of a letter to his excellency General Haldimand, dated from Detroit, the 18th of August, 1782:

"I am just honored with your excellency's letter of the 11th July, approving the conduct of the officers at the affair at Sandusky, and regretting the cruelty committed by some of the Indians upon Colonel Crawford, desiring me to assure them of your utter abhorrence of such proceedings. Believe me, sir, I have had my feelings upon this occasion, and foreseeing the retaliation the enemy would draw upon themselves from the Indians, I did every thing in my power to reconcile the Delawares to the horrid massacre their relations underwent at Muskingum, where ninety-three of these inoffensive people were put to death, by the people from American back settlements, in cool blood; and I believe I should have succeeded had not the enemy so soon advanced with the intent, as they themselves declared, to exterminate the whole Wiandott tribe, not by words only, but even by exposing effigies, left hanging by the heels in every encampment.

"I had sent messengers throughout the Indian country previous to the receipt of your excellency's letter threatening to recall the troops if they, the Indians, did not desist from cruelty.

"I have frequently signified to the Indians how much you abhor cruelty, and I shall to-morrow dispatch a person I have great confidence in to carry your injunctions to the southern nations. . . . .

"I have the honor to be with great respect, sir, your excellency's most humble and most obedient servant,

"A. S. DE PEYSTER.

"His Excellency General Haldimand, Commander-in-Chief, etc."

CHAPTER III.

1783.

ON CLINTON RIVER, MICHIGAN.

Wednesday, Jan. 1. In the forenoon we came with our brethren before the dear Lord, and were blessed by him, made a new covenant with him that we wished to be his, body and soul, his obedient children more than before, and we begged from him his nearness and blessing the whole year through. Ignatius, a poor sinner, who had grossly sinned against his teachers, was absolved amid many tears. Br. Heckewelder preached and Jungmann held the congregation meeting from the Scripture-verse: Zion heard and was glad. Since we had retained these Scripture-verses of the year '80, during our captivity, we take them for use this year.

Friday, 3. Most of the brethren went out hunting, for some snow had fallen, of which we have had little indeed thus far this winter. Adam straightway shot three great bucks, when he had hardly got out of town. Up to date we have yet no cold to speak of, for the ground in the bottoms is not yet frozen. We can cut and work with our hands unhindered, and this we have to do this winter.

Sunday, 5. Br. Edwards preached from Titus, iii, and then appeared the friendliness and graciousness of God, our Saviour. He made us blessed by the bath of regeneration and the renovation of the Holy Ghost. Br. Heckewelder held the congregation meeting from the Scripture-verse.

Monday, 6. We celebrated Epiphany with grace and blessing. The heathen's Saviour made himself sensibly known to us and blessed us and our little flock. Br. Jungmann conducted morning prayer, and asked the Saviour for his presence this day, particularly to bless us and our brown brethren; thereupon Br. David delivered the festival-discourse from the Scripture-verse: Truly my soul waiteth upon God; from him cometh my salvation. When doubts and fears, a gloomy band—Beset my soul on every hand. In the afternoon was a love-feast, for which the Indians had bought flour at the Fort; thereby we called to mind former times, and were thankful to the Saviour from our hearts that he had again brought us to peace and had again given us a place to rest our feet, and indeed a place so beautiful, so quiet, so remote from all the turmoil of the world, and especially from heathenish ways; and this is its charm, so that on the Muskingum it was not so quiet and still, for which we can not thank the Saviour enough. Only one thing is wanting—correspondence with our church, particularly with Bethlehem; this we have lost, and we must do without and deny ourselves much. Br. Heckewelder ended the day with prayer, kneeling: he thanked the Saviour for the blessing he had so richly let flow to us to-day and during the holidays; yes, during these days he has not let himself be unknown among the brethren. We thought also in our services and prayer of our scattered Indian brethren, and recommended them to the good Shepherd, that he may soon bring them to us.

Tuesday, 7. Br. Heckewelder went with William and Adam to the Fort; he, William, to get his rations of provisions, for as yet he had drawn none, for when he came through Detroit he could bring nothing with him, and Br. David wrote on this account to the commandant.

Wednesday, 8. Since we learned that a family of our Indians lay a day's journey this side of the Fort, which wished to come to us, but could not, and that they suffered hunger, three brothers went off to bring them here if possible. Sophia, Joshua's wife, brought forth a son, the first in this place.

Sunday, 12. In the sermon about the Gospel of to-day: When Jesus was twelve years old, but especially over the words: Wist ye not that I must be about my father's business, he spoke about the Saviour's great work for our redemption, which he always had in sight so long as he was on earth. At this time was mentioned the festival for the children, of whom but two are now here, and the little son of Joshua and Sophia, born on the 8th of this month, was baptized with the name Christian. Heckewelder, with the Indians, came back to-day from the Fort, and brought the two widows, Susanna and Maria Elizabeth, who had already been for a time in the Fort, waiting for an opportunity to come here. About the rest of our Indians we heard that many were wishing to come in the spring, but it is hardly to be written, the pains the savages take and the lies they invent to keep them from coming here, and our Indians have to steal away secretly if they wish to come here. Many white people from the States, who have been taken prisoners, have been tortured and burnt alive in Sandusky and among the Shawanese, for killing our Indians in Gnadenhütten. As soon as it is known that any prisoner had part in that affair, he is forthwith bound, tortured, and burnt.

Tuesday, 14. Early in the morning an earnest and applicable discourse of exhortation was delivered to all the brethren living here, owing to the fact that many of our people have comported themselves badly, and they were told this would not be permitted. This discourse was much talked about among our people, and it is to be hoped it will not have been in vain. Most of the Indian brethren went hunting for a week. A Delaware Monsey Indian has come here, and is encamped up this creek hunting; he begged permission in the spring to have leave to move here. He said he had long felt the call to this in his heart. He knew not well how to express himself or how he should speak when he asked to live with us; like many others, he could merely say that he liked to hear of the Saviour, and what he heard he believed to be the truth. Last summer in Detroit he spoke with us about this before we came here, and we could not refuse his request.

Thursday, 16. A Delaware family came visiting. Susanna Mingo went back to Sandusky to get her children, whom she had left behind.

Saturday, 18. Two more Delaware Indians came here visiting. They, namely, the Delawares, follow after us everywhere and seek us out, though we would rather see them remain away from us, for they are all people who have heard the Gospel, but have been unwilling to receive it, and they have troubled our church, and yet they can not keep away from us. Yes, we have to fear they will seek to do us further harm, and we can not trust them. At our captivity the Monseys have behaved the best.

Sunday, 19. Instead of the sermon there was read to the brethren from the History of the Days of the Son of Man, and Br. Jungmann held the congregation meeting from the Scripture-verse.

Tuesday, 21. The Indian brethren came back, who have been away hunting a good day's journey off. In that neighborhood they found hilly land, met with plains and clear, open bush, which country pleased them very well for hunting. In the same place, too, they came upon white cedar and white pine. They were lucky, too, in hunting, and brought in about twenty deer, for the bush there is not so thick and wild as here in this neighborhood. From Detroit came wandering Delawares, who hunt us out wherever we go. A woman wanted to live with us, but we advised her to remain away from here, for it is something very ventursome with women without husbands.

Saturday, 25. We had the holy communion, in which this time only four Indian brethren had part. Things will not go right with them. It is as if they could not find their way to the sinners' Friend, and we see very well that they have suffered great harm in their hearts and have lost all. From this can be plainly seen what a poor people they are; when they no longer have a brother with them they again become heathen and dead in their hearts. We must have patience with them until the Saviour again touches their hearts with the image of his sufferings and melts them.

Sunday, 26. The communion liturgy was read early, and then Br. Edwards preached. Sensemann held the con-

gregation meeting from the Scripture-verse : Peace be with
you all that are in Christ Jesus.

Monday, 27. Samuel, the assistant, went to the Fort,
likewise Sensemann and Michael Jung, on business, returning Wednesday, 29. We heard here to-day loud firing
of cannons, but knew not what it meant, but now we hear
it was the birthday of her Majesty, the Queen, which was
celebrated.

Thursday, 30. Most of our people went to Lake St.
Clair with meat, where a trader from the Fort will take it
and pay them for it what they wish in exchange for it, especially corn. Some came back Friday, 31, and others afterwards. This week we begin to make our preparations
for boiling sugar, for which purpose there is here no lack of
trees. In this country for the most part this kind of sugar is
used, only a little West India sugar. The traders take it
from the Indians and sell it again for three shillings the
pound.

Sunday, Feb. 2. Brs. Samuel and Abraham came from
the settlements with other brethren, whence they brought
home corn, and in the afternoon we had a meeting. While
they were away the cold was so intense that they could
not endure it, and had to go into every house to warm
themselves. Samuel came near freezing, and if he had
had to go a couple of hundred steps more he would have
fallen; the people had trouble in bringing him to again.
Upon the lake and ice, however, there is much keener cold
to encounter on account of the wind than in the bush, and
since we here are surrounded by the bush, we are not so
conscious of the cold.

Wednesday, 5. Chippewas came, as they are often wont
to do, but generally they come into our houses, and since
we white brethren were not at home, save the sisters,
Abraham was forced to tell them to avoid our houses, and
rather to go visiting in the huts of the Indians—that we
considered it improper for men to visit women when their
husbands were not at home.

Friday, 7. Most of the brethren are several days out
hunting. The skins are worth little here, but, on the

other hand, the meat much more, four and five dollars for a whole deer, and for this they can get every thing.

Saturday, 8. There came two white people, one a trader, named Isaac Williams, from the Fort, to visit us and see this country. This whole week it has been very cold, and it snowed every other day.

Sunday, 9. In the forenoon the sermon was about good seed in the field, where the enemy sows tares. Br. Hecke-welder held the congregation meeting from the Scripture-verse.

Monday, 10. The two white men, Isaac Williams and Cassedy, started for home; the last has already been here once before, and in Detroit has talked much about our towns and Indians, about their devotion and singing in the meetings, over which he wondered much and was edi-fied. He said he would not have believed the Indians could have learned to sing so finely; he could not himself boast of being an earnest and devout church-goer. Then, too, there was no opportunity except in the French Cath-olic church, but this time he had come for no other reason than to be present at our meetings, for it charmed him to see the Indians so assembled, and he liked to listen to them.

Tuesday, 11. The strong cold came to an end after lasting nearly two weeks, and it was somewhat milder, so that the following days of the week we had fine, spring-like weather; thus the snow went quite away, partly from rain, partly from warm winds.

Friday, 14. Two white men arrived. One, a German prisoner, brought in by the Indians, asked for a New Tes-tament as a loan, for here such books are not to be had, and it is a blessing for us that we have still kept our books, about which the warriors have not much troubled themselves. This week we made the first sugar.

Sunday, 16. A sermon in the forenoon, after which most of the brothers went back to their sugar-huts, the weather was so fine.

Sunday, 23. This whole week the brethren were in the bush at their sugar-huts, so also we, white brethren, except that Br. Jungmann and the sisters stayed at home alone by day. In the evening we all came home except the two unmarried brothers. The sermon was about the Epistle, that our fathers were baptized in the sea and with the clouds, but we with the precious blood of Christ that washeth and cleanseth us of our sins.

Tuesday, 25. Br. Jungmann, during a strong gust of wind, experienced the evident protection of the Saviour and of the dear angels, for, as he was getting water at the spring, a tree fell directly in front of him and another behind him, so that the branches whirled about his head, and if he had gone one step only, forwards or backwards, he would have been struck to the ground. He remained standing in the very spot where first aware of the danger, and said within himself: "Dear Saviour, thy will be done," and no ill was done him. Likewise our brethren, during the same storm, had wonderful protection, for, in so thick a bush of unusually high trees, it is very dangerous during such winds.

Wednesday, 26. All the Indian brethren who went off hunting two days ago, a day's journey from here, came home with nothing, for the snow is gone, and all the land is full of water, so flat and even is it. At times they had to go a long way through water and marsh knee-high, and thus were in no condition to accomplish any thing.

Sunday, March 2. The brethren came together for the sermon, which Br. David preached from the Gospel about the sower, saying that Satan, although he can not prevent the preaching of the word of God, is not indifferent and lazy about it, but much more seeks either to deprive people of what they have heard, or to fill their hearts with other and wordly things, that they may think nothing about it, and that he may turn their hearts therefrom. For some days such extremely cold weather has set in again, that nothing is to be done in sugar-making. Meanwhile, the brethren make preparation until the trees run again, so as to be ready.

Some went to the Fort to buy corn, for many have nothing left to eat. They drew in the autumn the same

quantity of provisions for six months that we drew, but
they have no idea how to manage with it. If they have
any thing, they eat much and spare not till it is gone.
They care not for the morrow what they shall then eat,
if to-day they can eat their fill.

Monday, 3. The Indian brethren, several days ago,
went off hunting, for the most part to get meat, which
they take to the settlements and buy corn with. This is
now enormously dear, and costs even now more than three
pounds a bushel, for last summer there was a failure of the
crop, and this winter the grain is spoilt by frost.

Tuesday, 4. Sensemann also went to the Fort to get
necessities, namely, corn, for now corn can still be had, but
in the spring none at all. He came back—

Thursday, 5, and with him two white men to see this
place and neighborhood. As we hear, many people purpose coming this spring to the mouth of the river to settle,
now that we have made a beginning.

Saturday, 8. For two days we have fine, mild weather,
the trees run, and sugar is again made, but this running
varies and lasts not long. We must watch for our chance,
and now the brethren are all scattered in the bush in their
sugar-camps, so that some of us white brethren only are
alone at home.

Sunday, 9. There was a sermon, for which the brethren
came home, and in the afternoon betimes went back again.

Tuesday, 11. William went to the Fort with some
others to get their monthly supplies.

Thursday, 13. He came back, and at the same time
two widows, Martha and Henrietta, from the Shawanose
towns. They remain here, but the latter will first get her
cattle and things. From them we learn thus much about
our Indian brethren, that they are much scattered in the
bush, here and there, but that Mark, with the Mohicans,
had gone away farther, and had settled with the wild Indians of the nation alone, and will not come here. They
are entertained there industriously with lies and fed with
them, that they may not come here. This place and
neighborhood are described to them as bad and danger-

ous; their friends among the savages watch them, and do every possible thing to prevent their coming here. They are in the hands of wolves, who plague and worry them all, and many of our Indians are blinded and let themselves be led like fools. There is, as it were, a judgment upon them, and punishment follows ever after them. Had they come, when last spring they got their summons to come, they would have been free and have escaped further punishment, but now, on account of their disobedience and perverseness, they must suffer, and what they yet hold of their cattle and effects will yet all be stolen, but yet they are still blind, and can not resolve to get away from the race of the wicked. We hear, however, that in the spring many will yet come here; but Mark, who plays the chief, and wishes to build up again his nation, which is really at an end, flatters himself that he will get a brother for their teacher. The times have changed, and we have learned how it is when we with our mission are among heathen chiefs, who wish to lay down rules for us; to whom unclean people complain when we reprove them for their wicked life, for the chiefs, the devil's generals, abet them, and so persecute us. How does that do for us? They are blind heathen. Our affairs and theirs go not together. Praise be to God that we are out of their hands, for we have nothing more to do with them, nor they with us.

Saturday, 15. We had the sacrament of his body and blood in the holy communion with hungry and thirsty souls.

Sunday, 16. The sermon was from the Gospel about the Canaanite woman: the brethren were present, but soon went back to their sugar-huts after our to-day's Scripture-verse had been treated of: Whom having not seen ye love, in whom, though now ye see him not, etc.

Towards evening three young people of our Indians came from the Shawanese towns, Matthew, Cornelius' son, and Jacob, the son of the Rachael who died last autumn in Lower Sandusky, and had agreed with him that he, with his two sisters, should come here to the brethren. With them came

Andrew, a single man; these three stole away, and came here simply to see and hear us, and with their own eyes to look at the country where we live, since they have heard so many lies from strange Indians who have been here and gone there: namely, that we lived in a place surrounded by water and marsh, so that we could plant nothing, and must starve, yes, we would yet all perish, for we were not sure of our lives, and yet many more lies, which were always told them to frighten them from here. They also said, as we had already heard, that they were all scattered, and could, therefore, say with no certainty who of them had it in mind to come here, and they who indeed wished to be here, must keep their wish secret from fear of the savages, who seek to hold them back, and watch over them that they may not escape them. The poor widows, who, alone as they are, can not help themselves, and have no confidence to come away, even if they wished to begin the journey, they are the worst off. Others again live without care for the day, and can not bethink themselves nor come to any resolution, and meanwhile let the heathenish life please them, and are again become heathen. Thus are they now circumstanced, they have got into great misery, and have no longer among them the word of God, for the old among them, as it seems, are the worst. It is thus worthy of note to observe that the Saviour urges on our young people, makes them anxious and distressed for their teachers, and they long again for God and for his word. We rejoiced much to see them, and it gave us new courage and hope that our Indian church shall again assemble and be edified.

Tuesday, 18. Most of the Indian brethren went off hunting for a few days, and the three who have lately come to examine the country, but the rest of the brethren were all in the bush, busy making sugar. They came

Thursday, 20, back home, and the assistant, Samuel, went with them visiting about the sugar-huts and to see the brethren, who also rejoice as much as we do, to hear something about our scattered brethren, and inasmuch as the three brethren wished to have a meeting, the brethren who are near by came home mornings, and we had daily meetings so long as they were here.

Sunday, 23. In the forenoon a sermon, in the afternoon a congregation meeting from the Scripture-verse : For the gifts and calling of God are without repentance.

Monday, 24. Two of the lately arrived brethren went away to their friends to bring them here as soon as possible. With them went also Abraham, Samuel, and others to the Fort to get corn. Every thing here has pleased them. They have seen that all they heard of us was a lie, but above all it did them good again to have an opportunity to hear God's word, which for so long a time they have had to do without.

The others in the Shawanese towns await meanwhile with longing for their return, to hear what sort of news they bring with them about us. We sent word to them that we invited hither all brethren who were distressed, in trouble about their salvation and longing for comfort, for here we were right quiet and undisturbed, seeing and hearing nothing of war. And since some of those there still continue to cherish a vain hope that some one of us will again come to them, we let them know that as long as the war lasts, this can not be, and we could not promise it, even should there be peace again in the land. They were a week on their way hither, and expect to make their journey back in the same time, but Andrew begged to stay here.

Tuesday, 25. Br. Conner arrived from the Fort to build himself a house, and soon to bring his family. For the sake of his maintenance he has had to stay there till now, and circumstances have forced him.

Thursday, 27. Brs. Abraham and Samuel came in from the Fort, where they saw the two young brethren depart, after having been provided with provisions for their journey by the major, to whom Br. David wrote. Our Indian brethren made the major a present of a couple of deer, which he very graciously received.

Friday, 28. There was a great thunder-storm, the second one since winter, with hard rain, and we had the finest spring weather, lasting several days.

Sunday, 30. The brethren came together for the sermon, and afterwards in the afternoon there was a congregation meeting, held by Br. Jungmann, from the Scripture-verse.

Monday, 31. A white man came from the Fort and bought from our Indians sugar for corn and flour, a good thing for our people, who are very short of food for a long time. All which they get here they can sell for a good price, be it what it may.

Thursday, April 3. The widow, Henrietta, went back to the Shawanese town to get her cattle and things she had left there. It makes us sad to see how they have quite fallen away from the Saviour, and again become heathen as soon as their teachers were taken from them; they see now what a poor people they are, if they have not a brother with them. None is subject to another, nor does one give heed to another, but each one is for himself, and there is no fellow-feeling among them. Each one considers himself shrewd, and accepts no advice from others. Those, however, who yet stand fast must be silent, and dare not speak; thus each one must see for himself where he will abide. Therefore it is hard with many a one to come away, for he has no suitable help, and can not help himself, for hitherto we have always had to seek to help them get here.

Saturday, 5. Early service, most of the brethren being at home.

Sunday, 6. In the forenoon, there was a sermon about our High Priest, who offered himself for our sins, and is entered into the holy place not made with hands, into heaven itself, to appear for us before the face of God. The congregation meeting was held by Br. Heckewelder, from the Scripture-verse: Him that cometh to me I will in no wise cast out. Since the warm weather already lasts for some time and sugar-making is ended, we stopped it to-day, for the sap is no longer sweet, and indeed there is little of it.

Monday, 7. Some Indian brethren went to the mouth of the river to help block-out his house for a white man,

who wishes to settle there, and invited them. In this way
they earn corn, which they much need.

Wednesday, 9. Abraham, with several others, went by
water to the settlement for corn, and came,

Saturday, 12, back again; so also the brethren from the
mouth, where they have blocked out a house and brought
it under roof. This whole week there were heavy rains,
with thunder, so that the creek rose higher than it has
been since the snow went off.

Sunday, 13. The sermon was about the Saviour's entrance into Jerusalem for his passion. The brethren were
exhorted to follow him, to go with him, step by step, and
to observe him in all the scenes of his passion. In the
afternoon there was a service for all communion brethren,
who before had part therein, but not for two years. They
were told to search their hearts, to be straightforward and
upright, and with all their troubles to go to the Saviour
and seek forgiveness, for that he was gracious and merciful to all those of humble and contrite heart.

Thursday, 17. After the brethren had all been addressed, the communion brethren, after the reading of the
history of to-day, had the washing of feet, and thereupon
the supper of our Lord in the night, when he was betrayed. Two sisters, Sophia and Salome, and one brother,
Adam, were readmitted after receiving absolution with
the laying on of hands.

Friday, 18. Throughout the day there were readings
of the history of the sufferings of our Lord and Saviour,
and this was listened to with moved and melted hearts.
At the words, "Jesus bowed his head and gave up the
ghost," we fell upon our knees and recited the liturgy.

Saturday, 19. We kept the Quiet Sabbath. We could
have no love-feast on account of our poverty, but in the
evening Br. Jungmann held a service about the blessing,
which through his rest in the grave has come to us and
become our portion.

Sunday, 20. After we had early greeted the brethren
with the words, "The Lord is arisen," we prayed the
Easter litany in the chapel, since we yet had no regular

God's acre. Afterwards the history of the resurrection was read, and then a sermon from Br. Heckewelder. In the evening was a congregation meeting from the Scripture-verse.

Monday, 21. Br. David wrote to London. We repaired our boat, and set out,

Tuesday, 22, for Detroit, for the time was favorable for getting provisions and ours were at an end. We came,

Wednesday, 23, there, as also our Indian brethren the 25th, and after Br. David had spoken with Major de Peyster, and got an order from him for us and our Indians, and had received the provisions, we went away again on the 26th. The major gave us two cows and three horses, which he had already promised us the year before, but which we had left behind, because we had not believed we could bring them through; these we now took. Mr. Askin informed us at once that he had received an answer from Montreal, and he paid us the £100 sterling. We bought two cows from this, but these are very dear here, namely, thirty to forty pounds New York currency. Br. David gave to the major the letters to be forwarded to London, as soon as the next ship sailed for Niagara, and this he promised to see to. At the upper end of Germantown, Br. David, by request, baptized four children.

Monday, 28. We got back home again, having been much hindered on the lake by head-winds, and having had much trouble to row against them. But the Indians had to lie still. Both their canoes were filled by the waves. We brought with us in our boat Br. Conner and his wife, with the provisions which now they get as we do, but which before they did not draw so long as they were in Detroit.

Thursday, May 1. Our Indians got home. They brought the following news: The Chippewa chief, whom they met on their way, spoke with them, and said that they lived on his land; it had not been his intention that we should settle here; he thought we would live the other side of the river further down. This land, however, they had already made over to white people, just as this on which we live belongs to Mr. Bawbee, as the major himself told Br. David, but it is probable that the thing has a more distant cause, and that the nations, Delawares, Shawanese, etc., have put an idea into the heads of the Chippewas and aroused them against us, in order that the Gospel may no longer be preached in the Indian land. They see that we here find protection and support under the English government, that we are settling down again, and that our Indians begin to come together again; this vexes them and they will not cease to think upon ways and means to hinder this, if not utterly to destroy us. Brother David wrote, therefore, Friday, May 2, to the major in Detroit, and informed him of this. This letter, a white man, our neighbor, who settled several weeks ago on this river below us, took with him to Detroit. We do not doubt that the major and Bawbee, who recommended this country to us, will do their best in the matter to have us remain here. Otherwise things were in their usual order. As soon as we got home, we again set about our labor of clearing the land. Of garden stuff we had already sowed a good deal.

Sunday, 4. The sermon was by Br. Heckewelder about the good Shepherd, who lays down his life for his sheep, and the congregation meeting by Br. Jungmann from the Scripture-verse.

Tuesday, 6. Br. Heckewelder went eight miles down the river to Mr. Tucker, whom he met on the way here to us. He was sent by the major with a letter for Br. David, an answer to his letter of the 2d Inst. In this he told us to continue our labor undisturbed and to plant; that we should be without anxiety, he would arrange the affair with the Chippewa Indians to our satisfaction, and if they came to us and said any thing, we should hand to them the string of wampum and the piece of tobacco he had sent us, and say to them that their father wished to speak to them about this, and invited them to come to him.

Wednesday, 7. Two messengers came, Matthew and Renatus, to tell us that some forty of our Indians were on

10

their way here, whom they had left on the Miami (Maumee), but that they had nothing to eat, and must maintain themselves on the journey by hunting. Since now planting-time is so near, and we should like to prevent their neglecting it, we sent to them on the 8th a canoe and with it Br. Edwards to the Fort, and Br. David wrote to the major about them, telling him this and asking him to send on some provisions to them, that they might get here as soon as possible and plant at the right time.

The rest, who are still among the Shawanese, have in part no wish to come here, and a part can not come on account of the savages, though they would like to come, for as soon as the savages observe that any one of our Indians would come here, they prevent him and will not let him go. But Mark, who, as we hear, has made himself chief of the Mohicans in that neighborhood, got them together and moved away with them farther, and has founded a separate town, but only two of our Indians are with him, Gabriel and Isaac. Sensemann held, on the 8th, the early service. The Indian brethren, who went in the boat to Detroit several days ago to get provisions, came back from there to-day.

Friday, 9. Br. David held the early service from the Scripture-verse. The brethren were encouraged to plant industriously and not to be lazy.

Saturday, 10. Br. Heckewelder held early service. This whole week we and our Indian brethren have been busy clearing the fields, but it is hard work, on account of uncommonly large timber.

Sunday, 11. Br. David preached in the morning, and in the afternoon Br. Heckewelder conducted the funeral of little Augustina, daughter of Samuel and Sara Nanticoke, three years nine months old, who died yesterday of consumption. Br. Edwards returned to-day, and not on the 12th.

Monday, 12. Br. Edwards returned from Detroit, where he received supplies for our Indians now on their way here, and sent them to them. At the same time he brought word that peace would certainly be made.

Wednesday, 14. The first of the brethren got here by land, namely, Luke, with his family, and,

Thursday, 15, came also some by water. They were all very glad to see us again and to be with us. Many soon came and told us their need, that their hearts had not been well since we were taken from them, and that on this account they wanted to come here. We could not but have hearty compassion with them, addressed them to the Saviour, to approach him again, and with him they would find comfort and forgiveness. After the chiefs in the Indian land observed that they wished to come to us here, they took all possible pains to hinder this, saying to them they should yet have patience for a little while, and not be in such haste; that they had much to consider and their affairs to put in order; they were not opposed to their going again to their teachers, and knew well enough they could not be without them, but as yet they knew nothing about the Chippewas, among whom they wished to go, and to whom they were perfect strangers, but they should send an embassy to them, and if the matter were first arranged, they had nothing against their going again to their teachers; they would be glad to have their children and young people show desire and inclination for this, and hear the word of God; they said to them therefore to wait until autumn, when all would be made clear. They did not, however, permit themselves to be longer retained, for they saw very well that they only wished to hinder their coming here this spring, and if they should first do their planting there, they would be quiet for a while, and this indeed the chiefs wished. Others who wanted to come here let themselves be held back till autumn, but wished to come then if they should see their time. The heathen will yet see and rue what they have done, to their own great harm, however; they begin already to see this, and are at discord with one another about it, and they accuse one another of having driven away the believing Indians with their teachers. The chiefs sent to prominent Indians whose friends wished to come here, and said to them they should stop their friends and hold them fast, but they got for an answer from Lennachgo: "I will neither prevent nor forbid any one to go to his teachers. Why have you driven their teachers away? Did I not tell you beforehand that if you drove away their teachers, their Indians also would not remain, yet you have done so, and thus you have driven away the believing Indians with their teachers. You would so have it, therefore I will prevent no one from going to them again, but I am glad of it. Who brought to destruction the believing Indians on the Muskingum? Have the white people done it, whom we call Virginians? Answer, No. They have not done it, but you are they who have killed them. Why have you not left them in peace where they were? They were quiet, and have done wrong to no man. Had you let them alone, they would all now be alive, and we could yet see our friends, but you would have it so, you wished to ruin them, and have so done." Thus spoke many of the chiefs. Half of the Delaware Indians are against the brothers and half for them. There are two parties of them, and both wrangle all the time about the brothers and their Indians. Especially the Goschachgünkers, whose neighbors we were at Lichtenau (near Coshocton, O.), in a manner consider themselves ours, since they, too, have suffered much and have not taken up the hatchet against the Americans, and they quarrel with the other party about this. They will on that account talk about this, in order to show what sort of effect and influence our circumstances, captivity, and fate have upon the Indians, and that it is not so lightly looked upon.

Friday, 16. Now that our little congregation was once again nearly as full as it was, we had to enlarge our chapel, at which the brethren went at once to work and built on a piece.

Saturday, 17. Br. Heckewelder went with some Indian brethren in a boat to Detroit, to get supplies for the brethren lately arrived, about whom Br. David wrote to the major asking for them. Meanwhile the brethren took a view of the place, to clear land where they could plant, for it is the proper time.

Sunday, 18. Br. Heckewelder preached. Br. David

conducted the service for the children, to whom he said he was pleased to see them together again and to have an opportunity to talk with them about the Saviour; they had now been a year among the savages, and would doubt-less see a great difference between us and them, and since they could now again hear about the Saviour, they should be thankful to him therefor, should love him, seek to live for him, give over their hearts to him, put away all their heathenish, thoughtless ways, forget what they must have heard, give heed to the word of God, and be obedient to him; thus would they be happy and contented children. We spoke with some of the brethren lately come, and ad-vised and encouraged them to start afresh and to make a covenant with the Saviour, to live for him. Many said: "We regard ourselves as nothing but heathen, for we have lost the Saviour, and our hearts have no life and feeling from him." Br. Jungmann held the congregation meeting. We see among them the Saviour's labor still, who has indeed not forsaken them, for if the old among them were dead and indifferent in heart, he aroused the children and young people so that they longed again for the brothers to be with them, and when they heard Br. David's message this spring, that we invited to us all brethren who were anxious about their salvation, and un-easy in regard to the Saviour, a little child answered, five years old, at once, when they were assembled, and said to his mother: "I will be the very first, and go to the teachers." The mother, who before was somewhat indifferent, and yet was always uneasy, made up her mind also and came here.

Wednesday, 21. Br. Edwards returned from the Fort, where he received supplies for the brethren lately come, given to him without hesitation. He brought back news that on the 25th of next month, June, the Americans would take possession of Detroit,[1] in accordance with the articles. And the major had told him it would be well and neces-sary if meantime some one of us came to the city to see

---

[1] But this did not happen till July, 1796.

how things went, that he might give us news betimes and care for us before he went away.

Friday, 23. A lost sheep came back to us here, namely, Renatus, the Mohican, who for many years has been in error and at last is come to this place. He begged very earnestly to be received again, to live with us, and since we saw it to be a thing which concerned the salvation of his soul, we had no hesitation in receiving him, for which he was glad, and went back at once to the lake, where he had left his wife and children, and next day brought them hither.

Saturday, 24. We began to plant corn, after having hitherto always been busy clearing land, and therein shall we continue so long as time permits.

Sunday, 25. Br. David preached from the Gospel: Whatever ye shall ask the Father—he will give it you. I came forth from the Father, and am come into the world: again I leave the world and go to the Father.

In the communion quarter-hour the Lord's supper was announced for next Saturday. Br. Edwards held the congregation meeting.

Wednesday, 28. The brethren helped us plant corn.

Thursday, 29. We prayed to our unseen, dear Lord, who is gone for us to heaven, and now sits at the right hand of God, and intercedes for us. We begged from him his blessed nearness feelingly and the holy walk with him at all hours of our life. Thereupon, in another service, the little son of Jacob and Christiana, born on the journey hither thirty days ago, was baptized with the name Joseph. Several brethren who have lately come complained to us of their wretched condition, in that they had departed from the Saviour since they have been among the wild Indians, and in part had been punished with heavy and gross sins, which now give them much to do, and cause them more need and anxiety in their hearts than all the distress they have outwardly suffered, and they long for comfort and forgiveness of their transgressions. We could not but have compassion with them, pray to the Saviour for them, to have mercy upon them, and direct them to him, the Physician of their souls, who alone can heal them.

Saturday, 31. After the brethren had been addressed, we had the holy communion. The Saviour was so merciful as to send us five brethren, whom he allowed to be re-admitted, four of whom were of those lately arrived, who received this mercy with humble and contrite hearts, for they had had no communion for nearly two years, and they were all absolved with the laying on of hands. The Saviour was manifest in a wonderful way to us, blessed us with his near presence, and gave us his peace.

Sunday, June 1. After the communion liturgy, Br. Heckewelder preached. The Holy Spirit was busy among the brethren, and brought it home to many a one's heart to see and understand his destructive and satanic position; this brought them to the Saviour, and they sought to find forgiveness and rest for their hearts.

Tuesday, 3. David held early service from the Scripture-verse: Take the helmet of salvation and the sword of the Spirit, which is the word of God. Thus would neither sin, nor the world, nor Satan with all temptations have any hold upon us.

Thursday, 5. Michael held early service. He spoke with several of the brethren lately arrived, who opened their hearts, confessed their guilt, that they had lost their Saviour, were dead in heart, and had polluted themselves with sin, for which they now sought forgiveness.

Sunday, 8. Upon our knees we prayed to God, the blessed Holy Ghost, thanked him for his pains, care, and oversight, which until now he has bestowed upon us, to adorn us for the Bridegroom of our souls. We acknowledged to him our shortcomings, and asked forgiveness of all our transgressions, that often we had given no heed to his voice, thereby making our hearts unblessed and discontented. The sermon treated of the office and service of the Holy Spirit, in the first place among the children of the world, and especially with the children of God, in whom he dwelleth since they have received sonship. In the service for the baptized, Cornelius was absolved with

the laying on of hands, for which we had much longed
and begged.

Monday, 9. Most of our Indians went off hunting for
a few days, for their provisions have come to an end, and
they want to get meat. Meanwhile, the brethren at home
were busy planting. They came,

Wednesday, 9, home with meat, and thus must they try
from time to time to help themselves through.

Thursday, 12. McCormick came with another white
man. He was present when we were made prisoners, and
since he saw that it went hard with us, he laid the greatest blame for our captivity upon the Indians, but we well
knew by whom they were instigated; he pitied us, and
showed compassion at our being put in such wretched circumstances, and that now we must seek to get along so
painfully and with such hard labor. He took his boy,
who had been with Conner, to put him in school.

Saturday, 14. We were busy planting.

Sunday, 15. Br. David preached from the Gospel about
Nicodemus, who came by night to Jesus, and spoke with
the Saviour about the new birth, which he has gained for
us, and to which all the Holy Trinity has contributed, that
we now again should become God's children through belief in Jesus Christ. In the children's hour Br. Heckewelder baptized the little daughter of Adolphus and Susanna, two months old, born among the Shawanese, into
the death of Jesus, with the name Susanna. Michael held
the congregation meeting from the Scripture-verse. To-
day a party of Chippewas went by, the first since spring,
on their way back from hunting.

Wednesday, 18. There came another family here from
their wandering, namely, Thomas, with his wife and five
children, very meek and humble, asking to be received.
They said: "We consider ourselves unworthy to live
again with you; we have lost our Saviour and are no better than other heathen and have befouled ourselves with
sin, but since our well-being and salvation lie upon our
hearts and we can have no peace, we resolved to go again
to our teachers, thinking that although we did not get
leave to dwell again with them, it would in some measure

be a comfort to us merely to see your town from afar."
We had no hesitation in receiving them, and let them feel
our hearty compassion.

They, too, had something to arrange before they could
come to us, for he springs from one of the foremost families, and is grandson of the former chief, Netawatwes:[1]
thus the heads of the Delawares watched sharply over
him and wished to keep him from coming to us, and many
who had not themselves courage to speak bribed Indians
to advise him to desist, and they used all their art, but
in vain. When they could effect nothing with him, they
turned to his wife and threatened to take away her children from her if they went to us, but she answered: "If
you take away from me not only my husband but my children, yet you shall know that I will go. I am determined
to go, and nothing can stop me, for what particularly
drives me to my teachers is the everlasting salvation of
my soul. What good does it do me if you give me a
houseful of clothes, silver, and other things and my soul
be lost?" We heard at the same time that Niagara[2] is
garrisoned by the Americans, and that already also some
are come to Detroit.

Saturday, 21. This week the Indian brethren helped
us hoe our corn. This whole spring until the present time
we have been hard at work, almost beyond our strength,
for we wanted to have our maintenance from this in the
future.

Sunday, 22. The sermon was about the rich man, in
which it was said the Saviour would show us how it is
with those who care only for their bodies and for the
world, but are unconcerned about their souls and their
eternal salvation, that our only necessity is to strive after

---

[1] Netawatwes was ever a steadfast friend of Zeisberger. He died at
the beginning of the Revolutionary War. He was much perplexed at
the differences among Christians, and had thoughts of consulting the
King of England about the matter. De Schweinitz' Life of Zeisberger,
p. 387.

[2] Niagara, Oswego, and other frontier posts were not given up to the
United States till 1796.

righteousness and to seek to obtain peace with God, then had we nothing to fear from judgment, for our debts were paid here. Br. David held the children's service and Jungmann the congregation meeting.

Monday, 23. We went with the boat to Detroit, Br. Heckewelder remaining at home, the Indians also with us, to get supplies. We got there the 24th, and since we had heard from there all sorts of reports that a great change and overturning in regard to authority had already begun, it was pleasing to us to find every thing in statu quo.

Br. David spoke with the major about the maintenance of us and our Indians, and informed himself by him how long he would furnish us from the king's store. And since the major wanted to hear Br. David's ideas about this, he told him that if it were pleasing to him, and he had nothing against it, we should be best helped if he would supply us with provisions until autumn, when the corn is ripe, namely, towards the end of October. We should receive this with appreciation and gratitude, in order that the Indians might not have to use at once the corn they had planted before it was yet ripe. He agreed to this at once, and made no difficulty about granting us provisions for four months, gave to Br. David the proper written order on the commissary, from whom we had to receive them, and since our boat could not hold a third of the whole, he ordered also a large transport for us, so that we could carry every thing, and with which we could go up to our towns. Since now, as he said, he had no trustworthy news from Quebec, for as yet no packet has come from there, he said to Br. David it would be well and needful if he would soon come back to the city, that if any change took place, of which there is no doubt, for they have received the articles of peace, he could confer with Br. David and make arrangements if he should be called away, for from the articles of peace it is plain to be seen that Niagara, Detroit, and Michilimackinac will be ceded to the States.

Thursday, 26. After every thing was ready we went

again from Detroit. Br. Edwards, in the great transport,
had already sailed away the day before with some Indians.

Friday, 27. We all came with a good wind over the
lake home successfully. As the river was very low, the
great transport, which had run aground, had to be lightened when already in sight of our town, so that it could
come all the way up. The Indians had this time for four
months fifty-two barrels of flour, twenty-five barrels of
pork, and also a good quantity of corn and other things
besides, so that they are certainly well provided for, and
have never been so well off in their lives. Our wish is only
that they may use it with thankfulness. They were again
ashamed, for when we went away from here, it was said
that in the Fort we should all be put in irons, that the rest
here would be taken away, and that we should get no
provisions.

Sunday, 29. Br. Edwards preached and Michael Jung
held the congregation meeting.

Monday, 30. Br. David delivered an earnest discourse
of admonition to the brethren on account of the bad conduct of some who went to the Fort with us, and Ignatius was
put out of the church. He, after receiving absolution,
had sinned more than once, and thus it is with many who
wish to draw near us again, and fall thereby again into
the mire, as if their punishment were not yet over.

Wednesday, July 2. The brethren helped us about our
corn plantation, for we are overwhelmed with work.

Saturday, 5. There came an express from the commandant in Detroit, who told us in a letter to Br. David that
two brothers had come there in a ship from Niagara, who
wished to see and speak with us as soon as possible. We
saw from his letter that one of them was Br. Schebosh.
Br. David, with Br. Edwards and some Indian brothers,
got ready at once and went thither in the boat, where they,

Sunday, 6, arrived betimes, and to their no common joy
met Br. Schebosh and John Weigand (messenger of the
Mission Board), whom a merchant there had taken into
his own house. At the same time, on that very day, an

American, Col. Douglass,[1] came by land from Pittsburg,
by whom we received a letter from Br. Ettwein.[2] What
joy, praise, and thanks held our hearts towards our dear
Lord is hardly to be described, after so long waiting and
such long separation from the brethren ; when he sees the
right time he certainly helps.

Br. David went at once to Col. De Peyster, who has
been promoted, and announced his arrival. He was extremely friendly, and asked Br. David whether he knew
Br. Schebosh, and whether he was an honorable man.
Answer. He need have no doubt of it. He told us why
he asked. He had heard he had instructions from Congress
for the Indians. Br. David answered him, that he did not
believe it, and had heard nothing nor learned any thing of
it, for the brethren received no such commissions. He said :
"That is quite enough for me. The two brothers can go
with thee and dwell with you. I will also give them supplies as long as you have them [and he gave at once to
Br. David a written order], only they shall communicate
to the Indians no information or news about the bounds
of the land, but be silent." Two officers from Congress
came here to treat with the Indians, but he permitted them
to do no more than announce the peace to them, for as yet
he had no orders therefor from higher quarters. Br.
David thanked him very politely for his beneficence and

---

[1] Ephraim Douglass, an Indian trader before the Revolution. He was
sent out, in accordance with a resolution of Congress, to treat with the
Western Indians, being well fitted for the purpose by his familiar acquaintance with the Indian tongues. He died in 1833, at the age of
eighty-four.—Letter from Hon. Wm. M. Darlington.

[2] John Ettwein was the successor of Bishop Seidel, and was consecrated Bishop in 1784. "Of humble descent, a shoemaker by trade,
he became a prince and a great man in Israel." He was born in June,
1721, converted in 1738, ordained deacon of the church 1746. In 1754
he came to America, was a missionary among the Indians, pastor of
the church in New York City, and afterwards in North Carolina. He
visited New England, preaching in Boston and laying the corner-stone
of a Moravian church at Newport. He was a man of extraordinary
executive ability. His death occurred early in the year 1802. See De
Schweintz' Some of the Fathers of the Am. Mor. Church.

kind intentions, that he had so well provided both for us
and our Indians now for nearly a year, and had given
orders for supplies till the end of October, and had cared
for us as a father would have done; we were indeed in no
condition to make him any return, but should always think
of him with appreciation and thankfulness; there was,
however, One above us all, our Father in heaven, who
would not leave him unrewarded. He answered that the
thing in itself was reward enough for him, for he saw that
what he had done had not been done in vain, and that
therefore he did it with all pleasure. Since now he had
become acquainted with us and he was not likely to remain
here, he would make the request that after he was replaced
and called away, Br. David would write to him from time
to time and give him news about our health and how we
got on, for as long as he was in the army and Br. David
addressed him a letter, it would certainly reach him, be he
where he might be; he did not know certainly that he
would be called away, but thus much he conjectured, that
it would not happen before June of next year, and before
that time he would speak further with Br. David and make
arrangements with him. After Br. David finished his
business he took leave of him in a friendly way, and we
departed,

Monday, 7, with the two brothers from Detroit, and
came,

Tuesday, 8, to the joy of ourselves and of all our brethren, back home. Tears of joy and thankfulness were
shed at seeing again, after two years, brethren from our
church and receiving news of it. We soon refreshed ourselves with our letters and news from the church, which
we read with melted hearts, especially about the death of
our venerable, dear Br. Nathaniel (Bishop Seidel), in whom
we lost a true father, and of many other man-servants and
maid-servants of our Saviour.

Wednesday, 9. At the early service from the Scripture-
verse of the day, which, to our joy, we have now again
received: The Lord hear thee in the day of trouble, the
brethren were saluted by the church and were told on this

occasion that the Saviour had heard the prayer of so many congregations for us, in his mercy had thought of us, and had opened the way for our again hearing from each other. The brethren were admonished to think back a little, to search and converse with their hearts, perhaps much would there be found, and their hearts would tell them that our all falling into such need and misery was in great degree brought about [for this was reason enough to be found] by our being sinners, and they were urged to seek comfort and forgiveness with the Saviour. We white brethren afterwards read some letters and journals, where-from we saw the hearty sympathy of our dear brethren in our sufferings, for we perceived with modest and affected hearts their distress and perplexity about us, whom may our dear Lord and Saviour comfort in regard to us. The rest of the day the two brothers told us by word of mouth how it stood with the church and what had happened meanwhile, so that we forgot all else.

Thursday, 10. After early service by Br. Heckewelder, in the communion quarter-hour, announcement was made to the brethren for the following Saturday that the Saviour would give us food and drink of his body and blood in the holy sacrament.

Saturday, 12. After the brethren had been addressed, we enjoyed his body and blood in the holy communion with hungry and thirsty souls. At the love-feast the letter of Br. Ettwein was read to the brethren and the greeting from the church made known. The Saviour gave us back two brothers, Cornelius and Peter, and two sisters, Magdalena and Agnes, who were readmitted, to whom it was an unspeakable blessing. Again to others who yet remained behind, it was a blessing that they entered their hearts, where the Holy Ghost disclosed to them their faults and deteriorations.

Sunday, 13. Br. Edwards preached after the communion liturgy and Sensemann held the congregation meeting from the Scripture-verse of the day. Those who were re-admitted yesterday came and showed their joy and thankfulness for the mercy which the Saviour had let them feel.

Monday, 14. Br. Michael Jung held the early service. The changeable weather for more than a week now, for it has been very hot, but is now so cold that we had to seek out our thicker clothes, causes among us white brethren indispositions and fevers, for if north winds blow here, it is not only cool, but at times cold even in summer.

Tuesday, 15. Many of the brethren went to the lake to get rushes for making mats; they came back the 16th.

Thursday, 17. Our neighbor from the mouth of the river came and asked that some Indians might help him, he paying them, to hill his corn, and this was promised.

Sunday, 20. Br. David preached from the words: Depart from me for I am a sinful man. Br. Heckewelder held the children's hour, Michael the congregation meeting. In the afternoon we read papers and letters we had received.

Monday, 21. Some brothers and sisters went down to Hasel to help him on his plantation, as we had promised.

Tuesday, 22. Br. Conner came back from Detroit, where he had got supplies. When we last got provisions there, and he at the same time went with us, Col. de Peyster refused to let him have them longer, and so he had to provide himself with them by buying them.

Thursday, 24. Br. Heckewelder held the early service. Some Indian brethren went off hunting. John, Luke's son, came from Sandusky, where he had been living.

Sunday, 27. Br. Heckewelder preached. We laborers read together the weekly journal[1] of last year's synod at Berthelsdorf (near Herrnhut), with sympathetic hearts, and gave thanks to the Saviour who was with them, imparting to them his council and aid. Br. David held the congregation meeting from the Scripture-verse: He hath made his wonderful works to be remembered: the Lord is gracious and full of compassion, about the wonder of wonders that God became man and for us gave up his life unto death that we might have life everlasting.

Monday, 28. Some went to Detroit to sell canoes they

[1] See introduction.

had made. A white man, named Homes, came from the settlement here visiting with his wife. He remained over night, and went back Tuesday, the 29th.

Wednesday, 30. From the brethren who came from the Fort we learned that Oswego[1] is now garrisoned by Americans. If this was true it was pleasing to us, for it will further the return of Br. Weigand. Also some friendly Delawares came here visiting.

Saturday, Aug. 2. Some Frenchmen came, and also two Germans from Detroit for a visit. Heckewelder held early service.

NOTE—Fine prospect for a good harvest.

Sunday, 3. Br. Edwards preached, David held the children's service, and Sensemann the congregation meeting. We read together the weekly journal of the synod.

Monday, 4. Brs. Sensemann and Conner went to the Fort, the latter for provisions.

Wednesday, 6. Br. David spoke with A. Charity, bade her turn altogether to the Saviour, and not to use her time in the church without blessing, but to give herself entirely to him, to ask forgiveness from him; but for that a childlike heart was needful, uprightness towards her laborers and the Saviour.

Friday, 8. Brs. Sensemann and Schebosh from the Fort, we had a letter from Br. Shewkirk,[1] from New York, dated Aug. 24th of last year.

Saturday 9. Tucker came with his wife for a visit. They asked for an Indian sister to be at the lying-in of their negro woman.

Sunday, 10. Br. David preached, thereupon the communion quarter-hour. We laborers continued our reading aloud of the weekly journal of the synod, and Br. Edwards held the congregation meeting.

Monday, 11. We refused an Indian woman who wanted

---

[1] See under June 18, 1783, p. 153.

[2] Ewald Gustavus Shewkirk' born at Stettin, Prussia, Feb. 28, 1725. He came to America in 1774, and served the church in various capacities, and at one time was pastor of the Moravian church in New York City. He was made bishop in 1785, and died at Herrnhut, in 1805.

to place her child with us, for by such children we have always hitherto been cheated and deceived.

Wednesday, 13. We had the holy communion, at which our dear Lord came very graciously to us and blessed us with his near presence.

Thursday, 14. Joseph and his wife, also Magdalena, went to the Fort to sell canoes.

Sunday, 17. Heckewelder preached, thereupon we read the weekly journal of the synod, the end of which we reached to-day, and we thanked the Saviour for having been with the members of the synod, for having imparted to them his advice and intelligence for the blessing and advantage of his churches, who now enjoyed them together, and we also. Br. David held the congregation meeting from the Scripture-verse: Blessed is the man whom thou choosest and causest to approach unto thee that he may dwell in thy courts. We shall be satisfied with the goodness of thy house. Also the children of the church shall fully enjoy it. O Lord, let them be thine own through the shedding of thy blood.

Monday, 18. Br. Jungmann held the early service, and Tuesday, the 19th, Br. Edwards. Some brethren, went to the settlements, with baskets and brooms to sell.

Wednesday, 20. Michael held early service. In our conference we considered which one of us should go with Br. Weigand to Bethlehem; inasmuch as none of the married brethren wished to go this time, except Br. Jungmann, who declared himself ready, but this did not have our approval, our choice had to be made from the two unmarried brothers. They let it rest upon the choice and approbation of the Saviour, and it fell to the lot of Br. Michael Jung to go with Br. John Weigand to Bethlehem.

Friday, 22. Some brethren who had gone to the settlement came back. Sensemann held the early service. Both we and the Indians were busy farming.

Saturday, 23. Br. David held early service.

Sunday, 24. Br. Edwards preached. In the service for the baptized, in the afternoon, Thomas was absolved

11

and again admitted to the church. Br. Jungmann held
the congregation meeting.

Monday, 25. Br. David held early service.

Tuesday, 26. The child of Thomas and Sabina, some
nine months old, was baptized with the name Rosina.
Heckewelder and Schebosh went to the Fort, among other
things, to find out about the sailing of ships for Niagara.
On,

Thursday, 28, they came back, bringing news that in a
few days a ship would sail for Niagara.

[So far the diary to Bethlehem.]

Saturday, 30. The brothers, David, Edwards, and
Sensemann went with Brs. John Weigand and Michael
Jung to Detroit, the last two to sail for Niagara on their
journey to Bethlehem. In the early service we committed
these brethren to the remembrance of the brethren during
their journey, that the Saviour should bring them, with
good fortune and health to their destination, that our
brethren might have perfect information about us. On
account of stormy weather, however, by which they were
kept back on the lake, they got there,

Tuesday, Sept. 2, and since the ship had already sailed
two days before, they must wait for another. Thus, after
a tender separation, we came back to Guadenhütten,[1]

Thursday, 4, on the same day Jeremy, son of Samuel
and Sarah, was buried. A frost that fell on the night of
Sept. 1, did much damage in the fields and gardens, but
yet not to the corn.

Saturday, 6. Sent an express to Detroit, with a letter
to Brs. John Weigand and Michael Jung, for Bethlehem.
The messenger returned the following forenoon, when we
learned from their letters they were still waiting for a ship,
and did not know when they should sail. We had to-day
a visit from Mr. Isaac Williams, of Detroit, his wife, and
some others, who made a journey here for their health by

---

[1] This is the first time in this diary that the settlement on Clinton
river is spoken of by name. Usually it is called New Gnadenhütten
for the sake of distinction.

the lake, but were very sea-sick. In the evening was the burial of the departed Anna, Abraham's wife, who died yesterday evening. Jan. 6, 1771, a widow, she had followed us from Goschgoschünk,[1] in the year '70, to Languntoutenunk (on the Beaver), where she was baptized by Br. Jungmann, and on the 11th of April, 1772, came to the enjoyment of the Lord's supper. Jan. 16, 1774, she was united in holy matrimony to the assistant, Abraham, then a widower. She always went a blessed way, so that we could always rejoice in her. But when her children, a son and a daughter, were grown up, and had married in the church, she gave all her care to their children, forgot herself and suffered harm in her heart, and though she was often reminded of this, she could not forbear, whereby she grew cold and dry in heart, and at times had to remain away from the supper of our Lord. Thus was she always variable, for in the disposition of heart she was pleasant and good. She had a lovely gift of speaking with sisters, of giving them good advice, and of directing them to the Saviour. She was wonderfully loved among the brethren, and this was especially evident during her sickness, for the sisters visited her very assiduously. From her whole conduct it could be seen she was chosen of the Lord, who led her, and did not let her go from his hand. In all our calamities of the last two years she stood firm and steadfast; nothing had might or power to turn her from the church. She was also among the first to come to us in Detroit and help make the beginning here. Two months ago she fell sick and has so continued since. All relief she tried was of no avail. In her sickness she invited different sisters to come to her to whom she thought she had spoken too directly, when she had only spoken the truth to them, and begged them all for forgiveness. One sister, Martha, a widow, answered her it was not so, whereupon she said: "Now I am ready, and nothing else keeps me from going to the Saviour." She admonished her children to remain with

---

[1] This town was on the Alleghany, near the mouth of Tionesta creek, not to be confounded with Goschachgünk, Coshocton, O.

the church and the Saviour all their lives, and her daughter she committed to her husband to act towards her as a
father. The brothers and sisters often went to her and
sang hymns, which she liked to hear. But for her the
Saviour was too long in coming and taking her to himself
and in bringing her to her blessed hope. At ten o'clock
last evening she had Br. David called, but she could say
little more, but said with difficulty, only that she wished
to go to the Saviour. He sang to her some hymns, and
during the words: I shall as my Master be—Clothed with
humility—Simple, teachable, and mild—Changed into a
little child—he blessed her, and she fell asleep in a moment
under his hand, softly and blessedly.

Sunday, 7. The married brethren celebrated their festival. At morning prayer, Br. Jungmann asked for us the
Saviour's near presence and bloody blessing for this day,
thereupon was the consideration of to-day's text: They
shall be all taught of God. Every man, therefore, that hath
heard and hath learned of the father, cometh unto me;
about learning to pass over to blessedness, not to vex
ourselves vainly in the church and to make life hard, but to
seek to make serviceable the merit of Jesus, from which
we have all that is good and blessed, and to have a share
in it. In the afternoon was a love-feast, and in the
evening Br. Edwards held the congregation meeting.

Monday, 8. Most of the brethren went to make canoes,
by which they can earn something, for they get a good
price for them.

Wednesday, 10. A Mohican, a friend of Christina, came
here visiting; his brother has remained in Gnadenhütten.

Saturday, 13. This week many were busy building. It
was again beautiful, warm, pleasant weather, but the frost
has already done much harm to many crops, and many
brethren will get no corn, for the frosts came this year much
earlier than is usual at other times. Besides, our Indian
brethren did not plant the right sort of corn, but a sort which
does not ripen here, which they brought as seed from the
Shawanese towns. Now we find the difference between here
and the Muskingum very noticeable, and here corn must be

planted which ripens earlier. Beans, cucumbers, and pumpkins have hardly begun to bear, and yet are frost-bitten.

Sunday, 14. Br. David preached about the foremost commandment: Thou shalt love the Lord thy God. Sense-mann held the children's service, and Heckewelder the congregation meeting.

Monday, 15. Most of the brethren went to make canoes. Br. David held early service.

Wednesday, 17. Chippewas came to trade some corn they brought.

Saturday, 20. Schebosh returned from Detroit and brought word that Brs. John Weigand and Michael Jung had already sailed on the 6th Inst., which was pleasant for us to hear.

Sunday 21. Br. Edwards preached, Br. David held the communion quarter-hour from the text, and Br. Jungmann the congregation meeting from the Scripture-verse of the day.

Wednesday, 24. Several houses have been blocked out this week; the weather has been fine and warm, so that we have good hope that our corn, which was planted quite too late, will yet get ripe and dry.

Friday, 26. Br. Jungmann and his wife talked with the brethren yesterday and to-day about the Lord's supper, and to our joy found them hungry and thirsty for this great good. We laborers had a conference, and at the same time a thorough and earnest talk together, so that we were somewhat hard upon one another, which was yet not without a blessing. Two white people came.

Saturday, 27. We had the supper of our Lord, and enjoyed his body and blood with hungry and thirsty hearts. A brother, Ephraim, and a sister, Sabina, were again readmitted, to whom it was an unspeakable blessing.

NOTE.—John Heckewelder administered[1] it. A sister, Agnes, received it on her sick-bed.

Sunday, 28. Br. David read the communion liturgy and

---

[1] This word is conjectured.

held the children's service. Br. Sensemann preached and
Br. Jungmann held the congregation meeting. The assistants, Samuel and Abraham, encouraged, edified, and
exhorted the brethren here and there in their houses to a
holy life and to walking with Christ.

Wednesday, Oct. 1. Most of the brethren and sisters
went to Detroit with canoes they had made to sell them,
for they get a good price, and with this can buy something
there, most of them being as badly off for clothes as they
have ever been, for during the war and famine they had
to make every effort to support their families. Br. Edwards also went to Detroit on business.

Saturday, 4. Two Frenchmen came here with apples to
sell. We white brethren were busy building, and partly,
too, in the fields, otherwise few brethren were at home.

Sunday, 5. Instead of a sermon Br. David read from
the History of the Days of the Son of Man something
from the sayings of the Saviour. Br. Edwards returned
from Detroit, by whom we had a letter from Br. Ettwein
from Bethlehem of May 20th, from which to our hearty joy
we had the pleasure of learning that Br. John,[1] from Europe,
was expected in Bethlehem for a visitation of the American church. David held the congregation meeting in the
Indian tongue. We read the proceedings of the synod.

Monday, 6. Most of the brethren came back from Detroit, where they sold a dozen canoes, some of them quite
large ones, and with the money from these they provided
themselves with clothes for the winter; thus by the guidance of our heavenly Father the brethren find the means

---

[1] Baron John de Watteville, the son of a clergyman, was born in
Thuringia, in 1718. While a student of theology at Jena he became
the friend of Count Christian Zinzendorf. In 1739 he was ordained a
clergyman, and in 1747 was consecrated bishop. His wife was the
daughter of Count Zinzendorf. He first came to America in 1748, visited various missions on the continent and in the islands, and carried
into effect changes in the government of the church. In 1783 he
made a second visit to America, and was here four years. Soon after
his return to Europe he died (1788).—De Schwinietz' Some of the
Fathers of the Am. Mor. Church.

of supporting themselves and their families. The widows make baskets, brooms, and mats, all of which they can sell at a good price, and since there are now this year many acorns in the bush, they gather them and sell them at a good price, and thus, if they are industrious, they can earn something in one way or another, and seek to help themselves.

Wednesday, 8. John (Heckewelder) held the early service from the Scripture-verse: The Lord is round about his people from henceforth even forever. Rejoice little flock. Br. Edwards went with a boat load of potatoes, cabbages, and turnips to Detroit, for which we thought to pay some debts we had to incur in our need.

Saturday, 11. David held early service. This week the brethren began to harvest in the fields, and to parch and dry the green corn, not yet ready, from being planted too late.

Sunday, 12. David preached, Sensemann held the children's service. We read from the journal of the synod about the churches and choirs. Heckewelder held the congregation meeting.

Monday, 13. Br. Edwards came back from Detroit.

Tuesday, 14. The Chippewa chief came here; as he was from the bush, and had nothing to eat, Br. Abraham collected some corn and pumpkins for him among the brethren and gave them to him, for which he was very thankful. His wife is the cousin of the late Netawatwes, and the near friend of our Thomas here. Thomas told them for the first time something about the Saviour, for he knows Shawano; they listened but kept quite silent.

Thursday, 16. Some brethren went to the plains for the autumn hunt; the sisters at home were industriously at work in the fields harvesting.

Sunday, 19. Br. Edward preached and Sensemann held the congregation meeting.

Wednesday, 22. Chippewas went through here, up the creek, on their way hunting. They observed how our town had grown. Our Indian brethren hunting.

Sunday, 26. Heckewelder preached. In the afternoon was a reading of the synodal proceedings. Edwards held the congregation meeting. After this to the communion brethren was announced the supper of our Lord in the holy sacrament.

Monday, 27. The Indians went to their hunting camp. They came in to the Sunday services, for the autumn hunt is on. A white man came from Detroit, from whom we learned that Niagara is garrisoned by Americans. Sensemann and Schebosh came back from Detroit.

Wednesday, 29. Br. Zeisberger and his wife spoke with the brethren to-day, and the following days, about the Lord's supper, and the others likewise, and found to their comfort and joy the Holy Ghost busy with their hearts.

Friday, 31. In our conference we had the joy of having the Saviour again send us four brethren, whom he permitted in the holy communion to enjoy his body and blood, which we the day after,

Saturday, November 1, enjoyed with hungry and thirsty hearts.

Sunday, 2. David read the communion liturgy. Edwards preached about the marriage feast, whereto men were invited to appear in the garments of righteousness. David held the congregation meeting.

Monday, 3. Agnes died in peace.

Tuesday, 4. Her remains were buried. She was baptized by Br. Martin Mack,[1] in Old Gnadenhütten (Carbon Co., Pa.), on the Mahony, Sept. 5, 1751, and came afterwards to the enjoyment of the Lord's supper. She went through all the fatalities, difficulties, and changes through which the Indian church passed. In the year 1755, in

---

[1] John Martin Mack was by birth a Würtemberger. In 1734, at the age of nineteen, he went to Herrnhut, and was disposed to remain there, but two years later he came to America. Here he had part in all the undertakings of the brothers, laboring in the Indian missions for nearly twenty years. In 1762, he sailed to St. Thomas to serve in the mission among negro slaves. To this work he gave the rest of his life, coming to Bethlehem in 1770 to be consecrated bishop, and visiting Germany ten years later. He died in 1784.

Nov., when Gnadenhütten was destroyed and burnt by the
Indians, she went to Nain, near Bethlehem, and in the
year 1763 into the barracks in Philadelphia. In 1765,
when peace and quiet were again established, she moved
with the Indian church to Friedenshütten on the Susquehanna. In the spring of 1772 she came with others to the
Ohio, first to Languntouteniink (Friedensstadt on the
Beaver), and the year after to Gnadenhütten on the Muskingum, from which she had to flee and return to Lichtenau
in the year '78, on account of the war troubles; here she remained a year, and in '79 again went to Gnadenhütten.
In the year 1781, when the Indian church on the Muskingum, with its teachers, was carried away captive, and
brought to Sandusky, she had part in all the hardships we
encountered, and since she was a widow, for her husband
had died not long before in Gnadenhütten, she had a hard
time, suffered hunger, as did all of us, but in all our need
she hung upon the Saviour and the church, and nothing
separated her from him and the church. In 1782, when
the Indian church was altogether robbed of its teachers,
for they were all taken to Detroit, she clung to the greater
number, and lived a year in the Shawanese towns. When
she heard that the brethren, her teachers, with some Indian brethren, were again settling, with others also, in the
spring of 1783, she got ready, and in the beginning of May,
this year, came to us here, sickly as she was, with the intention rather to die in the church than among the savages, and this the Saviour also advised. She came again
to the enjoyment of the Lord's supper, and was right
blessed, but in her body she was no longer well, but wasted
away until on the day before mentioned, easily and blessedly she died in his arms and bosom. She is a clear example and proof that whoever has a true heart, him he
helps through all tribulations, and upholds him also to
the end of all need through himself and his wounds.

To-day went Brs. Heckewelder and Sensemann with
many Indian brethren in the boat to Detroit to buy some
necessities for the winter, before the strong cold comes on
and the lake is frozen. They came back on the 8th.

Friday, 7. By one of our young Indians, Daniel by name, who came here from the neighborhood of the Shawanese towns, we had news that Mark had suddenly there gone from time.

Sunday, 9. Br. David preached from the Epistle, Eph., vi, 10 : Finally, my brethren, be strong in the Lord and in the power of his might.

Br. Edwards conducted the children's service and Heckewelder the congregation meeting.

Monday, 10. The above mentioned Daniel, an unmarried man, son of Philip, the Mohican, who perished at Gnadenhütten, asked to be taken back to live in the church. He told to Br. David quite sincerely his course of life since our departure from Sandusky; whereupon Br. David asked him how it was now and what his thoughts were. He answered : "I am sick and tired of the heathen life and conduct, and will now live for the Saviour; formerly when I lived in the church I could not say this, for I always thought to find pleasure in the world. I knew not how to value what it is to be in the church, but it is now my intention to make better use of it." We had no hesitation about receiving him and to use pity, confidence, and diligence with our young people, for we have found from repeated experience that the pains we have taken with them, even if we must have trouble and vexation with them, are not in vain, and that the Saviour lets them thrive and come to a blessing. We must especially wonder that our young people, even when they had their freedom and nobody hindered them from running straight into heathenism, more than the older people, have yet stood fast, have not forgotten their teachers, nor thrown them aside, but have longed for them again and have pleasure and inclination for God's word ; from this can be seen that the Saviour holds his hand over these, our youth, and that his eye watches over them.

To-day were the remains of the little Rebecca buried, six years, nine months old, who died yesterday, a dear child, that loved the Saviour and willingly went to him, as she said to Br. David, whom twice she had called to her, and only an hour before her death said that she was going to the Saviour.

Thursday, 13. At morning prayer the feast of the Elder of his church was announced and we asked for his near presence this day and for his bloody blessing in our hearts. Br. Heckewelder delivered the public sermon, and then the baptized brethren had a festival-discourse, and last we prayed to our Lord and Elder, thanked him for his guidance and recognition of us, begged pardon for all our sins, and that we had given him trouble, vowed fealty and obedience to him, and he let his friendly face shine over us, blessed us and sent us his peace.

To-day we again made a beginning with our Assistants' Conference, which has hitherto been omitted, for we have had only the two assistants, Abraham and Samuel. Now these two and Cornelius, Schebosh, and Bathsheba, with us white laborers, form the Assistants' Conference. They were exhorted to love and unity among themselves, as something in which they had failed before this time, to treat the brethren with love and compassion, not to be stern and harsh towards them [which is a peculiarity of the Indians] if with one another things went not well, but to let them feel their loving and sympathetic heart.

Friday, 14. Since a fine, fresh snow fell last night and the hunters went out, there was brought in to-day a fine number of deer, which are now quite fat. Abraham took a rare animal and quite unknown to our Indians. It was larger and heavier than a raccoon; its head and mouth are just the same, but its feet and legs are short and shaped like those of a mole or a beaver's feet. The Chippewas say they run under ground like moles, although they are so big, and they are very fat. This was the English badger.

Sunday, 16, Sensemann preached. We had a reading service,[1] and Jungmann held the congregation meeting.

---

[1] By this is meant a public reading of reports from missions or of lessons from the Scriptures.

Monday, 17. Many sisters went to seek for hemp with Samuel and other brothers, into the hilly land where they found enough of it, wherewith and also with meat they came home heavily laden on the 22d. Since they are not used to a flat country, they have always much pleasure in seeing hills again, which begin a good day's journey from here. Chippewas encamped not far from here, near a dead horse, and they stayed until they had eaten it up, for it is their custom to eat dead cattle.

Thursday, 20. Conner came back from the Fort, and also an Englishman, named Homes, came from the settlements, who remained until the 23d. They are all, however, either somewhat honest, simple folk or men of this world. In none of them are found desire and inclination for any thing good or for God's word, but it is a place quite dead and dark, where men live for the day only, undisturbed about their souls, and seek only for money and goods.

Saturday, 22. Absolution was given to Renatus, the Mohican, at his request, upon his sick-bed. He said: "Three things distress me; the first is the forgiveness of my sins, the second to know that my wife and children will remain with the church when I am gone, and the third that linen fails me for my shroud." After he was absolved, he said: "Now is it well with me, and I rejoice to go to the Saviour. I wish not to be again restored to health, but my wish is that he may take me to himself."

Sunday, 23. Br. David preached from Phil. iii, 17: Mark them which walk so as ye have us for an ensample. Heckewelder held the congregation meeting. For two days it has been very cold. The river and lake begin to freeze. We read to-day from the synodal journal about church conferences.

Monday, 24. We recalled the calamity on the Mahony[1] twenty-eight years ago.

Thursday, 27. Our people went to the hills for their autumn hunt; for the most part, only sisters are at home.

---

[1] Where, in 1755, perished ten persons at the hands of the Indians. For full account see De Schwineitz' Life of Zeisberger, Chap. xii.

Friday, 28. By the Indian, Adam, from the Fort, I had a letter dated July 4, from Br. Shewkirk, in New York, by way of Quebec and Niagara, which the commandant, Col. de Peyster, sent to me.

Sunday, 30. [1st day of Advent.] Br. David preached in the Indian language, for no interpreter was present, about the joy of the children of God at the incarnation of the Saviour, that he had taken our flesh and blood that he might offer himself for us upon the cross to reconcile us with God. Heckewelder held the congregation meeting. To-day and yesterday it snowed, as it has already done several times this autumn, but no snow has yet remained.

Monday, Dec. 1. Some brethren went off to the hunters to get meat. They came,

Wednesday, 3, home, and also many of the Indian brethren from the hunt, but they got little, since many Chippewas are also off hunting in that neighborhood. Thus our Indians earn little hunting, and yet they find it necessary, in order to get corn for their families, and they must try to get something by their labor.

Thursday, 4. There were among our people unpleasant things to arrange. A sister wished to go from the church, but she thought better of it, and found her heart.

Sunday, 7. In the sermon by Br. Heckewelder, about the wicked, last times which would come over the whole circle of the world, two white people from the mouth of the river were present. In the communion quarter-hour about the text: Come for all things are now ready, the brethren became as it were reconciled, their hearts were washed with the blood of Christ, and they were clad with the cloak of righteousness; they were invited to receive his body and to drink his blood next Saturday. Sensemann held the congregation meeting from the Scripture-verse: Let thy priests be clothed with righteousness: and let thy saints shout for joy.

Tuesday, 9. For a time we have had quite cold weather and a good deal of snow has fallen, but now a thaw sets in and the weather is so warm that the snow has all gone off.

Friday, 12. To-day and yesterday we spoke with the brethren about the Lord's supper. We found them walking with the Saviour and longing for his body and blood. Bathsheba spoke to some Chippewa women, encamped near us in the bush, about the Saviour, but they did not understand very well. The brethren repaired our chapel, and caulked it with moss against the winter.

Saturday, 13. Br. Schebosh returned from the Fort. We heard that this autumn in a storm three ships in Lake Erie and four in Lake Ontario had been wrecked and entirely lost. At the Lord's supper, Sabina, Adam's wife, was present for the first time.

Sunday, 14. After the communion liturgy Br. Edwards preached from the text: The poor have the gospel preached to them. A wonderful movement was observed among the brethren who are not yet quite in order, being still behindhand, so that they begin to long to come into the right way. David held the service for the children, whom he encouraged to give their hearts and to receive the childlike Jesus. Br. Sensemann held the congregation meeting.

Monday, 15. Br. Edwards went with several of our Indian brethren to Detroit and came back the 18th.

16. Peggy Conner became the mother of a daughter that, Sunday 21st, was baptized with the name Susanna. At the sermon our neighbor, Edward Hasle, was present with his wife, who came here visiting last evening. Afterwards was a service for the baptized. They were reminded of the covenant they had made with the Saviour at baptism, were urged to search themselves to see how they had kept it; that the Saviour would not let himself be put off with fine promises, but required upright hearts from those with whom it was truth and who showed it by their works. Heckewelder held the congregation meeting from the Scripture-verse on St. Thomas' day: That ye may tell it to the generation following. For this God is our God for ever and ever. I place my hand in Jesus' side and say: My Lord and my God.

23. For the first time a Chippewa woman was at the early service, who understood Delaware.

Wednesday, 24. We began Christmas with a love-feast and rejoiced in God, our Saviour, who for us became man, was born in a stable in Bethlehem in a manger, and we thanked him for his blessed incarnation and prayed to him upon our knees. He made himself known to us, made us feel that he was with us. Our hearts were aroused and many tears were shed.

Thursday, 25. Br. Heckewelder preached from the Epistle: For the grace of God that bringeth salvation, hath appeared to all men. Two white people came to hear the sermon. In a service for the baptized afterwards three brothers and a sister were absolved by the laying on of hands, who, since they came to us last spring, could not be refreshed and healed, namely, Luke, Joshua, Andrew, and Sister Amelia, Cornelius's wife, a service especially blessed by the Saviour, and above all there was a thorough work of grace among the children and adults, as we had already often wished; and others who yet longed to come, but must still wait, came more to their own hearts and learned to know themselves.

Friday, 26. Last night came much snow and cold weather.

Sunday, 28. Br. David preached from the Epistle: But when the fulness of the time was come, God sent forth his Son, made of a woman, etc., so that we might receive the adoption of sons. Sensemann held the children's service. It was cold to-day. Heckewelder held the congregation meeting from the Scripture-verse.

Wednesday, 31. We assembled at the usual time at the end of the year, thankfully called to mind the mercy and kindness we had enjoyed during the past year from our dear Lord, acknowledged to him our shortcomings, and asked forgiveness of all our transgressions and the comfort of his grace. In a prayer upon our knees we remembered our brethren yet wandering in error and begged him to assemble them and bring them again to the flock. He showed himself to us, his poor and little people, and kindly looked down upon us and sent us his peace.

What has happened to us this year is briefly the following. At the beginning of the year we were still but a handful, but in the spring, about the first of May, we were increased by a fine number of brethren who came to us from the Shawanese towns. Of the rest, however, who have remained behind, we have heard nothing since, how they are, save that Mark has suddenly gone from time.

At the beginning of July, to our hearty joy, came Brs. Weigand and Schebosh from Bethlehem to us, by whom once again we had letters and news from the church. The first with Br. Michael Jung went away August 30th. We hope the Saviour has brought them fortunately to their destination.

The Saviour has not left himself without a witness in our brethren's hearts. With longing eyes we have seen that the Lord is with us and walks in our midst. The Holy Spirit was busy in our hearts and has brought many a one to the Physician of his soul, that through his wounds he should be cured and made well. Twenty-six brethren have this year been absolved and sixteen readmitted to the holy communion. The Saviour has also shown us that in regard to his supper we ought to manage with the brethren more prudently, for they have generally suffered countless injuries in their hearts; which also happened, and he has made it become an especially true blessing.

In regard to the maintenance both of ourselves and of our Indian brethren for the present year we have a bad outlook. We got provisions until the end of October and had hoped also that we should harvest enough from our plantations for our needs, but this hope has failed, since in the first place we were ignorant of the climate, and secondly, we planted corn which in this land does not ripen, and besides we planted it somewhat too late, so that some indeed harvested something, but many nothing at all, and must try to get through by hunting and by the labor of their hands, and it is also a good thing that our Indian brethren have occasion to earn something by their hands. We trust in our dear heavenly Father that he will give and bless our daily bread. Five children have been born and baptized. Three children have died, namely, Augustina, Jeremy, and Rebecca, and two sisters, Anna, Abel's wife, and the widow, Agnes.

12

CHAPTER IV.

1784.

New Gnadenhütten, on the Clinton, Michigan.

Thursday, Jan. 1. Br. Edwards preached from Gal. iii: Ye are all the children of God, for as many of you as have been baptized have put on Jesus. The baptized brethren renewed their covenant with the Saviour, who in baptism had made them with him, gave themselves anew to him to be the reward for his woes, and so to remain. Two sinners were absolved, Daniel and Adolphus, the first born in the church at Nain, who was likewise taken into the church, for which the Saviour showed himself gracious, as especially during the holidays a new life came among the brethren, and the Saviour, through his Holy Ghost, during these days has done a good work, and many have been borne to the Lord, for when he begins to work, it speeds. We took for use last year's Scripture-verses and texts.

Friday, 2. Some Indian brethren went to the swamp bear-hunting.

Sunday, 4. Br. Sensemann preached from Tit., iii, 5: He saved us by the washing of regeneration and renewing of the Holy Ghost.

Rainy weather came on; thus far it has snowed much, and now the snow cannot get deep.

Tuesday, 6. Br. Heckewelder conducted morning prayer, and asked in the name of all our little flock, out of the bloody fulness of Jesus, his blessing for this day. In the service for the baptized, from the Scripture-verse and text for the day, Christiana Schebosh was admitted to the church, and an unmarried sister was absolved, namely, Esther. At the love-feast afterwards the brethren were reminded that our church made it its business, and had thereto a call from the Saviour, to announce the Gospel to those poor, blind heathen, that we had our life in peril herefor, and lived not even to death, and that we should think ourselves richly rewarded if we brought to the Saviour one soul which learned to know its Redeemer, for he became the Saviour of the heathen, and that the day is therefore named Epiphany, for after his birth men came from distant lands, worshipped him, and brought him gifts. All the services were blessed and accompanied by his presence, for which, at the end of the day, Br. Jungmann, in a heartfelt prayer, gave him praise and thanks, and in this the whole company united.

Wednesday, 7. Some of our Indians went out bearhunting; it began to snow hard, and kept on the following days, and then very severe cold weather came on, so that,

Saturday, 10, some gentle people came in sleighs from Detroit, on the ice over the lake, to visit us, simply to see our town, who say that by the thermometer it has not been so cold for twenty-eight years as it is now, it being seven degrees lower than in the whole time.

Sunday, 11. The four gentlemen were present at the service, who have looked at our town and visited in our houses. They said that if they should say in Detroit there was such a settlement here on the Huron river, as there really is, no one would believe them; they must themselves come and see whether they had spoken the truth. In the afternoon they went away quite content, and said that they thought their trouble and journey well rewarded in that they had seen our town. The boys and children had a blessed service for their festival, to them was pictured the boy, Jesus, as a model and example for them, in whose footsteps they should follow.

Tuesday, 13. Most of our Indian brethren went to the Milk River, on the way to Detroit, to make a bridge, for it is now frozen, and it is easier to make a bridge now than in the summer, likewise over other creeks to do the same. They came back on the 16th, and likewise Br. Sensemann back from the Fort, bringing news that we might expect a

visit from Col. de Peyster with several other gentlemen
next week.

Saturday, 17. A Chippewa came here and remained
over night, and with him the next morning went Thomas,
both of them after a bear, which the former had lost trace
of when night came on, but it went over the lake.

Sunday, 18. Heckewelder preached. To the communicants the Lord's supper was announced for next Saturday,
and open-heartedness was recommended them. Br. Edwards held the congregation meeting.

Tuesday, 20. Sensemann held early service. Frenchmen came with two sledges up the river on the ice; they
brought corn and victuals which they exchanged for venison, and went,

Wednesday, 21, back again. To-day it snowed again,
and the snow gets always deeper. For a week now very
cold weather.

Saturday, 24. At the Lord's supper, Joshua, Amelia,
and Susanna were readmitted, and one sister enjoyed it
on her sick-bed. This week it snowed several days in succession, and the snow was now three feet deep, so that it
was hard to get fire-wood.

Sunday, 25. Heckewelder read the communion liturgy,
Sensemann preached. In the marriage service, Andrew,
an unmarried man, and Sister Anna, an unmarried woman,
daughter of Samuel and Sara, were married. Br. Edwards
held the congregation meeting.

Tuesday, 27. Sabina, Adam's wife, came to bed with a
daughter.

Wednesday, 28. The assistants, Abraham and Samuel,
spoke to Ann Charity about her conduct. Two white
people came here from the settlement over the lake, from
whom we heard that the snow there is deeper than here,
and that outside the track one cannot get through, for it
is deep, and has a hard crust above.

Saturday, 31. We ended the first month of this year
with thankful hearts to our dear Lord that to the present
time he has graciously aided us and our Indian brethren
in this hard winter and deep snow, which through the

whole country lies full three feet deep, so that our Indian
brethren, though they have really no food, yet can not go
hunting, for there is no getting out, and many have now
nothing at all left to eat, but they live from what is given
them by those who have still something left. We are also
overrun and cannot but give to them when we see their
need, but in a single day we could give away all we have,
and then hunger and perish with them. All were therefore busy making snow-shoes, with which they can overtake the deer upon the snow, and in this way was the first
brought to town lately. But most of them are not accustomed to use these and must learn how. We have, however, thought of breaking a road to the settlement, also
by the use of snow-shoes, of getting the means of life.

Sunday, Feb. 1. During the sermon Br. Heckewelder
baptized the little daughter of Adam and Sabina, born on
the 27th, with the name Cathrine, into the death of Jesus.
In the service for the baptized, two single brethren, Zachary and Joseph, were absolved in the name of the Holy
Trinity, whereto the Saviour showed himself gracious and
mighty, so that many tears were shed. At every absolution of this kind there is universal joy and sympathy
among the brethren, as if such were now first baptized, and
all those who again come back to us are, through absolution, again admitted to the church.

Wednesday, 4. The severe winter still continues, and
it has snowed nearly every day, and the snow gets ever
deeper. Our Indian brethren, about whom we are most
anxious and distressed, have many of them nothing more
to eat. Their need grows, for which they are also themselves much to blame, since it is their custom never to have
care beforehand, but to eat as long as they have any thing,
and when it is all gone, and need presses upon them, they
seek to get something. No one had thought there would
be such a winter. Old settlers in Detroit say that as long
as they have lived there the snow has never been so deep.

Saturday, 7. Within three days, by the use of snow-
shoes, more than one hundred deer have been shot, for
which, in our hunger, we were very thankful to our

heavenly Father. The cold, however, was so searching, that many froze their feet, which happens sooner and easier on snow-shoes than in the snow.

Sunday, 8. Br. David preached from the Gospel about the good sower in the fields, whereby it was remarked that each heart had to watch over itself, so that their enemy might not again cast into their heart wicked seed, from which the Saviour has redeemed it, forgiving its sins and purifying it from them, and again pollute it, whereby such a poor heart becomes a weed in the church, and if it does not soon hasten to the Saviour and let itself be cured, it is in danger of being rooted out and cast into the fire.

Monday, 9. One of our Indians went with the sledge to Detroit, over the lake, for upon the ice there is hardly any snow and good travelling. We sent a message to a couple of Frenchmen about bringing here corn and provisions to exchange for venison, for our Indians cannot well go into the settlements on account of the snow. Ignatius came on the 11th in a sledge, laden with corn, back from Detroit.

Thursday, 12. Frenchmen came with corn and provisions on two sledges, and exchanged their supplies for venison.

Friday, 13. Mr. McKee and Elliot came with two sleighs to see our town and settlement, of which they had heard much, and had to wonder at the labor already done. They pitied us and our Indians that on account of the early frosts our corn had failed, which is hard indeed for us in this severe and long-lasting winter. In the evening they went on to our neighbor. With them was also McKee's brother from the Susquehanna, by whom we sent letters to Litiz and Bethlehem. Br. Schebosh went in the sledge to Detroit to get corn.

Sunday, 15. Br. Edwards preached. In the quarter-hour for the married, Br. Jungmann married the assistant and widower, Abraham and the widow Martha, with whom we afterwards had a love-feast. Br. David held the Congregation meeting from the text: The Father hath not

left me alone: for I do always those things that please
him.

Wednesday, 18. To-day and the three preceding days
many white people came here, English and French, in
part for a visit, and in part they brought food to exchange for meat. All who came carefully examined our
town and had much to say about it.

Sunday, 22. Br. Jungmann preached from the Gospel:
Behold, we go up to Jerusalem, about the Saviour's approach to his passion. In the marriage service Br. David
married the widower Renatus and the single woman, Anna
Regina. A merchant from Detroit, who with his family
has come here visiting, was present and asked for the
baptism of his two children. Thereupon in a common
service they were baptized, the one with the name John,
the other Mary. Both parents sat before the table and
held the children for baptism, which conduct was very re-
spectable and impressive. As there is no ordained preacher
of the Protestant church in Detroit, the Justice baptizes
the children also, or the commandant, if it be asked of
him, but to many this is not satisfactory and they are
scrupulous about it.

Tuesday, 24. They went back again to Detroit well
pleased with their visit. Christiana brought forth a son.

Thursday, Feb. 26. To-day and yesterday came here
more French and English, all in sledges upon the ice. They
make the winter useful, for with a sledge they can come
in one day, which in summer can not be done in a single
day, unless the wind be very good.

Saturday, 28. Many Indian brethren came back from
the settlement where they have been to get corn, but have
found little. The winter, since the new year, has been very
severe, the snow three feet deep, and the cold weather lasting. Old settlers say they have never had so hard a winter here. Many cattle perish in the settlements for want
of fodder, and they who have corn must use it for their
cattle, and therefore none is to be had. We are in great
distress about our Indians, who have nothing to eat, and

it goes hard with them, their need always getting greater.
May our Father in heaven give us our daily bread.

Sunday, 29. Br. David preached. In the afternoon
service Br. Edwards baptized into Jesus' death with the
name of Henry, the little son of Ignatius and Christiana,
born on the 24th Inst. The Lord's supper was announced
to communicants for next Saturday. Again came Frenchmen here in sleighs.

Wednesday, March 3. Again snow has fallen a foot
deep upon the old, so that now it lies four feet deep, and
without snow-shoes we could go nowhere, except upon
the ice to Detroit. There is great want of food among
our brethren, who can by no means get any thing.

Thursday, 4, and Friday, 5. Brs. Zeisberger and Jungmann and their wives spoke with the brethren about the
Lord's supper, whom we found in all their need content
and walking with the Saviour. We had,

Saturday, 6, the Lord's supper, accompanied with his
near presence. A sister, Sabina, enjoyed it with us for the
first time.

Sunday, 7. Br. David read the communion liturgy,
Heckewelder preached, Sensemann conducted the children's service, and Edwards the congregation meeting.
The assistant brethren were directed to speak with Andrew,
which was done.

Monday, 8. Schebosh, with his daughter and her husband, went with the sick Joseph to Detroit to the doctor,
as also for provisions for their family. Likewise many
Indian brethren went to the settlement for food. William,
who also went there, broke into the lake with his horse
where it is deep enough for a ship to sail; he sprang at
once from his horse and held him two hours, until the
people living in the neighborhood came to his aid and
helped get his horse out.

Wednesday, 10. We went to our sugar-huts to make
preparations for boiling sugar, but the snow was still
more than knee-deep, though it is a month later than it
was last year when we began.

Friday, 12. Many came home with corn from the settlement and from Detroit. It is very dear, 20–32 shillings a bushel, and not to be had, for everywhere there is want after so severe a winter. The Chippewa chief, who was here over night, said that a day's journey from here to the north the snow was up to a man's arms, and further northward it lay deeper than a man's height, so that many Chippewas had perished from hunger, for they could neither hunt nor support themselves in other ways; many had for a time lived upon birds and woodpeckers they had shot, and maintained themselves until they could get home. Now for several days we have had rain and a thaw, with thunder, so that we have hope of its being milder and easier to get along with.

Sunday, 14. Br. David preached, and then we got together some brethren, and held an inquiry and investigation in regard to some gossip and talk about Abraham's marriage; this is usually the way with the Indians, for a wedding can not occur without there being much gabbing about it.

Monday, 15. A Frenchman came here in a sledge, from whom our Indians got some provisions. He wanted to go farther to the Chippewas, but we advised him to turn about, the ice being untrustworthy, which to-day he did.

Wednesday, 17. For two days it has again been very cold; many cattle from the settlement that go about the bush here, also many wild animals, perish. Deer are found in the bush lying dead, for the snow is so deep, and moreover hard, that they can not get along. For us, too, it is hard to bring our cattle through, since we had made no preparation for such a winter, last year there being little snow, none of consequence.

Thursday, 18. The brethren are all at their sugar-huts, but the weather is still too cold to do any thing.

Sunday, 21. Br. David preached, and Jungmann held the congregation meeting from the Scripture-verse.

Monday, 22. The brethren went out again to their respective places in the bush. They were told to come home on the 25th. We went out to get rushes for our cattle, wherewith we seek to take them through.

Wednesday, 24. To our joy we had a thaw, with rain, which, however, lasted no longer than to-day, and our joy was again checked. Different Indian brethren came back from the settlement with some provisions; but every thing is very dear and hard to get, corn not at all.

Thursday, 25. Most of the brethren came home. We assembled, called to mind the incarnation of our Saviour in the body of the Virgin Mary, and thanked him with melted hearts that he had so condescended on our account to embody himself in our poor flesh and blood. Martha, William's wife, became the mother of a son last night in her sugar-hut.

Saturday, 27. To-day and yesterday fine, mild weather, and if there were no deep snow we could call it spring weather, but this makes it so cold and keeps it from melting.

Sunday, 28. Heckewelder preached. Now for a week Br. David labors with the rheumatism, and can not go out.

Sunday, April 4. During the whole week both we and all the Indian brethren have been busy making sugar, for the weather was fine, and the deep snow becomes slowly less, but since it is so deep, little effect is produced upon it in the bush. Most of the brethren were present at the services to-day. Br. David preached about the Saviour's entrance into Jerusalem. In the service which followed Br. Heckewelder baptized, with the name Anton, William's son, born March 25. To the communicants the Lord's supper was announced for Maundy Thursday, and there was read to them what St. Paul says (Cor. ii.) to the church.

A man sent to us from the neighborhood, and asked that one of us would come and marry him, but this we utterly declined, sending word to him that we did not concern ourselves with the marriages of others. After the services the brethren went back to their sugar-huts. This morning many came here over the ice, but with danger to their lives, for the river is again quite open, so that they can sail to and fro in canoes.

Thursday, 8. In the evening there was a reading of the history, for which all the brethren had come together from the bush. The communion brethren, after they had been addressed, had the washing of feet, and thereafter the Lord's supper, to which Luke and Adolphus were re-admitted.

Friday, 9. We read the story of the passion, in four parts, with moved and melted hearts, and this was listened to with great attention and eagerness by the brethren. At the words, Jesus bowed his head and gave up the ghost, we all fell upon our knees, and sang: Lamb of God, thy precious blood, healing wounds and bitter death. The brethren, after the history was ended, were dismissed, for they are compelled to earn something to eat. Mamacke's Shalachzink asked permission to live here. She has already several times lived with us, and her child was baptized by us and died.

Sunday, 11. We read the Easter litany, partly in our chapel and partly in the grave-yard, and at the proper place thought of those brethren who, during the year, have gone home, Anna and Agnes, together with their children, and prayed for eternal communion with them. Afterward we read the account of the resurrection. Br. Heckewelder preached from the text: He showed unto them his hands and his side. After consideration of the Scripture-verse and text in the congregation meeting, which Br. Jungmann held, we dismissed the brethren to their work again.

Tuesday, 13. Different brethren came from the settlements, where they had been for provisions, exchanging for them the sugar they had made, but they could get little, for everywhere it is a hungry time. They got as many pounds of flour as they brought pounds of sugar.

Thursday, 15. Now that the corn was gone, our brethren sought to live on wild potatoes, going to the lakes, where there are many of them, and bringing back as many as they could carry. The lake, however, is yet closed, and there is no getting to Detroit by water. Schebosh went down on his way to Detroit, but had to come back again on account of the ice.

Monday, 19. Schebosh went by water to the Fort for supplies.

Thursday, 22. Zipporah died, she was,

Friday, 23, buried. She was baptized by Br. Jungmann, April 12, 1772, in Languntoutenünk, and already
in Goschgoschünk had become acquainted with the brethren, where she visited the meetings, and after the brethren
left the place and moved to Languntoutenünk, she followed them with her husband and children. Afterwards
she went also to the Muskingum, to Schönbrunn, where,
on the 11th of November, 1775, she came to the supper
of our Lord. Her husband, Jephtha, died there in 1776.
She was from the time of her baptism blessed and content,
so that we could rejoice in her. A dream, however, which
she had about her son, who had been baptized and died,
caused her much doubt, so that she was not sound in the
faith, and always had a certain doubt left in her mind
whether the brethern had preached the true learning and
the way to blessedness. This could be seen also in her
conduct, especially during the disturbances of the war, so
that we could have no satisfaction in her. Yet the Saviour did not leave her, but went after her and brought her
near to us. All this in her very wearisome illness gave her
much to do, and she had no peace until she was again absolved, whereupon she was quite comforted, and with much
longing awaited her call. This came on the day mentioned, with the blessing of the church.

This same day, in the morning service the child of the
Mohican, Renatus, was baptized Jacob, and the child of
Jacobina, Agnes.

· Saturday, 24. Brs. David, Jungmann, Heckewelder, and
Sensemann went to Detroit, Br. Edwards remaining at
home with the sisters. Most of the Indian brethren went
to the lake to dig wild potatoes, for they have nothing to
eat, and the men make canoes to sell for food. The first
party,

Sunday, 25, arrived there, and they went at just the
right time to have no trouble from ice, for had they gone
a day sooner they would have had to lie over on account
of ice.

Br. David's business there was chiefly to speak with the
commandant, and to set forth our need and our Indians'

need, and to beg him to help us with supplies. This time
he was well disposed to this, although supplies were few
in the king's store, and of flour there was none at all, for
last autumn three or four ships were wrecked on the lake.
Both we and our Indians got some beans and pork, and we
were glad enough, especially that our Indians were helped
in their want, for now seed-time is near, when they most
need help. Br. David baptized in the city the children of
two merchants, namely, Sara, daughter of Nathan Williams, and Isaac, the son of Loveless, and Br. Heckewelder
baptized outside the town in the settlement likewise two
children, Maria, Hessen's daughter, and Jacob, Graonrad's
son.

Wednesday, 28. Br. David baptized on the island a
child of Tafelmeger's with the name Eva Maria.

Thursday, 29. We again went away from Detroit. On
the way in the settlement Br. David baptized the child of
a man named Frank, with the name John, and thus we
came Friday, April 30, back here to our friends. On the
lake we met many of our Indian brethren digging wild
potatoes, on which they lived; therefore there were few at
home.   •

Sunday, May 2. Br. David preached. The Indian
brethren were for the most part come home, and they got
ready to go to Detroit for provisions.

Monday, 3. The Indian brethren went to Detroit. We
began to work on our plantations and to make preparations to plant. Br. Sensemann and his wife had many
things stolen from them last night, provisions and clothes.
We could not be quite sure who the thief was, unless we
conjectured him to be Daniel, Christian's friend, who went
away from here two days ago.

Tuesday, 4. We had the first thunder-storm of this
spring. The Chippewa chief was here over night; he said
to our Indians, since this summer few deer were to be had,
that he would tell them how and where they could catch
fish enough, namely, if they would block up the creek a
few miles above us, where it is narrow, that the fish, which
are very large, could not get back into the lake, and in

this way, all summer long, they could have fish enough if
they wanted. He said further that they would do no harm
to our cattle, we should have no fear about them. We
answered him that we also had confidence in them, for we
wished to have firm friendship with them, but we were
very sorry we were so poor as to be unable to give them
any thing to eat when they came here, but should we be
in better circumstances, we would also do them good. He
answered that he knew this very well, and that he was
aware that when we lived on the Muskingum we had done
much good to the Indians who came there.

Thursday, 6. The Indian brethren returned from the
Fort with eleven barrels of pork and beans, which came
just right for planting time, for if they had not got help
they could not have worked from hunger, nor have
planted. Thus our dear heavenly Father helps us from
one time to another, in the winter by the many deer they
got, then by the sugar they made, and afterwards by the
wild potatoes, by which they kept themselves alive.

Saturday, 8. Since the brethren were all at home yesterday, and divided their provisions, they all set about
planting and clearing the land. They had to buy all their
seed-corn in the settlement, for their own of last year had
not ripened. They were urged to be industrious and observe the time well, in order that they might once again
have bread, as on the Muskingum. They knew how hard
it was to hunger, as they had for three years.

Sunday, 9. Heckewelder preached; Sensemann conducted the children's service; David held the congregation
meeting.

Wednesday, 12. Our Indians made fish-dams in different places; they stopped up the creek so that the fish
could not go down, in which way they could have fish all
summer if they wanted them. They brought in at all
times many of these of uncommon size and of all edible
sorts, and this is another great help for them.

Friday, 14. We were done with planting, but since our
seed-corn was not good and did not come up, we had to

plant a second time, but our Indians, who are also busy at this, have not yet done planting.

Sunday, 16. David preached from the text: Whatsoever ye shall ask of the Father, etc., that the Saviour has revealed and made known to us the Father, that he so loved us that he gave his beloved Son, his only joy, to death for us. Then the holy communion was announced to the communicants for next Saturday. Sensemann held the congregation meeting from the Scripture-verse.

Wednesday, 19. Two rangers came here from Detroit to get McKee and Elliott's cattle, for which they asked the help and aid of the Indians.

Thursday, 20. On Ascension Day of our dear Lord we prayed to him, looked to him, had ourselves blessed by him, and inasmuch as he is no longer visible in the world, we begged for his unseen nearness for all days and hours according to his promise: I am with you alway. Br. David preached.

Saturday, 21. After the brethren had been addressed we enjoyed his body and blood in the holy communion in the most blessed way. One brother was there present for the first time. To-day we had the great joy of getting by way of Detroit letters from Brs. Simon Peter, Matthew, and Grube,[1] from which we learn that our dear Br. John (de Watteville), who was at sea in need and in danger, had not yet arrived; we thought much about him and his company and prayed to the Saviour to bring them safe to land. We likewise learned that they, as well as we here, had had a very severe winter. For a week we have had severe rains, and consequently most of our fields are under water, so that in this hungry planting-time we have a bad outlook that any thing will grow, since what is planted rots in the ground and does not come up.

[1] Simon Peter of Friedberg, Forsyth Co., North Carolina, 1784–1791. A Moravian clergyman.

Perhaps Bishop Matthew Hehl, an eloquent preacher, at this time in Litiz, Pa., where he died 1787, having retired from his office in 1784.

Reverend Adam Grube, at this time in his seventieth year, probably at Litiz, where he had officiated at Zeisberger's marriage, 1781.

Wednesday, 26. Since the supplies our Indians got are almost exhausted [and yet these have helped them to be able to plant without delay], many of them went to the lake to dig wild potatoes, and the men also to make canoes, from the sale of which they will have provisions.

Thursday, 27. Brs. Sensemann and Schebosh came back from Detroit, bringing news that Col. de Peyster, commandant there, is upon the point of leaving the place. We wish him every good thing, for he has done well by us, and our Indians would not have been alive here if he had not interested himself in us and helped us. Who will come in his place and how further it stands in regard to government we can hear nothing certain until we see, for the people are kept in uncertainty. From the Illinois, where usually the winter is mild, we learn that from the severe winter very many cattle, and also the wild buffaloes, have died in the bush from want of food and from the deep snow; thus the hard winter extended throughout the land.

Saturday, 29. We were quite done with planting, and hoped this year to have a better harvest than last year, for at this season, then we had planted nothing. But it is a long time before we can get any thing for food from our plantations, and till then we and our Indians have to support ourselves, and we get along with difficulty.

Sunday, 30. The sermon treated of the office and work of the Holy Ghost, not only generally, but also especially with believers. With our baptized brethren we prayed to God the Holy Ghost upon our knees, thanked him for his unwearied, true care, patience, and long-suffering for us, begged him to forgive us all our sins, when we had not regarded nor listened to his voice, and had grieved him, vowed to him obedience and faithfulness, whereto he sent us his blessing and peace. Br. Jungmann held the congregation meeting. In all our services he let himself be sensibly felt among us.

Monday, 31. We heard that the commandant, Col. de Peyster sailed away yesterday from Detroit for Niagara, but who comes in his place we know not.

Thursday, June 3. Gottlob (Sensemann) went to Detroit. Since we had heard of an opportunity to send to Pittsburg, Br. David wrote to Litiz a letter, which he took with him.

Friday, 4. He came back from there with the news that they were repairing the Fort there, that the Indians in Michilimackinac were said to have killed eight soldiers and traders, that they were said to be very proud and ill-disposed towards the English for compelling them to go to war with the Americans.

Saturday, 5. Several of our Indians returned from Detroit, where they had taken and sold canoes to get again some few necessities of life. They were, however, very much deceived in their expectations, and had to pay enormously dear for every thing. We finished hoeing corn to-day.

Sunday, 6. Heckewelder preached from the Gospel about Nicodemus, and David held the congregation meeting from the text of the day.

Monday, 7. Br. Jungmann held the early service.

Thursday, 10. Joshua and Adam, who have come back from Detroit, met there Potawatomy Indians; one of them, an interpreter, who knew many Indian tongues, said to our Indians that we should come to them and live on their land, that the Chippewas did not like to have us on their land on account of the hunting and fishing—they did not like to see others hunting and fishing on their territory. They live a good day's journey westward from Detroit, and said there was much game there, more than where we lived. In many places there has been a frost, but here little was to be seen of it.

Saturday, 12. Abraham, Zachary, and others came back from canoe-making.

Sunday, 13. Br. David preached, Sensemann held the children's service, and Edwards the congregation meeting.

Monday, 14. Abraham, with others, took the canoes they have made to Detroit, to get food in return for them. Others went to the settlement to earn something by their

13

labor among the white people and French. The sisters make baskets and brooms to take there, and thus our brethren have to strive to get along. There is no hunting this year and no meat to be had, for deer are few.

Wednesday, 16. Gottlob held early service. The sisters went for wild cherries, of which there are many this year, on which in part they live.

Saturday, 19. There was a bad storm, which threw down many trees, and did much damage to our fields. There are usually such storms every spring, but this year it was greater than last. The insects, mosquitoes, ponkjis,[1] and horse-flies are very many more and more troublesome than they were last year, so that when the wind is still it is about impossible for man and beast to live.

Sunday, 20. Edwards preached from the Gospel about the great feast, and David held the congregation meeting from the Scripture-verse.

Monday, 21. Abraham and many others went to the settlement, in part to get provisions and in part to earn something by their labor in the fields, for here they have nothing to eat; nothing can be had this year by hunting, for there are hardly any deer and game; these perished last winter. Those who remained at home were very busy about their corn in the fields.

Thursday, 24. There came some white people here, one a French trader, who, however, could dispose of nothing here. After quite dry weather, lasting some time, we got a fine warm rain; here usually after rain very cool weather follows.

Saturday, 26. Some of our Indians came back from the settlement, where for some days they have worked in the fields and earned some provisions. They could not describe how badly the inhabitants live and what dreadful famine is among the people, so that they live only by fishing and from weeds, while they work. This week we hilled our corn, and for the most part were done with it.

---

[1] In Zeisberger's Delaware Spelling-Book, pongus means sand-fly, and in Brinton's "The Lenâpé," etc., p. 246, pungusak is rendered gnats.

The Chippewas, Tawas, Potawatomies, and four other nations also, as we hear, wish to go to the Americans, hold a council with them, and make their excuses, saying that they have been compelled to take up the hatchet against them, but even then had not done it except that some runners-about had gone into the war; since their fathers had made peace with them and had given them all the land belonging to the nations, they wished now to seek friendship with the Americans.

Sunday, 27. Br. Jungmann preached from the Gospel about the lost sheep, that the Saviour came to bless sinners. David held the communion quarter-hour, and announced to the brethren the Lord's supper for next Saturday.

Monday, 28. Sensemann held early service.

Tuesday, 29. John held the early service.

Thursday, July 1, and Tuesday, 2. Brs. Zeisberger and Jungmann and their wives spoke with the brethren, whom we found content, in spite of all their outward need and want. Many came from the settlement, where they have been working for food with the French, who have themselves very little.

Saturday, 3. Two Frenchmen came from the settlement visiting, and with them a German, to see our town and neighborhood; they went back on the 4th. They could not wonder enough at the fair prospect of our fields for a good harvest, for in the settlement there is a very bad outlook. They said that most people there had no bread, and lived from the weeds they cooked and eat. We heard from them that Detroit will be garrisoned by French from France. The communion brethren had the holy communion of the body and blood of our Lord. A sister, A. Charity, partook of it for the first time since she is here, after receiving absolution.

Sunday, 4. After the communion liturgy there was a sermon by Heckewelder. David conducted the children's service, and Jungmann the congregation meeting.

Monday, 5. All the Indian brethren went away, some to the settlement, the others for whortleberries, a day's journey from here, for at home they have nothing to eat, and each one must look about to find something. Luke, who remained at home, expressed himself about the famine in this way: "We have brought this need upon ourselves, we are the cause of it; on the Muskingum we had enough to live on, and no want in any way, and yet we were not content, but we sought and thought to find things yet better, but as soon as we came away from our towns on the Muskingum, hunger began among us, and since then has never ceased. When I look at our teachers, they have nothing better than we; I see how thin they are, and that they go about here in such clothes as we were not wont to see them in. We are to blame for this also; they suffer on our account. If I reflect farther I see what harm and that nothing good comes from our suffering hunger. In the first place comes thieving, to which hunger drives them; in the second place, many suffer harm in their hearts if hunger forces them to the settlement or to the Fort, for they fall into all sorts of bad ways and bring back home a defiled heart; thirdly, hunger is the cause of our town being deserted; this was not our way formerly, but we were glad to be together as much as possible, and we refreshed ourselves together in the meetings from God's word and the sweet Gospel. We were formerly accustomed to be summoned to the meetings by the church bell, instead of which, however, now the servant must either call the brethren together or ring a cow-bell. If one looks at our brethren, famine can be read in their faces, they look so thin and lean as hardly to be able to work or to do any thing.

"When, however, I think that we have suffered hunger so long, and yet that none of us is dead from hunger, it seems wonderful to me, for I see that, in spite of all, the Saviour has always helped us to find something to relieve our pressing needs. Last summer the commandant gave us provisions until autumn, and last winter, when we had to look out for ourselves, God sent a deep snow, which lasted the whole winter, so that we struck the deer dead with the hatchet and lived upon them. As time went on

and we could no longer find support in the bush, since
the snow was gone, we got along very well with wild potatoes and by selling the canoes we made, and now that
we can no longer earn any thing in this way, the dear Saviour has already cared for us beforehand by letting the
whortleberries grow in such quantities that we shall have
enough to eat until our corn is ripe. Thus we have, although not too abundantly, yet always something to eat,
so that we remain alive. I believe, too, that this want will
not always last, but that our dear Saviour will again give
us enough to eat; whoever then is steadfast and lets not
himself be led away from the church in the hope of better-
ing his condition, he will in the end be glad, can thank and
praise the Saviour."

Sunday, 11. The white brethren read something from
the Idea Fidei [1] together, for none of the brethren were at
home.

Thursday, 15. Samuel came back from the settlement.
His wife was brought to bed there with a daughter, but
this child died after living one day, and was buried there
on the Frenchman's land. He had been working there to
earn his food.

Sunday, 18. In the forenoon we again read together,
and in the afternoon, since the brethren came here, there
was a meeting and discourse from the Scripture-verse.

Br. Schebosh, who came from Detroit, brought news
that twenty boats from Albany were on their way here
and had already got to Oswego, so that we hope to get
letters from the church by the occasion; further that there
is great scarcity in Detroit, and nothing to be had for cash.
With his own eyes he saw a Spanish dollar offered a
baker for a pound of bread and refused. A hundred
weight of flour costs £7, 13s., and is not to be had. We
were so fortunate as to have a Detroit merchant in the
spring lend us money to buy flour with, when we could
still get it cheap, namely, £6. (£3, perhaps.)

Monday, 19. Our Indians again separated, some going

---

[1] "Idea Fidei Fratrum, or Short Exposition of Christian Doctrine."

to the settlement, others for whortleberries, and thus our town was again empty, and we white brethren were left almost alone at home.

Saturday, 24. Some were again here, and we had,

Sunday, 25, services. Day before yesterday and to-day we had rains again, after quite dry weather, so that all our crops look promising and give us a good prospect for a fine harvest.

Monday, 26. More than a week ago Abraham's daughter came here, who left her husband several years since, went away from the church and afterward, on the Muskingum, was sometimes with us and sometimes away; she now gives out that she would like to live in the church. Since now we had different opinions about this, some having compassion with her and maintaining that mercy should be shown her, others opposing her coming into the church, since she can cause harm, and we should only take trouble upon ourselves if we again admitted her, we took the Saviour's advice as to what should be done, and he was not in favor of her coming into the church at present. She was therefore advised to go elsewhere, and this she did.

Tuesday, 27. Abraham, Schebosh with his whole family, and others, went to the settlement to support themselves by reaping in the harvest and gathering ears; thus our town was left except by Luke and his mother who remained at home. This makes the wolves, which have already destroyed many cattle, as bold as if they knew that no Indians are at home, so that at night they come into town for our cattle, on which account we have to shut them up.

Saturday, 31. Some Monsey Indians arrived, who had come from Niagara to Detroit, and did not themselves know where to go. They went through here on their way to the whortleberries for they had nothing to eat.

Sunday, Aug. 1. As no Indian brethren were at home we had service for ourselves, and read together out of Instructions in Spiritual Doctrine, Idea Fidei.

Monday, 2. Gabriel came here visiting from the Shaw-

anese towns where most of our Indians live together. He
said that many wanted to be here and talked at times
about it, but could not make up their minds; they always
hoped that perhaps brothers would come to them. Some
Delaware chiefs, Twightwees and others, had counselled
about this where the believing Indians with their teachers should live [for they are not pleased that we live here],
had also made propositions, but as yet had come to no
determination.

We stay here and await until a door be opened, for till
now all is closed. We have been driven away by them,
thus they must call us back again. He related that last
autumn all the corn in that country was frozen in the milk,
that, on this account, everywhere among the Indians there
is great hunger, and that the snow there last winter was
as deep as here.

Friday, 6. Edwards and Sensemann went to Detroit,
returning,

Sunday, 8. Br. David preached, and likewise held the
communion quarter-hour, and announced to the brethren
the Lord's supper for the 13th of this month. Jungmann
held the congregation meeting. The brethren all got
back home yesterday from the settlement, where they
have been at work harvesting, and had earned something
to eat.

Friday, 13. Early this morning Sister Heckewelder
gave birth to a daughter, which, in the afternoon, was
baptized into the death of Jesus, with the name Anna
Salome. After addressing the communion brethren the
day before, we enjoyed his body and blood in the holy
sacrament. To them was related first the history of this
day, what the Saviour had done in his church fifty-seven
years before,[1] had grounded it upon his flesh and blood,
which grace had since come upon the heathen and upon
us, so that we now also, by this grace, belonged to his
church, which the gates of hell could not overcome.

Sunday, 15. Br. Edwards preached. In the evening

---

[1] Particular visitation of grace in the congregation of Herrnhut, at
the holy communion in the church at Berthelsdorf, 1727.

David held the congregation meeting from the Scripture-verse.

Monday, 16. Our Indians again separated, some going for whortleberries, others to the settlement to earn something by their work in the harvest, and thus they will get along until their corn is ripe.

Friday, 20. By Schebosh back from the Fort, we heard that ten Delaware Indians had been killed over the Ohio in Kentucky, probably because they had done damage or wished to do it; that therefore all traders had taken flight from the Shawanese towns to Detroit, and had to leave every thing behind to save their lives, for the Indians wanted to kill all the traders. Thus there is yet no peace among the Indians.

Sunday, 22. David preached from the Gospel: Jesus beheld the city, and wept over it. On account of hard thunder and rainy weather there was no congregation meeting.

Thursday, 26. Matthew, Cornelius' son, came with a couple of Indians, one Gottlieb, on a visit from Gigeyunk (now Ft. Wayne). We heard from them thus much about our Indians, that the greater part of them lived by themselves in a place which Mark had chosen for them; that an Indian, Masktschilitis by name, from those of Goschachgünk, was with them, who was like a chief, whom they gave heed to, who had promised to make it right with the Twightwees about their dwelling there, and to get permission for them to have a brother with them. If this was arranged, he wished to call the brothers there as their teachers, that is, at least two hundred, if not three hundred, miles westward from here.

Friday, 27. To Abraham, who came back from the whortleberry place, Chippewas came where he was encamped, who said that their chiefs, the commandant, and Mr. Bawbee had agreed in Detroit, and arranged that the believing Indians, with their teachers, should live here. Mr. Bawbee, to whom the land belongs, said to them we should live on his land as long as we wished, and if peace should come again, and we wished to move elsewhere, we could do as we pleased. These Indians said they were not so ignorant about us, that they knew that their grandfather [thus they called the Delawares], the believing Indians, were good people who had done much good to the Indians.

Sunday, 29. Heckewelder preached from the Gospel about the Pharisees and tax-gatherers. Sensemann conducted the children's service. Chippewas came in, asking for something to eat on their way; this we gladly gave them, for now we have our own bread, but until now we have been in no condition to do this.

Friday, Sept. 8. We recalled to-day our captivity of two years ago, with thankful hearts to our dear Lord who has rescued us from so much danger and need, and has sent us deliverance, so that now we live again in peace and quiet, and can edify ourselves. We remembered also our flock, scattered in the Indian land, and wished the Saviour might again assemble and bring here his elect, of which we are still always of good hope.

Saturday, 4. A party of Frenchmen came here from Detroit, by way of the river, for a visit, who have never been here. They examined very carefully our town, and everything, and took notice of all. They said they had not thought of seeing here such a town and settlement; we had done so much work in so short a time, and such good work, such work as the French never do. They soon inquired whether there would be preaching to-morrow, which they,

Sunday, 5, attended, and then turned homewards. Br. David preached, and Jungmann held the congregation meeting.

Tuesday, 7. The married brethren celebrated their festival with grace and blessing. At morning prayer Br. Jungmann prayed for us the close nearness and presence of our dear Lord and his blessing out of his bloody fulness for this day. Thereupon was the discourse from the Scripture-verse: I will guide thee with mine eye. In the afternoon was a love-feast for all the inhabitants. Br. Heckewelder ended the day with a short discourse and the

New Testament blessing (2 Cor., xiii, 14). We white brethren strengthened ourselves at the end by the body and blood of our Lord in his supper, and bound ourselves ever to remain by his cross, to bear God's sufferings until we see him face to face.

Saturday, 11. This week the Indian brethren have been building their houses, and every thing was therein considered how they would have place to store their corn, a good harvest of which they expect. Now also the famine is ended, and we have enough to live on, for which we cannot thank enough our dear heavenly Father.

Sunday, 12. Sensemann preached, Edwards held the children's service, and Heckewelder held the congregation meeting.

Monday, 13. A Shawano came here with his family visiting. His wife is our Amelia's sister. This night we had the first frost, and thus fourteen days later than last year. We find, moreover, only a very slight difference between here and the Muskingum, for there, even at this time, we had frosts every year.

Tuesday, 14. Jungmann held the early service from the Scripture-verse: My cup runneth over.

Wednesday, 15. Heckewelder held early service,

Thursday, 16. David, from the Scripture-verse: He shall give his angels charge over thee.

Saturday, 18. This week we began harvesting. Edwards held the early service.

Sunday, 19. Jungmann preached; afterwards was the communion quarter-hour, and this was announced for next Saturday.

Thursday, 23, and Friday, 24. There was speaking about the Lord's supper, which we,

Saturday, 25, enjoyed. William and his wife, Martha, had the grace of enjoying it with us for the first time since they have been here, whereover there was great joy among the brethren, and no less with us laborers. With Schebosh, who came yesterday from Detroit, we hoped to hear of brothers from Bethlehem, or to have letters from there, but again there were none. He heard there that the

Americans will not come, having received in exchange for this government two islands in the West Indies.

Sunday, 26. Br. David preached, after the communion liturgy had been read by Heckewelder. Jungmann held the congregation meeting.

Monday, 27. Both we and the Indian brethren have been busy harvesting our fields, kept it up the successive days of the week, and were done with it. What a difference we found between last year and this, not only in regard to our fields, but also in the weather, for we have thus far had fine, warm, dry weather. We have a very rich harvest, and every thing has ripened and thriven to the best advantage, as well as on the Muskingum, more and more. How glad and thankful we are that our Indian brethren have once more enough to eat, and that the famine is ended, through which they often became listless, and thought it would always be so here, and not otherwise.

Friday, Oct. 1. Our neighbor, Tucker, came from the mouth of the river, visiting. We were done with our corn harvest. A deer was brought to town to-day, a thing rare this year, for they became very few from severe weather last winter, so that the hunters seldom see them. Raccoon-taking is now their best hunting, of which there are many.

Sunday, 3. Edwards preached. It rained all day. Two Frenchmen came here, Mitchel's son for a visit.

Saturday, 9. Since we had news from Detroit that a certain gentleman, Major Smallmann, was going to Pittsburg by way of Sandusky, we wrote to Bethlehem. The Indian brethren were very busy building, and are almost done with it. The Chippewa chief went through here. Adam, who examined his musket, had bad luck with it, for it went off in his hand, and he was hurt a little.

Sunday, 10. Heckewelder preached, after this Br. David, with Jungmann and Sensemann, set out for Detroit over land, arriving there the 11th. First on the 12th he visited the Lord Geo. Hay,[1] spoke with him, and told him the agreement he had made with Col. de Peyster, and

---

[1] De Peyster's successor at Detroit.

asked him about our living here, and complained to him
of our situation, that it looked as if we should not be
here long, since we lived on land belonging to Mr. Bawbee;
in the two years we had been living there, we had done
much work, clearing land and building many houses; if
now we should be driven away from there, as he had yesterday heard said by Mr. Bawbee, we should be ruined
anew; moreover at present we knew not where to turn,
for we dared not go into the Indian land, having been
driven from it, elsewhere we knew not where to go. He
answered Br. David that we should be altogether easy and
undisturbed, and remain where we were; no one could or
should drive us away; we were the first settlers on the
land and had improved it; we had the nearest right to
it : no one could make pretensions to lands, given by the
Indians, but whoever first lived on them had the nearest
right to them; should the Chippewas be troubled that we
lived there, he would set them right and make them content; should it happen contrary to all his expectations,
that we could not live there, they would find a new place
for us. Br. David thanked him for his good-will, and
after speaking to him about different matters and recommending himself and our Indians to his protection, took
leave of him. He was otherwise very friendly and showed
his inclination to us, and promised to visit us sometime.
Br. David with the brethren came,

Wednesday, 13, home again.

Friday, 15. Mr. Dolson, our friend, came here from Detroit, returning on the 16th. During the week all the
Indian brethren were making canoes in order to get clothing for the winter, since nothing is to be got by hunting.

16. The brethren were urged to pay punctually their
debts in Detroit.

Sunday, 17. Br. David preached, and baptized in the
afternoon John, the son of Zachary and A. Elizabeth,
born on the 14th Inst. Br. Jungmann held the congregation meeting.

Monday, 18. The Indians all set again to making

canoes, to get them ready and bring them to Detroit before the cold weather begins.

Wednesday, 20. From Detroit we have news through Conner, who is come from there, which a man coming from Pittsburg brought with him, that the brethren in Bethlehem have petitioned Congress for 2,000 acres of land on the Muskingum, which was read a second time in Congress; we heard of this some time ago by way of Pittsburg.

Friday, 22. A Shawano came here visiting with his wife; he has already been here; both are lame and cannot longer support themselves.

Saturday, 23. Ignatius' mother, in whose heart the work of the Holy Spirit has already been seen, expressed her longing for the bath of holy baptism.

Sunday, 24. Br. Jungmann preached about the marriage garment, Christ's blood, and righteousness, which we get by grace, and without which no man can stand before God.

Monday, 25. The Indian brethren went again to their work in the bush; different sisters into the settlement to sell baskets and brooms.

Saturday, 20. The above-mentioned Shawano intends to pass the winter here with his family, on which account he wanted to make a hut near by, but after consulting with the conference brethren we did not find it well to give them permission, since the Chippewas might on this account be discontented with us if we let strange Indians, with whom they do not stand well in friendship, settle on their land.

Sunday, 31. Edwards preached. David conducted the children's service. We had a conference with the assistants. Heckewelder held the congregation meeting.

Monday, Nov. 1. The Indians brought to-day and to-morrow (sic) the canoes they have made, nine in number, into the water, and took them to the fort to sell.

Wednesday, 3. Br. Heckewelder went to Detroit on business.

Sunday, 7. Br. David preached and held the congregation meeting in Indian, for no interpreter was present, and indeed only three brethren and a few sisters were at home. In regard to climate, we have thus far as fine, warm weather as a man could expect, and lately thunder with rain.

Monday, 8. Br. Heckewelder came back from Detroit. He baptized there Hasle's child, on the 6th.

Tuesday, 9. Since it had several times come to our ears, and now Br. Heckewelder had heard much about it from the merchants about the streets in Detroit, that the Chippewas had expressed their discontent at our Indians dwelling here, saying that they did them great harm and damage in their hunting, and this went so far that they said we would not go away until they had killed a couple of us, which would be the occasion for their getting us out of their land. Since now Br. Heckewelder who called upon the Governor, and, among other things, had told him at a proper time that we thought of building a regular meeting-house this autumn, had this answer from him, that we should let this alone, and especially build nothing further, since no conclusion was yet reached either about the land or the government. The Governor sent him this message by a colonel. This gave us occasion for considering together what we should do and whether we should undertake any thing in this matter on our side, so that, by waiting longer, we might not come to straits nor waste our time. Thus we begged the Saviour to advise us, and we asked him. He gave us for answer that he wished to be asked something about our conduct and outcome with our Indians. After further consideration we made two lots. The first the Saviour approved, that we should consider and resolve to go back over the lake with our Indians. The second the Saviour did not approve. We added yet a blank thereto, and drew the first. We considered further, in case we went back over the lake, where we should turn, and we asked him about this too. He pointed out to us the country on the Walhonding to settle in. We thanked him from our hearts for his gracious advice and direction; they were also after our own hearts, although any thing like this had not before occurred to us, but we were altogether here. We see now, however, that that is best for us, for if we move on this side the lake to another place, the Chippewas would not be satisfied, and our Indians would still be in their way, and since they wont have us here, it is best that we go elsewhere. Inasmuch as we have the winter before us, we have time to arrange matters for departing in the spring, as soon as the weather and the ice in the lake permit.

Friday, 12. We spoke with the brethren. We sent letters to Bethlehem by Mr. Wilson, who is going back to Pittsburg.

Saturday, 13. We did homage to our Elder, and deemed ourselves happy in being under his rule, and finding ourselves so blessed. We prayed to him and thanked him for his being among us, for his care and trouble with us, asked him forgiveness for all our faults and shortcomings, and vowed to him fidelity and obedience. At the end of the day the communicants enjoyed his body and blood in the holy communion.

Sunday, 14. After the communion liturgy Br. Heckewelder preached, and in the afternoon, towards evening, in the congregation meeting, Ignatius' mother, a widow, was baptized into Jesus' death with the name Elizabeth; this was the first baptism of an adult in this place, and was blessed business over which all the brethren were glad, thankful, and much enlivened.

Monday, 15. Brs. Sensemann and Schebosh went off to Detroit. Most of the Indian brethren went hunting to try to get only one or a couple of deer to make shoes with, for the hunting is not at all good, and there is nothing to gain by it.

Saturday, 20. During the whole week we have had windy weather and rain, as is usual here in the autumn and winter, for a fine day is rare.

Sunday, 21. Br. David preached, and Jungmann held the congregation meeting.

Monday, 22. Sensemann and Schebosh came back from Detroit by land. Upon the lake they had very stormy weather, and had to lie still for ten days. Their canoe was split by the waves, so that they had to come home afoot. By a letter which Br. Sensemann received in Detroit from Br. Brucker,[1] from Hope, in New Jersey, we learned that things for us from Bethlehem must be on the way here this side of Albany, which could not get through this summer, because the passage to the States was not then open; it will be a wonder if these things and letters be not lost.

24, or thereabout we wrote to Bethlehem.

Saturday, 27. By Br. Edwards, who, with Abraham and others besides, went to Detroit, Br. David wrote to the honorable Governor, telling him that since we and our Indians heard time and again that the Chippewas were discontented at our living here, and indeed had threatened to kill some of our Indians, we intended to leave their land as soon as possible; he would be so good as to make known to them that next spring we intended to move back again over the lake. Our hunters all came home, their whole hunt being two deer, a bear, and several raccoons; most of them, however, had no sight of a deer all the days they were gone.

Sunday, 28. Br. Heckewelder preached and told the brethren we were now entering Advent time, when we especially brought to our minds that the Saviour of all men was born into the world.

Tuesday, 30. We ended the month with praise and thanks to the Lord that he had so graciously helped us through the summer and autumn during the great famine, and that he had now so richly blessed us in this, that although our Indians could gain little by hunting, they had not only enough to live on, but also something to sell, so as to provide themselves with clothing for the winter.

Friday, Dec. 3. Br. Edwards returned with the Indians from Huron Point on the lake, where they met so hard a storm that their canoes were filled, and for the moment

---

[1] Probably an agent of the Moravian mission at Hope; perhaps son of the Rev. John Brucker, a missionary in New Jersey, who died 1765.

sunk, and much of their lading was lost. They had to remain quiet twenty-four hours, during the cold in one place where they hastily landed till the storm should be over, where no wood was to be had, for they were surrounded with water.

Saturday, 4. The Indians drove cattle to Detroit for the merchants.

Sunday, 5. Br. David preached. Edwards went to Detroit. In the afternoon the married sister, Anna Sophia, daughter of Samuel Nanticoke, sick with consumption from which she suffered two months, suddenly died from bursting a blood-vessel. Her remains were buried on the 8th. She was baptized in Lichtenau by David, Jan. 1, '78, already a well-grown girl; from that time she was always a quiet, orderly maiden, who loved the Saviour and had a tender heart, and often bewailed with tears her wickedness and sinfulness, and then she was directed to the Saviour. January 25th, of this year, she was married to the single man, Andrew, but for two months it could be seen that she had consumption, which made rapid progress, so that we could perceive she was nearing her end. In her sickness, when she could no longer get up, she was quite resigned and gave herself to the will of the Saviour, and showed her willingness to go to him. Yesterday, as also on the 5th, she burst a blood-vessel and departed very quietly and suddenly with the blessing of the church.

Tuesday, 7. Br. Edwards came back from Detroit, where he had gone by land. Br. David had written by him to the Governor, telling him that for many reasons we intended in the spring to leave this place and to move back again over the lake; that he would be so good as to tell this to the Chippewa chiefs, that they might have no uneasiness on our account. He had nothing against this, but said that before that time we should hear more from him.

Sunday, 12. Br. Jungmann preached; in the afternoon all our brethren were informed that in the spring we intended to move back again over the lake, wherefor they

14

should prepare through the winter, that we might go away
as soon as the lake was open, which most found to their
liking, and there was real joy.

Tuesday, 14. After the Indian brethren had yesterday
taken advice together, and divided themselves for the
work, they went to-day in five parties to make canoes for
the journey, of which they aim to make fifteen, and to
have them all done before they take up any other work.
They came,

Saturday, 18, back home, and had already several done.

Sunday, 19. Br. Heckewelder preached about the joy
of believers in the Lord and Saviour, who for our sake put
on our poor flesh and blood. To the communicants in their
service the Lord's supper was announced for Christmas.
Br. David held the congregation meeting, and made to
the children an address of exhortation.

Monday, 20. The brethren went again to their canoe
work, and came,

Wednesday, 22, home again for the address given the
next day, and the Saviour gave grace that many a one
among the brethren was aroused and brought into the
right path.

Friday, 24. We began Christmas with a love-feast, rejoiced in God, our Saviour, who is also the heathen's Saviour, and thanked him for his incarnation, birth, passion,
and death, and adored him in his manger. At the end
candles were given the children, wherewith they joyfully
went home. [We thanked him that he had made this
known and revealed it for our salvation, for else we were
blind as are other heathen.]

Saturday, 25. Br. David preached. In the afternoon,
during service, Br. Sensemann baptized the little daughter
of Br. Thomas and his wife Sabina, born on the 23d Inst.,
with the name Judith, into the death of Jesus. In the
evening the communion brethren enjoyed his body and
blood in the holy sacrament in a blessed way.

Sunday, 26. Br. David preached from the Epistle: For
the grace of God that bringeth salvation hath appeared
to all men, and in the afternoon exhorted the children to

praise and gratitude for the little Jesus in his manger,
that he had clad himself with our poor flesh and blood,
and was born man; this they did, and sang to him praise
and thanks in his little manger. Br. Heckewelder held
the congregation meeting.

Monday, 27. To-day and the following days the brethren kept up their work, coming home at night, and encouraging one another, when they came together, to praise
and thank the Lord. Jungmann, who wished to go to
Detroit by land, had to turn back again on account of
ice, marsh, and water, for there was no getting through
until it was frozen harder.

Tuesday, 31. Our second horse died, so that thus, in a
few days, one after the other, our two best horses are gone.
The reason of this is the rush-grass, of which there is
much here, on which cattle live in winter and grow fat,
but it is no uncommon thing that they die from it, if they
cannot be kept away from it. Towards midnight we assembled for the end of the year, and brought him our filial
thanks for all the kindnesses shown us this year, and for
all the good he had done us body and soul. It stands
especially fresh in our remembrance that our dear heavenly
Father has so graciously and wonderfully brought us
through the famine which last summer fell upon us and all
this land; that our Indian brethren, in the spring, supported themselves, partly by labor, partly by wild potatoes
for a while, and when time went on, and they could earn
nothing more, our heavenly Father sent them whortleberries, which grew in such abundance, a day's journey
from here, that they had their fill of them, and could live
on them till their corn was ripe; this was, indeed, no nour-
ishing food, but yet they could live on them. Now it is
usual for sickness to follow famine, as we have often observed among the Indians, and so we consider this the
greatest kindness, that the Saviour has lent us health, and
of sickness we have seen no sign. As regards us white
brethren, we had to feel it too, but the Saviour aroused a
merchant in Detroit, who in the spring lent us money so
that we could buy much floor against the want in the

summer, so that we just got along until our corn was ripe; if we had not got the loan then, we should have been without resource, for soon after nothing was to be had for cash. The dear heavenly Father afterwards, in autumn, gave us a blessed harvest, so that we and our Indians have again enough to eat, which we thankfully acknowledge and praise him for with joyful hearts and mouths. That our hearts could daily feed and be refreshed on God's word, we recognize as a great kindness and mercy from him, for still so many, belonging to us, are robbed of this, and must perish. We therefore beseech our dear Lord to give us yet more in the future, and lend to those who are absent the grace to come again to the flock, and that to them again his divine word may shine a clear light. We thanked him also for the quiet and peace which for more than two years we have enjoyed; with all our hearts we were altogether here, it had also never occurred to us that we should again so soon take into our hands the pilgrim-staff, but since the Saviour had given us advice to go back over the lake with our little band of Indians, it is also after our own hearts, for when we consider the journey lying before us, we see many difficulties which are coupled with danger in getting over the lake. We do not doubt, however, that he will move with us, go before us, and prepare the way, that his advice and wish will be carried out for the praise and glory of his name. In conclusion, we asked his forgiveness of our faults and transgressions, which we confessed to him; he comforted us, and let his peace rest upon us, with which we entered upon the new year.

We have had the holy communion nine times this year, whereto one came for the first time.

One woman has been baptized who came to us this year.

Eight children have been born, four boys and four girls.

Three couples have been married.

Two adults have died.

CHAPTER V.

1785.

NEW GNADENHÜTTEN, ON THE CLINTON, MICHIGAN.

Saturday, January 1. Heckewelder preached; afterwards all baptized brethren had a service. We gave ourselves up to him anew to be entirely his own, renewed our covenant which we had made with him in holy baptism, and begged his mercy, that through nothing, be it life or death, might we be separated from him and his people, and vowed to him fidelity and obedience. Since we had received no Scripture-verses and texts for this year, we took for use those of 1782, and Br. Jungmann held the congregation meeting from the first Scripture-verse of this year: And it shall come to pass that before they call I will answer, and whilst they are yet speaking I will hear. Complete thy work and crown thy grace—That I may faithful prove. And the text read: Jesus Christ, the same yesterday, to-day, and forever. In this we ever rejoice. Name and deed are one. He is called and is also Jesus, which we had already considered in the service for the baptized.

Sunday, 2. Br. David preached; Br. Edwards held the congregation meeting.

Wednesday, 5. For some days now we have had severe winter weather and cold. The snow is over a foot deep; the creek has been frozen for two weeks, so that sledges can be used on it with safety.

Thursday, 6. On this day, Epiphany, the Saviour of the heathen made himself especially known to his little flock, which he has got together from the heathen, held fast by the doctrine of his sufferings and his death, which he has also guarded and protected from all temptations, and held for his glory through all the trials that have befallen it; for this we adore him and cannot thank him enough. ['Why then should we not cheerfully have patience with their weaknesses, since the Saviour has had so much patience with them and shown them grace, and since we are eye-witnesses that they are an object of his mercy, and above all they are his, dearly bought with blood, the price of his woes, with whom he will sometime be adorned?]

In the morning prayer Br. Jungmann asked his bloody blessing for this day, and committed us and all heathen churches to his mercy. Then was the service for the baptized, in which still another discourse from the Scripture-verse: The Lord is exalted, for he dwelleth on high. He hath filled Zion with righteousness, and the text: Rejoice, ye Gentiles, with his people. Two, namely, Ignatius and Joseph, were absolved, kneeling before the church amid many tears, whereby a blessed feeling and the Saviour's nearness were noticed. In the afternoon at the love-feast the brethren were reminded that on this day all our churches thought of them before the Saviour, and sympathized in the grace he had shown them, that as he had especially intrusted to his church to announce the Gospel to the heathen, they rejoiced and thanked him, when they saw that the Saviour blessed their pains and work; that they must look upon our church in Bethlehem and beyond the great waters as their mother, for from them the word of God was come to themselves, therefore also we were glad to have fellowship one with another and liked to hear from one another, that the Saviour might have praise and thanks for what he had done to us and among us. In the concluding service, which Sensemann held in the evening, we thanked him for the blessing he had let fall upon us this day from his bloody fulness, and ended with the blessing of the church.

Saturday, 8. They brought into town the canoe the brethren have made for our journey. Our third horse died, so now we have none.

Sunday, 9. Br. Heckewelder preached, and then the

---

[1] This paragraph in brackets is struck out of the original.

boys had a service; they were exhorted to take the boy
Jesus for their example, to beg from him above all, obedient hearts, as he was obedient and·subject to his parents.
At the end we recommended them and our youth to him
in prayer, to his grace and protection.   Br. Jungmann held
the congregation meeting.

Monday, 10.   David held the early service.   The brethren came together to consider and set about the work they
have to do for our journey.

Tuesday, 11.   Most went again about their work of
making canoes, which is indeed a hard task, but seems not
so to them, for they want to go back over the lake.

Wednesday, 12.   Sensemann returned from the Fort,
bringing news that the brethren had got 10,000 acres of
land[1] from Congress, which was brought by a gentleman
from Pittsburg.   We heard that the wolves become very
bold, go in packs, and destroy many.   In this neighborhood, on Wolf creek, they eat up a Chippewa Indian
and his wife, and followed several others, who could barely
save themselves; this happens because there is almost no
game for their support; thus it is unsafe for a man to go
alone into the bush.

Saturday, 15.   The brethren came home from canoe-
making ; they have ten ready, and five yet to make.

Sunday, 16.   David preached, Edwards held the congregation meeting.   A Chippewa family came here, and remained over night; they were well received and entertained, and presented also with some corn.   The Indian
brethren spoke much with the man, saying to him, among
other things, that next spring we were going away from
here; we had often heard they were·discontented at our

---

[1] May 20, 1785, Congress ordered that "the said towns (on the Muskingum) and so much of the adjoining towns as in the judgment of
the geographer of the United States might be sufficient for them, be
reserved for the sole use of the Christian Indians formerly settled
there." Two years later Congress added 10,000 acres to this grant.
The Moravians had petitioned Congress on this subject as early as 1783,
and hence Zeisberger's statement of the rumor. See Taylor's Hist. of
Ohio, p. 396.

living ou their land, therefore we now wished to let them
know we were going away. He answered : Yes, it was
indeed true that one of their chiefs, who lived on the east
side of Lake St. Clair, where he had land and his town,
had been dissatisfied, and had made the young people ill-
disposed towards us, but that they had killed him. Thus
it goes among the Indians—some are for and others against
a thing.

Monday, 17. A Frenchman came here in a sledge, with
all sorts of things to trade. The wolves followed Renatus,
who had gone down to the lake, upon the ice. Inasmuch
as he had on skates, he waited a little to see whether they
were really aiming at him, and when they got reasonably
near, he hurried away.

Saturday, 22. Mr. Dolson came with his wife and four
others, among whom was a captain from the navy, from
Detroit. They left their sleighs at the mouth of the river,
because the ice was not trustworthy, and came here by
land. On the 23d, they were very attentive during the
sermon, and afterwards, among themselves, spoke much
of what they had heard, for the discourse was in English.
A ship's captain felt himself touched, and went about
afterwards thoughtfully, and said the minister in his sermon had to do with him alone; that the whole sermon
was aimed at him; that he had shown him clearly and
plainly how things stood with him, and had spoken the
truth. To-day they visited us in our houses, and the first
had the desire, since we were going away, to hold a farm
here and give us something for our improvements, if it
could be done. They went away on the 24th. On that
same day came Mr. Wilson, with a German named Charles
Turner, and a Frenchman. The German is a schoolmaster
in Detroit,' was a prisoner in Bethlehem, from Burgoyne's
army, a private soldier. The first earnestly asked us and
persisted that we should marry him, and since both he
and those with him gave sufficient grounds and moving
reasons, against which we had nothing to urge, the marriage took place on the 25th, to the content and satisfaction of all present. They returned home on the 26th.

Thursday, 27th. Frenchmen came with three sledges, bringing apples to exchange for corn, and in this way is the corn got away from our Indians, so that in the end they will have to suffer for their imprudence, and then when they have no longer any thing to eat, they will over-run us, and we must give them bread.

Saturday, 29. The brethren finished the canoes for the journey, seventeen in number.

Sunday, 30. Br. Heckewelder preached, David held the communion quarter-hour, Sensemann the congregation meeting. From all we learn from Detroit we see that both the Justice and several of the most prominent men, English and French, stand in the background, but are the real instigators of the Chippewas, and use them as tools to get us away from here in order to make themselves masters of our settlement, and they have themselves fallen into strife about the land we live on, and each one wishes to be the owner of it.

Monday, 31. From Detroit, a sister visited us from New York, Cornwall by name, who left New York in October and got to Detroit in November, where her husband is in the king's service in the navy here. From her we first learned that our dear brother, John (de Watteville), and his company, came prosperously to Philadelphia last summer. She went back the 2d, taking leave of us with tears, and wished she could stay with us.

Tuesday, Feb. 1. Mr. Dolson, his brother, and some others came here from Detroit, and carried away corn, since we were in debt to them. They, and also Mrs. Corn-wall, went back on the 2d.

Saturday, 5. We had the holy communion, accompanied by the blessed Saviour's near presence.

Sunday, 6. Edwards preached after the communion liturgy, read by David, wherein the importance of the Lord's supper was dwelt upon, and the brethren were admonished not to regard it superficially, nor as a common thing, nor through unworthy matters to deprive themselves of the communion, whereby they would become dry and dead in heart. In the afternoon in the service Br. David baptized the little daughter of Renatus and A. Regina, born yesterday, with the name Anna Justina. Br. Jungmann held the congregation meeting.

Monday, 7. Heckewelder and Schebosh went to Detroit, the Indian brethren partly hunting, partly making canoes.

Wednesday, 9. Mr. Tucker came here with his family, he asked for the baptism of his child, whom Br. David baptized. Heckewelder came from the fort.

Sunday, 13. David preached. Jungmann held the congregation meeting.

Monday, 14. Justice Nathan Williams[1] and others came from Detroit to see our place. The first spoke with us apart about our moving away, and said that it was a pity that we who had done so much work here should now go away and turn our backs upon all our labor, and he offered, if we would remain, to take upon himself to arrange matters with the Chippewas, and to satisfy them so that they should not molest us. We answered him it was too late, we were now ready and determined to go.

Tuesday, 15. Mr. Capt. McKee came with a large suite, who bought cattle, hogs, hay, corn, and all sorts of things from us. Capt. McKee was particularly friendly to us; he approved our departure over the lake, saying that he saw very well that our Indians could do nothing here, they had no hunting, and though they were quite able to support themselves by working, yet they were cheated out of their own by Detroit merchants, this he had himself often observed; he wished also, he said, by a good opportunity, to send a message to the Indians over the lake, to announce our return, and at the same time to advise them to give us a good reception—not in the least to molest us [for he may well have been conscious that he formerly has blackened us among the Indians]. He wished at the same time to clear himself of having had any hand in our being taken captive, as he plainly gave

---

[1] A justice of the peace, by trade a carpenter.

us to understand, laying the most blame on Col. de Peyster, and he again denies it.   Let him have it as he.will,
we know well enough how the matter stands.   Each one,
however, who had a hand in it would now like to clear
himself; it is evident they are sorry to have broken up
the Brothers' Mission, and would willingly seek to make
all good again if only they knew how, but not even kings
could do this, much less they.

Sunday, 20.   Jungmann preached.   David held the congregation meeting.

Monday, 21.   Most of the Indian brethren went off to
make canoes to sell, and thus pay the debts they were
forced to incur during the famine, and this is their only
way.

Wednesday, 23.   Adam, who came back from Detroit
and spoke there with McKee, related that news had come
from the Indian land, that Indians of all nations were retained in Pittsburg, and kept like prisoners, on which account some had again gone to war, and McKee had said
to him that peace was not yet established in the Indian
land; we should therefore do better to wait and plant
one more year here, although he had said nothing like this
to us here.   This news spread among our Indians, and
there were different opinions, so that many wished not to
go away, but to plant here, but we kept silent in the matter till we should get more exact news and information.
He also said to Adam that he had sent a message to the
nations about our moving over the lake, to open the way
for us.

Sunday, 27.   Edwards preached, and Heckewelder held
the congregation meeting.

Monday, 28.   Sensemann held early service.   The Indian brethren brought their canoes from the bush into the
water.

Wednesday, March 2.   We laborers had a conference
and considered about Br. Jungmann and his wife who
wanted to go to Bethlehem, and about Br. Sensemann and
his wife who wished to send their child there, and since
we intended to move back over the lake with our Indians,

and must again begin anew, we could oppose nothing to
their wishes, as enough of us would yet remain here.
We found the best and easiest way for them to take was
through Niagara, Oswego and Albany, for we had no
horses to go by way of Pittsburg. Br. Jungmann and his
wife undertook at the same time to take with them to
Bethlehem little Polly Heckewelder.[1]

Friday, 4. Mr. Dolson came from Detroit, from whom
we heard that Capt. Pipe, who had much to do with
our captivity in Gnadenhütten, on the Muskingum, and
had there been especially prominent, had been killed in
Pittsburg.[2] If this should prove true, it would cause uneasiness among the Indians, particularly among the Wolf
tribe of the Delawares, whose head man he was, although
the other tribes were not pleased with his conduct in this
war, and especially with regard to our captivity, and not
at all satisfied with him.

Sunday, 6. David preached and Jungmann held the congregation meeting. Most of the brethren had come home
from making sugar or canoes, but the weather is yet too
cold for making sugar, and this night a fine snow fell.

Monday, 7. Br. Edwards held early service. Heckewelder returned from Detroit, where he spoke both with
the Governor and with McKee. Both expressed themselves in regard to our moving over the lake as follows:
they held it best, and therefore only wished to advise us
to wait a little until autumn for the two following reasons:
first, since the Americans and nations were yet engaged
together in negotiations on the one part about their land
and had not yet come to terms, that also disputes and
disagreements about lands had arisen among the nations
themselves, and therefore it would not be the best thing
for us to be mixed up in them. He, the Governor, and the
colonels had strict orders from England to protect our

---

[1] Joanna Maria Heckewelder, born April 6, 1781. She died in 1868,
over 87 years old. For a time she was thought to be the first white
child born within the limit of the present State of Ohio.

[2] His death was not until 1794.

mission in every possible way; therefore they wished to expose us to no danger, but to advise us to wait until autumn, for then every thing would be arranged and in order. Secondly, it was not advisable for us to go this spring, for we should have to cross the lake already in April, and then it was hazardous and very doubtful whether we should reach our destination at the right time and be able to plant. The month of April was a very stormy month, and it would be dangerous at that time to cross the lake. They advised us for these reasons to plant again here, and to go away in the autumn, but if we wished to go now after they had imparted to us their advice, they would not and could not retain us. We laborers considered thus the circumstances, and at the same time the direction the Saviour had given us, but that we also then, when we had this direction from the Saviour, had a lot that it was also unnecessary to hurry. If then no important circumstance had arisen, we should have gone this spring, but since now there was a weighty cause, we could still wait without acting contrary to our lot, for we were not bound to go this spring. That the Saviour had so early given us and let us know his directions, was necessary for this reason, since both we and our Indian brethren were in debt, which we were forced to incur during the famine, and which required time for payment; for this we had done our best during the winter, and praise be to God, had brought the matter so far that we were all free from debt and could go where we would. We resolved, therefore, to plant once more here. It might be that before that time we should get better and more favorable news from the Indian land over the lake. Capt. McKee, who, on our account, had sent a message to the Indians there and informed them that we thought of going back again, was expecting an answer, which he would communicate to us upon its receipt.

Saturday, 12. Our Indians came home from the bush, part from making canoes, part from their sugar-huts. The weather is always too cold for this last work, and there is nothing to be done at it. If for a day we chance to have fine weather, it is sure to snow the next, and so it keeps on. As it seems, we shall have a late spring.

Sunday, 13. Heckewelder preached and Senseman held the congregation meeting. He spoke with the assistant brothers, and told them our thoughts about going away and staying here; that we thought of waiting until autumn, and this was afterwards made known to all the brethren.

Monday, 14. Jungmann held early service. Samuel and Stephen drove cattle to Detroit. It snowed again. They came back Wednesday, the 16th, bringing news that in the Indian land there was nothing noteworthy and nothing to be feared.

Sunday, 20. Brother David preached from the Epistle, Phil., ii, 5: Let this mind be in you, which was also in Christ Jesus, and he announced to the brethren the approach of passion week and the holidays, saying that as our Saviour humbled himself and became obedient unto death, even the death of the cross, so also we should be obedient to God's word for our eternal salvation. To the communicants the Lord's supper was announced for Maundy Thursday. Br. Heckewelder held the congregation meeting from the Scripture-verse of the day.

Tuesday, 22. By William, who came back from Detroit, we had, quite unexpectedly, but to our excessive joy, a package of letters from Bethlehem, by way of Niagara, together with Scripture-verses for this year. The most noteworthy thing was a letter from the U. A. Conference,[1] and also a writing in his own hand from Br. John (de Watteville.) Col. de Peyster, in Niagara, got the packet from an Oneida Indian, wrote to us about it, inclosed the packet with his own letter, and forwarded it to Detroit. This gave us all extraordinary joy.

Thursday, 24. In the evening there was a reading of the history; then the communicants had the washing of feet and afterwards the holy communion, whereby Jacob was a candidate.

[1] See Introduction.

Friday, 25. We read the history of the passion in four parts, which was listened to with great attention and eagerness, and with moved hearts. At the death of our Saviour we read, kneeling, the liturgy, and many tears rolled down our cheeks. Also early in the first service mention was made of the day, that God, our Saviour, had come into the flesh that he might offer his life as a sacrifice for our sins, and that by his death he had brought back eternal life and blessedness.

Saturday, 26, was a love-feast for all the inhabitants. At the service the brethren were greeted, both by Brs. Joseph and John,[1] whom some among us were found to know, and by the brethren this side and the other side of the sea, and they were assured of the recollection and prayers of all our churches, which aroused wonderful joy among them.

Sunday, 27. We read the Easter litany, partly in the chapel, and partly in the graveyard, and at the proper place thought of the sisters, Zipporah and Anna Sophia, who had died since last year. Afterwards a portion of the history of the resurrection was read. Br. Jungmann preached, and Heckewelder, in the evening, held the congregation meeting from the Scripture-verse.

Tuesday, 29. The brethren again got ready and went to their sugar-huts, but this year the spring is very bad, nothing but snow-squalls and rain, and as it seems, a late spring. Our creek broke up and gave us higher water than we have ever had.

Saturday, April 2. The creek was always rising, and the weather was very stormy, but the lake is yet frozen, so that there is no getting to Detroit.

Sunday, 3. Sensemann preached, Br. David held the quarter-hour service for the baptized from the text of the day, and brought to memory this memorial day of those who have been baptized this year. Here only one has this year been baptized. At the end the brethren were told we should not move away from here this spring, but wait

---

[1] Spangenberg and de Watteville are here referred to.

until autumn. Besides, we see no possibility of this, for
now would be our time for departure, and the lake is yet
frozen, though other years it has already been open at this
time. Three years ago we came on the 20th of April to
Detroit, and no longer was ice to be seen.

Monday, 4. Most of the brethren went to their sugar-
huts, but this year is bad for sugar, so that there will be
little of it made, for we have always either rain or snow-
squalls, and very seldom a fine day.

Wednesday, 6. The Indian brethren brought the canoes
they have made out of the bush into the water, and got
them here. Jungmann held early service.

Thursday, 7. Heckewelder held early service. It rained
and snowed all day.

Sunday, 10. David preached. In the afternoon the
Indian brethren went to the lake to bring their canoes
into the water, and the sisters to the sugar-huts, for the
trees ran to-day.

Monday, 11. At a love-feast we laborers had together,
we congratulated Br. David on his sixty-fifth birthday, and
our hearts blessed him.

Sunday, 17. Heckewelder preached.

Monday, 18. Since the lake is now open, Brs. Jungmann,
Sensemann, and Heckewelder went to Detroit—the first
two to set their affairs there in order before their departure for Bethlehem, and likewise to learn of some ship
sailing. At the same time went most of the Indian brethren, and also many sisters, to sell the canoes which they
have made this winter, and to pay their debts. We heard
the next day, however, it was so stormy on the lake that no
canoe could go, and they had to encamp at the mouth of
the river.

Thursday, 20. Last night and all day yesterday it
snowed, and was also very windy, and so it kept on to-
day. It is a very late spring, still always cold, and every
day stormy, so that we very well see that we should have
been in no condition to get over the lake before planting-
time.

Sunday, 24. Br. David preached in Indian. In the

afternoon Brs. Jungmann, Heckewelder, and Sensemann came back from Detroit, likewise also the Indian brethren. In a few weeks there will be an opportunity to sail for Niagara.

Thursday, 26. After early service was the communion quarter-hour. This was announced to the brethren for next Saturday.

Thursday, 28. We planted our bread-corn.

Friday, 29. Both yesterday and to-day we spoke with the brethren, and the Saviour gave us the grace of finding more in them to rejoice in than to be sad over.

Saturday, 30. At the Lord's supper Zachary was for the first time a partaker, and Christina, Jacob's wife, was a candidate.

Sunday, May 1. Br. Heckewelder preached. In the afternoon all the baptized brethren were told that we found ourselves compelled to send away Joseph on account of his bad conduct, for he is a blemish in the church, so that we feel ashamed of him before the world, since he brings us into ill repute and makes us a bad name.

Monday, 2. Br. Edwards and several Indian brethren went off to Detroit.

Tuesday, 3. Ignatius' brother came visiting.

Thursday, 5. After reading the history of the Ascension, we prayed to our dear Lord, asking for his unseen presence and daily and hourly walking with him. The sermon thereupon was preached by Br. David from the text of to-day: Lo, I am with you alway even unto the end of the world.

Friday, 6. Br. Edwards came back from the Fort; no ship had yet come from Fort Erie (opposite Buffalo), and every one conjectured that the ships that sailed had been prevented by ice from coming to land, for the ice there always breaks up later than in Detroit. From the Indian land we learn that the Shawanese and Cherokees have not yet come to peace, nor did they go to the treaty to which they were asked.

Saturday, 7. Yesterday and to-day we planted our fields and got done with them.

15

Sunday, 8. Sensemann preached, David held the children's service, and Edwards the congregation meeting. After a long time, for during the winter we hardly saw a strange Indian, Chippewas came here again, down the creek, on their way to Detroit, remaining here over night. The brethren entertained them, gave them food, and spoke to them also words of the eternal life.

Friday, 13. From Detroit we have news that a council with the Chippewas has been held, and that they have been told the Americans would take possession of the place, at which they were very much alarmed, and, after the end of the council, prepared for war. What will follow upon this we have to wait for. Further we heard that the Shawanese upon the Miami had moved away and left their former towns, when they took council whether they would begin war or receive peace, that therefore the Detroit merchants called in all their traders in the Indian land. On the other hand, our Indians have been busy planting, they are all striving to make a good crop of corn that they may sell it in the autumn, therewith to provide themselves with the means of life across the lake, and in this we have encouraged them.

Sunday, 15. In the first service was to-day's festival announced, of God, the Holy Ghost, and Br. Heckewelder preached. In the second service two grown women were baptized, one by Br. David, with the name Mary Magdalene, and one by Br. Jungmann, with the name Helena, into the death of Jesus. In the service for the baptized we adored God, the worthy Holy Ghost, and asked absolution for our manifold faults and transgressions, thanked him for his care and the trouble he had taken for us, begged from him obedient hearts and fidelity, and that he would remain with us and would further show himself strong and mighty among us.

[Thus far to Bethlehem.]

Tuesday, 17, in the forenoon, the whole church had a love-feast at the departure of the brethren, Sensemann and Jungmann, with their wives, who, with the two children, Polly Heckewelder and Christian David Sensemann, set out for the church in Bethlehem. We blessed them with our hearts and committed them to the eye and guard of Israel to accompany them successfully to their destination. We laborers bound ourselves by the cup to love and hearty remembrance, since the Saviour had helped us through so much need, danger, and hardship, which makes our thinking one of another pleasant, and excites and encourages us to praise and gratitude towards the Lord. Thereupon these brethren started for Detroit, accompanied by Br. Heckewelder and some Indian brethren, and the whole town stood on the shore, taking leave of them and seeing them depart.

Saturday, 21. Heckewelder came back from Detroit, whither he had accompanied the brethren. No ship had yet come from Fort Erie, although two, and the first one certainly a month before, had sailed hither, and no one can conceive what is the reason of their remaining out so long, yet it begins to be thought they have come to misfortune in a storm, but the Governor intended to send another in a few days, if none comes in, by which the brethren will go. They got free passage in the cabin, and a merchant, our friend, will provide them with what is necessary, not only as long as they are in Detroit, but also on the ship. We heard at the same time from the Indian land, that among the natives all appears well, and nothing is to be feared of a new Indian war; but that the land from Pittsburg to the Shawanese towns was all in the hands of the Americans. The Wyandots, before they went to the treaty in Pittsburg, had taken counsel together, as they usually do if they go to a treaty, to deliberate and prepare what they wish to say and to answer. Among other things, also, they had deliberated about the believing Indians, since they expected to be asked about them, why they had treated them so badly, and they had resolved that before they were put to question about this, they would come forward and openly testify that the Six Nations were upon the point of blotting out the Indian church of believers, and since they, the Wyandots, perceived this, they had themselves taken them away from

their towns to save them from destruction, but since now
again there was peace, they wanted to put the believing
Indians back again in their towns. The Americans, however, had given them no time to make this speech, but
declared they would take possession of all the land, and
hereupon the Wyandots were cut short, and could say
nothing about the matter.

Saturday, 21. We were quite done with planting.
Our Indians have planted much more than they did last
year, and have cleared much more land.

Sunday, 22. In the forenoon the sermon was from the
Epistle to the Romans, xl. 33: O the depth of the riches
both of the wisdom and knowledge of God, and about
the Holy Trinity, that Father, Son, and Spirit have stood
by and worked together to bring about the redemption of
the human race, wherewith God, the Holy Ghost, is yet
ever busy, bringing it to the belief in Jesus Christ, and
to convince it of its unbelief. Heckewelder held the congregation meeting.

Wednesday, 25. There came here a Chippewa Indian,
whose father is chief in this neighborhood, and both had
come back from the treaty in Pittsburg. He was here
several days ago, and had promised the Indian brethren
to return and tell them what was done at the treaty, but
inasmuch as Tucker told him we did not concern ourselves
with such matters, he said he had brought nothing with
him. However, he told us a good deal, saying, among
other things, that his father was away among the Chippewas, to take them the news, but had told him he should
come to us and tell us something; when the Americans
should be in Detroit, they would consider where they
could show us land to live on, but this he spoke not
plainly about; that a few days before he had had a letter
from Pittsburg, in which he was told that in two months
the Americans would be here. He was a very intelligent,
fine-looking man, the like of whom we have not yet seen
among the Chippewas. He said it was well we remained
yet a day here, no peace was yet made with all nations;
we should not listen to what some of their foolish people

said, but quietly plant here. He went away on the 28th, and we gave him some corn for planting, of which he stood in need.

27. The Indians hoed our corn.

Sunday, 29. Edwards preached, David held the children's service, and Heckewelder the congregation meeting.

Tuesday, 31. From the Fort we learn that Brs. Jungmann and Sensemann, with their wives, sailed several days ago from Detroit for Niagara.

Sunday, June 5. Br. David preached from the Gospel, about the great feast. The Lord's supper was announced to the brethren for next Saturday. Heckewelder held the congregation meeting. With the assistant brothers we held a conference, and considered about sending two brothers over the lake to examine the neighborhood where we wished to go, but since we heard that the Americans were taking possession of all the land between Pittsburg and the Shawanese towns, we shall have to give up our plan of going to the Walhonding, and must perhaps remain on a creek flowing into the lake. We are somewhat perplexed about this; the whole matter of our moving is yet dark, for we do not rightly know where and how we shall be, and therefore we wish further news and information. Above all, may the Saviour make us a road thereto, open the way, and send us certainty in the matter, for he gave us the direction thereto. Capt. McKee, who in our behalf sent a message to the nations and informed them of our return over the lake, said to us that they received it well, but that as yet he had no answer from them, and that this was no bad token. We, however, think otherwise. The natives will not indeed suffer the word of God to be preached in their land; that shall cease, as they have already said; therefore it will indeed be hard to get an answer.

Monday, 6. Br. Edwards held early service.

Tuesday, 7. David held early service. He said, by occasion of the Scripture-verse, that we, with all our concerns, let them have what name they would, should go to the Saviour and talk them out with him, not alone what troubled our own hearts, but if things went not well in our

families, we should lay our house and family affairs before
him, and commit them to him.

Wednesday, 8. Heckewelder held the early service.
The assistants spoke with Luke and his wife, between
whom there was a difference. They were so fortunate as
to make peace between them, for which they used more
than three or four hours. This sort of work we are glad
to make over to the assistants, who take time for it to hear
the brethren through, and this requires time, for if we laborers wished to do it, it would use up all our time, and we
should not be in condition to contend with all. The assistants can also sooner tell them the pure truth and bring
them to acknowledgment, for if we tell them of their bad
conduct and faults, they take it very loftily, and often cannot bear it.

Thursday, 9, and Friday, 10. There was speaking with
regard to the Lord's supper. We found the brethren in a
blessed way, and saw with pleasure the work of the Holy
Ghost in their hearts, and when something had occurred
to disturb their love one to another, the Saviour had given
grace that all in love was arranged and done away with.
There came a couple of women, A. Johanna and a
single woman, Lea, from the head of the Miami, from
whom we got news of our Indians there, that they had
heard of our moving over the lake, and said we should
come to them. We heard too that Helena and Benigna
were gone from time. The first of these (Johanna) is a
bad person, and took away with her one of her children,
John, and Lea remained here. We had, thereupon,

Saturday, 11, the Lord's supper accompanied by his near
presence; of which one sister, the young Christina, partook for the first time, and Anna Elizabeth, who was not
indeed born in the church, but for the most part had
grown up therein, saw it for the first time, though from
weeping she could see little. After the Lord's supper
many brethren came to our house, as is always usual at
such times, greeted and kissed the two sisters, rejoiced and
showed their thankfulness for the Saviour's grace.

Sunday, 12. The communion liturgy was read early. Br. Heckewelder preached. Edwards held the congregation meeting. In the spring we had already held it needful to send some Indian brethren across the lake this summer to inform themselves about the water-ways and rivers, that we might know what river or creek we should have to take when we had got over the lake, since none of our Indians was acquainted thereabout. This matter we had therefore repeatedly considered, for it was now time to execute it, and we had also spoken with our assistants about it, but it always remained to us somewhat undetermined, and we were in uncertainty and still in the dark in regard to our moving over the lake. We have direction by lot to the Walhonding, but we hear that the States have either already taken possession, or are about to do so, of all the land upon that side except a small stretch along the lake. Now our thoughts were ever turning to the head of the Walhonding, but should what we hear be true, we must be in doubt whether it is advisable for us to think of settling there and whether then we should not do better to remain on a creek that falls into the lake if we found a suitable place, and thus regard the lot, that our Saviour only wished to point out the course we had to steer. In order to come from our uncertainty to clearness, we resolved to-day through the lot, with the approbation of the Saviour, that Br. Edwards, with three Indian brethren in our behalf, should go not only over the lake, but also to Pittsburg, to inform themselves there at the proper place of all circumstances, and in regard to our moving there to get information and advice. This direction of the Saviour was to us in our circumstances, whereover for many days we had so much thought, prayed, and wept, a great consolation, and aroused our hearts to praise and thank the Saviour, our only friend and counsellor. The lot read: The Saviour favors that Br. Edwards with some Indian brethren shall in our behalf make a journey to Pittsburg.

Wednesday, 15. A Potawatomy Indian came here, who after the manner of the Indian chiefs, by a string of wampum, asked for tobacco and some powder, which we gave him. We heard that the Delawares and other Indians are going in large numbers up the Miami (Maumee), and wish to live there. The Delawares and Shawanese, who no longer have any land, are now taking counsel whither they shall go.

Friday, 17. Br. Edwards and the Indian brethren, Samuel, Peter, and Jacob, started for Pittsburg, for which purpose they had made a bark canoe to go over the lake in, and these are the best to go through the waves. We heard on the 18th, by William, who came back from Detroit, that on that day they had gone away from there and have now probably come as far as the mouth of the Miami. We received to-day, before Br. Edwards left, letters from Brs. Jungmann and Sensemann that they on the 29th, but in twice twenty-four hours, had come to Fort Erie and the same day to Fort Slosser.[1] They met there Col. de Peyster, who promised to help them on further, and wished to send them on to Oswego by a ship that lay ready.

Sunday, 19. Br. David preached and held the children's service in Indian. Heckewelder held the congregation meeting.

Wednesday, 22. Several Indian brothers went to the settlement to get provisions, for already they have again nothing more to eat. So has it been with them every year here. Even if they have planted corn enough, they would sell it during the winter for a trifle, already in the spring would have nothing, and in the summer must buy it again dearer, and suffer, as we have an example this year.

Friday, 24. From Detroit, whence our Indians came back with some provisions, we learned that a man in Detroit had met Br. Edwards, with the three Indians, in Miami bay, where they had fortunately arrived.

Saturday, 25. The Indians hilled our corn.

---

[1] "The transport of goods by land to Fort Slausser, two miles above the east side of the falls" (of Niagara). Heriot's Travels through the Canadas, Chap. VIII.

Sunday, 26. Heckewelder preached. David held the congregation meeting. |Br. Schebosh, who came back from Detroit, learned there that in regard to peace among the nations the prospect was still bad ; that the Twightwees and Cherokees, which last in this war have been driven from their lands, and now wander about among the other nations, excite them and are still always going out stealing and murdering; likewise that Pomoacan has sent forty men to the Scioto. where the white people from the States have gone and wish to settle. How this hangs together, and what will follow hereupon, we must await.

Friday, July 1. This week all the brethren were busy in the fields, and are now for the most part done with hilling corn, which this year again furnishes a fine prospect for a good and rich harvest. For a time we had very hot weather. The insects, mosquitoes, ponkjis, and horse-flies are worse and more troublesome than they were last year, so that neither man nor beast can have any pleasure in life,.and here, say the Indians, it is yet tolerable, but around the lake they are said to be in such numbers that it is nigh impossible to live, and that these plagues of the land will ever cease there is no hope, on account of the many great swamps and marshes.

Sunday, 3. David preached from the Epistle to the Romans, vi. 3 : Know ye not that so many of us as were baptized into Jesus Christ were baptized into his death? and afterwards conducted the quarter-hour of the married. Heckewelder held the congregation meeting from the Scripture-verse.

Tuesday, 5. We heard through the Chippewa, who often comes here, that something bad was going on among the nations; that a black belt had come to the Chippewas from the Shawanese, Twightwees, Delawares, etc., with a hatchet concealed within ; that these same and the Cherokees had already murdered many white people. One hears such stories here without knowing their foundation ; therefore it is well and needful that Br. Edwards is on his way to Pittsburg with the Indians, from whom, upon their return, we shall get trustworthy news.

Wednesday, 6.   Came Kaschajem, and with him Thomas, a boy, whose father, Philip, was killed in Gnadenhütten, from Gigegunk, but they had little to say about our Indians in that quarter.   Some of the news we had from that quarter is true, that the Cherokees and Twightwees are going to war, but not so bad as we anticipated.

Friday, 8.   The Scheboshes and many besides went to Detroit to seek corn, for many had sold too much and must now buy it at a higher price.

Sunday, 10.   David preached and Heckewelder held the congregation meeting.   Few brethren were at home, but they came,

Monday, 11, for the most part.   We had news that Br. Edwards, with the Indian brethren, seventeen days before, had arrived in Pittsburg, from Pettquotting (Huron River, O.).

Tuesday, 12.   David held the early service, and thereupon the communion quarter-hour.   He announced to the brethren the Lord's supper for next Saturday.

Saturday, 16.   After the brethren had been spoken to the day before, we had to-day the holy communion, in which a sister, A. Elizabeth, had part for the first time.

Sunday, 17.   David read the communion liturgy and held the congregation meeting.   Heckewelder preached.

Monday, 18, and Tuesday, 19.   We heard from Detroit, which swarms with Indians, that they are very restless, and have held a war-dance.   We heard, at the same time, that an army is expected in Detroit, which is already on the march.[1]   We were, therefore, concerned about our brothers, and wished the Saviour might soon bring them back home to us.   Moreover, we know not how to account for the preparations for war.

Wednesday, 20.   We learned something more exact about the above-mentioned circumstances, namely, that an army is marching from Pittsburg to the Shawanese towns, from there to the Wyandots, to make peace with the nations; first to quiet them, and then to come to Detroit,

---

[1] This was false.

which was to us the most probable. Meanwhile our Chippewa, the chief's son, said to us that the war-belt had already gone to all the nations, and that they wished to meet the Americans. We hoped, however, that all would yet be peacefully arranged without bloodshed. The above news a Wyandot had brought from Pittsburg, in a letter to them.

Thursday, 21. Br. David held early service, and,

Friday, 22, Br. Heckewelder. To-day, and for a few days, most of the brethren went to the settlement to earn the means of life in the harvest among the French.

Sunday, 24. David preached, few brethren were at home.

Monday, 25. John, Luke's son, came from Sandusky. William and several besides, with their families, went to the settlement to work.

Saturday, 30. We had the great joy to see Br. Edwards with the three Indian brethren again among us, in good health and with success. It was a very special joy also that he brought with him a packet of letters for us from Bethlehem, Litiz, etc., which Mr. Wilson had in charge to forward to us, with whom the brethren had lodged, and who, in Pittsburg, took them into his own home. When they went away from us, and had gone across the lake, they landed at Pettquotting, the other side (i. e., east) of the mouth of the Sandusky, from which place they went by land, by way of Tuscarawas, to Pittsburg, and they came back again by way of Cuyahoga. On their way back, on the Tuscarawas creek, they made a bark canoe, and went up the creek as far as they could. Then they left their bark canoe, and went by land to the Cuyahoga, where they made another bark canoe and went as far as the mouth of that river, left their canoe and went by land along the lake to Pettquotting, where they had left their first canoe, in the hope of being able to use it on their way home, but since it was warped by the heat of the sun, and quite useless, they were forced to make a new one, which they did at once, and for which a Chippewa Indian who was there pointed out a tree, so that they were not

compelled to seek a long time for one; from there then in
two days and two nights, they came over the lake to the
mouth of the river, or to the straits below Detroit, but
they travelled day and night, and were quite worn out·
Br. Edwards, who had hurt his hip, came home quite
lame from weariness, and could hardly go from the canoe
to his house when they got here, but he was quite well
again after resting a couple of days. As to the business
for the sake of which he made the journey, in the first
place this is the main thing; we now know certainly that
there is no more Indian land across the lake, and that the
States own all the land, and take possession of it; that
they will not altogether drive away the Indians, but yet
will not permit them to live in their neighborhood, that is,
on the Muskingum and in that quarter, but they must remain at a distance. In Pittsburg, also, he read in a newspaper that the Christian Indians have their towns on the
Muskingum, namely, Gnadenhütten, Schönbrunn, and
Salem, confirmed to them by Congress, with so much land
as the geographer, the surveyor general, shall hold fit;
this also we knew, in part, by letters from Br. John and
Ettwein, of May last, although it had not then been confirmed.

Through this news our minds are now clear, and we see
plainly enough that we shall not have to look about for
another place to settle in than in the country on the Muskingum. It would not be well received from us, and we
might soon be driven away again if we settled elsewhere;
on the other hand, no one can drive us from our towns on
the Muskingum, since now we know our way and have it
before us. Br. Edwards and the brethren have no need to
find out about another way than by Cuyahoga, though
they found no creek or river which goes from the lake far
into the country except the Cuyahoga. He spoke also
with some people in Pittsburg, who are very willing to furnish provisions at a cheap rate if we go over there this
autumn, whether we are forced to winter on the Cuyahoga,
the Muskingum, or the Tuscarawas. They see with pleas-

ure there that we shall soon live in our towns there
again.

Sunday, 31. Br. David preached, Heckewelder held the
congregation meeting. Most of the Indians were in the
settlement.

Wednesday, Aug. 3. Br. Heckewelder went to Detroit
on business. Sister Sara Heckewelder has for a week had
intermittent fever [every other day], which weakens her
very much. He came,

Friday, 5, back from there, bringing a letter from Jungmann and Sensemann, written June 11, in Niagara; in this
they told us they had made arrangements to go in boats,
which had come from Schenectady, and were soon going
back there. We hoped that by this time already they were
come to Bethlehem. As regards peace among the Indians,
it is still uncertain, and there is nothing trustworthy to be
judged about it. We hope for the best. The Indians in
Michilimackinac are said to be much excited, and the
dwellers there fear a hostile inroad from them. Heckewelder brought news of the Governor's (Hay) death. He
was buried on the second of this month.

Sunday, 7. Br. Edwards preached and David held the
congregation meeting. Most of the brethren who have
been working at the harvest in the settlement and earning
food, came home yesterday and to-day.

Monday, 8. Heckewelder held early service, thereupon
to communicants was announced the Lord's supper for Saturday, the 13th. Some brethren went whortleberrying.

Tuesday, 9. David held early service. Since the Indian
brethren were now all at home, we made known to them
what Br. Edwards and those with him in Pittsburg had
told us, and how they had found circumstances; also we
read to them from the letters from Bethlehem they had
brought, all of which was pleasant for them to hear, especially that Congress had given them their three towns.

Friday, 12. Both to-day and yesterday there was speaking; we found the brethren, in spite of their halting and
failing, attached to the Saviour, and longing always to become better.

Saturday, 13. To the brethren in the early service and also to the communicants in the evening the occasion and peculiarity of this day were told, and we related to them what the Saviour had done for his church fifty-eight years ago; the hearts of all the brethren were purified, and they bound themselves to abide by the word of Jesus' death and passion, and to announce this both to Christians and heathen, which he so blessed that already many thousands had received it, and through belief in his merits had found forgiveness of their sins and everlasting salvation and blessedness, whereof we also bear witness, and through grace have become members of his church and partakers of the blessing and happiness which he has gained. We asked for his gracious absolution, and then had the holy communion.

Sunday, 14. Communion liturgy. Heckewelder preached, Edwards held the congregation meeting.

Monday, 15. Brethren whortleberrying.

Tuesday, 16. Schebosh went with several brethren to Detroit, coming back Thursday, the 18th.

Friday, 19. Sara Nanticoke bore a daughter, that was,

Sunday, 21, baptized with the name Anna Maria. Edwards preached, David held the children's service, and Heckewelder the congregation meeting.

Wednesday, 24. Joshua took a Nanticoke boy, who is not quite right in mind and had run away here to the brethren, back to the settlement, where his friends are, but the next day back he came again.

Thursday, 25. From the Miami came Christian Gottlieb with his wife and child visiting, as also, Saturday, 27, the cripple, Thomas, to see and hear what we have in mind and how we are disposed. There the past year the stout Helena, the old gray-haired Paulus, and Benignus, and this summer Anna Justina, have passed from time. In regard to peace among the nations, nothing is yet settled. This month they hold a great council, to which a thousand Indians will go, it is said, and now we await what shall then be determined. Our Indians are yet considering what they shall do. They have heard that we again move back over the lake ; they keep themselves together, and if any one of them will come to us, they dissuade him. Neither the Wyandots nor Delawares knew where to settle us when they got McKee's message about our moving over the lake.

Sunday, 28. David preached. Edwards held the congregation meeting.

Tuesday, 30. By Thomas, who went back to the Miami, we sent word to all our Indians in the Indian land, greeted them, and said to them that this autumn we should make our journey by way of Cuyahoga to the Muskingum; that we invited them all to unite themselves with us, either in Cuyahoga, Tuscarawas, or at Schönbrunn on the Muskingum. If this autumn or winter they should go hunting there, they would meet us. He said he believed this news would be pleasant for all to hear, and that they would all like to come. We laborers had already conferred together, for we wished to tell our Indians something certain and trustworthy, and as we again had a lot that we should go, which is a certain thing, we asked whether we had yet any thing to ask the Saviour in regard to our going away this autumn. We got for answer that we had to ask the Saviour about nothing further. We saw from this that we should have no hesitation to go this autumn. What induced us to make this inquiry was this, that through the summer we had heard all sorts of weighty news about the nations, on which account we were advised by the Governor in the spring to wait until the times should be better cleared up, and if we took every thing together, it was not favorable, and the nations were secretly going about something, but now, as it seems, this is removed, and soon there will be perfect peace.

Wednesday, 31. The widows, six in number, had, on their day and festival, a service, blessed and accompanied by his nearness. The brethren were reminded to provide themselves with canoes, not to be negligent by waiting until the last hour, and most of them thereupon went out to make some.

Saturday, Sept. 3. By occasion of the Scripture-verse : He shall give his angels charge over thee to keep thee in

all thy ways, the brethren were reminded of our captivity
four years ago to-day, and were exhorted to praise and
thank the Lord, who, through the service of the dear
angels, had turned away from us much evil, danger, and
hardship; that the brethren, above all, had to be on their
guard not to murmur against their Saviour, if any thing
did not go to their liking, but to think and believe that
what he does and lets happen, that is well done, and takes
a blessed end. Many brethren thought about this, and
said to us how sad in mind they then had been, how their
hearts had been oppressed—had thought all was over with
them, and that the church was utterly ruined and rooted
out.

Sunday, 4. Heckewelder preached; Edwards held the
congregation meeting. In the evening came Matthew,
Cornelius' son, from the Miami, from whom we learn that
Abel there, about two weeks ago, passed from time.

Monday, 5. A party of Nanticokes came here visiting;
they had come to Detroit lately from Niagara out of the
Mingoes' land, and were on their way to the head of the
Miami, where now assemble Indians from all sorts of nations. These were,

Tuesday, 6, at the early service, very attentive. During
the day others came also, among whom were some Mohicans, so that some forty Indians were here visiting, the
first visit of the kind here on the Huron. We soon saw
that among them were some who had ears to hear, and
were not indisposed for the kingdom of God, but we
thought at the same time, if only they were not Nanticokes. One of them, Samuel's own brother, told the
others who had come first, what he had heard in the meeting, and what he had retained, namely: that we had to
seek our help, eternal life, and blessedness from the Saviour
alone, who had gained and earned all that through his
bitter passion, and through his blood and death; that he
was the only true God, and except him there was none
besides. "A good deal more was told," he said, "but this
much I was able to bring away."

Wednesday, 7. For the sake of friends who wished to

hear, there was a common service early in the morning. Afterwards the married brethren had their festival and service from their text, and in the afternoon was a love-feast for all the inhabitants, and in conclusion we brought to our dear Lord our filial thanks for the grace and blessing he had given us to enjoy, through his recognition of us and his invaluable nearness.

Thursday, 8.   After the early service most of our friends set out for Detroit. Samuel's brother had spoken alone in confidence with him, and told him his thoughts, namely: for a year and a half he had the desire to come to the church, and now he believed he had the oppor-tunity to carry out his inclination, for his nation was now about to move; as yet he had told no man, not even his nearest friend, what he thought, and wherewith he was busy; he was perplexed about his happiness, to ob-tain this he saw no desire or way among the savages, but he believed he could attain it among the believing In-dians; one thing, however, caused him perplexity and doubt, he was a great sinner, and in this war had shed the blood of many men ; when he thought about this, it was ever as if some one said to him, "It is vain for thee to be concerned about this, thou canst not turn, thou hast too many sins lying upon thee, give up the thought;" he had therefore determined, since he was come to Detroit, to visit the believing Indians and to find out whether it were possible for him to find mercy from the Saviour, and whether among the believing Indians there was one who had been so great a sinner as he, and if this were so, he could think there was yet hope for him. Samuel showed him then the way to salvation, and told him no one was so great a sinner, nor so corrupted, as not to find mercy and forgiveness from the Saviour, who had shed his blood for the sins of the whole world. He spoke yet farther, telling Samuel how he had thought of arranging matters to get away from his chiefs, who if they suspected this of him, would watch and guard him carefully lest he should get out of their hands; ten of them were his

16

friends of whom he believed they would be of his mind should he tell them his purpose. Thus must most Indians steal away, if they wish to come to us.

Saturday, 10. Wischnasch came from Sandusky to visit us, from whom we learned that it is still doubtful whether peace will be made among the nations.

Sunday, 11. David preached. At break of day Heckewelder set out for Detroit taking letters with him for Bethlehem. Two Frenchmen were present at the sermon, and also several strange Indians.

Monday, 12. From Detroit Heckewelder did not bring us very favorable news about moving away for the present, for the Indian land seems very restless and confused, and the Indians in all quarters are arming for a new war, for which the nations are already quite unanimous. This is the common talk in Detroit, and every one advises us against going over the lake in such existing, unsettled circumstances. It is said a treaty will be held with the nations at the mouth of the Miami of the Ohio, but it is said they will come there in arms, and that, therefore, we shall soon hear something exciting from that quarter. We have also heard that if we went over the lake now, the Indians would again make us prisoners, and take us where they wished in the Indian land, that they will not permit us to go to the Muskingum. If an Indian war should break out, it would not be advisable for us to break up here, and certainly we should have something to fear. They state that if we go over the lake, they have orders from M(cKee) to take us prisoners and hold us fast. The Indians, also, who come here, dissuade us from moving away, should there be war. The nations wish to fight for their land and hold it, but we hope that this unrest will be quieted, although it might be too late for us this autumn.

Tuesday, 13. By the Indian, Gabriel, who came from the Miami, we had a letter by way of Pittsburg, which he got in Detroit, from Br. Ettwein in Bethlehem, of June 15th. From this we see that they then knew nothing of Brs. Jungmann and Sensemann and their wives, but of

them we have news through Cassidy[1] that on the 25th of
June they were yet a day's journey from Schenectady, and
had lodged with him on the Mohawk River.

Friday, 16.   There came a whole party of Nanticokes,
Mohicans, and Monseys, visiting, who all wanted to go to
the Miami.   This week we began to harvest our corn,
which is this year ripe much later than it was last, probably on account of the drouth this summer, for the whole
summer through we had not one good rain, and only two
or three little thunder-showers.

Sunday, 18.   Heckewelder gave the sermon, at which
all our strangers were present.   Thereafter was the communion quarter-hour, and Edwards held the congregation
meeting.   To these strangers, here visiting, the Indian
brethren praised the salvation the Saviour has won for us
by his blood and death.   Among others was a Mohican,
who begged the brethren to speak to him about the
Saviour, and then he came to Abraham, who, with Br.
Samuel, discoursed to him with great earnestness, and not
without effect, for he was much convinced of the truth,
but before they were done a Nanticoke came as messenger
from Detroit, to call away his people, and brought bad
news from there, that the nations over the lake had all declared war against the Americans, which should last thirty
years.   At the same time we got a message from an Indian from the Miami and the Shawanese towns, they having heard that this autumn we wanted to go back over the
lake; he sent word to us to remain here still and to wait,
for there was now no peace, and it was not advisable for
us to go there, and if yet we did so, they were determined
to get us all together, to hold us fast, and to bring us to
the head of the Miami; for the present, we should stay
here and remain until perfect peace should be made.   We
heard, also, that the nations intend to begin hostilities at
this treaty, which is to take place this autumn in that
neighborhood.   They have much to say, and make boasts,

---

[1] Perhaps this is the man called Cassedy on p. 130.

as is their custom, but the Lord can soon bring their plans to nought.

Monday, 19. Immediately after the early service the strangers all went away to Detroit, and now their heads were full of war, and they forgot again the good they had heard. Thus does Satan to many inquirers, that they may not hear God's word, but be held in uncertainty and blindness.

Saturday, 24. The brethren had lately been spoken with, and we enjoyed his body and blood in the holy sacrament. This week besides we have made a good beginning with our harvest [see 16th], and on Thursday, 22d Sept., we had this year the first little frost, thus three weeks later than last year.

Sunday, 25. After the communion liturgy Br. Edwards preached and Heckewelder held the congregation meeting.

Monday, 26. Br. David held early service. To-day many brethren went to the salt-springs to boil salt, not far by water, and by land only some seven miles.

Thursday, 29. After the early service, in which, likewise, mention was made of the protection and manifold oversight of the Saviour for us through the service of the dear angels, we experienced the same in an extraordinary way. A musket went off in a boy's hands, and the ball went under the arm of another boy who stood in front of the first, but only grazed him, so that the fright was greater than the harm. The boy who was hit screamed so that everybody thought he must be mortally wounded.

Our Chippewa, who often comes here, when he came to-day, asked an Indian brother whether we still thought of going away this autumn, and when he got no for an answer, for the Indians had told us not to go away, there being yet no peace, and that we should do best to stay here, the Chippewa replied: "I knew that very well, and therefore I told you it was good you should stay here a day longer. The Indians, however," he said farther, "are not the cause, they would not stand in your way, but the blame is Mr. McKee's, who, in council in Detroit, has made you over to the Shawanese, and told them he did not like to see us going again to our towns. If then they saw us going over the lake, they should take us, turn us about, and bring us into the Indian land, wherever they saw fit. The Shawanese wished to give us over to the Wyandots, who live near Detroit, and told them they were near at hand, and if they saw us going by, they could stop us, and show us another way, but they refused, and would have nothing to do with it." The Chippewa said he had heard this with his own ears, and been present at the negotiation. We had already, at different times, and from different Indians of all sorts of nations, heard the same thing, had also spoken with McKee about it, but he disclaimed and denied it, and assured us of his friendship, but now we see it is true, and he continues, behind our backs, secretly to stir up the Indians against us, as he has been the head-leader of all the Indian hostilities against us. If this is so, how is it advisable and possible for us to go away? We are given over to the Indians, that they may again plunder us and treat us according to their will, for this would not remain undone since the power is given them so to do. We cannot believe that the Indians could so have thought out all these lies, and that every thing is unfounded. We must, therefore, yet delay and wait for better times. It is as if Satan sought to hem in our way over the lake, and as if it pleased him not that we should again go there. We have further heard that he is reported to have said that if the Wyandots had known that Br. Edwards was going to Pittsburg they would have killed him. This also he denied. As soon as Br. Edwards started, however, he let the Wyandots know, and gave them a hint they could do something if they wished, and Samuel heard this on this journey.

Saturday, Oct. 1. The brethren came home from the salt-lick, having boiled a good lot of excellent salt, which is just the thing for them, salt being here a scarce thing.

Sunday, 2. David preached. Edwards held the congregation meeting.

Saturday, 8. This week all the brethren were busy harvesting their fields. In spite of a very dry summer we have a moderate and yet quite good harvest, though not so good as it would have been if it had rained more, but we are thankful for it. This week Ignatius, Renatus, and John went over Lake Erie hunting. Some went out salt-boiling. By land it is only six or seven miles.

Sunday, 9. Heckewelder preached, and David held the congregation meeting. The (chapel) servant's office was again given to Luke and A. Charity. They had already served in Schönbrunn.

Monday, 10. Several began making canoes, therewith to earn clothing for the winter, instead of hunting. The sisters were at home, industriously harvesting, with which this week they will for the most part be done, and have had on the whole a very good harvest, so that they have all wherewith to live.

Friday, 14, was the burial of the little child who died yesterday, A. Maria, daughter of Samuel and Sara Nan-ticoke, two months old, less six days. Last night, as also two days ago at night, we had hard thunder-storms, one after the other, till morning, and in our grave-yard a tree was struck and torn to splinters. The autumn this year is unusually warm, like summer, and thus far we have had only a light frost, but much stormy weather.

Sunday, 16. David preached, and Edwards held the congregation meeting.

Thursday, 20. Yesterday Peter, with two others, went to Sandusky to get our bell, there buried, but to-day we had news from Detroit that the Wyandots had killed the traders in the Tuscarawas and seized all their goods. We heard at the same time that the Americans had come already to the Shawanese towns, and that another party was on its way to Lower Sandusky. Since now the country seems so restless, we sent an express to call back Peter and his company, that they might not come to trouble, for in these troublous circumstances it is no time to go there. The States, as we hear, offer the nations both peace and war, to choose which they will.

Sunday, 23. Early in the morning Samuel and Adam came from the Fort, and confirmed the above news. Edwards preached about the king's reckoning with his servants, and David held the congregation meeting.

Wednesday, 26. Some brethren came back from Detroit. McKee asked Joshua, who came from there, whether we should go over the lake this autumn. He answered no, that we had heard from the Shawanese, Mohicans, Delawares, not to go, but to stay here, as there was yet no peace. All, however, agreed in this, that he, McKee, would not have us go to our towns, and had said to the Indians that if we went, they should lay hands on us and bring us another way. The Chippewas had also told us this, and since all nations spoke in the same tone, it must indeed be true. None of us white brethren could well tell him this without incurring danger, but he must have heard it from an Indian, for they can tell him what they wish and think, but he denied every thing, saying the Indians told horrible lies. We see that we have a secret foe in him. The Governor, who was our friend, is dead, and there is then almost no authority that regards right. He can do what he will, without giving account to any one. The way is closed to us. How is it possible for us to go away from here? We shall always be held in captivity. Yet if men close the way, Jesus opens it with might; herewith must we console ourselves.

Thursday, 27. Br. Edwards went to Detroit on business, from which place came,

Saturday, 29, Peter, by whom we heard it had been very stormy on the lake, and that Br. Edwards did not get out of the river until this morning.

Sunday, 30. David preached and Heckewelder held the congregation meeting.

Monday, 31. Abraham, Samuel, and several others went to Detroit to sell canoes; others went out hunting, so that few remain here.

Wednesday, Nov. 2. Edwards returned from Detroit. He had a good and successful journey, considering the stormy weather of this time of year.

Sunday, 6. Edwards preached. Through Samuel, who came from Detroit, by way of Pittsburg, by the kindness of Mr. Wilson, we had letters from Br. Ettwein, one from Br. Reichel from Europe, and others, to our heartfelt joy. In the afternoon was the communion quarter-hour, and the congregation meeting from the Scripture-verse: O Lord, how great are thy works, and thy thoughts are very deep.

Monday, 7. A trader's wife, Sally Hans, came here to sell goods, and stayed until the 10th. She took in from the brethren seventy bushels of corn for goods. She spoke with Samuel about her land on the east side of St. Clair, whereof she would be glad to give us a strip.

Thursday, 10 and Friday, 11. We spoke in regard to the Lord's supper. We found the brethren, to our joy and thankfulness to the Saviour, in a blessed way, walking with him. The brethren repaired our meeting-house.

Saturday, 12. We had a gracious communion, blessed by his dear presence. Jacob was present, partaking for the first time. The Saviour gives us especial joy in our young people, so that five are now communion brothers, one after the other, and a joy to us.

Sunday, 13. We asked from our dear Lord, the Elder of his churches, gracious absolution for our faults, transgressions, and shortcomings, adored him anew with our whole heart, and begged him farther, as a true shepherd and head, to make himself known to us, to show himself to us, to interest himself in us, inwardly and outwardly, and to help us, that his will may be done on earth as in heaven; during this tears spoke more than the mouth. He made himself known to us, and was evidently among us. In the evening Br. Edwards held the congregation meeting.

Monday, 14. By Br. Heckewelder, who went to Detroit, we wrote, by way of Pittsburg to Bethlehem. [These letters did not go through.] We had reason for doubting about these letters getting through, since we had very bad news from over the lake, namely, that between Pittsburg and Cuyahoga six traders had been killed and robbed, so that the passage is inevitably stopped. Ah, may the Saviour soon send us his noble peace!

Tuesday, 15. Most of the brethren went hunting. Br. Schebosh and some others went to Detroit; a few remain at home.

Wednesday, 16. Heckewelder returned from Detroit. The above news that traders have been killed is false, and, as we hear, things are not so bad in the Indian land as we have heard, but the trouble is, the Mingoes and Cherokees are making a plot. It is said the Indians are not hostilely disposed towards whites, but only towards Kentuckians. There is something in this whole matter which we cannot well make out. Traders go into the Indian land from Detroit as many as will, and nothing hinders them, but we dare not, we are not permitted to go away, and we must still have patience.

Saturday, 19. Three days ago the first cold weather came; up to that time we had a very fine, warm, dry, pleasant autumn; but the Detroit people prophesy a hard winter and deep snow.

Sunday, 20. Br. Edwards preached, and David held the congregation meeting from the Scripture-verse:

Wednesday, 23. Schebosh and A. Johanna, who went to Detroit a week ago, came back, having been much delayed by stormy weather. In Detroit there is much talk about a new war, and many would like to see it. Be this as it may, we see that it is better to be here than to be again in danger of falling into the hands of the savages; for this they have long been encouraged, and we are given over to them if we cross the lake. Upon what grounds we are held here like prisoners we know not.

Thursday, 24. We got the first lasting snow, which was just the thing for our hunters; thus far we have had a very dry autumn.

Sunday, 27. Heckewelder preached the advent sermon about the coming of our Lord into the flesh, and Edwards held the congregation meeting.

Monday, 28. Most of the brethren went hunting, and the sisters at home provided themselves with wood.

Wednesday, 30. By the Scripture-verse: Lord, thou hast been favorable unto thy land ; thou hast brought back the captivity of Jacob, the brethren were reminded that we have experienced similar circumstances, which are not yet quite passed, and have reason to recommend ourselves anew to him, to remind him that in former times he has done much for us, and has shown us compassion, and to entreat him to do yet more and more, that we may not lose hope and confidence in him.

Saturday, Dec. 3. Many of the brethren came home, and for the most part had all shot something, so that they have meat and shoes, which last is a prime article, for until now they have had to buy skins for shoes in Detroit.

Sunday, 4. David preached about the Saviour of the heathen, who is come to fulfil the prophecies given to the heathen by the prophets. Edwards held the congregation meeting Yesterday and the day before the snow fell a foot deep, and last night came on a thaw with rain, so that the snow almost all went off.

Monday, 5. The brethren got in wood for us, for we have no horses.

Tuesday, 6. Most of the brethren went off bear-hunting, and Brs. David and Edwards to build a sugar-hut, the weather was so good.

Wednesday, 7. Samuel and Adam to the Fort, whence the latter came back on the 9th, bringing news that in the settlement and in Detroit bad sicknesses and the small-pox prevailed from which many died. People in Detroit, who wish us well, wrote to us we should let as few of our Indians as possible go there, that the pest might not be brought to our town. The English people in Detroit at last begin to become pious, and believe the sickness is a punishment from God. They came together in the Council House, and had something read to them and are thinking about a church and a preacher.

Sunday, 11. Instead of the sermon Br. David read to the brethren something from the Gospel. This week there was rain and a thaw. The snow went off and the ground was quite bare.   Edwards held the congregation meeting, and Joshua translated for the first time.

Monday, 12.   David held early service.   Samuel came back from Detroit, bringing news that a couple of strange Indians, who had bought something in the town and of whom no one knew whence or of what nation they were, for they spoke not a word, killed two merchants below the town when they went away.   What will come from this, or what it means, time will show, but this circumstance caused much alarm and fright among the people.

Thursday, 15.   Most of the brethren came back from hunting.   This year they have made something by it, at least that they have meat to eat and skins for shoes, for last year they never once got so much.

Saturday, 17.   Since the weather was very fine, and for this time of year warm, the sisters were away generally this week, and made some sugar.   The ground was clear of snow, and the weather extraordinarily fine.

Sunday, 18.   Br. David preached about the joy of believers in the Lord, who was clad in our poor flesh and blood, and has reconciled us to God through his sufficient sacrifice, and has brought us the peace of being in God's mercy.   To the communion brethren the Lord's supper was announced for next Saturday, and they were invited thereto as thirsty souls.   Heckewelder held the congregation meeting from the Scripture-verse.

Monday, 19.   Some brethren went to lay out and make a new and straight road to Detroit.

Tuesday, 20.   It rained all day.

Friday, 23.   From Detroit we got the cheerful news that the last treaty with the Indian nations on the Kauawha[1] had been well and good for the benefit of the country, so that there is good hope of a lasting peace with the nations.   This news was of importance to us,

---

[1] Zeisberger probably refers to the treaty made with the Indians early in 1785 at Fort McIntosh (Beaver), Pa.   This treaty, and the act of Congress in pursuance thereof, wherein provision is made for the Moravian Indians, can be found in Albach's Western Annals, pp. 433–438.

for we now could hope that this circumstance would build us a way over the lake, which till now has been closed to us.

Saturday, 24. Christmas we began with a love-feast, rejoiced in the birth of our Saviour, who for love of us, poor and wretched beings, clad himself in our poor flesh and blood, thanked him for his blessed incarnation, sufferings, and death, whereby he hath brought us eternal redemption, and adored him upon our knees. Thereupon the communicants enjoyed his body and blood in his holy supper with comforted and joyous hearts.

Sunday, 25. After the communion liturgy, the sermon which Br. Edwards preached, was about the announcement of the angels to the shepherds: Behold, I bring you good tidings of great joy. Then the children in their service showed their joy over the little Child in the manger, sang to him with joyful hearts, and brought to him their childish thanks for his birth and incarnation. To a poor Shawanese family in our neighborhood our brethren gave somewhat for their necessity, each one contributing, for which they were thankful and glad.

Tuesday, 27. Learning that Mr. Duncan, of Pittsburg, was in Detroit, we sent to him Br. Schebosh with a letter, and also to converse with him; he came back Thursday the 29th, bringing us a letter from him also, and a letter from Br. John Jungmann from Pittsburgh, from both which we perceived that things for us were come there, but that we could not get them this winter. What made us feel worst was that he had forgotten in Pittsburg a packet of letters he intended bringing us, and now we know not after how long a time we shall get them. We heard at the same time that two days ago two whites had been murdered, and that the Chippewas had done both these and the former murders.

31. Towards midnight we assembled for the end of the year, thanked our dear Lord for all the kindness, goodness, and mercy we had enjoyed from him, that he had cared for us, soul and body, and had given us the grace that our hearts could daily feed on the word of his atone-

ment and passion, and we begged him to grant us this again, and to send us such hearts that we should ever hunger and thirst more and more for this; that he in outward matters had blessed the work of our hands, and had lent us a good harvest, so that we might not starve nor complain of want; that he had let us, who are only strangers among strange people, enjoy peace and quiet, has been with us, and has shown himself among us a gracious, loving Saviour; that the Indians among whom we live and to whom we are strangers, have put nothing in our way, much less molested us. We asked his forgiveness of all our faults, failings, and shortcomings when we have lagged behind and could have done better, whereupon we held comfort and assurance from him through his Holy Spirit, and entered then joyfully upon the new year.

There were baptized this year two adult women and two girls; to the communion were admitted two brothers and two sisters; one has died here, a child, A. Maria, daughter of Samuel and Sara Nanticoke; the inhabitants here on the Huron River are 117 Indian souls.

CHAPTER VI.

1786.

CLINTON RIVER, MICHIGAN—VOYAGE OVER LAKE ERIE—ON THE CUYAHOGA.

Sunday, Jan. 1. Heckewelder preached about the name of Jesus as our Saviour. In the service for all the baptized brethren, we gave ourselves anew to be entirely his own, in all our faults and failings to hold fast by him, and not to leave him. We promised him with hand and mouth that nothing should separate us from him, nor tribulation, nor danger, nor fear, nor fright till we saw him face to face. For our daily Scripture-verses we took in use last year's, and in the evening Br. Edwards held the congregation meeting from the first Scripture-verse : Cause me to know the way wherein I should walk : for I lift up my soul unto thee. Lead us in accordance with thy grace and the Gospel.

Monday, 2. By Samuel, we sent letters for Bethlehem to Mr. Duncan, in Detroit, to forward. This occasion was one much wished for, and we were glad of it, for here people are few to whom letters can be intrusted. We heard from Tucker that the Chippewa chief sent us word that he would come here soon after New Year's day, and had something to say to us. Of this we were glad, for we had long wished an opportunity to speak to him or them.

Friday, 6. Early at morning prayer was sung for the first time in Indian : Peace be to this congregation—Peace to every soul therein. We asked for the near presence of the Saviour, his blessing, and his bloody fulness for to-day; and recommended ourselves and all churches among the heathen to his mercy. Thereupon was a service for the baptized from to-day's text : That which had not been told them shall they see, and that which they had not heard shall they consider.

Welcome, dear brothers, welcome—To the life from Jesus'
wounds. Since he has announced to us salvation in his
wounds, and has also sent us hearts to receive and to
believe, and since through belief we are come to enjoyment of the same and rest therein, we can, and will also,
wheresoever we have opportunity, confidently preach to
those heathen who are yet in darkness and blindness, that
grace is to be found in Jesus only, that they shall be welcome to salvation in Jesus' wounds, which he has won for
them also, and we will invite them thereto. At the love-
feast, at which also a white man was present, our brethren
were reminded of our other heathen churches, and what
the Saviour had done among them, in so many places, by
his grace and the service of the brothers. Br. Heckewelder ended the services of the day with a short discourse
over the Scripture-verse: Turn away mine eyes from beholding vanity.

Ah, give us dull eyes for things of no profit, and eyes
full of clearness in all thy truth. It was a day of grace
and blessing for our brethren. Those who had their baptismal day on this day, came together and invited the assistants to a love-feast, sang together, and rejoiced in their
election, just as also happened during the holidays, for
they celebrate the day of their baptism as their birthday in
the church, not knowing their real birthdays.

Sunday, 8. Br. David preached about giving over the
heart to the Saviour for the sake of the mercy he has shown
us, that he has sacrificed himself on the cross for our sins,
and had reconciled us by his blood. To the boys, on their
day, was the history read: When Jesus was twelve years
old, etc., and by occasion of the text: Jesus increased in
wisdom and stature, and in favor with God and man, they
were reminded to take the boy, Jesus, as their model and
example, who was obedient and subject to his parents, and
since they were come to those years when they were capable and began to think about things, they should not
think about bad and sinful things, but about good things,
as they heard the boy, Jesus, had done, who went into
the temple, listened, and inquired about the Scripture.

Tuesday, 10. Yesterday and to-day some went out again hunting.

Saturday, 14. Three Chippewas came here, one a chief's son, the other a captain, to speak with our Indians. Before this already we had heard that the chief himself would come to tell us something, and, as it seemed, these were sent. They said the chief of the land on the river was dead [for among the Chippewas each chief, and there are many of them, has his own district. of land which he owns], and his son was now chief, for with them the position of chief is hereditary. This one had it in mind to say to us towards spring to go over the lake again away from his land; that they indeed thought not thus, for they loved their grandfather, and wished him to remain firmly seated there; they wanted to tell us this, so that if it happened, we should already know about it, and it would not come upon us unexpectedly. They said farther, that to the north-west were bad Indians, who had already killed many white people, whom they called Virginians, and to the objection that no Virginians lived in this neighborhood, but English only, they answered that they called all white people, English and Americans, the French only excepted, Virginians; that they had already sent a message to the bad Indians to cease, but they gave no heed, and if they did not cease they would be compelled to fight against them ; that our Indians should not go far in that direction, so as not to come to harm, but should they hear they had designs against us, they would inform us and tell us that we might rather go away. Though our Indian brethren spoke much with them, they could not so perfectly understand every thing as we should have been glad to have them, and as we wanted to say something to them, and had something to say, we invited them to come again after a few days, and to bring with them our neighbor, Mr. Tucker, who knows Chippewa well, and this they promised to do. They were present at the sermon Sunday the 15th, about which they inquired yesterday when they came. They brought with them a cask of rum, which they gave to our Indians, asking for corn, this we gave them, the whole town bringing them a fair supply together, more than they had expected, for which they thanked us much and often. When they went away we gave them again their cask of rum on the way, and this they were also glad to receive.

Sunday, 15. Edwards preached; David held the congregation meeting.

Tuesday, 17. Susanna came from the bush, where her husband was hunting, and said there were many Chippewas·in the neighborhood. Our people began again to bring up all sorts of stories and lies, to make one another afraid, saying the Chippewas would do us harm.

Thursday, 19. The Chippewa chief came here again, as he had told us, with three others besides, and the day after,

Friday, 20, Mr. Tucker also, who understands Chippewa, but he said at once that, so far, as they spoke by strings or belts, he could not and dared not interpret, for he incurred danger. They came together, and the chief first delivered a long introductory speech; that their father had ,invited us here, and had arranged with them (the Chippewa chiefs) that we should live here on this river, and they had established us here so long to dwell, until there should again be peace. When he had spoken thus far he drew out a string of wampum, and now we should hear what he had to say; but he was stopped by Tucker, who told him he dared not interpret such speeches, if they had any such thing to say, they must go to the Fort to McKee, and arrange their matters there, and thus it ended, and we could hear nothing, but it is probable they wanted to tell us to go away from here in the spring. Thus Indians dare not once speak together and say any thing one to another, except in the presence of McKee, for none of us white brethren was present; and yet the Indians are a free people, they counsel together, do and act without control; and so they went away again, having accomplished nothing.

Sunday, 22. David preached and held the children's service. Heckewelder held the congregation meeting.

Tuesday, 24. A couple of Mingoes came here, who told

16

again war-stories, that in the spring, without fail, an Indian war would break out; at the same time they said the Americans would come to Detroit in the spring. Edwards held early service.

Wednesday, 25. Heckewelder held early service. Several Indian brethren went to Detroit.

Sunday, 29. Heckewelder preached about good seed in the field. To the communicants announcement was made of the Lord's supper for next Saturday. Edwards held the congregation meeting.

Wednesday, Feb. 1. A pair of English people, who came here yesterday in a sleigh from Detroit, namely, a man and a woman, entreated us to marry them. As we could not well refuse, there being no clergyman in Detroit, and if there was, one could not justly put the people off, we had to give our consent, and since they brought from Detroit testimonials, and bound themselves to protect us from damage, we did it, and Heckewelder married them,

Thursday, 2, whereupon the next day they went back to Detroit.

Friday, 3. Yesterday and to-day was speaking, to which the Saviour gave grace,

Saturday, 4, and we had thereupon a very blessed communion, accompanied with his near presence. We were very much put to shame, for it had looked as if some brethren would have to remain from it, but the Saviour so brought it about that no one remained away. Three sisters, Jacobina, Anna Paulina, and Helena, were candidates, to whom it was a great blessing.

Sunday, 5. After the communion liturgy Br. David preached. Heckewelder held the congregation meeting.

Monday, 6. David and Heckewelder went to Detroit, whence they,

Wednesday, 8, came back. They spoke there with the new commandant, Maj. Ancrum, and told him that Col. de Peyster had settled us with our Indians on the Huron River, in the year '82, until there should again be peace. The year before, in the spring, we had thought of moving back over the lake, but had been advised by Gov. Hay and

McKee to wait until autumn, as no peace had yet been made among the Indians; this we had done, but in the autumn, seeing and hearing that there was no better outlook, we had remained, and our departure now depended upon what he should advise; he would best know how things looked in the Indian land and how the nations were disposed; if no cause for alarm or danger was at hand, we should be glad to settle in our appointed place next spring, for we saw we could not stay here, and the Chippewas would gladly see us away. He answered that at present things looked as favorable among the nations as ever. The Shawanese, who hitherto had come to no treaty with the States, had now consented, and also the other nations, and he hoped soon to have good news from them; he saw no difficulty, and no cause for anxiety, why we could not go; if we went he would send in our behalf a message to the Indians that they should not molest us. To the same purport spoke also Capt. McKee, whom we called upon, so that we saw circumstances would arrange themselves if it should be true, for hitherto it has not been time. Every one had told us that he was a man hard to treat with, but we found him quite otherwise. Moreover, Br. David baptized on the 7th, in this city, Elizabeth, Nathaniel Williams' child, and Heckewelder one, by name, Peter.

Saturday, 11. Some gentlefolk came from Detroit visiting, among others Mr. Dolson, to look at our settlement, who has a wish to buy it.

Sunday, 12. At the sermon were present some of those who came yesterday from Detroit, but these, like those here generally, are merely people of the world, who inquire neither about religion nor God's service, but are worse than heathen. In the afternoon service Br. David baptized the little daughter of Br. Jacob Schebosh and his wife Christiana, born day before yesterday, on the 10th, with the name Elizabeth, at which service also the white people were present. Br. Edwards held the congregation meeting.

Monday, 13. The Detroiters went back to Detroit.

Wednesday, 15. The brethren began to make preparations for sugar-making, going to their sugar-camp, for the weather was beautiful and mild.

Saturday, 18. Both to-day and yesterday Frenchmen came here to buy meat from the Indians. We heard that murdering Indians are said to be again in the settlement, who are out for murder, and are said to have again killed two whites [was false]. So the murderers are said to have grown to six, when before they were only three. The Chippewa chief had us warned of them.

Sunday, 19. Heckewelder preached about the sower, and David held the congregation meeting.

Tuesday, 21. We heard from Detroit, that on account of a band of Chippewas it was unsafe in that neighborhood, and that the Governor had issued a proclamation, warning all the inhabitants not to go far from the city without a guard and arms. We also learned, as was said to us, from one McCormick, who came from Pittsburg, that there was given to our Indians land on Licking creek, which falls into the Muskingum some forty miles below Lichtenau, instead of Schönbrunn, Gnadenhütten, and Salem, but how far this story has truth we must wait farther to learn.

Thursday, 23. Frenchmen came here to sell flour and apples for all sorts of things, and had a good trade.

Saturday, 25. Mr. Dolson came from Detroit and also two Frenchmen for the same purpose, remaining here over Sunday. An English woman from the settlement came here with her child, five months old, and asked for its baptism, and Br. David baptized it Sunday, the 26th, with the name John. Br. Edwards preached, and David held the congregation meeting. This whole week cold and snowy weather.

Tuesday, 28. We ended the month with praise and thanks to the Lord, who, during the winter, had done us great good, outwardly and inwardly. Thomas' child in the bush got the measles.

Thursday, March 2. Some people had offered to buy our improvements, in case we got permission from the major. We applied to him and asked, and now we had

news from Detroit that Maj. Ancrum, the present com-
mander, would come here with Mr. Askin to make us a
visit.

Saturday, 4. The major came, with a couple of officers
and Mr. Askin, in their sleighs. We had prepared for
them a separate house and room, and furnished them as
well as we could. They looked about our town to-day,
visited in the Indian houses and took notice of every
thing, examined a part of our fields, and especially the
country, which was the main object of their visit. Our
town and its situation and the whole neighborhood pleased
them exceedingly well. They had not thought of finding
such high and dry land here, and the work we have done
here in three and a half years was a wonder to them. The
major and Mr. Askin, each of whom had a grant from
the king of 2,000 acres, wished to have it taken up here
for them and to pay us and our Indians for our improvements and work what was fair and right. The major will
in the spring, as soon as the lake is open, take us all over
to Cuyahoga in the king's ships. He and all with him
were exceedingly friendly to us and showed us their good-
will. The next morning they went back again, very well
satisfied.

Sunday, 5. Br. David preached, and afterwards in the
second service announced to the brethren the Lord's supper for next Saturday, and Heckewelder held the congregation meeting.

Monday, 6. Heckewelder and Schebosh went on business to Detroit to arrange all kinds of things about our
departure. They returned on the 8th, Heckewelder having arranged with Mr. Askin provisionally, it being agreed
that we and our Indians shall have 400 dollars for our
houses and improvements, we whites one half and the Indian brethren the other. Heckewelder baptized on the
7th Isaac Jones' child, George David, and another, Dr. An-
tony's, Louisa Dorothy.

Wednesday, 8. We had, by way of the Shawanese
towns, letters from Br. Schweinitz (John C. A. de S.) of
Oct. 12, '85, from Brs. Jungmann and Sensemann, of Oct.

8th, and his son, John Sensemann, of Nov. 1st, from Pittsburg.

Thursday, 9. The surveyor, Lieut. Frey, came with his
company to measure off four thousand acres of land, in
which shall be included all our fields and our town; of
this they made the beginning the next day.

Saturday, 11. We had the holy communion, accompanied by the near presence of the Saviour. Our dear
Lord blessed us in an extraordinary way. Three sisters,
Jacobina, Anna Paulina, and Helena, were for the first
time partakers, and three others, namely, Renatus, the
Mohican, his wife, Mary Magdalene, and the widow, Elizabeth, looked on for the first time, and this caused great
joy with all the brethren and with us. There came again
four sledges with Frenchmen here, who brought with them
their wives and children, merely to see our place, which is
now quite the fashion since the major and Mr. Askin have
been here.

Sunday, 12. After the communion liturgy, during the
sermon from the Gospel about the Canaanite woman, were
present Lieut. Frey and the ship captain, Mr. Anderson.

Monday, 13. Our Indian brethren, who have already,
during the winter, laid out and cut through a straight road
to Detroit, went out to clear the same, so that sleds and
carts can pass through, and to meet a party of road-makers
whom the major has sent up from below for the same
purpose, that the road may be ready as soon as may be.
The sisters all went to the sugar-huts.

Thursday, 16. The brothers got done road-making.

Friday, 17. The surveyor, Frey, and Capt. Anderson,
who have done here all they wished, went back to Detroit, measuring, on their way back, the road with chain.
They have measured the creek, which is still frozen, with
all its turnings, half way to the lake, of which, as well as
of the appearance of our town, he has made an accurate
chart and sketch.

Sunday, 19. Heckewelder preached; few of the brethren were at home, being in their sugar-huts, for the trees
were freely running. The brethren who have helped

make the road came home, and it has been found to be twenty-three and one-half miles from our town to Detroit, straight through the bush. The Indian brethren were well paid for the work they have here done. This forenoon the brethren from over the river came here from their sugar-huts, on the ice, and in a couple of hours it was all open; they went over in canoes on their return.

Tuesday, 21. Two Frenchmen came to look at the place, sent by Askin and the Governor, for in the future they will live here, each one renting a plantation together with a house. As we hear, our place will remain a town, and those who come here will live together, in this way all our houses being used.

Friday, 24. To-day and yesterday the weather was very stormy, and some brethren in the bush, in their sugar-camp, experienced the manifest protection of the Saviour and the dear angels, for the wind struck down many trees, which fell on A. Johanna's sugar-hut, crushed it in, and she was in the greatest danger of being struck, but suffered no harm.

Sunday, 26. Br. Edwards preached. Inasmuch as most of the brethren were not at home yesterday we celebrated to-day yesterday's momentous day (Annunciation), read the history, and brought to him our joyful thanks for his meritorious holy incarnation, in which all of us, children, young and old, have so great part, and yet enjoy it. Thomas' family came here; two children who have had the measles have recovered, and they go no farther.

Monday, 27. We congratulated Sister Sara Heckewelder[1] on her birthday, at a love-feast.

Tuesday, 28. The Indian brethren went to the lake to get their canoes into the water.

Friday, 31. We got news that the Chippewas have brought the two murderers to Detroit and surrendered them, that thereupon they were held under guard, when

---

[1] Sara Ohneberg had been married to John Heckewelder, July 4, 1780, by Grube, at Salem. "It was, doubtless, the first wedding of a white couple in the present State of Ohio." De Schweinitz' Life of Zeisberger, p. 478.

one of them, trying to get away, was shot by the watch, the other is under guard.

Sunday, April 2. Early at the break of day Heckewelder and William went to Detroit. Br. David preached about the effectual sacrifice of Jesus for our sins. In the second service he baptized, with the name Philippina, the little daughter of Adolphus and Susanna, born day before yesterday.

Tuesday, 4. Heckewelder came back from Detroit, bringing us news that we could celebrate here in quiet the holidays, but immediately afterwards we must break up here and go to Detroit, where a ship would be ready to take us and our Indians to Cuyahoga.

Wednesday, 5. There came here a couple of strolling Germans, who came from the States to Detroit to see the country, and they are disposed to settle here.

Saturday, 8. The brethren got done making sugar.

Sunday, 9. Br. Edwards preached. Thereupon was a service for the communion brethren, and David held the congregation meeting. Two white people came here and examined the place and fields, wishing to settle here.

Monday, 10. The brethren went to the lake to get the canoes they have made, into the water.

Wednesday, 12. Speaking with the brethren. People from Detroit visited the place; many wish to move here.

Thursday, 13. On Maundy-Thursday we read in the evening the history of our Saviour's atonement struggle, agony of soul, and bloody sweat on the Mount of Olives, and of his being taken prisoner, whereby our hearts were melted at our debt of thanks towards him. The communion brethren had afterwards the washing of feet and then the holy sacrament of his body and blood in the night of his betrayal. Two sisters, Mary Magdalene and Elizabeth, were for the first time partakers, and Ignatius and his wife, Christina, were readmitted, he coming thereto for the first time since he is here.

Friday, 14. We passed Easter Friday in contemplation of all his sufferings, his bonds and buffets, his crown of thorns and scourgings, his countenance spit upon, and

what scoff, scorn, and revilings, passed over him in his crucifixion and martyr-death to the grave, and the reading of
the story was listened to with moved and melted hearts.
At his death, falling upon our knees, we read the liturgy,
brought to him our common thanks for all he had done
and suffered for us, and as we were in no position to make
him compensation therefor, we vowed to him that his
death, passion, and what he suffered for us, should never
leave our hearts till we saw him face to face.

Saturday, 15. The whole church had a love-feast, the
last one here.

Sunday, 16. Early in the morning we read the Easter
litany, partly in our chapel and partly in the grave-yard,
and then a portion of the story of the resurrection was
read. Heckewelder preached and David held the congregation meeting.

Monday, 17. In the evening came Capt. Anderson, whose
ship lay at the mouth of the river, which on Tuesday the
18th was laden with corn our Indians brought, which Mr.
Askin had bought here.

Wednesday, 19. We got ready for departure. White
people were already here, and among them one Cornwall
(from Connecticut), to whom over night our town and settlement were given, and who took possession.

Thursday, 20. After we had early, for the last time, assembled in our chapel, and thanked the Saviour upon our
knees for all the goodness we had enjoyed from him, and
farther committed ourselves to his mercy upon the journey, we loaded our canoes, and all went away together in
the afternoon. None of us all remained behind, save
Conner's family, who himself knew not whither to go, nor
what to do. In the evening we camped at the mouth of
the River Huron. It was just four years to-day that we
landed in Detroit, and in truth we could not do otherwise
than give the Saviour to recognize our thankful hearts for
all the kindnesses he had shown us, and that he had done
every thing so well with us. Our Scripture-verse read:
Casting all your care upon him. He who has chosen us

for himself well knows in what we are lacking,[1]—a proof
that he will farther be gracious to us, and that we shall
not find it needful to be anxious how things will go with
us in the future.   We left Conner's family behind.   How
strong we are ! How many have died, how many been born !

Friday, 21.   Early in the morning we went into Lake
St. Clair, and in the afternoon, with a good wind, came to
the outer end of the settlement, but the wind getting
strong and the waves running high, we had to lie still
to-day and all of the 22d.   The people in the neighborhood, French and English, came to visit us, and were
sorry at our moving away, and would rather we remained.

Sunday, 23.   The strong wind lessening, we started
early, and at noon came to Detroit with a fleet of twenty-
two canoes, most of them quite large.   Here we were well
received.   Since the ship in which we were to go had to
be repaired, we must wait some days here.

Wednesday, 26.   Br. David went to Capt. McKee and
told him our Indians would like to say something to the
Chippewa chiefs, many of whose people were in the city,
before they went away, and begged him to give them an
opportunity for this; this he did, telling the Chippewas to
keep themselves sober, for their grandfather (i. e, the
Delaware Indians) had something to say to them and
wished to shake hands with them.   They came, Thursday
the 27th, together, and our Indians made a speech to them,
expressing to them their thankfulness for receiving them
and allowing them to live near them on their land quietly
and peacefully more than four years ; they told them they
were now going back again over the lake to their former
home, and for confirmation of their speech gave them a
bunch of some 1,000 wampum.   One of the chiefs [they
were not all present] stood up with a string of wampum
in his hand, and said : "Grandfather, we love thee and
see not willingly that thou goest away from us.   We bind
thy legs together that thou canst not go forth, and say to
thee : "Turn again and abide by the River Huron.'"   We

---

[1] Collect.

looked upon this speech as a compliment, for hitherto we had ever heard that they would like to see us go away again, since our Indians took away their hunt. In the evening, however, came another chief from over the river, who was not in the council, who said to our Indians that they should give no heed to what the drunken Chippewa chief had said; he knew very well that from the beginning it was arranged that we should remain there until there was again peace; it was well we were again going over the lake and should be out of the way, and he gave us to understand they had yet something to settle with their father (i. e., the English) after we were gone. We sent back again to the chief his string of wampum.

It was resolved that one ship should take all of us to Cuyahoga, but we saw that one alone could not hold us all, and spoke about the matter to Mr. Askin, to whom sole charge herein was given by the commandant, who ordered that another one should go. All people in Detroit showed us their sorrow, not only that we, but also that our Indians were leaving them. These left a good reputation behind them, for all merchants in the city report that they have paid all their debts to the last penny, saying it could well enough be seen that they were an honorable people and better than all the inhabitants around Detroit, who do not like to pay their debts, and add thereto; that this was the fruit of the missionaries' labor. We were ourselves glad and thankful to the Saviour that none of our Indians remained a penny in debt, having always urged upon them to be mindful of this. This was pleasant. One family, namely, Thomas', who is very poor, but rich in children, was somewhat in debt and had nothing to pay with, for which he was much perplexed, complaining to us of his situation. His wife went walking with the children on the commons near the town, where she found a guinea, but did not know whether it was copper or gold until she heard from us. Thereupon he paid his debt and had still somewhat left, and we were as glad about it as he was.

Friday, 28. After we got our pass from the Major, who

gave us and our Indians provisions for the journey, and
had thanked him for the good services he had done us,
we went away at mid-day in the Beaver and Mackina
sloop. At first we had much difficulty in getting off on
account of the weeds with which we were surrounded,
and when we were come some seven miles, with a good
wind, we went aground under all sail, and had two hours'
work, with the help of the other ship, to get off again.
It was Capt. Anderson's written order, given in our presence, that he and all the ship-people should show themselves friendly to us, and treat us well, and that we should
inform them how they behaved towards us and our Indians;
that the captain should use all forethought and not put
us in danger, yes, if the wind were strong, rather to lessen
sail than to frighten the Indians; in short, as far as lay
in his power, to land us fortunately in Cuyahoga. In the
evening we came to anchor at the mouth of the river. The
captain put all the Indians ashore, for the ship was much
crowded, where they made them a fire and encamped. A
man by the name of Hasle, who lives there, and whose
child Heckewelder baptized, came from the Wyandot
town which we had gone by. The chief, who knew us,
and who two days before had come from the treaty with
the States, sent us word he wished to call upon us in the
morning before we started, probably to tell us something
about the treaty, for he had said to Hasle that never had
so stable and good a peace been made with the Indians as
was this; this was satisfactory and pleasant for us to hear,
but he had no sooner seen us than the captain lifted,

Saturday, 29, anchor early in the morning, and we went
into the lake, having wind from the side, quite a strong
wind too, and with few exceptions everybody was sea-sick.
Yet we came, towards evening, after sailing forty miles,
to Pudding (Put-in)-Bay, among the islands, when the
captain came to anchor in water six fathoms deep, for
from this point he had to change his course, and must
wait for a suitable wind, and here, moreover, the harbor
is good and safe protected from all winds. Here we stayed
till May [23d], for the captain would not venture to run

out unless he had a good wind, it being dangerous to come
on the coast except with a west or south-west wind. We
landed on the island every day, and remained till evening,
when we again went aboard ship. Two nights, also, we
encamped on land, for both ships were much crowded,
and if we passed the night on shipboard, half of us had
to sleep on deck, and it was well the weather was good
and not cold. In the evening, whenever it was possible,
we had our services. The Indians shot ducks and pigeons, and found wild potatoes and onions in abundance.
The captain and ship's crew fished, and got fish enough
for us and everybody. The island is good and fertile,
three miles long by two wide. South of it, about a mile
off, is another much larger, indeed there are many islands
here in the midst of the lake. There is much red cedar
timber here, much of which is taken to Detroit for ship-
building. The bank round about the island is quite a
high bank, like a fortification, which the sea-waves have
thrown up and formed. Our Indians started up deer, but
had no sight of them. There are many raccoons, but no
other game.

May, 5. The wind changed to the north-west and blew
hard. We were all ashore. The ships raised anchor, and
went to the east side of the island, out of the wind. Some
Indians wept, saying they were abandoned and left upon
the island, and that would be fulfilled which the savages
had always predicted, but we explained to them, and
changed our camp to the other side of the island, where
the ships lay.

Saturday, 6. Early, about two o'clock, we had a thunder-storm from the south. At break of day we were ordered to come aboard, but hardly was the first boat-load
aboard ship, when the wind sprang around to the north-
west, and it came on to blow hard. The ship nearest
land, the Beaver, was in danger of being driven on the
rocks, she was so near land ; she had to let her anchor go,
and by good luck she got by the rocks, and came to
anchor on the east side.

Friday, 12. We encamped on the east side. Towards

evening, when the wind went down, the captain got up his anchor again. Some of our Indian brethren began to be short of provisions. The 13th and 14th we encamped on the island.

Monday, 15. Early in the morning we saw three ships lying at anchor. The sloop, Felicity, from Detroit, had come in during the night, on her way to Fort Erie.

Wednesday, 17. The Felicity sailed with a north-west wind for Fort Erie. She had the Chippewa murderer aboard in irons; some of our Indians were there aboard and saw him. We remained at anchor, for the wind was not good for us, since it bore down directly upon the coast of Cuyahoga, making a high sea, so that the captain could not run in, for there is a sand-bank at the mouth of the river, and ships must have still water, if they want to get in, otherwise they are in danger of being wrecked on the bar, or we must then run to the north shore.

Thursday, 18. The wind was for a while favorable, but varied so much as to run all around the compass. Some Indians talked of making canoes to go to the nearest land south, and to leave the ship, but this would have been very venturesome, for, if a storm had arisen on the lakes, they would all have perished.

Friday, 19. Since the captain perceived the wind was changing to the south, we all had to go aboard in the afternoon. He made every preparation to put out into the lake, hoisted the boat on deck, and ran down to the extreme east end of the island, and came to anchor. Here we lay till two o'clock, and as the wind held, he ran out to sea, Saturday, the 20th. But, at ten o'clock, when we had come half way to Cuyahoga and saw the coast before us, the wind again veered to the east, and was very strong and the sea high, and almost everybody was sea-sick. The captain could do no better than turn about and seek our former haven. He signaled the Mackina, and we turned about, and came in the afternoon, fortunately, to our island again, where the brethren refreshed themselves.

Sunday, 21. We white brethren landed, and in the

evening went aboard again. We gave of our corn to the needy.

Monday, 22. In the night it blew very hard. The captain had his second anchor ready to let go should need require it.

Tuesday, 23. We had all to go aboard early. Both ships ran towards another island lying to the south, opposite the first, into a better harbor, where no wind could get at them, come from what quarter it might. Here they fastened the ships to the trees, so that we could go from the ship ashore, for the bank is quite steep and the water deep. Here the Indians got a new place to hunt, for they had already quite exhausted the game on the other island, and there was little more to be had, though there is no other game here than raccoons and pigeons. This island is as large again as the former. The harbor is called Hope's Cove, for the ship, Hope, passed the winter here, being frozen in. Our crew also began to run short of provisions, although till now they have caught fish for themselves and for us, if only they could. Here we built us huts, and thus we have always something to do. In camp we had our service.

Wednesday, 24. On Ascension Day we were comforted with the promise of our dear Lord that he would ever be with us, by sea and by land, also upon the islands in the midst of the lake. In our service we were made assured and aware of this.

Friday, 26. Wind and weather continued always as before—east wind, with rain. Our Indians got many fish and raccoons and shot ducks. To-day they saw Rocky Point, not far from Sandusky, very plainly over against this island. Ginseng root grows here in abundance, as if planted.

Saturday, 27. Early in the morning the wind was south-east. The captain prepared to run out, but it turned back again to the east, and we stayed still.

Sunday, 28. In the forenoon a boat came from Detroit, with three men, sent out to hunt us up, since the ships which they had long expected back stayed out so long, and

they conjectured they must have met with trouble. The
Beaver, the larger ship, got orders to go back to Detroit,
and the sloop, Mackina, to take us in two trips to Cuyahoga. This made us very uneasy, for in this way we saw
nothing else before us than to use up the whole summer
here on the lake in making our journey, and where should
we get any thing to eat for so many people? Still it was
well that we got some few supplies sent on with us, but
what were they among so many, for we had already supported our Indian brethren a week from our own stock,
and hoped day after day for relief. We took counsel with
both captains, for the reason of the order they had now
received was not evident to us, and proposed to them that
the Mackina in two trips should take us to the Sandusky
shore, and should then go to Cuyahoga with the baggage
as soon as the wind was favorable. This the captains not
only approved, but also held for the best. Both ships were
to-day unloaded, the Beaver for her return and the Mackina in order to take the people to Sandusky.

Monday, 29. Early at daybreak the Beaver was towed
out of the harbor, and then got under sail for Detroit.
She belongs to the North-West Trading Company, and is
not a royal ship, on which account she was to go back and
without delay to Michilimackinac. The captain had expressed his sorrow to us that he could not take us to Cuyahoga. In the afternoon Br. David and his wife, with the
greater part of the Indian brethren, went aboard the Mackina and sailed away. Br. Heckewelder and his wife and
Br. Edwards remained with the rest on the island till the
ship came back to take them. We sailed around the south
side of the island. The captain hoped with the wind to
reach Sandusky, but it was impossible. We were forced
to cast anchor at the point of the island, and since in the
evening the wind got too strong, and he did not consider
it advisable to lie at anchor in the open lake, we had to run
a piece of the way back below the island out of the wind,
where we lay till morning.

Tuesday, 30. The wind had gone down, and it was
very calm, but contrary. The captain saw no possibility

of coming to Sandusky with the wind, and wanted to run back again to the harbor. We begged him to set us ashore on the nearest land opposite us, which he did at our request, holding towards the land, and as the wind was very weak the sisters and brothers took the paddles, a store of which they had made on the island, and towed the ship to the land. By mid-day we were all landed, and the captain turned straightway back to get the rest. Hardly had we encamped when ten Tawas, out hunting, came to us, who were much amazed to meet such a number of people in a place where far and wide was no way nor road. We told them our situation, and pointed out to them our ship, which could yet be plainly seen, that had brought us hither. We gave them food, and they shared their meat with us and showed us also how to steer through the bush to Sandusky, for near the lake or strand we cannot get along. We learned that it was some sixteen miles to the mouth of the Sandusky. In the evening we had our service and consideration of the Scripture-verse: The Lord shall increase you more and more, you and your children. We still saw our ship at anchor near a little island. Here those who came after took more fish than they wanted or could bring with them. The water swarmed with fish, so that with a sharp stake we could not strike without hitting some.

Wednesday, 31. We made up our bundles early and prepared for departure. Each one had to carry his full burden, for we had to provide ourselves for two weeks, as we did not know when the ship would get to us. Br. David and Susanna, as well as the others, moved off. Samuel went ahead and was pilot. The hindmost had the easiest time, for they found a beaten way before them. At noon we came to a deep, swampy creek, and as there was no chance to make a canoe, all had to get wet up to the arms and take their bundles on their heads, that they might not be wet. David and Susanna were carried over by four men upon a litter, hastily made. In the evening, as we were getting our camp ready, a deer was shot and

18

distributed about the camp. Though the journey was
hard and the brethren weary, yet were they cheerful and
pleased to be again on firm land and in their element.

Thursday, June 1. Early in the morning we soon came to
Sandusky Bay, which we had to cross. It is quite wide
[a mile], and then we had to lie still, the wind being
strong and the waves very high. Many French live here
about the bay and on the islands in the bay, to whom Br.
David went, to see if they could put us over, but they had
neither boats nor canoes suitable for this, none in which
more than two or three persons could go, and we had to
turn to the Ottawas, who lived on the lake, who were
willing to lend us their canoes, in part bark canoes, for
pay.

Friday, 2. We had still to stay in camp here, the wind
blowing from the east straight into the bay, and the waves
running very high. In the forenoon Abraham came with
two families after us, and joined our party. Heckewelder,
with the rest, came by water, in bark canoes, which they
made, as soon as wind and weather were favorable.
Brs. Schebosh and Edwards, with the Indian brethren,
Cornelius, the blind Ephraim, and the aged Beata, remained on the ship, being unable to go by land, and came
to us in Cuyahoga with the baggage. To-day and yesterday we had many visits from Ottawas, who live just by us.
In the evening they had a dance, and when none of our
Indians went to the dance, at the end of it they came out
into our camp, seeking to lead astray our women. Some
came to Br. David and said to him they would like to have
some of our women. He told them, for one understood
Delaware very well, that they must know that our Indians
no longer lived in the heathenish way they did; that they
should not trouble themselves about them, that we would
not grant them their wish, whereupon they went away.
In the evening we had our service and consideration of
the Scripture-verse: For thou hast delivered my soul from
death, mine eyes from tears, and my feet from falling.

Saturday, 3. At daybreak we got ready, for the wind
had somewhat gone down, and after we had gone full three

miles upon a point of land, on both sides of which was the lake, we crossed over in the little canoes, which had to make several trips, till at eight o'clock we had all got over. We went then the whole day along the lake shore in the sand, until in the afternoon we came to the Pettquotting,[1] a great creek, by which Indians live. Here we asked the Chippewas, who lay here, to set us over, who would have us encamp with them, for they wanted to put us over the next morning. Meanwhile Samuel and three other brethren had swum over, and gone to a French trader, a mile up the creek, who lent us his batteau, in which we very soon got over, and then encamped in the first suitable place. Br. David went to the trader to see if he could get a horse for Susanna, but he was not himself at home, but only his servants, and so he got none.

Sunday, 4. We lay still and celebrated Whitsuntide. Strange Indians from the Monsey town, one or two miles from us, attended the sermon, many, friends of our Indians who were visiting us. Here we heard that William had been here, who with several others had come by land from Detroit, and now came here from Cuyahoga to see if he could learn any thing about us. The Indians told them lies enough, saying to them they had seen a ship on the lake that had lost her masts, and that they saw her go down, and it must have been we. William, we heard further, had gone back again hunting. In the evening Heckewelder came to us with the rest by water, so that we were now all together. We heard cannon fired on our island.

Monday, 5. We set out again, some by water, and Br. David, with those who went by land, made a good day's journey; they had to pass many creeks, over which we were carried, going to-day for the most part along the strand, and we came at night to where the steep rocks overhang the lake, on which heights we encamped.

Tuesday, 6. Br. David hired a horse from an Indian for a good price, that we should have had yesterday at Pett-

---

[1] The Huron River, O., where two years later, near the present Milan, Erie Co., our Indians settled.

quotting, but it did not come, so that Susanna, who thus far
has had to go afoot the whole way through swamp and
water, could better get along, though even on horseback it
was often very hard travelling through the dense bush. We
went over a very deep creek,[1] where the canoes helped over
those who were going by land, and where also Chippewas
lay. We encamped here and the Indians went out hunting, but brought back only some wild turkeys. We saw
our Mackina far out in the lake making for Cuyahoga, and
knew her, and they also saw our white tents. We wished
her good luck. Samuel, who went yesterday to Cuyahoga
to see if he could find any of our people or whites, came
back, having met no one.

Wednesday, 7. Hitherto for the most part we have
travelled along the strand, but now that the steep rocks
overhang the lake, we went above on the height along the
lake, and saw with great amazement and not without awe
the great and wonderful works of the Creator. For the
rocks stand in part perpendicular and smooth, like a wall,
straight upon the lake, where from above is a view down
into the depths of the lake, so that one grows giddy as he
looks. In part they are undermined, and so little black
bays run up into the land, and if these were not here they
(the undermined places) could not be seen from the land,
but only from the lake. On the rocks are streaks of different colors, in a line, as if made by the hand of man by
a cord, white, red, blue, black, yellow, etc. If now the
wind blows from the lake toward the rocks, no transport
or canoe can be saved, but must be dashed to pieces. They
must, therefore, wait for wind and weather suitable for
getting by. It was well for us that wind and weather were
favorable, especially for them who went by water. Those
on land had a bad road to-day all day, long, wading
through swamp and water. We passed another large, deep
creek, where without canoes we could not have got over,
and encamped upon the rocky height. Heckewelder, with

---

[1] Perhaps Vermillion River. .

some others, was ahead of us and Thomas, who came by
water with us.

Thursday, 8. As the horses could not be found, Susanna had again to go afoot till noon, when we came over
the last great creek, and after that had quite a good, dry
road. Now again, after four years, we saw mountains
and had. the pleasure of going over them. We came in
the afternoon to Cuyahoga, where we found Heckewelder,
who this morning at daybreak had passed the last cliff
with good luck some nine miles from here, where in a
storm or even in a strong wind no cat could save herself,
and where in the last war Bradstreet[1] with his army was
wrecked and many people left in the lake. Joshua, who
last evening came upon Chippewa Indians, who also wished
to go on, and invited him to go with them, did so. These,
when they came to this dangerous place, offered and strewed
tobacco about in the water, so as to get by successfully,
and this is always their custom. Heckewelder had hardly
got into the river this morning, when a wind sprung up
and a canoe which lagged behind came to grief from the
rocks and had to run ashore. It was broken up, but all
others were rescued. Our Mackina day before yesterday
had already arrived in good, calm weather, at the mouth
of the river, which was great good luck, for when they
sounded and found on the bar not more than three feet
of water, there was no possibility of getting in. The
channel was stopped up, and where last year this same
sloop came in, having eight feet of water, there is this
year dry land, or a heap of sand thrown up by the lake.
The captain was on the point of turning back to Detroit
without landing the baggage, but was finally persuaded
by the words of Brs. Schebosh and Edwards to try it, and
thus with much trouble, from the open lake, for it was a

---

[1] Col. John Bradstreet, in 1764, returning from his expedition against
Detroit and other French posts, came to trouble here.

"As the boats of the army were opposite the iron-bound precipices
west of Cuyahoga, a storm descended upon them, destroying several,
and throwing the whole into confusion. For three days the tempest
raged unceasingly." Tayler's Hist. of Ohio, p. 144.

good mile from land, they brought every thing ashore at
last. Had it not been calm, it could not have been done.
The sloop had to put back into the lake. After she was
unloaded and lightened she made another trial and came
into the harbor all right, though with trouble enough, that
she might be out of danger from a storm. Now it became
somewhat clear to us why we had to stay so long on the
island, and could not get away until at last things so fell
out that we had to make quite a different tour, for both
ships and we too would have come to grief or we should
all have had to put back to Detroit. Last year the captain came in here with this same sloop, and had eight feet
of water on the bar, where now are only three feet. We
could not but be thankful to the Saviour that all had
gone well with us, that we like children were carefully
watched over here on earth.

Friday, 9. Our Indians went out hunting and came
upon deer and elk enough, but none brought any thing
back, though we much needed something, and many had
nothing left to eat. We had good hope of finding white
people here, who could have helped us with provisions,
but when we sought we found no one; there was a house
stored with flour, intended for Detroit, but there was no
one with it, and we knew not what to think. We resolved
for the first thing to make canoes, most of them of bark,
and as soon as possible to get away from here and to go
up the creek to find out how far we could go, and if we
should come upon old fields, to consider whether we should
plant something. Thomas with his family who was behind,
and whom the storm fell upon, gave up his canoe and
came here by land. We then on the 10th all set about
making canoes, To-day a deer came into camp, which
was divided among us all.

Sunday, 11. As soon as day broke we helped the
Mackina out of the river and brought her fortunately
over the bar, though she often stuck on the sand, and we
left her a mile from shore out of all danger, when she got
under sail; this was the captain's greatest trouble, and he
often said he feared he would have to give up the ship.

We were ourselves right glad and thankful to the Saviour that all had passed off so well and without damage. He could not permit the Detroiters to suffer any loss or harm on our account. It rained all day to-day very hard, as it has every day since we got here. We are also very thankful to the Saviour for the fine weather he gave us on our journey since we left the island.

Monday, 12. Our people made canoes. Hunger begins to fall sharply upon us. May the Saviour soon help us out of our need! Chippewas came to us, who have been hunting along the lake; they went and took away secretly many horse-loads of flour from that stored in the house above us. No one of our people took any of it, though they have much want and suffer hunger.

Tuesday, 13. Wrote to Bethlehem by Schebosh, who is going to Pittsburg, and on the 14th to Pittsburg to Duncan and Gibson.

Thursday, 15. Heckewelder made a beginning, and set out with several families that had canoes, and on the 16th Br. David started with a party, and on the 17th overtook the former. The first day we had still water, and good travelling, but the second day bad, for the creek was full of falls, and the further we went, the worse it was. Br. Edwards remained behind with the last to depart.

Sunday, 18. We came to an old Ottawa town, where we stopped to examine the neighborhood. We considered what would be best for us, and found that we and our Indians could not hold out to keep up our journey as we had thought, namely, to come to Thuppekünk, where we had thought of planting yet. We saw that we should yet have several day's labor, that our people had nothing to eat, and we dared not then think of planting. We resolved, therefore, to stay here this summer, when our matters would become clearer, for at present we are confused, and know not rightly how things are with us. We laid out our camp upon the east side of the creek, upon a height, and the day after,

Monday, 19, we sowed the land on the west side, where we wished to plant, and found good and, in part, quite clear land for this purpose, only it was very wild, the weeds standing as high as a man, which we had to cut down, thus having much trouble and labor.

Tuesday, 20. All our Indian brethren came here, and we were now all together. All were busy building themselves huts hastily, for it had rained every day since we broke up from the lake, and they began at the same time to clear the land and to plant. In the evening we had a service for praising and thanking the Lord for all his goodness in this new place.

Wednesday, 21. White people came through with a hundred pack-horses laden with corn and provisions, from Pittsburg, on their way to the mouth of the river, from whom we managed to buy some flour, and they told us they should continue the whole summer to bring on provisions for Detroit, and we could thus get all we wanted. They asked for a couple of Indians for a couple of days, to find out for them the way to the lake, and these were given them.

Saturday, 24. We were, for the most part, done with planting, as much as we could do at this time. The Indians were quite lucky hunting, shot deer and bears; they needed them too, and got them in the nick of time.

Sunday, 25. Wrote to Bethlehem by the pack-horse men who came back through here. Br. Heckewelder held service. Some Indians also went to Pittsburg to buy cows and drive them here.

Monday, 26. Weschnasch out hunting came through here, remaining over night, and thus many lies were spread among our people, among others, that the Cherokees wanted to come and kill us, likewise on account of our moving to the Muskingum, yet many Indians were against it.

Wednesday, 28. A white man, one of the pack-horse men, who got lost while looking for horses, and had wandered about three days and nights, came at last to us. We gave him to eat and provisions for his journey, whereupon he went to Pittsburg. He could not say enough as to how many bears he had found in the wild-cherry trees, the cherries being now ripe, two and three in one tree, and our Indians resolved to go at once for them.

Friday, 30. We early learned a sad circumstance, Thomas, who was scalped (at Gnadenhütten, March 8, 1782), went down the creek fishing, day before yesterday, and when he remained out over night, it was supposed he had gone down to the lake. This morning Jacob went down the creek, where he shot a deer, and found his canoe, which had floated down, but not him. But when search was made, he was found dead in the water. Since he was scalped, he has often had fits, and this was doubtless the cause of his death, for he was one of the best swimmers. He came from the Shawanese towns to us on the Huron River, loved the brothers, and wished not to remain among the savages; this he often said to Br. David, that he would like to be with us. He was buried here the next day. Abraham, with others, who wished to go to Pettquotting to get corn, and for some days, from stormy weather, lay by the lake, waiting for good weather, came back again, having accomplished nothing, and with him two white people from Detroit, on their way to Pittsburg, who remained with us over night. We heard from them that many white people lived in our town on the Huron River, English and French, but that it was a perfect nest of drunkards.

Saturday, July, 1. All our Indian brethren went off on the bear-hunt. A party of Chippewas, among whom was a chief, came up the creek, and encamped near by us. They came here from a hundred miles beyond Michilimackinac, and intended going to Pittsburg; they were orderly and friendly.

Sunday, 2. Isaac Williams came with an Englishman and a Frenchman from Sandusky, in order to go to Pittsburg with the next pack-horses, for which he would wait here. He had heard that we came over the lake and passed by Sandusky, and had wished to see some one of us, to give us a little news, that we might act accordingly, and not come to harm and into difficulties, for he was troubled about us, lest we might continue our march to

the Muskingum, and it would not be well for us so to do.
He had heard among the Indians that they had spoken
much against our moving there, since it was not yet time,
and since even this last May, in Thuppekünk, traders have
been plundered and murdered. We thought not a little
about this, as we lay on our island in the lake, what might
be the reason that we could not go forward; we believed
the Saviour, whose own we are, who certainly thinks of
us, and to whom it is not a matter of indifference how
things go with us, must have his own reasons for this,
and so it was; this we saw and felt afterwards. Had our
passage in the ship been ordinarily good and quick, we
should certainly have gone straight to the massacre on the
Muskingum, and have had a bad welcome, but, through
our long voyage, our time was so used up, that, for this
reason, with other circumstances added thereto, we had
to give up this plan, and we resolved to pass the summer
here, which was certainly for the time being best and
safest for us. The Indians, as it seems, are not opposed
to our going again to our towns, only they say it is not
yet time, since there is yet no thorough peace among them,
and many, if not the most, still await a new war. They
are not opposed to, as far as we hear, but are quite in
favor of, our remaining here, and no one will put any
thing in our way. We are here so out of the way that no
Indians come here except those who are out hunting, or
those who wish to visit us.

Monday, 3. Br. Schebosh came back from Pittsburg
with Andrew, his companion, bringing orders from Messrs.
Duncan & Wilson, to their agent at the mouth of the
creek, to let us have every thing we needed on credit, or
for cash, on which account, in all probability, he had gone
there. He brought us the packet of letters, which Mr.
Duncan, who in the winter was in Detroit, had forgotten,
and also the Scripture-verses for this year. To be sure,
the letters were partly two years old, and partly of last
year, but to us they were new, pleasant, and cheering.
We had news, however, that a packet for us had gone to
Detroit, which Isaac Williams would have liked to stop in

Sandusky and send to us, but could not; we were sorry for this, for they may readily be lost. They could not have come to Duncan or Wilson, or we should certainly have had them.

Tuesday, 4. We sent a canoe down to the lake with Duncan's order to his agent. The next day they came back, bringing first ten sacks of flour for the Indians, charged against Mr. Askin's bill of exchange for two hundred dollars, so that the Indians now have something to eat.

Thursday, 6. The flour was divided among the brethren. Peter, Renatus, and those who had come with them from Detroit with the horses by land, and had staid for some time hunting in Thuppekünk, came to us. They had heard of our arrival here from two Indians, who had come hither with us from Pettquotting, and made their way to us. They knew of the massacre which had taken place there, not far from them.

Friday, 7. William went to the fort to get provisions there with his horses.

Saturday, 8. This week our Indian brethren were busy building, and the sisters in the fields. We hold our services in the open air when the weather is good.

Sunday, 9. We kept Sunday quietly for the most part, and enjoyed the rest we need through our heavy and hard labor. Had service.

Monday, 10. Goschachgünk Delawares came here from the Shawanese towns, from whom we heard that the Indians did not yet know where we remained, that they had heard of our sailing away from Detroit, but since, after so long a time, they could hear nothing of us, they believed we had all gone to the bottom, that, at last, they learned from the Ottawas that two ships had foundered on the lake, from which all the Indians inferred that it must have been we; that they finally heard we had passed Sandusky, but nothing further as to where we had come and remained, but that all the Indians wished us not to go to the Muskingum for the time being, but to remain in Cuyahoga, since there was yet no stable peace. From this we

perceive it will be pleasant for all the Indians that we
stay here. A trader from the States, whose friends perished on the Muskingum, came here through the Shawanese towns on his way to Pittsburg, whom the Cherokees
and Mingoes are on the track of, and in that way we may
have trouble from them.

Thursday, 13. I wrote by Isaac Williams, who went to
Pittsburg, to the commandant there, Col. Hermann,[1] telling him our arrival, and, at the same time, our want of
food, and recommending us to his protection, since we are
now again come into this land.

Saturday, 15. Now comes again all the usual trouble,
with which hitherto we have had to contend in the Indian
land, though, during the few years we were at the north
side of the lake, we had none of it, until now that we
are come here again, namely, that the savages, friends of
our Indians, come and seduce weak, often confused, minds,
and lead them from the church, as we had, to-day, an example. Strange Indians came and enticed away from her
husband a woman with her children, for she was poor
here, had nothing to eat, and was starving; they told her
that if she would go with them, she would want for nothing. Her husband, who could very well have taken away
the children, from vexation gave them all up and let them
go. He repented of this afterwards, and wished to have
back, at least, his children. We gave him two courage-
ous brothers, and they went the next day,

Sunday, 16, to get them. They brought her in on the
17th, and she was glad to be back again. It has happened
to us in several cases that those who have been seduced
from the church and again brought back, have become
afterwards dear and firm brethren. Withstand the devil
and he flees from you. David held service in Indian.
15th (marginal note) Capt. Godfrey, who came in the
Mackina to the mouth of the creek, inquired about our
condition through one of his sailors, who came here and

---

[1] Thus plainly written in the original, but probably Gen'l Harmar is
meant.

stayed over night. After she left us and went away, she
was driven from her course to Fort Erie.

Monday, 17. There came strange Monsey Indians here
for a visit. They came first upon Br. David quite alone
on his plantation. He sat down with them, and they
asked him many questions; for example, whether we
should move to Thuppekünk, and how many white brethren there were, and whether David was there, of whom
they [must have heard, though they did not know him.
These were Indians who, during the war, had been in
Niagara, and did not know us. They went into town, or
rather into camp, and asked the Indian brothers to preach
to them and tell them about the Saviour, saying they had
never heard about this. This was done, and the next day
they went back to the lake, whence they had come. 18th.
The Indian brother, Samuel, with others, came back from
Pittsburg. We got letters from Br. Matthew,[1] of Litiz,
of Sept., 1783. They also brought with them one of our
Indians, Michael by name, from his wandering. They
met him in the bush. He was glad, indeed, to see us, and
at once asked permission to live with us, and this was
granted.][2]

Thursday, 20. Pack-horses came from Pittsburg with
flour. We got for ourselves and our Indians nineteen
casks. Michael spoke with Br. David, asking to be received again, and we cheerfully complied with his request.
We laborers had a conference about arrangements for our
place of abode, and consulted the Saviour by lot, and we
had for the time being to come to no conclusion, yet we
laid out a road from the town, that in building we might
make no waste.

Friday, 21. Most of the brethren went out elk-hunting.

Sunday, 23. Br. David preached from Romans, vi, 3:
Know ye not that so many of us as were baptized into
Jesus Christ, were baptized into his death? Pack-horse
men went back, by whom we sent letters to Bethlehem

---

[1] The venerable Bishop Hehl.
[2] Passage in brackets is from Beth. MS.

and Litiz. They encamped not far from us, and had stolen from them last night by the Indians nine horses.

Monday, 24. Done with hilling the corn, which stands very fine.

Tuesday, 25. Indian brothers came from the hunt, having shot four elk and five deer. Susanna, who went away yesterday, came back to-day. All sowed turnips and many. We have service every evening, when it does not rain.

Friday, 28. William came from the Fort. We had hoped for letters, but he brought none, and our things are still there, too.

Saturday, 29. Several brethren went by water to Pet-quotting, others to Sandusky to get corn; others again off hunting, and so must strive to get their families through. Heckewelder held service. Cathrine went to her husband.

Sunday, 30. David preached, and as it rained in the afternoon there was no other meeting. We read meantime the Bethlehem Diary.

Monday, 31. Several went away hunting. The Chippewa chief here in our neighborhood, with some women and children, visits us daily to get something to eat, for all their men have gone to Pittsburg, and they who are here have nothing to eat and we have little ourselves, but when they come we always give them something to eat. We ended the month with consideration of our Scripture-verse.

Tuesday, Aug. 1. There was a thunder-storm.

Wednesday, 2. Samuel and several others went out hunting and to boil salt, their families with them. Very few remained at home. A German from Redstone (Fay-ette Co., Pa.) came here, who has been for some time in Detroit and last in Sandusky. He had fever and nothing to eat. He will wait here for a chance to go to Pittsburg. David held service in the evening.

Thursday, 3. Mr. Neal, from the mouth of the river, came here. He complained that the Indians who come here are very insolent and he feared they might kill him.

On this account he will not stay there longer, but go back to Pittsburg with the pack-horses the next trip.

Friday, 4. The Chippewas came, who have been to Pittsburg, leaving their wives and children here. They had nothing but good news to give. The most noteworthy was that the Chippewas, Ottawas, Potawatomies, Wyan. dots, and Delaware nation have concluded a stable peace with the Americans, only two who did not wish it being excluded, the Shawanese and Cherokees. The Six Nations, however, wanted to put them in and force them to agree.

Saturday, 5. Several Chippewas were present at our evening service, quite devout, but it is a pity we cannot speak directly to them. There are many among them who understand Shawano, and one can speak with them in case of need, but this is not enough. They are much better Indians to get along with than the Delawares, Wyandots, and Tawas, also not so thievish, nor are they plunderers.

Sunday, 6. Heckewelder preached and David held the congregation meeting from the Scripture-verse. The Chippewas, who have been encamped here as long as we, went away to-day down to the lake. We read together the Bethlehem Diary.

Monday, 7. Wittigo, with two white people and some Wyandots from Sandusky Bay, went through here on their way to Fort Pitt.

Tuesday, 8. The sick German, who came here sick six days ago, and now is better, started for Fort Pitt.

Wednesday, 9. Joshua came from the Fort. The Pittsburgers, as we hear, have great pity for us, and consider together how they can help us and our Indians in our famine until orders come from Congress, which would delay too long if they should now first make the announcement there. They spoke with Joshua about this, and must gladly help us. Our brethren suffer great hunger; this can be seen in their faces, and this depresses their spirits much. We cannot but pity them, but we cannot help them, for we have nothing ourselves. An Indian said to him we should be called away from here, and then all the white brethren be sent away home, except David, who would remain; he belonged to the Monsey nation, who adopted him.

Thursday, 10, and Friday, 11. There was speaking in reference to the Lord's supper. To our comfort and heartfelt thankfulness to the Saviour, we found the brethren cheerful and content, with a hearty longing for Jesus' body and blood in the holy sacrament, which now we have not had for nearly five months, since Easter on the Huron River, and since we have been here, from the want of a chapel, for the Indian brethren have enough to do to support and maintain their families by hunting, and they cannot be expected to work until we have something to eat from our plantations.

Saturday, 12. Contrary to our expectations, many brethren were at home who had been to Pettquotting for corn, whence indeed they brought some, though not much. We had thereupon, upon the 13th, a very blessed communion. This gave the brethren new courage. The body and blood of our dear Lord revived their hearts anew, so that we gave ourselves up again to be entirely his own, to live for his joy. Owing to rain we could have to-day no general meeting.

Monday, 14. Some went again by lake to Sandusky to get corn where there is said to be much. Since we heard that letters, which had gone to Detroit in the spring, on account of which we wrote there, were come to the mouth of the river, we sent there to get them and received them. There was a letter from Br. Schweinitz, of May 4th, this year, together with a little book of Scripture-verses and texts for this year. The packet had been opened, but not the letters, and a calendar and two papers were missing, according to the letters.

Tuesday, 15. Brs. Heckewelder, Edwards, and two Indian brothers, went to Old Cuyahoga, where. they waited for Mr. Wilson, with cattle, to buy some of them and drive them here. Service in the evening.

Wednesday, 16. A party of sisters went again to the Lick to boil salt, where Messrs. Duncan and Wilson sent many kettles, which they offered to our Indians to use.

Thursday, 17. Heckewelder and Edwards came back with cattle they had got from Mr. Wilson, who came himself afterwards, on the 18th, remained over night with us, and on the 19th went down to the lake on business. He said we had done well in staying here and not going to the Muskingum; thinks also that it would not be advisable to move there in the spring or next year, for well-grounded reasons. Mr. Hutchins, with his surveyors and people, is out to measure and declare the boundary between the land of the States and of the Indians. It is generally believed that the undertaking will cause uneasiness among the Indians and indeed much murdering and killing sooner or later. Thus it is truly best we are far away. He says we have hit the best place on this creek, where the most excellant land lies, for he is well acquainted here.

18. Mr. Neal came here, from whom we learn this: a royal boat, with an officer and eight soldiers, had come there (the mouth of the river). He, who knows us and has been with us on the Huron River, wanted to visit us, but when he heard he could not get here in his boat, he gave up the plan. By a letter from Mr. Askin, of an old date, when we had hardly left the island, we learned that the commandant had sent another ship with provisions to the islands, which was to bring us and our belongings to Cuyahoga, but had not found us.

Sunday, 20. Heckewelder preached in the forenoon, and baptized the little son of Br. Adam and his wife, Sabina, born yesterday, Augustus. We brethren, the laborers, read the journals, Br. Reichel's discourse at the end of the year '82 and beginning of '83, also about the captivity of Brs. Jorde and Pfeiffer upon the English king's ship, and finally the release of the first, of all which we had never heard a word. Br. Edwards held the congregation meeting from the Scripture-verse: I have declared and have saved. Jesus, how shall I thank thee. I acknowledge that my salvation rests with thee.

Wednesday, 23. We got at last, by the pack-horses, the

19

things sent by the church for us and the Indian church; all their things have come, and nothing is destroyed, but our things were in part destroyed, and in part much was wanting, and doubtless much was lost on the way here from Pittsburg. These, on Thursday, the 24th, were distributed among the brethren, and awakened generally much joy and thankfulness, after they had first been told that the brethren in Bethlehem already three years ago, upon hearing of the loss they had suffered, and of the want in which they were, had thought of them and sent them these things for their bodies' needs, while we were over the lake, but since they could not come to Detroit, the brethren had found another way, getting them back and sending them to Pittsburg, and now at last we had them. Many brothers came forward and expressed their thankfulness. Some said: "We are not worthy that the brethren in Bethlehem should have so much love for us, and think about us efficaciously. We are not worthy of having teachers given us, to whom we have so often caused much trouble." Others again said: "None of the white people would have given themselves so much trouble to send things such a long way and forward them to us, except the brothers; they would have given them up and let them be. We see that it has been to them a matter of concern, and has cost them much trouble to do us good."

Friday, 25. Brs. Schebosh and Edwards went down to the lake on business, some Indian brethren to Pettquotting and Sandusky.

Saturday, 26. Brs. Schebosh and Edwards returned from the lake.

Sunday, 27. David preached about the saving Gospel Paul had preached to the heathen, that the word of our Saviour's death upon the cross is the strength of God to all those who receive it in faith. We laborers continued our reading of the Bethlehem diary of '83, which we ended to-day. Br. Edwards held the congregation meeting.

Monday, 28. The salt-boilers all came back from the Lick, and some came from the Fort. Samuel had, in both places, met some of our Indians, from whom he heard that not only they, but many others, wished to come to us, who for a long time already had only been waiting till we should again have come to this side of the lake. Among them he met one named Anton. He said to Samuel: "Thou hast been with our teachers these four years they have been away from us, or near them, therefore I think thou knowest them well, and canst tell me the truth about them." Samuel answered him: "Yes, indeed; I know them right well, and if now first I might hear from thee what thou willst particularly hear, perhaps I can tell thee." Then said Anton: "I have had thoughts about our teachers, of which I cannot get rid, and if I do drive them from my mind they always come back again, namely, I think that they are the cause, and have given occasion that so many of our friends perished in Gnadenhütten; they have betrayed us, giving notice to the white people of our being there, whereupon they came and fell upon us. Now, tell me the truth, is it so or not? Thou must necessarily know about them." Samuel said: "I must first ask thee one thing before I answer, Art thou right in mind? If thou art failing there, I would rather answer thee nothing." "I am of good understanding, thereof thou needst not doubt, and so I should be glad to know thy thoughts about this." Samuel said to him then: "Thou thinkest so, indeed, but I say to thee the truth, thou thinkest falsely, and thou makest against our teachers accusations of which they are innocent; this I know certainly, for I know them." Then Anton farther said: "I have ever now, all the time, a wicked heart, and so I think badly and wickedly; as thou seest from looking at me, so is my heart also." He was painted red all over, and said farther: "What does it help or profit me if I deceive myself by outward show, and make myself like a believer, when yet my heart is bad? In spite of this I will yet soon visit you, and then also greet our teachers. Thou canst meanwhile greet them from me and tell them what I have said to thee, and how thou hast seen me." He had in Gnadenhütten, by the

massacre, lost all his children, and almost all his friends,
but he had himself gone away from them secretly to Pittsburg, saying nothing about it to any one, whereby he escaped the massacre, where he, but without shoes and
almost naked and destitute, had fled, when the militia had
fallen upon the Indians there and murdered some of them.

30. At the service from the Scripture-verse, Br. David
made an earnest exhortation to the brethren on account
of the bad course they lead when away.

31. Sisters went to Sandusky to get corn and harvest
the fields given them by their friends.

Friday, Sept. 1. Edwards held the evening service
from the Scripture-verse: Upon his kingdom to establish
it with justice.

Sunday, 3. David preached from the Epistle 2, Cor.
iii., 4, about this, that of ourselves we can neither think
nor do what is good but that God gives us power therefor,
and through his Holy Spirit must work in us good works,
and make us fit therefor. We read the Bethlehem diary
for the month of May, '84.

Monday, 4. Ignatius returned from Sandusky, where
he got corn; on the lake he was sunk with his canoe and
cargo, but yet he saved every thing.

Tuesday, 5. In a conference with the assistants we considered about sending a couple of Indians as messengers
of peace to our Indians [in error] scattered here and there
in the bush, to visit them, to encourage them, and to learn
their mind and disposition. We found it best to invite
some of them here, if it could be done, for then we could
talk out the matter with them, learn their plans, and consider what we had best resolve for their good. We had
thought indeed whether it would not be well for one of us
white brethren to go with them, but the assistants opposed, saying it would attract too much notice among the
Indians, and, at the same time, they would draw this in-
ference: "He comes to persuade the Indians to move
again to the white people, bringing them again into misfortunes and danger." Therefore, we had to give up this
plan. We resolved, then, that the assistants, Samuel and

Thomas, should make this journey, who were also willing and ready for it.

Wednesday, 6. Adolphus, with a canoe-load of sisters, started for Pettquotting to earn some corn among the Indians in the corn-harvest. Jacob and William went off hunting to the Tuscarawas. By Renatus we had letters from Bethlehem, one from Br. Ettwein, of Aug. 10, by which we learn of Br. John's (de Watteville) presence in Bethlehem, of whom we had already heard he had departed for Europe; at the same time, we perceive that letters of the month of June are still on their way. Both Renati, who were hunting in Thuppekünk, had again to flee on account of white people, who always swarm about there.

Thursday, 7. Samuel and Thomas began their journey to our Indians scattered here and there, after we had blessed them the evening before in the service for this, and had recommended them to the brethren. We gave them instructions of somewhat the following import: that we had not forgotten them over the lake nor here, but constantly thought of them, and had always wished we could visit them; we looked upon them as belonging to us and merely separated from us, wishing they could again be in communion with us; since now we believed that most of them would not have forgotten that they had received God's word, as we also, and were troubled about the salvation of their souls, we should like to learn their thoughts about this, how to make it possible for them again to hear it and come to the enjoyment of it; we would not just now bid them come to us, but they who wished to come would all be welcome here, but we should like to see some of their intelligent people, and to consider with these what could best be done on our part for them, that this should not fail, and for this they should make us proposals which we could understand and consider; they should not give up courage, thinking, "All is in vain; nothing will come of the plan of our all together making one church again; we have become savage, have deeply sinned, the Saviour and the brethren have cast us

away, and we are incurable." No, they should take new
spirit, and turn to the Saviour, who is merciful and gracious, and so willingly forgives sins; we did not invite
them that we might speak with them about their bad
condition and their sins, and learn exactly about them;
besides we knew how this was when they lived among
utter heathen, but we wished to speak with them about
this, how they could be put into a blessed life, away from
their unblessed state, which could happen as soon as they
would turn again to the Saviour, who had poured out his
blood in satisfaction for their sins.

Saturday, 9. William's Martha bore a son.

Sunday, 10. Br. David preached in Indian, there being
no interpreter. We read the journal, Memorabilia from
Bethlehem of '84.

Tuesday, 12. Christina bore a daughter, who, however,
died as soon as born.

Saturday, 16. William returned from the head of the
Tuscarawas, where he had been hunting. He found there
eleven swarms of bees, from one of which he brought the
honey, and the rest he let alone till he could get them.
Others besides have found from eight to ten and more.
The bush swarms with bees. In the same neighborhood
there had been not only slight frosts, but heavy ones,
though we here have had none. Our corn is yet very
backward, and should we get a hard frost, it would all go,
and all our trouble and labor would have been in vain,
and as it is, some will get no corn, either planting not the
proper kind or too late.

Sunday, 17. Br. David preached and baptized Matthew,
the little son of William and Martha, born on the 9th.
We read the proceedings of the U. A. Conference of '83.
Heckewelder held the congregation meeting.

Wednesday, 20. Weschnasch came here from his hunt-
ing-hut. We were busy yesterday and to-day bringing
blocks for David's house. A bad and inflammatory fever
prevails among our Indian brethren, with which many
are already down. Heckewelder held evening service.

Thursday, 21. Pack-horses came through here from

Pittsburg on their way to the lake. These people brought bad news, that an Indian war would break out. The Shawanese, who are always murdering, took away captive a woman with her children, cut off their legs at the knee, put them alive into fire and burnt them.

Friday, 22. We heard unpleasant news, that without fail an Indian war would break out. The Indians are said through the summer to have murdered as wantonly in Kentucky and to have done as much damage as in the last war.

Saturday, 23. Mr. Neal was here over night.

Sunday, 24. We got by the pack-horses our things which yet remained behind, in good condition. Br. Heckewelder preached, and Edwards held the evening service. David went to his bed sick.

Monday, 25. Br. Edwards was also badly attacked by the fever prevailing here.

Wednesday, 27. By Mr. Neal sent letters to Bethlehem. [Thus far to Bethlehem.]

Sunday, Oct. 1. Heckewelder preached. Two white people came here from Detroit on their way to Pittsburg. They were robbed of their money by an Indian, who gave himself out as belonging to us and wishing to come properly to the sermon. Ignatius came back from Sandusky. It is reported that all white people have been ordered to go to Detroit. Abr. Kuhn,[1] who is our enemy and a Wyandot chief, told him that we had closed his ears and let him know nothing about our coming over the lake; we had acted like fools in coming over the lake; he knew for a certainty that there would be a new war, for he learned it in Canada, where he had himself heard it.

Wednesday, 4, and Friday, 6. Brethren came from Pett. quotting with corn, so that for a time they have something to live on, but of those in Sandusky they knew nothing.

Saturday, 7. Samuel and Thomas came back from their journey. During almost the whole trip the first had to withstand a severe illness [coming home sick], for in all

---

[1] From Lower Sandusky, according to Heckewelder.

Indian towns a severe fever rages. They were heartily welcomed by many of our Indians, who were again encouraged by the brethren, and the longing to come to us is anew awakened among them, and some want to come in the spring and to wait no longer. Those on the Miami, however, were indifferent, to whom they sent a message from the Shawanese towns, in order to speak with them, but none wished to come. One, however, Samuel's brother, Augustus, blasphemed and said, among other things : " I was in Philadelphia,¹ in danger of my life, and have seen with my own eyes those who made attempts upon my life, and I got out of danger with difficulty. On the Muskingum the white people have at last attained their purpose, murdering so many of our friends ; therefore will I keep far enough from them ; no one shall take me to them ; and I say to thee, nevermore will I come to you and live with you ; I will hear nothing about the Saviour. Perhaps if you lived near by I would sometimes come to see you and visit you, but that will all be as it will. My forefathers have all gone to the devil; there will I go also ; where they are there will I also be." Samuel heard him quite through, and answered him : I have heard thy mind and was horrified at it, but I will tell thee my mind. Nothing shall take me from the Saviour and the church so long as I live ; neither trouble nor fear, neither hunger nor persecution nor danger to my life ; all this I reckon as nothing, if only I have the Saviour and from him also the salvation of my soul, as I surely shall, if I stay by him, and that can no man take from me, even if they take away my life." At this he was quite still and had nothing to say.

They were everywhere received in a friendly way by the savages. No man gave them a harsh word. I will, however, by a few examples, show how, by many sorts of craft and by fine words, they sought to induce our Indians to

---

¹ In 1763, probably, when the Christian Indians from Nazareth and Nain were taken by a sheriff to Philadelphia, where they were received with the yells and shouts of an excited mob.

fly to them. Thomas is well known among the Indians to
have been a wicked man among the savages, whom his
grandfather, Netawatwes, had to drive away, which was the
occasion of his coming to us. He came to his acquaintances and friends in the Shawanese towns, who had prepared a feast and sacrifice; they also invited him thereto,
but he declined. They persisted, however, that he should
merely come and eat with them, but this he did not do.
When they were together in performance of their ceremonies they came again and asked of him to come, rattle
with the tortoise shell and sing, as is their custom. He
answered that he had forgotten that and could no longer
do it, he had not done it for so many years. They answered he would soon hear how the others did it. He
said : "That is your way, but I have found another way to
live, which is better. I cannot go two ways. I remain in
that where I now am." Then they let him alone. In
Sandusky he met one of his former comrades, who was a
counsellor. He took him to his house, many young people
following him, so that the house was full. The counsellor
said to him that since he had not seen him for a long time
and rejoiced in his coming, he wished to make him right
welcome, and taking a cask of rum he put it before him
and told him he should drink. Thomas, after they had
discussed the matter a while together, took the cask of
rum, thanked him for it, and placed it before the young
people, saying they might drink it if they would, but he
might not, and he went away. Another also wished to
treat him in the same way, and welcome him, to whom he
straightway said: "You Indians are thus. You are
very willing to ask the believing Indians to drink, and if
you can make them drunk, you have joy therein, laugh at
them, and always jokingly say: 'The believing Indians
are no better than we.'" Another, the counsellor, took
him to his house, and gave him a fine scarlet-red coat.
Thomas thanked him for it, and begged him to be so
good as to hang it up on the nail again. When the
other asked him why, saying he gave him the coat, and
he should put it on. Thomas answered: "I see very

well it is a captain's coat, and I am neither a captain nor wish to be one." Another time this same man came to him with some fathoms of wampum, which they do to put a man under obligations to them, who does not easily dare refuse if 'any thing is asked of him—a thing they understand among themselves without words. Thomas took the wampum, held it awhile in his hands, and before he went away gave it back to him, saying to him : "Thou art a counsellor and always needest wampum, but I can make no use of it, but I thank you for the present."

On their return they met Capt. Pipe, who was friendly towards them, and with a belt gave them a message which was as follows : "My friends, ye believing Indians in Cuyahoga, I have lately had news from the Goschachgünkers in the Shawanese towns, that a great council will be held there, whereto all nations assemble, which shall decide whether we shall have war or peace. Thereto also are ye invited to hear what the conclusion shall be." He turned the belt around and said to the other assistant: "Friends, ye believing Indians in Cuyahoga, ye ·have been moving about for several years, from Sandusky over the lake to the Chippewas, and now you have come back again to Cuyahoga, of all which ye have let us know nothing. While now the times are portentous and it seems as if a new war would break out, ye are in danger where ye are, of being again fallen upon by the white people. Therefore I take you by the hand, and set you in the neigborhood of the Pettquotting, which is intended for you ; there seek ye out a place that pleases you and is suitable for you ; there can ye keep your cattle. No one shall disturb you or put aught in your way, there shall ye dwell in quiet and hold your worship of God since ye go not to war. Accept this proposal for we mean well by you. I know well that your towns on the Muskingum are given to you, it may sometime happen that ye go there, but for the time being it is not advisable, not good for you."

Sunday, 8. Br. Heckewelder preached, and as he intended to go away to-morrow with his family to the church,[1] he bade us farewell, and many tears were shed, a proof that they love their teachers. In the evening white people came here, who accompany Br. Heckewelder and his wife to Pittsburg. Among them was also John Leeth,[2] who during Br. Grube's visit was baptized by us, and also his wife Elizabeth, who had been a prisoner since she was half a year old, and had grown up among the Indians. He asked very earnestly to be received again, saying he could not remain away from us, and had waited with great longing till we came over to this side of the lake; that he was resolved to live with us and nothing should retain him. We pitied him, but told him it was a well fixed rule with us in all our missions to receive no white people, and so we could not promise him before we had inquired of the brethren in Bethlehem about it and had their opinion; we had examples that we had fared badly with such people, and had afterwards much repented of having received them. All remonstrances and representations, for we made it right hard for him, telling him that even if he should get permission to live with us he must submit to our rules, and could have no preference above the Indians, yes, he must very often be their servant, if he wished to get along with us—all was of no avail, but he said he would willingly endure any thing if only he could be with us, for the sake of his soul's salvation. We laborers, with Br. Heckewelder and his wife, strengthened ourselves in the evening once more with the body and blood of our Lord in the holy sacrament, bound

---

[1] i. e., to Bethlehem.

[2] John Leith's Biography, with annotations by C. W. Butterfield, was published by Robert Clarke & Co., in 1883. Leith was born in South Carolina, in 1755. When seventeen years old, he was taken prisoner by the Delaware Indians, and adopted by them. Even after his marriage to Sally Lowrey (in regard to his wife's name, see under Dec. 14 and 18, 1788) he lived two years in Gnadenhütten, O. By his own statement he was converted in 1793. He married his second wife in 1802, and died 1832.

ourselves to abide by Jesus' cross, to bear his sufferings,[1] thereby to love one another from our hearts, though absent one from another.

Monday, 9. At noon they went away after a tender leave-taking, whereby tears were shed on both sides. Many Indian brothers and one sister, too, accompanied them to Pittsburg, and nearly the whole town a part of the way. Brs. David and Edwards were still very weak and in no condition to go out.

Tuesday, 10. Petty, Job Chilloway's former wife, came here from Detroit to see her sister, and also a white man from the same place, captain of a boat, which takes flour from here, by whom we had a friendly letter from Mr. Askin, to whom Br. David wrote back. An Indian brother who went with our friends as far as their night-quarters and came back again, brought us word they had so far gone well and fortunately.

Wednesday, 11. All the brethren who are at home and well, went out hunting to get meat to eat while building the meeting-house, and some sisters for chestnuts, of which there are many this year. Many sisters came back from Pettquotting and Sandusky, where they earned corn in the harvest. Some of them were seized by the sicknesses prevalent everywhere among the Indians, such as fever and swollen necks, on which account they were so long away. Two sisters went to our Indians in the Shawanese towns and on the Miami. In the first place, and in the neighborhood of Sandusky, they were received with joy by the greater part, and whole families, children and the old, wept together, especially Nathan. Davis' family. Since spring he has been sick, quite paralytic, and said if he could only get well enough to sit horseback, that he would come to us with his family, but should he go from time, his wife and children should go to the church without delay.

In the latter place, namely, on the Miami, people were very shy, no one wished to have any thing to do with them,

---

[1] A quotation from a hymn.

until they had been there a couple of days, when they became kinder, and began to talk with them. They even found some young people who said they would no longer delay, but would come to us, so also in other places, some leave parents and friends, and come to us, a fair sample of our young people; one sees there is more life and feeling among them than among the old, who are like the dead. Also those who have been assistants are the most indifferent of all, but the Saviour will yet gather them to the flock, one after the other.

Friday, 13. Isaac Williams came through here from Pittsburg, bringing us news that they had met the Heckewelders, all well, but that three war-parties were out, whom they must meet, who had murdered and scalped a man on Salt Lick, whom Isaac and his people had buried; likewise that Congress had declared war against the hostile Indians in order to force them to peace, that already a thousand men had invaded the Indian land.

Inasmuch as we had been requested by Pipe to send some one to the council in the Shawanese towns, whereto we and the assistants had not the least inclination, but inasmuch as Heckewelder, both at his departure and from his first night-quarters, had sent word to the assistants that they should listen to the chiefs and do what they told them, and send a couple of brothers, we laid the matter before the Saviour, asking his advice, but he did not approve, and this was exceedingly to our wishes, and we thanked him for his good advice.

Saturday, 14. From Sandusky all the brethren now came home except one family, and that is on the way. The brethren spoke there with Titawachkam, a Monsey captain and head-man in his town, who told them he was going to the council, and when he came back he would call upon us, and give us news of what came up and what was decided; that we ought to have settled either upon the Sandusky or the Pettquotting, when we came over the lake, but had passed them by; we should now settle at the latter place; they should not be uneasy about any harm happening to their teachers [among them David]; he was his friend and in his family and race; whoever did harm to him did it to himself, and he would interfere. This is the same man[1] who, at the time of our capture in Gnadenhütten, wished to make him free and his own, but that did not then succeed, for we brothers would then have been separated, therefore Br. David gave him no answer. By this circumstance I must still mention that the Indians had divided among themselves our three towns, namely, this Titawach-kam wished to have those in Schönbrunn, for mostly Monseys lived there; Pipe, Gnadenhütten, and the Gosch-achgünk Indians wanted to have those in Salem. But among themselves they were discordant and hostile, and thus nothing came of this plan, no one daring to make much pretension from fear of the others. Somewhat like this is also the occasion for Pipe's message to us, about which we now have somewhat exact information. At the treaty he said to the commissioners: "Ye desire your flesh and blood of us, that is, all prisoners, but I have heard nothing of your wishing to give or make satisfaction for the loss of our friends, which we suffered at Gnadenhütten, where ye murdered unoffending men, women, and children, who yet never went to war nor troubled themselves about the war." Now we hear that Pipe wishes in their place to own us, wherefore he will have us nearer him, and has called us to the Pettquotting. This pleases our Indian brethren not at all, they would rather go over the lake, where they were free.

Sunday, 15. Br. David held again the Sunday services for the first time, having so far recovered. After the sermon came some white people here on their way to Pittsburg. They asked for an Indian to go out with them as far as Salt Lick,[2] for the way was uncertain; this we could

---

[1] See before p. 10.

[2] "Col. James Hilman entered into the service of Duncan & Wilson, of Pittsburg. They were engaged in forwarding goods and provisions upon pack-horses across the country to the mouth of the Cuyahoga, now Cleveland, thence to be shipped on the schooner Mackinaw to Detroit. During the summer of 1786 he made six trips, the caravan consisting of ten men and ninety horses. They usually crossed the

not well refuse them, though only a few were at home, and
of these some were sick, and the well had necessary work
to do. So we gave them one to go with them, for which
they were glad and thankful. One of them was quite an
old man with a white head, the brother-in-law of Capt.
McKee, of Detroit. He told us that Brant,[1] who is a Mohawk and colonel, and has this summer come back from
England, and is now at the great council in the Shawanese
towns, was earnest for peace, that the nations wanted to
have a line fixed and established as far as the land of the
free States should extend, and if Congress were contented ˜
with this, there would be stable peace among the nations.

Monday, 16. The brethren worked earnestly at the
meeting-house, making a good beginning,

Tuesday, 17, but late in the evening came a messenger
from Pipe, in Sandusky, telling us the Americans[2] had
made an incursion upon the Shawanese towns, killed ten
men, among them a chief, and wasted and burnt every
thing. They conjectured the women and children were
all taken prisoners, as they knew nothing about them;
that they stayed there one night and then went back again;
that they came to within four miles of the Delaware
towns, when they turned about [which shows they have
no intentions towards us]. Farther, that a couple of
Wyandots had brought in word they had seen many white
people in Tuscarawas, and that more were always getting
together, from which they conjectured an army was coming
here this way. He had us told therefore; that he had

Big Beaver, four miles below the mouth of the Shenango, thence up
the left bank of the Mahoning, crossing it about three miles above the
village of Youngstown, thence by way of the Salt Springs, in the township of Weathersfield, through Milton and Ravenna, crossing the Cuyahoga at the mouth of Breakneck, and again at the mouth of Tinker's
Creek, in Bedford, and thence down the river to its mouth, where they
erected a log-hut for the safekeeping of their goods, which was the first
house built in Cleveland."—Howe's Hist. Collections of Ohio, p. 338.

[1] The famous Joseph Brant, a warm friend of the English, whose life
by Wm. L. Stone has been published in two octavo volumes.

[2] Under the command of Col. Ben. Logan, probably. Albach's Annals of the West, p. 447.

already before sent us a message, and now again said to us
we should be upon our guard, and flee before we were overtaken. This news caused much fright among our Indian
brethren. We could not, indeed, believe that an army
was advancing this way without our having heard any
thing about it, at the same time that Br. Heckewelder and
the Indian brethren would now already be at the Fort,
who certainly would have given us news of this by a messenger. We conjectured rather it must be the surveyors
who have come to the Tuscarawas. All the objections,
however, by which we sought to set the brethren right,
helped not at all; fright and dread were too great, they
got ready and the sisters all fled to the bush till morning,
when they came again.

18. We considered with the brethren and found it best,
for we saw them filled with fear, to bring the sisters and
children into the bush some distance from town, where by
day they could go to and from. It was also not well to
say much to them about the matter, having before us the
example in Gnadenhütten. The brethren could partly remain at home or go to and fro until, through our brethren,
we had more exact news. This they did, and most of the
sisters, with the children, went camping in the bush, but
we remained at home, giving ourselves over to the providence of the Saviour. Abraham, while he wished to flee,
thought of his teachers, and fled not, but resolved with
them to leave body and life.

Thursday, 19. We sent a couple of Indian brethren to
the Tuscarawas to find out whether the above news was
true or false, or if they met Indians to inquire about this,
in order that we might bring the brethren to themselves
again out of their dream. Some went also to examine the
way to the Fort, but they found no trace of any thing like
what we had heard. A family of white people, a woman
and children, who came from Detroit, on their way to
Pittsburg, came and begged us much to help them with a
couple of horses, and to give them two Indians for escort
for pay. Glad as we should have been to help them, for
we saw that if they stayed long here they would become a

burden to us, and we must support them, yet we were in no
condition to persuade any one to go with them, and could
not well do so, for if any misfortune should happen, we
should have to bear the blame. White people came up here
from the lake, among whom one had come only a few days
before from Sandusky, who told us and our Indians that
it was certainly all lies. Meanwhile, some impure spirits,
who were glad to seek friendship in the world and among
the savages, and whose hearts hang thereupon, as we had for
some time observed, found occasion during these troubles
to tear themselves from us and to take refuge among the
savages, and these were Luke's whole family. It could
not be seen that it was fear of danger which drove them
away, for when our sisters fled to the bush with their children, they remained at home, and were untroubled, as if
they well knew that what we had heard was all lies. Br.
David spoke longer than two hours with Luke, but he saw
he was fully determined to go, and at the same time that he
tried to cause nothing but trouble among the other brethren, running from house to house, trying to persuade them
to go with him; so Br. David let him go in peace, bidding
him hold us in love, and not to forget the Saviour and
put him wholly aside, and thus he went, Saturday, the
21st. Many Indians believed he was the author of the
lies, and through his wife had contrived this in Sandusky,
and one of them told him this to his face when he went
away. Meantime most of the brethren came every morning from the bush home, remaining during the day and
taking care of their plantations. Br. David spoke with
Samuel and Abraham, who visited him, about the meeting-
house, which was at last ready, even to the roof, pointing
out to them Satan's labor and hinderances the whole summer that we might get no meeting-house. Br. David had,
during the summer, got together timber for his own house,
which he now gave for this.

Sunday, 22. In the sermon, to which most of the
brethren came, Br. David exhorted the brethren, and
begged them not to let themselves be too much overcome

20

by fright, nor seek to help themselves and find safety, but
to take refuge with the Saviour, to place in him their hope
and trust, who would not bring them to shame, by whom
they would find comfort and advice. We were not as the
heathen, without hope. We had a Saviour, the All-
powerful, to whom there was no want of wisdom, means,
and ways to take his children through trouble, fear, and
danger, but whoever sought help of himself, he would fall
short, and must afterwards be ashamed. We saw that
this had effect upon our brethren's hearts; they were encouraged and found comfort in the Saviour. Some Chippewas came from the lake and asked us for corn, to
whom each one gave from his fields, for which they were
thankful.

In the evening, when it was already dark, we heard
from afar a great uproar from white people and horses'
bells. We supposed it was the pack-horses with flour, but
to the Indians, with all our persuasions, this was not trustworthy, but they believed it to be the army of which we
had heard, which would surround us, and no one would
venture out to see, but every soul of them fled to the bush,
and left us quite alone until, at dawn, Br. Schebosh went
out and found it was the pack-horses, who by good luck
had an Indian with them, a near friend of Pipe's, who
told them that all they had heard was a lie. Then they
were convinced, and recovered from their fear and tim-
idity. If the Indian had not been with them, they would
never have believed the white people, so incredulous were
they.

Monday, 23. The brethren came to their senses, and
began to assemble again, although those who were in the
bush had fled still farther away at the news.

Tuesday, 24. Thomas and Zachary came from the
Tuscarawas, where they had found no trace of white people, nor of Indians, although they examined the road from
there to the Fort. Their journey gave them recompense
in that they found things.

Wednesday, 25. The pack-horses went away again,
storing here their flour, seventy horse-loads, for no white

people were at the lake. The family of white people from Detroit had now a good opportunity, and went away with them, of which we were very glad.

Thursday, 26. Most of the Indian brethren went out hunting, since for some time they had not courage to go out, nor to shoot in the neighborhood, even if they could shoot a deer, so as not to be disclosed.

Friday, 27. Sara Nanticoke bore a daughter, which was baptized Sunday, the 29th, at the sermon, with the name Amelia. The Indian who came with the pack-horses from Pittsburg, then went to Sandusky, and yesterday came back again, met Luke with his family on the lake, not far from here, and told him that all he had heard was false and lies, and when he asked him if he had not better turn about, he answered, no, that he was travelling, and turned back no more.

Monday, 30. The brethren again set to work at the meeting-house to get it ready.

Tuesday, 31. Chippewas came in, who go up the creek hunting, and encamped here a couple of days.

Friday, Nov. 3. Our Indian brethren, who have been expected for several days, came back from Pittsburg, whither they had accompanied Br. Heckewelder and his wife. They brought us the pleasant news that the Heckewelders had gone so far with good health and fortune, and had gone away from there into the country before their own departure. By them we had, at the same time, letters from Bethlehem and Litiz, to our great joy, of Jan. 18th and Aug., likewise Sept. 10 and 11 of this year. Besides they brought none but good news with them, and nothing in the least alarming. They could bear witness that no army was coming out this way, and that nothing dangerous was to be feared. The letters of Sept. held important news and account of the conference in Bethlehem, but thereto must the Saviour help us make path and road.

Sunday, 5. We had our services, accompanied with the nearness of our dear Lord, whereby it was well with us and our brethren. The brethren were greeted from

Bethlehem, especially from John.[1] In the evening a messenger came to us from Luke's camp on the lake, to whom
a messenger from Sandusky had come, who brought us
again the message ; we should now go thither, and when
we should be there they would consider where we should
dwell. Thus they would drive us about, and as soon as
we should be in their hands and in their power, we should
have no end of moving about. When we asked the messenger how it happened that they wanted to have us there
again, he answered : "Some one of our own number was
the cause, who had sent them word that Pettquotting was
still too far away from them ; we should rather live with
them in Sandusky. "This can be no one but Luke, who is
going thither, for there is no one among us who wants to
go thither, even if we must, but since he wants to do so, he
bids them bring us all there, and he has contrived the
whole thing which gives us so much perplexity.

Tuesday, 7. As the messenger was going back we sent
the string of wampum back, thereby announcing: "We
could not dwell near unbelievers, much less among them."
They knew very well that we had ever lived apart from
them.

Wednesday, 8. One, Wilson by name, came here from
Detroit on his way to the States. He wanted to borrow a
horse, and have with him one or two Indians for escort,
but we could not so immediately help him.

Friday, 10. We had the first services in our new chapel
from the Scripture-verse: Look down from heaven and
behold from the habitation of thy holiness. Thereupon
was the communion quarter-hour, in which the holy communion was announced to the brethren for day after to-
morrow.

Saturday, 11. Chippewas came here and stayed over
night. Our Indians tried to find out where they were
going, but they did not want to say exactly. The next
morning, however, one came after them to get them back

---

[1] Either John de Watteville or John Ettwein.

again, when we found out they were going to war, and the chiefs wished to stop them.

Sunday, 12. Br. Edwards preached, and in the afternoon was a love-feast for all. After the brethren had been spoken to yesterday and the day before, we had in the evening the holy communion, accompanied by the near presence of the Saviour with his poor, sinful flock, which confessed itself sinful before him, and acknowledged its guilt.

Monday, 13. After consideration of our Scripture-verse: And to our God for he will abundantly pardon, and of the text: For thus saith the Lord God: Behold I, even I, will both search my sheep and seek them out, we prayed to our dear Lord, the Elder of his church, thanked him for his blessed rule, under which, by his mercy, we find ourselves so blessed, for he feeds his little sheep upon his holy wounds, which he felt for us; we asked forgiveness where we had not done right, nor always followed and fulfilled his good and gracious advice and will; that he would be further interested in us, and especially take upon his true heart our outward circumstances, opening and showing the way for us, putting aside all the hinderances made by Satan, that through us he might accomplish his holy will. We got the assurance in our hearts that he would do for us all this and yet more.

Wednesday, 15. Many got ready for the autumn hunt after they were done with work in the fields and with the building of their houses and huts. There are but few houses built, most getting through this winter in huts, since we know not how soon we must go hence.

Thursday, 16, and Friday, 17. The sisters helped us get in our crops, turnips, and potatoes, of which each one has planted freely.

Sunday, 19. Br. David preached from the words of Paul: I count all things but loss for the excellency of the knowledge of Christ Jesus.

Monday, 20. There was in the evening another slight alarm. Sisters, who were gathering chestnuts, brought home a piece of board they had found in an old house a few miles from here, on which were painted six warriors, with two prisoners and five scalps. Many believed that the six Potawatomies and Chippewas, who went through here a week ago, had fallen upon the pack-horse people, soon expected here, killed and taken prisoners some of them, and had then painted this board to let our Indians know about it. We could not, however, believe this, for the pack-horses could not yet have gone so far out, and we hoped for the best.

Tuesday, 21. Abraham went with some sisters to Pett-quotting to bring into safety some corn they had got there, and to bury it, for all the Indians have moved thence.

Saturday, 25. Many brethren came home from hunting, content, with horse-loads of venison and bear-meat, and casks filled with honey they had collected in the bush, for there are many bees here; thus our Indians, after the hunger they have endured, will again for a time have enough to eat, and more, and can live well; they cheerfully gave to us, too.

Sunday, 26. Br. Edwards preached, and Br. David held the congregation meeting in the evening.

Monday, 27. Wrote to Bethlehem and Litiz. Br. Edwards held early service.

Tuesday, 28. David held early service: But because ye are not of the world, therefore the world hateth you. By Samuel and Thomas, who went with horses to the Fort, we sent a package of letters to Litiz and Bethlehem.

Thursday, 30. Two Tawa Indians came in from hunting in the bush, staying here two days. The sisters cut wood for us.

Friday, Dec. 1. As the weather was fine and mild, the sisters went out to try to make some sugar for all at the love-feast.

Sunday, 3. 1st of Advent. Br. David preached about our Saviour's coming into the flesh, who, by his incarnation, passion, and death for our sins, brought back to us eternal life and happiness, wherefore we should be glad and thankful, rejoicing in our Saviour.

Tuesday, 5. Last night a fine snow fell, which was just the thing for our hunters.

Friday, 8. To-day, and several preceding days, it snowed so that the snow is knee-deep, and shows yet no sign of stopping.

Saturday, 9. Two white people came here from Pittsburg on their way to Detroit, by whom we had letters from Brs. Ettwein and Sensemann, from Bethlehem and Heidelberg (Berks Co., Pa.) From a Pittsburg newspaper, sent by Mr. Duncan, we learned the resolve of Congress about our Indians, just as we had already had news of it by letters from Bethlehem.

Sunday, 10. Br. Edwards preached; David held the congregation meeting.

Monday, 11. The white people set out on their way to Detroit. Br. David wrote by them to Mr. Askin about the letter of credit which Br. Wollin had sent for us to Mr. Dobie in Montreal, which Br. Ettwein had mentioned in his letter.

Tuesday, 12. It has snowed now for several days, and again to-day steadily. The snow always gets deeper, so that we are in a good deal of trouble about our cattle, while at this time of year on the Huron River (Michigan) we saw little snow, or almost none. The sisters brought our turnips from the field to the house for our cattle. Some of the hunters came home, for the snow is too deep for hunting, and our Indians are preparing to get snowshoes ready, a thing they had not expected, for on the Muskingum they never needed any, no deep snow ever falling.

Thursday, 14. Rain fell, and a thaw set in, which continued several days, so that the snow, which had been two and a half feet deep, almost all went off. There came seven Tawas and Chippewas from the lake here, remained over night, and inquired about the flour which had been stored here and not taken away. They were answered that the flour belonged to their father in Detroit. The morning after, as they went away, they observed the house where it was, for they passed through here not long ago, and therefore knew it. They took out three casks, two of which they took with them, the other they gave to our In-

dians, since it was too much for them, and they went away.
We, however, put the cask with the rest, and did not take
it. The evening before they had called upon Br. David;
one, a Tawa, knew English somewhat, and a Chippewa,
Delaware. They said they lived in Sandusky, on the lake.

Saturday, 16. The thaw kept on, for which we were
glad.

Sunday, 17. David preached, and then held the communion quarter-hour, which was announced for next Saturday. Br. Edwards held the congregation meeting.

Monday, 18. David held early service.

Tuesday, 19. Edwards. Abraham, with his wife, came
from Pettquotting, where he had been kept so long by the
deep snow. He had there met Luke and his family, with
A. Johanna, who pass the winter there, expecting us in
the spring. They think they will then have made the
journey, and be so far ahead of us. A. Charity came with
him.

Friday, 22. David spoke plainly with A. Charity, and
showed her how deceived she was in leaving us.

Saturday, 23. Having spoken with the brethren for
several days, we found cause in part for joy, in part for
sorrow. We had the number of thirty at the Lord's supper, which was accompanied by the Saviour's near presence. Three sisters and two brothers remained away this
time. Samuel and Thomas were not yet back from Pittsburg, and we cannot conceive why they remain away so
long. We conjectured that one of them must be ill, for
Samuel was not right well when he went away.

Sunday, 24. After the communion liturgy Br. Edwards
preached, and then David held the children's service, exhorting them to praise the infant Jesus with joyful hearts
and to glorify him with their mouths. We began Christmas with a love-feast. The history of our Saviour's birth
was read, and after consideration of the Scripture-verse
and text we prayed to the little Child in the manger. At
the end burning wax-tapers were given to the children;
whereupon all went joyfully home, and they sang afterwards in their huts Christmas verses.

Monday, 25. David preached from John, i : The word was made flesh. Br. Edwards held the congregation meeting. The brethren came to greet us and showed their hearts joyful at the Saviour's birth.

Tuesday, 26. At last came Brs. Samuel and Thomas from Pittsburg, whom we had very long and eagerly awaited, believing they must have met some misfortune or that they had been somewhat sick, but the deep snow had detained them, which in Pittsburg was much deeper than here, for they said it was over their hips, and it was not so deep here. We had by them a letter from Br. Heckewelder, in Carlisle, of Nov. 2, from which we learned they were in good health. From Gen. Butler, Superintendent of Indian Affairs, we had likewise a friendly letter, from which we learn his good intentions in offering us his services. Only it is a pity the winter is so hard and the way to him yet almost impassable, for I should like to see him to accomplish something for ourselves in the Indian land with the chiefs. Samuel told him the chiefs wanted to have us on the Pettquotting, but he advised him against accepting this call, telling him they would do ill to go there and would have an unquiet, pitiful life.

Friday, 29. The brethren got wood for us, a brother, sisters, boys, and girls. In the evening, since now the two brothers have come from the Fort, we made known to the assistant-brethren the resolve of Congress concerning our Indians and the orders sent out in their favor. Likewise that in the spring, by the grace of God, we should move to the Muskingum, it being the advice and direction of the Saviour and of the brethren. Br. David told them he was determined and ready to go and had thereby but one trouble, namely, whether all the brethren would be willing, but this he wished and hoped. He told them they had their choice.[1] The chiefs had summoned them and wished to have them with themselves, with no other intention than utterly to destroy the Indian church, for from them we had nothing good to expect, either bodily or

---

[1] This word is conjectured.

spiritually. If now they accepted the invitation of these chiefs it would not look well, Congress having made them such good offers and wishing to help them. If they went to the Muskingum, they would, perhaps, be done with the chiefs, but this would not hurt them, for they already knew from experience what they could expect from them. As long as we were among them we had never seen them give us any help, even in regard to the wild Indians; when they killed our cattle, stole our horses, and so on, we had never got satisfaction nor justice. We found that the assistants all agreed with us, thinking as we did. They believed also that most of the brethren would agree and that perhaps none would remain behind. As far as we have observed among the brethren, they have no desire for the Pettquotting, still less for Sandusky.

Sunday, 31. David preached. Towards midnight, we assembled at the close of the year, called to mind the kindnesses of his gracious guidance and direction, and his help through all difficulties. If it was at times hard and with distress, yet we cannot, at the close of the year, thank and praise him enough that he has done all so well and blessedly with us beyond our expectation. We remembered the grace and mercy the Saviour has shown us.

A year ago we knew not how we should fare, and there was little likelihood of our getting away from the Huron River this year, but when we spoke in February with the commandant in Detroit, we found that the Saviour was beginning to make us a way. He led the hearts of authority that it not only opened the way for us, but also helped us. We celebrated Easter in peace, having blessed holidays, but soon thereafter, April 20th, we broke up and started upon our travels. In Detroit, where we stayed several days with the Indians and had to wait, the commandant gave orders that two ships should be fitted out for us to take us to Cuyahoga; with these we sailed away April 28, and on the 29th, came to the islands in the lake, where, owing to adverse winds, we lay, and used up a whole month, until, at last, it was so arranged and the

Saviour helped, that we, partly by land along the shore, partly by water, all came, on the 8th of June, to the mouth of the Cuyahoga. Now was the trouble over, fortunately and without harm, but another met us, which was still harder than all, namely, famine, as we had also expected from the very beginning of our journey. We settled here in the bush, where far and near was no Indian settlement, and for a long time saw no ways or means of getting that by which we and our Indian brethren could live, but the Saviour helped, so that, in some measure, for a time, we were aided for pay, and also planted somewhat, which he so blessed, that, with what the Indian brethren have got here from other places, we shall have enough to eat until spring. We trust our heavenly Father further to care for us and to give us advice.

The Indian brethren, Samuel and Thomas, in September, made a visit to our Indians wandering in error, and were very well received by some, who, in return, were encouraged by them to turn back again to the church, which was not without blessing, and we can see that little by little many will again come back to the flock and again be found here.

We stayed here on the Cuyahoga quite quiet as regards the savages and their chiefs until October, when we got a message from Sandusky, and the chiefs sent us an invitation to come to Pettquotting and settle there, and soon after a second [that we should go to Lower Sandusky] was so involved in lies that it put our Indian brethren in such fear that for a week they fled into the bush, from fear lest the white people should fall upon them to murder them, which for a time made great uneasiness among the brethren. Luke took this occasion to go away from us with his family to Pettquotting, and A. Johanna, just twelve persons, whom, however, we do not reckon in the account. At last our brethren saw they had been deceived, and again came to their senses. After consideration of our Scripture-verse and text, we thanked the Lord upon our knees for all the goodness he had shown us, begged forgiveness also for all our faults and shortcomings,

and all this was accompanied by the tears of the brethren.
We were richly comforted by him and he let us feel his
peace. At the end the blessing of the Lord was laid upon
the church, and we gave the kiss of peace for the new
year one to another.

We have had the holy communion six times, thrice over
the lake on the Huron and thrice here, whereto five brethren have been admitted.

Five children have been baptized. One man has come
back to us again, namely, Michael.

Lately went to Pettquotting, Luke with his family and
Anna Johanna, in all twelve persons. One has died.

At present there are with us of married people sixteen
couples and one individual woman.

Single men 2, of whom one unbaptized.

Widowers 2.

Single women 6, of whom two unbaptized.

Widows 3.

Big boys 8, of whom six unbaptized. .

Big girls 7, of whom three unbaptized.

Boys 13, of whom two unbaptized.

Girls 21, of whom one unbaptized.

Total 95 Indian souls, among them 34 communion
brethren, without those in Pettquotting.

CHAPTER VII.

1787.

ON THE CUYAHOGA—JOURNEY TO HURON RIVER—SETTLEMENT THERE
(PETTQUOTTING).

Monday, Jan. 1. Br. Edwards preached about the name of Jesus as our Saviour. In the service following upon this, four persons, the single man, by name Lewis, and a young man, by name Benjamin, a single woman, by name Maria Elizabeth, and a maiden, by name Johannette, were baptized into Jesus' death, the two first by Br. Edwards, both the last by Br. David, whereby a mighty grace prevailed, and the near presence of the Saviour was to be noticed. In the concluding service Joshua's daughter, Salome, was admitted to the church, on which occasion Br. David laid down to our baptized youth the necessity of admission to the church, and impressed it upon them, and many wept bitterly. This caused quite a new movement and excitement among the young people of either sex, so that many tears were shed.

3. Two Chippewas were at the early service, very pious and devout, one of whom understood Delaware.

Friday, 5. Joseph, who had been sent by us over the lake, came here from Sandusky to see us, and secretly told an Indian brother, Thomas, that the nation had resolved upon war with the Americans, the Chippewas being the leaders, also that the chiefs had forbidden any one to let us know about it; that we missionaries would be killed, and not merely be made prisoners, as was before done; that the nations had all united for the war, and that the beginning would be made in the spring, in the neighborhood of the place where the Shawanese prisoners had been taken. They are now over the lake at a treaty, and when they come back they will send us a message once more, and if we do not regard it and yet go to the Muskingum, they will use force, killing us missionaries and carrying off our Indians, thus once for all the matter would be ended, and they would have no further trouble about us. Such is said to be the talk.

Saturday, 6. We celebrated Epiphany, accompanied by the near and perceptible presence of the Saviour. He showed himself great and mighty to his Indian flock that still remains and has been rescued from overthrow. At morning prayer we committed ourselves, as also all our churches among the heathen, to him for his blessing, and asked his near presence with us this day. In the second service of the baptized, after a discourse upon the Scripture-verse of the day, was absolved Michael, who came to us this summer, with a powerful outpouring of grace; and a grown maiden, A. Salome, was taken into the church. At the love-feast we thought of the churches among the heathen in Greenland, South America, and in the Isles.[1] The brethren were reminded and made to think that the Saviour had hitherto brought them through many trials, dangers, and temptations, and they were also told they should not think all was over now, they should not be so sure, but stand on their guard; we were not yet done with all difficulties and danger; a hard storm might still fall upon us; they should stand fast, and not indeed trust themselves, but believe that they are poor and weak, and so should cling the closer to the Saviour, and put their trust in him alone, who would never bring them to shame. In the service that followed upon this, a grown maiden, Ignatius' daughter, was baptized into Jesus' death, with the name Anna Maria; also to-day was baptized Cathrine's sick child, by name, Samuel, and A. Salome.

Sunday, 7. Edwards preached, and thereupon the children, especially the boys, had a blessed service. His history was brought to their minds: When Jesus was twelve

---

[1] At this time the Moravians had nine missions in the West Indies, three in Greenland, and one in Surinam.

years old, etc., and there was a discourse about their text:
And Jesus increased in wisdom and stature and in favor
with God and man. In the congregation meeting from
the Scripture-verse, Cathrine upon her longing request
and entreaty was absolved. Her husband brought her to
us on the Huron River in '85, but he went away himself,
and, as we learn, is paralytic and cannot walk, but as soon
as he is somewhat better will come to us.· She made clear
that she wished to live and die in the church, would willingly in the church share our joys and sorrows; however
things went with the Saviour's people, well or ill, she
wished to share them, and considered herself fortunate to
suffer hardship with the church. We could not but give
praise and thanks to the Saviour for the mercy he had let
our brethren experience and enjoy during these days.
There was a quite new comprehension, and thorough
awakening among them, so that none went away empty, as
if the Saviour had something especial in store for them, and
wished to prepare them for something to come. Pleasant
was it to us that they had heard none of these stories
about war, and would not hear them, for only two brethren had heard them and they kept silent. We laborers
had afterwards, late in the evening, a conference together
about them, for if the news were true, which we had a
while ago and again just now, we could not be quite
quiet and indifferent about it, without thinking and considering what we should do, and this soon, before it was
too late and we were caught unprepared. We thought
the news might be true, there was no impossibility
about it, for ever since we have been here we have heard
that the Indians are eager for war, and only wait for
things to go well for it. On the other hand, it may also
be deceit on the part of the chiefs, who secretly spread
abroad such news, and even forbid any one to tell us of
it on this very account, that we may the more readily believe it, they well knowing it would come to our ears,
and wishing to arouse fear and dread among our Indians,
so that they may take refuge with them and accept their
messages. Since now we were in uncertainty, and knew

not what to believe, and since we did not wish to waste
our time, for we had little now, and almost none to turn
ourselves in and to form a plan, we turned to the Saviour
and begged his advice. We asked him whether, consid-
ing our circumstances, we had now any thing to ask him,
and the answer was, yes. In the consultation hereupon
we made the following lots :

1st. The Saviour is for our soon going away from here;
hereto we put a blank and the first was drawn.

2d. The Saviour tells us to go to the place on the Muskingum pointed out by the conference in Bethlehem,
and hereto a blank, and the first was drawn. We had
still one matter of concern, namely, to know whether
we should soon set out upon our journey to the Muskingum, having for some time such fine weather, the
ground free from snow, and the Cuyahoga perfectly clear
from ice. The Saviour let us know that we had no need
of haste, but could await the spring.

We were from our hearts thankful to the Saviour for
advising us and helping us out of our trouble and perplexity. His word is truth, therein we trust, thereon depend. We should now no longer be disturbed by evil reports, nor pay heed to them, but go straight on and regard
them not.

Monday, 8. Joseph had us asked whether he would be
received again if he should come back to us with his wife.
We did not refuse him, but sent word to him he must first
know whether his wife was of his mind, and if thus he
came we would consider it.

Wednesday, 10. Salome, Stephen's wife, became suddenly ill with convulsions, so that it was feared she would
not come to herself again, but she got better the next day.
Many brethren went off to search for sugar-places and to
build huts.

Thursday, 11. A party of Chippewas came here from
their hunting-place, encamping near by for several days.
They were going to their sugar-place, were very friendly,
and said that those who took the flour here were Tawas,
and no Chippewas, for they did no such things.

Sunday, 14. Br. Edwards preached and David held the congregation meeting. The Chippewas near us gave our Indians a feast of bear's meat, having shot several bears.

Tuesday, 16. Br. Edwards held early service. In the marriage quarter-hour afterward the single brother, Lewis, Salome's son, and the single sister, Esther, the late Rachel's daughter, were married. Most of the brethren went into the bush to build sugar-huts.

Saturday, 20. Five messengers came from Pittsburg, sent to the nations with a message from Mr. Butler. Among them were two Senecas, one of them a chief, a Cayuga, an Onondaga, and a Wyandot. They made a speech to our Indians with a string of wampum, washed the tears from their eyes, comforted them for all the suffering they had passed through, and thereupon made known to them the directions given to them, whereto they had the order of the well known Cayashoto, the Mingo chief, who stayed much in Pittsburg. Their directions are to try whether they can bring the nations, especially the Shawanese, to incline their ears to peace, and if they perceive any inclination thereto among them, to invite them to a treaty; to promise the Shawanese also, if they wish to make peace, they shall recover the thirty odd prisoners whom they have in the States. Our Indians thanked them, through a string, as well for their comforting address and good wishes as for the information about their directions, encouraged them to do their best, that a stable treaty of peace may be made among the nations, for we were children of peace and wished them good success. This pleased them so much that they said that now they went twice as cheerfully and willingly about their work; they would do their best, and on their return would come here again to tell us how they found things and what they had accomplished.

Sunday, 21. Early in the morning they set forth again on their way after we had given them some provisions for the journey. Br. David delivered a sermon about: Lord if thou wilt thou canst, etc. I will. Br. Edwards held the congregation meeting.

21

Tuesday, 23. From the many rains and thunder-storms the Cuyahoga rose so high yesterday and to-day as to cover the lowland. Our Indian brethren contributed corn for the Chippewas and gave it them. The eldest of them is brother of the chief who was our friend over the lake. They wish to make sugar here with our brethren ; they are very friendly, and always asking when we shall go back home again over the lake, thinking we stay here only for hunting, as they do.

Thursday, 25. Most of the brethren went away to their sugar-huts, the weather being good and the water lower.

Saturday, 27. Late in the evening came a messenger from Sandusky, not for us, to be sure, but to summon home the Indians in the bush here and there off hunting. We learned from him that the Indians were come back from Detroit, and we inquired about the state of affairs, what was the common talk among them. He said he knew thus much, that ten nations there had declared for peace, to which they were exhorted, and that they had agreed to this : Whenever a nation from now henceforth should continue to do harm, all the others would look after it and force it to keep peace. This was very pleasant news to us, from which we. could see that the Saviour began to make ready for us and to clear hinderances from our way.

Sunday, 28. Edwards preached, thereupon was the communion quarter-hour. The messenger, by name Mamasu, who remained here to-day, and whom all the Indian brethren well knew to be a bad man, who, in Schönbrunn and Gnadenhütten, had designs against the life of the brothers, and when he long lay in wait for them, almost executed his murderous plans, (he) wished now to hear about the Saviour, and asked the Indian brethren to tell him somewhat, and this they were glad to do, and not without effect, for he said afterwards he was of mind to come to us, and to change his ways, that he had neither father nor mother, and with his other friends [there were some few of them, four brothers and three sisters] he had already spoken, and they were not opposed. The reason of their coming upon such thoughts was that they had an uneasy, pitiable life, nothing but drunkenness was cared for, al-

though he drank with them, yet not willingly, and as they
had heard they would be free from this if they came to us,
all would like to be with us. The 29th he still stayed
here, and was quite disposed to remain here at once, and
not to go away farther, for he said, the message with
which he was charged did not hinder him, he cared nothing about that, for Pipe would soon send another in case
he stayed out too long, but to this we did not advise
him.

Wednesday, 31.   The Indian, Mamasu, resolved to stay
here for good. He wished neither to deliver his message,
still less to go back, for fear he might be disturbed in
his purpose and hindered by the Indians. We advised
him neither the one nor the other, but awaited what
would happen, and only wished him firmness.

Saturday, Feb. 3.   Our dear Lord blessed us unspeak-
ably by the enjoyment of his body and blood in the holy
communion, after the brethren had first been spoken to.

Sunday, 4.   After the communion liturgy, in which the
brethren were recommended to have always in their hearts
and not to forget the suffering, passion, and death of our
Lord, and to interest themselves more therein [thus would
their faults and shortcomings be ever less, and the brethren ever more welcome and a greater joy and pride to the
Saviour], was the sermon by Br. David, and Br. Edwards
held the congregation meeting. The assistants spoke with
Mamasu, whom we wished to put on probation, and they
made known to him our ordinances, whereby he promised to conduct his life.

Monday, 5.   In the early service, where the discourse
was about the Scripture-verse : The sons also of them that
afflicted thee shall come bending unto thee, the brethren were informed that Mamasu had permission to live
with us, that we should all rejoice if he throve before the
Lord.

[Thus far to Bethlehem.]

Wednesday, 7.   The brethren all went to their sugar-
huts. There remained at home, of the Indian brethren,

Cornelius, almost blind, and Ephraim, who is quite blind, and two old widows, besides us white brethren.

Saturday, 10. Mary Magdalene was brought to bed in the sugar-huts—with a son.

Sunday, 11. Br. Edwards preached about the good seed in the field, and David held the congregation meeting. Quite a large number of the brethren came home, but,

Monday, 12, nearly all went back again. A. Charity remained for sugar-making, with our permission.

Wednesday, 14. By Peter, who went to Pettquotting, Mamasu sent back to Pipe his message and the wampum.

Sunday, 18. A good many brethren came home. Br. David preached about the Saviour, and Br. Edwards held the congregation meeting. In a book that came by chance into our hands last summer, we found instruction and direction how to reckon when Easter would fall this year, and we found it would be April 8th, according to our calculation, for we had neither calendar nor Scripture-verses for this year.

Monday, 19. The brethren went back early, each one to his place in the sugar-camp. For several days we have pleasant spring weather.

Wednesday, 21. Chippewas came in from their sugar-huts very fine-looking, friendly Indians.

Friday, 23. An Indian came through here as messenger to the Indians in Gokhosing (Vernon River, O.), to summon all those there to the Miami, whither now all the Indians are going, usually no good token of peace. We learn that the nations seem to incline to peace, but that all depends upon a treaty the nations will have held in Pittsburg.

Sunday, 25. Two Chippewas were present at the sermon, which Br. David delivered, one of whom understood Delaware somewhat. At the end of this the little son of Renatus, the Mohican, and Mary Magdalene, born in the sugar-camp on the 10th Inst., was baptized with the name

Timothy. Br. David held the congregation meeting from the Scripture-verse.

Tuesday, 27. By Stephen and Adam, who went to the Fort, we sent letters to Bethlehem.

Friday, March 2. Peter, with his people, came back from Pettquotting, where he saw Luke and Anna Johanna, who wish themselves back with us and are not at all pleased there. With them came here also Petty, who manifested her desire to be with us again, and she remained here.

Sunday, 4. The brethren who are not far off came home from their sugar-camp for the services. Br. Edwards preached and Br. David held the congregation meeting in the afternoon, and then most of the brethren went back again.

Tuesday, 6. Our Samuel became suddenly sick, had Br. David called in the night, committed to him his wife and children, and bade him not to permit them to be seduced into heathenism by their friends who live on the Tawa River, if he should die, and this Br. David promised him. He was let blood, whereupon the next day he was better.

Saturday, 10. Stephen and Adam returned from Pittsburg, gladdening us with letters from Bethlehem, dated last year, and from Br. Ettwein, of Jan. 6th, this year; also the Scripture-verses and texts for this year. At the same time we had a message from Lieut.-Col. Harmar from Fort Harmar, at the mouth of the Muskingum [who received the order from Congress and was to execute it], wherein he made known to us the resolve of Congress in our favor and told us we should send for the five hundred bushels of corn mentioned, twenty axes and twenty hoes and one hundred blankets in the aforesaid Fort Harmar.

Also Gen. Richard Butler, Agent (for Indian Affairs), sent us word in a letter to Br. David that he had good hope that during the summer all differences with the Indians would be put aside and every thing brought into good order. Trustworthy news from the assembly of the nations, he wrote, made this very credible to him. Messrs.

Duncan and Wilson, however, advised us at the same time in their letter to remain here a year longer and to plant. They did not, indeed, allege their flour business, which they thought safe under our oversight, but because they believed that during this summer a stable peace would be made again with the Indians.

Sunday, 11. Br. David preached and thereupon held the communion quarter-hour, and he told the brethren now that we had the news from the proper hand, for which we had always waited, what Congress had resolved in their favor and for which they had given orders for execution. This was communicated by the speech of Lieut.-Col. Harmar, which he sent to them in writing. At the same time they were told to prepare for departure for the Muskingum, and to be ready to do what was needful. We observed that most of them were glad and joyful to move to the Muskingum, but some few were doubtful about it.

Tuesday, 13. An Indian on his way from Sandusky to Pittsburg came here and stayed, on account of the high water, through the whole week, it raining much, son of the departed Jacob. We had always heard that the Indians were all moving from Sandusky to the Miami, assembling there, and this is usually no good token, and now we heard the contrary.

Friday, 16. Both yesterday and to-day the brethren were spoken to, for they had all come together from the bush. To our shame (at our lack of faith) we found that the Saviour, in regard to our wandering and moving to the Muskingum, had turned the hearts of the brethren, giving them courage and inclination thereto. None of them had any desire to move to Pettquotting or Sandusky; even the few who did not wish to go to the Muskingum, on account of their children and friends who were murdered there, had indeed no longing for this, but they wished rather to go with the greater part and remain with the church than again to put themselves under the savages.

Saturday, 17. At the Lord's supper were present as

candidates two sisters and two maidens, namely, Cathrine, Esther, Salome, and Anna Salome.

Sunday, 18. After the communion liturgy, Br. Edwards preached and David held the congregation meeting.

Tuesday, 20. A white man of Pittsburg, an acquaintance, came here from the head of Great Beaver Creek, where he had passed the winter among the Indians, bringing some wares and things, all of which our Indians bought of him. We heard among our people all sorts of unpleasant things about our moving. There appeared traces of obstinacy [and this made us sad] among those from whom we had not expected it, but we were not therefore cast down, but went comforted to work. Petty went to Sandusky, promising to come back to us again. Most of the brethren went,

Wednesday, 21, to work making canoes. They have one ready now and need yet still seven or eight.

Thursday, 22. The white man went back again.

Saturday, 24. Messrs. Duncan and Wilson came here and remained until the 26th. They spoke with us about our moving to the Muskingum, advising us to remain here, for, as they said, there was yet no peace with the Indian nations, and the times were still very uncertain; for this matter they had instructions from Mr. Butler to speak with us. Although we did not heed this much, and therefore had not much concern about it, yet through Luke's sons, on the evening of the 25th, we got very disagreeable news and threats from the Indians, that if we moved Br. David would be killed, and this caused us much consideration.

Sunday, 25. (Annunciation.) David preached and thereafter held the service for to-day's festival from the day's text: Forasmuch then as the children are partakers of flesh and blood, he also himself took part of the same, about the great blessing and the great grace which has become the portion of us all, small and great, through the Saviour's incarnation, passion, and death, that we now by Christ's will are in God's grace and through belief in him are become the children of God.

Monday, 26. Edwards held early service. Messrs. Duncan and Wilson set forth on their way to Detroit, one of our Indians going with them as guide as far as Pettquotting. Since we were now prepared to break up from here after the Easter holidays, but the news which we heard both from Pittsburg and from the Indian land, caused us much consideration and concern, inasmuch as we could not see plainly and clearly, indeed it seemed as if we were again hemmed in on all sides, we were anxious for consolation, and needed advice to know what we should do, for we saw no outcome for our Indian brethren about whose well-being, safety, and quiet we were most concerned, and where could we get us advice save from him who knows beforehand times and circumstances, to whom our situation and perplexity are better known than we can tell him, who alone is wise and the best adviser in all our needs. So we brought our circumstances before the Saviour, and begged him most earnestly and pressingly to advise us according to his own heart, and to make known to us his gracious, good, and agreeable will. After much consideration and after our moving to the Muskingum at present was not opposed by him, and our other plans fell through, we saw that the way thither was barred for the time being; to remain here was also impossible, and we had no other resource than to go again out by the lake, whence we came a year ago, and finally as we had but this one plan in reserve wherewith all our schemes, thoughts, and considerations came to an end, the Saviour approved that we should seek a place of refuge between the Cuyahoga and Pettquotting, and there remain. For this also we brought him our thanks and adored him, astonished and full of awe at his government, which he carried out among us, and for the ways which he went with us. We must place our hands upon our mouths, and say : " What he does and ordains is right and well done, for in his government has he never failed." This was indeed unexpected by us, and a perfectly new scene was spread open to us, something which now indeed we could not understand, but in the. future should better understand and comprehend, why it should so be and not otherwise.

Tuesday, 27. The Indian brethren set about getting some canoes ready, which they had already begun, after we had first spoken with the assistants and made known to them that we should not this spring go to the Muskingum, but back again to the lake, whence we came. Many were in thought thereover what it meant, and this we could not indeed quite plainly tell them, save only that times and circumstances were not yet settled, and as yet there was no stable peace. They accommodated themselves very well to this and were also quite content. We have lately observed among the brethren that many, especially such as lost their children and friends on the Muskingum, are not entirely willing to go thither, but yet we have also found that none of them would have remained behind, and wished to go his own way, if we had gone there, and all was already arranged to go there and not elsewhere.

Friday, 30. As it was rumored among the brethren that we do not go to the Muskingum, but back again, there secretly spread among them a report that Br. David and his wife would return to the church, that Br. Edwards would go with them, and this caused much unnecessary consideration [and some said to us they would go with us, whether we went into the land (of the States) or over the lake], for this had some only resolved, but it had also the result, that when they talked about it among themselves, they said, with tears in their eyes, that it would be no wonder should it so be, they had already caused us so much anxiety, but if this time only we would stay with them, they would so trouble us no more, but from now on would better themselves, through the Saviour's grace.

Sunday, April 1. Br. Edwards preached to-day from to-day's Gospel about the Saviour's entrance into Jerusalem. Thereupon was the communion quarter-hour, and towards evening the congregation meeting from the Scripture-verse: In thy presence is fulness of joy; at thy right hand there are pleasures for evermore. Afterwards, the brethren were told we had hitherto thoughts of going to the Muskingum, when we broke up here, but that we found our circumstances such that it was not yet time; to remain here we also found not well; we should then select a place for a temporary abode between here and Pettquotting, but meanwhile always consider our appointed place on the Muskingum the object of our endeavors.

I will here introduce an example to show how the Holy Ghost preaches among the brethren. Many brethren and sisters came together in a house, talking about to-day's Gospel. which they had heard. One brother said: "I have often already heard that which I heard to-day, but it has never been so clear to me as to-day, especially the words the Saviour spoke: My house shall be called of all nations the house of prayer, but ye have made it a den of thieves." He said: "Our body is a temple, a house of the Holy Ghost. The Saviour has washed us from our sins by his blood, and prepared our hearts and bodies, that he may dwell therein. Henceforth we should not defile God's temple, nor again let in the old sinful things from which our Saviour has washed and cleansed us; we must always bear in mind that we are not our own, but that we belong to the Saviour, body and soul, and therefore keep ourselves undefiled."

Tuesday, 3. Yesterday and to-day the Indian brothers got some canoes ready and brought them into the water, whereby Samuel dislocated his arm for the fourth time, which, with much trouble, was at last brought back again. From Pettquotting came Zachary, bringing a message from a Monsey chief to Br. David alone: "Grandfather, I hear thou willst go to Thuppekünk, but I advise thee not to go there this spring. I cannot plainly tell thee why, but this much, it is not yet time. I can also say nothing as to whether there will be war or peace; that depends upon circumstances. Think not that I oppose thy teaching the Indians God's word; that is dear to me, but I advise thee well. Go not to Thuppekünk, ye might all suffer harm."

Wednesday, 4. Both yesterday and to-day the brethren were spoken to, for there is much which is unpleasant, and this makes us grieve, yet the Saviour again sent us much peace in them.

Thursday, 5. Towards evening was read the heart-moving story of our Saviour on the Mount of Olives. Then the communion brethren had the washing of feet, and thereupon enjoyed his body and blood in the holy communion with hungry and thirsty souls. Michael was readmitted. Two young sisters and two grown girls were partakers for the first time. This was indeed something new, for hitherto we have always been on our guard about admitting such young people to the holy communion, but it seems the Saviour will show us that we should give more thought to our young people than hitherto. We have found many times from experience that they surpass the old in attachment to the Saviour and the church. They have no longer taste for the world and heathenism, nor pleasure therein. They will not remain among the savages, even those who are not baptized, but have grown up in the church.

Friday, 6. The story of our Saviour's sufferings, crucifixion, death, and burial was heard with moved and melted hearts. For his hard and bitter, suffering, for his buffetings and scourgings, for all the wounds he received for us, for his outpouring of blood, he received many tears of sinners, and the brethren could not hear enough; it was as if they heard for the first time.

Saturday, 9. We had a love-feast, whereby was a discourse about the Saviour's rest in the grave after his hard sufferings, and then about the Scripture-verse and text.

Sunday, 8. We read early in the chapel, having here no grave-yard, the Easter litany. Thereupon was a part of the story of the resurrection read. Br. Edwards preached, and, in the afternoon service, Esther, Cornelius' daughter, a single woman, was taken into the church, and her brother baptized into Jesus' death with the name Tobias, whose father Tobias had been a martyr at Gnadenhütten, on the Muskingum.

Monday, 9. By John Leeth and two Indians with him

we had a letter from Br. Heckewelder from Pittsburg, of
the 2nd of this month, telling us of his arrival there with
two brothers, Michael Jung and Weigand. We at once
made preparations, and sent,

Tuesday, 10, several brethren there with horses to help
them. The letters from Bethlehem, however, did not
come. Samuel went also with a couple of brethren a
good day's journey from here, to seek a place for our settlement, where we thought of staying as soon as they
came back.

Wednesday, 11. Anna Johanna came from Pettquotting. They were almost shipwrecked on the rocks in a
storm. These, especially Anna Paulina, when, the next
morning, they were at early service, could do nothing but
weep, at again hearing the word of God, of which they
had heard nothing the whole winter, but they accused
themselves and called themselves guilty, that they had let
themselves be so blind.

Friday, 13. Samuel came back with the two brothers,
Stephen and Adam, from their exploration. When they
went away from here, they went straight through the
bush to the head of the very creek where we wished to
go. There they met a party of Tawa Indians out hunting, who told them that farther down the creek they
would find excellent land. They made then a bark canoe,
went down the creek, and found it as they had been told,
namely, a great tract of good land, even better than here,
or than we have anywhere had; it was partly clear and
the rest easy to clear, some five or six miles from the lake,
but quiet and deep water so far, but straightway at the
upper end a strong current and rapids begin. Only they
said they could find no town-site, for on the creek there is
nothing but rich bottom land, but yet this lies so high
that water can never overflow it. This creek is half way
between Cuyahoga and Pettquotting,[1] the only place we
can make use of, and there is no other to be found, therefore we had no choice.

---

[1] Probably, then, Black River.

Sunday, 15. David preached, and thereupon held a service for the baptized. We had six brethren baptized this
year, and three taken into the church, whom we committed to the Saviour for farther oversight, and to God,
the worthy Holy Spirit, for his care, to let them grow in
the knowledge and love of Jesus Christ, and to thrive in
the church wholly for him. From Pettquotting came a
French trader, on his own business, in quest of a strange
Indian, and stayed over night. Br. Edwards held the
congregation meeting. One of our Indians, Mamasu, who
went to the Tuscarawas and lay alone in the bush, was
fallen upon at night by two wolves. One of them attacked his dog, which gave the alarm. The Indian seized
his musket at once, and while the other wolf was spring-
ing upon him, he jumped over the fire, and shot him dead
in his camp; he then ran at once to help his dog, whereupon the other wolf took flight, but his dog was so very
much hurt that he had to carry him the next day.

Monday, 16. David held the early service. He told
the brethren to hold themselves in readiness to start from
here within two or three days, as many as could, for we
could not all wait until those from the Fort had come
back.

Thursday, 19. After the early service, in which, at the
end, we thanked the Saviour in prayer for all the goodness, kindness, and blessing we had here enjoyed from
him, and had further recommended us to his grace and
guidance, and after we had thereupon loaded our canoes,
we went, some by water down to the lake, while, at the
same time, they who went by land began their journey
with Br. Zeisberger and his wife, but Br. Edwards with
those by water. We came,

Friday, 20, to Stone Creek (Rocky River, perhaps),
where we found some canoes, most having passed the most
dangerous place, namely, the steep rocks, and some had
already got a good distance beyond, but, on account of
high wind, had to come to land. A year ago to-day we
left Huron River.

Saturday, 21. There was a hard wind from the north

and north-west, on which account the canoes had to lie
still. The waves struck so hard upon the rocks that the
ground trembled at times, for the wind came straight
from the lake. Those on land also kept still on the 22nd,
for the night before they fished by torchlight, and speared
some hundred large fish, weighing from three to ten
pounds each, which they had to cook and dry on the way.

Monday, 23. We left the canoes and set forth upon our
way. It was yet too windy upon the lake to start. In the
evening we encamped.

Tuesday, 24. We turned from the way along the lake,
going some miles through the bush straight to our place,
and when we came to our creek where we wished to go,
we found ourselves on a high hill, from which down into
the plain we could overlook the whole country, as it were
a beautiful, pleasant garden. We went from there across
the land, pleased with every thing we saw. We found it
just as the brethren who had been here described it, and
even better, for there is almost as much clear land as we
shall all need. It is true, as they said, we have nowhere
had such good land. We encamped near the creek, which
is deep, and thus far no strong stream, for the lake checks
it thus far; a little further up, just above us, the stream begins. In the evening Samuel, the only Indian brother with
us, went fishing, and had in a short time more fish than
were necessary. They are a sort of pike, which now at
this time go in great numbers from the lake into the creek.

Wednesday, 25. Those who set out by water at the same
time with us got here. They started this morning with
still water from Stone Creek at daybreak, and came by good
luck this afternoon into this creek, when a strong wind
arose, and the lake was already quite rough. We found
now that we were some five miles from the lake, and if the
wind comes thence we can plainly hear it roar. In the
evening we unloaded our canoes and brought our things
where it was dry; pleasantest and best was it to have had
fair weather during the whole journey.

Thursday, 26. We got rainy weather, and each one
built himself a hut. The sisters dug wild potatoes, of which

there are many here, a very wholesome food for Indians.
Matthew, Cornelius' son, who came here yesterday from
the Miami, said that Titawachkam wanted to give him a
message for us, which he would not receive, but told him
he might deliver his message himself, whereupon so much
was told him by word of mouth; to say to us that soon
something would be told us by the chiefs to something this
effect: We should not plant here, but come to Sandusky,
where they had made a place for us. Many bad threats
were also added if we refused, and this again caused us
much anxiety. ·He said at the same time that the Indians
always held themselves ready for war.

Friday, 27. A canoe went to Cuyahoga to help forward
those who went to the Fort. David held evening service
from the Scripture-verse. The Indian brethren brought
in clear alum, which they got from the rocks on the creek,
and they said there was plenty to be had. Another canoe
went to Pettquotting to get corn, a good day's journey
from here, but before they came out of the creek into the
lake they were stopped by Titawachkam, who came here
with Luke, bringing us a message from the chiefs, Pipe,
Welandawecken, and Pomoacan, and as he was in haste
to turn back again he ordered the brethren to assemble at
once, saying he had something important to tell us. As
Br. David was not present when this occurred, he had him
called, for to him, he said, he had something to say per-
sonally. When he came he made first an introductory
speech, saying that he was sent by the aforesaid three
chiefs to make known to us quickly their mind and will
before it should be too late, since spring was at the door.
On our behalf they had held a council and considered for
our good and resolved how and where we could dwell
quiet, safe and undisturbed. The chiefs meant well by us
and wished much we might accept their message. The
message, accompanied by a string of wampum, was as follows: " Friends, ye believing Indians, we have thought
upon you for your good, considered and resolved that for
the present ye can nowhere live so quietly and securely
as near us on the Sandusky River, neither here where ye

are, nor in Pettquotting, nor elsewhere in Cuyahoga.
Our uncle, Pomoacan, gives you a piece of land between
the Lower Wyandot Town and Monsey Town, where
I live; there ye can plant and fish, settle, and continue
your worship of God undisturbed, and no one will trouble
you or put any thing in your way, for every one knows the
chiefs have made ready unanimously the place for you. If
you agree to this it will be well for you. I do not say
that ye shall first much consider about it, for it has all been
considered, and ye have nothing to do but to arise. I take
you by the hand and lead you to your appointed place,
which is made ready for you."

Thereupon he turned to Br. David and said farther,
likewise with another string: "Hear, my friend, my rela-
tive. Thou art my grandfather, my flesh and blood, of
my color. My forefathers, our chiefs, have adopted thee
into our nation. I know well, over what they have agreed
together concerning thy person. One of the then chiefs,
still in life, has given me a commission in thy behalf to
have care of thee, for no chief is here, and not to permit
any harm to happen to thee in these yet unquiet times;
this is not unknown to the chiefs here, they are perfectly
well aware that I am placed here by my chiefs to conduct
thine affairs, they know thus that thou art in good, safe
hands, and that no harm will happen to thee," whereupon
he handed the string to Br. David.

Afterwards we yet spoke much with him, telling him
our anxiety about living so near other towns; first, on
account of their drunkenness; secondly, on account of
the seduction of our young people; thirdly, on account of
our cattle. To this he answered they had thought about
this too, and come to an understanding about every thing;
their young people would be told not to be troublesome to
us, nor do us harm; therefore he was there if we had any
thing to complain of, it would not be needful for us to do
ourselves justice, but we should only tell him, he would
conduct our affairs at the proper place, and provide what
was right. Different brothers told him their thoughts and
fears. Abraham said that what the chief told us was al-

ways fair, if only we could depend upon it that they were
speaking the truth. When they took us away from our
towns on the Muskingum they had also said we should not
regard our plantations, we should find enough to eat
where we were going, but afterwards they gave us not a
grain of corn except what we had to buy enormously dear.
Another said they had already thus promised us Pettquotting, had told us to dwell on the Sandusky wherever we
pleased, but afterwards bade us get out of that country,
and Br. David said to him that they had also promised
them that they should have and keep their teachers with
them, and should continue to hold their worship of God
unhindered, but yet they had deprived them of their
teachers, and driven them over the lake. He had to hear
a good deal which he could not deny, but he said it was
all true, he knew well enough, but it should no more happen. Some said again that they should go not only with
great reluctance to Sandusky to live, but were quite opposed to going, from which he could see that our Indians
were more against it than we were, but yet afterwards
they went. After we had talked over all sorts of things
with him, and had also inquired how far the place
was distant from other towns, he told us we should be
seven, eight, or nine miles from his town, but from the
Wyandot town we should be much farther off; then we
separated, and, as he wanted to turn back towards home
to-day, we spoke with our Indian brethren, telling them
our mind and disposition, for we can plainly see that we
have no choice, we should cause ourselves nothing but vexation, trouble, and all manner of hardship if we wished to
oppose, and then should accomplish nothing; therefore we
advised them to give their consent and acquiescence for
going to Sandusky, and this they did, seeing that we consented. We gave our answer by a string of wampum that
we wished to do what they required of us, and would go
there when they had appointed. But to the clause concerning Br. David we added a clause, to wit: that the
brothers who were with him should have the same regard

22

paid them, and the same privilege as he had, or if he should pass from time, and another come in his stead, that there should be the same arrangement. The whole matter, as regards this point, is expressly to be seen in the diary of the Mission on the Ohio for the year 1770, in the months of May, June, or July.

Though we could not quite rejoice about this circumstance and occurrence, for it went against our mind, thought, and will, and was something we could not do willingly, and yet must do, we were comforted by to-day's Scripture-verse to thank the Lord therefor. It read: Give thanks unto the God of gods, give thanks to the Lord of lords, to him who alone doeth great wonders, and this we did, but for the present still in faith. Br. Edwards held the service in the evening.

Saturday, 28. We sent a messenger to Cuyahoga, to give the brethren still remaining there news of our situation, and to bid them follow us as soon as possible. Luke, who remained over night, went away, with whom Br. David spoke in a straightforward and earnest way, laying before him every thing, which he denied.

Sunday, 29. Br. David held service in the forenoon and Edwards in the evening.

Monday, 30. At noon came Br. Michael Jung, with the messenger from Cuyahoga, where, with Br. Weigand, he had come from Pittsburg three days before, by whom, to our heartfelt joy, we got letters from the church, wherewith we were busy all the afternoon and refreshed ourselves. He came to us even here in the bush on our pilgrimage. He had left Br. John Weigand in Cuyahoga with our brethren, who were behind and for whom we were waiting. In the evening service the brethren were greeted by the churches and brothers, and were told that Br. John, who much loved the Indian brethren, had sent them a message in writing, which they should hear so soon as they should all be together.

Tuesday, May 1. Michael Jung held evening service from the Scripture-verse.

Wednesday, 2. Last night and to-day was a high wind.

The lake was not to be travelled and we could not expect our brethren. Br. Edwards held service. We learned late this evening that Br. John Weigand had come to the lake below with Br. Schebosh and his wife, William and others, and encamped there. The first came,

Thursday, 3, early to us, as we were upon the point of breaking up to move on, yet we welcomed and greeted one another and rejoiced together. We then soon went away, leaving our pleasant place, which in every way pleased all who saw it, and we left our huts standing, which we had made, and went down to the lake, where we encamped; here we waited for the remaining canoes from Cuyahoga.

Friday, 4. It was very windy last night and to-day, but as the wind came from the south and did not hinder us, two canoes went ahead to Pettquotting to get corn. Five canoes came to us from Cuyahoga, for which we have been waiting, so that now Cuyahoga is quite deserted and we are all together. With them came to us John Leeth, with his wife and children, who came with the brothers from Pittsburg. As in the evening there was windy, rainy weather, we could have no service, but Samuel had in his hut an hour of song, at which many brethren were present. Mamasu, who has already often spoken with Br. David, being in great perplexity about himself, came of his own accord and from the restlessness of his heart, and had an upright, fraternal talk with him. Afterwards also he brought to Br. David his brother, who had come with the brethren from Cuyahoga, having gone there from hunting, and said that he too would like to live with us and become a believer; to whom Br. David said he should first learn about us by seeing and hearing, so that he could well consider and not afterwards repent.

Saturday, 5. Early the wind was still good for us. We made every preparation for running out and going to Pettquotting, but before we were ready the wind went around to the west and was very strong, so that the lake raged and roared. We had to remain encamped here, but got our cattle over the river, which is here quite wide, and

encamped on the west side, where we were somewhat out
of the wind.

Sunday, 6. Br. Zeisberger and his wife went on ahead
with those who were going by land with the cattle, so that
if the wind became favorable the canoes might not have
to wait for them and we might not hinder one another.
They came,

Monday, 7, towards noon, the wind not changing, to the
mouth of a deep creek (Vermillion River, perhaps), where
they swam the cattle over, and making a bark canoe, got
the men and baggage over, and then went along the lake
till evening. At the night-quarters we saw on the shore
of the lake an interesting occurrence, which may often
happen here on these lofty shores. A great mass of land,
together with the trees which stood on it, close and high,
was torn from the land and carried a good piece out into
the lake and made at once an island. The wood standing
on it was not in the least injured and continued to grow
as before.[1] From this one can form some slight idea of
the earthquakes in Italy, by which also tracts of land are
moved, but yet an earthquake was not the cause here.

Tuesday, 8. Since the bush in which we encamped was
very wild and thick, we had this morning long labor in
getting the cattle together. We came in the afternoon to
Pettquotting,[2] and encamped a mile from the lake on the
creek, where a French trader lives, who entertained Br.
Zeisberger and his wife with bread, butter, and bush-tea,
which tasted right well, for we were hungry.

Here the Indians, whom we met, advised us against
going to Sandusky. Among them was Weschnasch
[Frederick], one of our baptized, who told us we had been
deceived with the statement that the Monsey town was
eight miles from our place; that it was not over two miles
off, and that we should be much plagued there by sots.
This was indeed such good reason for alarm that we
thought much about it and our Indian brethren, who did

---

[1] I do not understand Zeisberger to speak as an eye-witness.

[2] Huron River, flowing through Huron and Erie counties.

• not want to go there, said we should all be ruined—first, through the drunkenness; secondly, because we came too late for planting, and we should again have to pass a whole year of famine.

In the evening came Benjamin from the brethren on the water, bringing a letter from Br. Michael Jung, who told us that late last evening some canoes ran into the creek where we swam our cattle over and made a canoe, that Br. Edwards with his canoe had sunk in the waves, and that others had to go back a part of the way in retreat before they could come.

Wednesday, 9. We lay still in Pettquotting, waiting for the canoes, to which some of our Indians carried some provisions and corn they had bought here; by these Br. David wrote to the single brothers, Edwards, Jung, and Weigand. At the evening service some strange Indians were present.

Thursday, 10. In the afternoon the three single brothers came to us, and also some canoes which had got to the river before the wind grew so strong, but the others had to run to land farther back, and first got to us in the evening, and then we were all together again.

They were so lucky yesterday when they had to lie still as to shoot an elk and a deer, so that they all had meat. We considered here what was farther to be done, for we saw that we were not lords of the lake, which so hindered us that we should yet use up a month in getting to Sandusky, and then first have to clear the land, and so we dared think of no planting. Since now we have before us here up the river old fields, which were planted last year, although not quite enough for us all, yet we found it unanimously best to remain here and to plant, though we could expect nothing else than to be harassed here, but we resolved to put the matter through with earnestness, for it is as if every effort were made to bring us again to misery and hunger. God help us out of this need! In the evening was a service from the Scripture-verse. We went up the river with a number of brethren to see the place, and found along the river many fine

plantations, and as far as we went deep and still water as
if there were ebb and flow.

Friday, 11. Our Indians in part bought, in part borrowed corn from the Frenchman, under the condition of
paying it back again in the autumn, which was very kind
of him, only it was a pity we had not much, but there were
in the place where we thought of remaining, some forty
or fifty bushels buried, which we could have for a dollar
a bushel, and this was just what we needed. In the afternoon we went some miles up the river, to the place where
we thought of remaining and planting, and encamped.
It was a solitary place, a wilderness where nobody lived,
but before it was quite dark a town of huts stood there,
and the place was lighted by fires. Our Indian assistants
and brethren, however, were not quite at their ease about
remaining here, fearing that we should soon get another
message, and that no peace would be allowed us here, but
that very likely we should be driven away by force, though
want urges us and we cannot possibly go farther. Under
these circumstances the worst and most oppressive is that
among the Indians it is hard to come behind a thing and
learn the truth, for as soon as one only knows how things
peculiarly hang together and are developed, it is easier and
we could resolve upon something, but before this occurs
we are in the dark. We heard here from strange Indians
as if Titawachkam were acting for himself, and would
make himself chief, but that the other chiefs knew little
about the thing; behind him Luke puts himself, and the
two work together, and, as it seems, it is they who make
us so much need, anxiety, and uncertainty. Br. David
therefore conferred with the assistants until after midnight, and it was settled that the two Indians should go
to Pipe, lay before him our necessity, and talk the matter
out with him in order to learn how we were situated, what
was truth and what was not truth, in short to come to an
understanding with him about every thing.

Saturday, 12. There came from Sandusky Pipe's
Longus,[1] as if summoned, from whom we heard much for

---

[1] See this word under Oct. 23, 1790.

our comfort, finding out also that Pipe was to be found at home. The brothers, William and Thomas, set out on their journey thither in the afternoon. Towards evening the Chippewa with his family came from the mouth of the Sandusky to visit us, who had passed the winter near us in Cuyahoga, and after his usual way he was very friendly, remaining over night. William and Thomas went on our business to Sandusky.

Sunday, 13. Br. David preached, and Weigand held the evening service under the open heaven.

Monday, 14. The Indian brethren divided the cleared land among themselves, and we found there was much more of it than we had supposed, so that they would not be obliged to clear more, but merely to plant. This is a great help. The plantations lie favorably, for we shall not have to make fences, and we dwell on the east side of the creek upon a considerable height. The place did not altogether please us as much as we wished, moreover, the water in the river is bad, especially in summer. We must, however, take it as it is, and still be glad, if we may stay here and can be quiet. Br. Michael held service from the Scripture-verse: Let the whole earth be filled with his glory.

Tuesday, 15. All went earnestly to planting to get seed-corn into the ground as soon as might be. In the afternoon Brs. William and Thomas came back from Sandusky, where they had heard that Pipe was not to be found at home, having gone away to the Wabash. They, therefore, found it best, from good reasons, to go to the Wyandot chief, at Lower Sandusky, and this they did, after having made known to him our arrival at Pettquotting by a string of wampum, and they represented to him that we could not possibly, this spring, go up to Sandusky over so many falls, that this would use up a month, and we should lose the time for planting, so that, at some other time, we could travel farther; in accordance with their request, we were come thus far, but could go no farther. The Wyandot chief showed by a string of wampum his satisfaction that we were come so far, and per-

mitted us to plant here, but not to busy ourselves much
in building, as we had elsewhere been accustomed, since
we should not long remain here, but meanwhile we must
be content with huts until we came to our appointed
place. This was very pleasant and agreeable for us to
hear, as we had also hoped that so much would be permitted us, should we go to the right man, and we were
now for a time somewhat comforted over our circumstances.
One thing, however, caused us trouble and perplexity,
namely, that we now saw that we had been deceived in being told that our place lay seven or eight miles from the
Monsey town, for it is not more than two miles in a straight
line, and this occasioned much consideration, since we saw
that great damage could therefrom spring up for us, yes,
that we might be eaten and swallowed by the savages, unless
the powerful and extraordinary hand and might of God
should rule over us. Therefore, we were discomforted,
and remained so, although the Saviour, who does what he
will in heaven and upon earth, may change time and circumstances. We were already well enough aware that
we are under the rule of heathen, and could now no
longer do in every way as we would and should. On this
point we find it hard that we are not our own masters.
On the contrary, considered from the other side, it is
quite in accordance with our purpose that we dwell among
them, it is indeed our calling to preach them the Gospel,
and that cannot be done if we are distant from them.
We must let ourselves be content to be in the midst of
Satan's nest, where he is visibly lord and king, and where
we are surrounded by devils, for in each of the wild Indians there lurk who knows how many, and this is not a
mere figure of speech, but it is really so. In the evening
we had thunder, with rain, and could hold no meeting.
From Gigeyunk (Ft. Wayne), where now all the Indians
draw together, the brethren brought news of there being
very great famine among the Indians, no corn nor means
of living to be had, that the children waste away from
hunger, and yet all go thither, where many will find their
graves. There is such confusion among the Indians that

it is impossible to describe it. They flee, and know not before what, and run straight to death.

Wednesday, 16. All were busy planting. There came some Chippewas here visiting, who stayed over night. Br. Edwards held the meeting.

Thursday, 17. We assembled early before our Lord, who for us has ascended into heaven, and begged for his blessing. After relation of the story, for there was no book at hand, and a discourse from the Scripture-verse: He is thy Lord, worship thou him, we begged for his presence, his wandering with us in our pilgrimage, his nearness and communion both with us in common and for each heart separately. We committed ourselves especially to his and the care and oversight of the Holy Ghost, of which, in our present circumstances, we have unusual need, and to the eye and watchman of Israel for grace in the future. At the end Zachary's and A. Elizabeth's son, born day before yesterday, was baptized Jonathan. There came a couple of Monsey women visiting here from an Indian party, on their way to the Miami, who, yesterday, came to the mouth of this river, and who have been invited into this country. Michael held service in the evening.

Saturday, 19. This whole week we were busy planting. Both yesterday and to-day strange Indians were here visiting, in part acquaintances from the Monsey nation. They had lived a day's journey from the Cuyahoga, on the Tschinque[1] creek, and some had thought of planting this summer on this river below us. Among them were also some who have been baptized.

Sunday, 20. On account of rain we could have no service until evening, and then Br. Edwards held it, at which were present some strangers, to whom afterwards, for they passed the night here, the Saviour was preached.

Wednesday, 23. Mamasu's brother got permission from the assistants to live with us, after our rules had been made known to him, by which he promised to conduct

---

[1] Perhaps the present Chagrin River.

himself. He had come to us here on our journey from Cuyahoga, and as soon as he came had asked of Br. David to be permitted to live with us, but he told him he should first inform himself, consider well, make a trial, and first be better acquainted with us ; but since that time he has stood fast by his resolution, and we had no hesitation in granting his desire. He is a well-minded man.

Thursday, 24. We learned from Detroit, from where a boat has come to the river, that Duncan and Wilson were under arrest there, together with their debtors.

Saturday, 26. Adam came back from Sandusky, where he had got corn. We heard that the Indians, towards autumn, are invited to a treaty at Tuscarawas; that at present they are all out hunting; that the Twightwees and other nations did not wish to have the Delawares there, who were on their way in crowds to Gigeyunk, but told them to go upon their own land to live, and not to ruin their hunting, for the Delawares shoot the deer for the sake of the skins, and leave the flesh lying in the bush. We have always heard that nearly all are hurrying thither, and are now again driven back. Michael held early service.

Sunday, 27. The sermon treated of the office of the Holy Ghost, of whom our Saviour told us that he would send him in his stead to remain with us forever. Thereupon we thanked him in prayer for his true and motherly care, for his unceasing pains and the labor he had with us to prepare us for the Saviour, asked his forgiveness when we had oftentimes grieved him and given no heed to his admonitions, and begged him to stand by us, to show himself mighty and powerful among us, and gave ourselves up farther to his true guidance, care, and oversight. He gave us in our hearts the assurance that he heard our prayer. In the afternoon service, held in the open air, from the text: Know ye not that your body is the temple of the Holy Ghost which is in you, Mamasu was baptized into the death of Jesus with the name Jeremy.

Tuesday, 29. A man from Detroit, Smith by name, visited us, and a woman came here from Sandusky, who had buried here forty bushels of corn, all of which our Indians paid for with goods. We recommended the brethren to consider about a meeting-house as soon as possible. The next day they straightway made preparation and began upon it. Br. David wrote to Mr. Askin, in Detroit, by the French trader.

Wednesday, 30. It was extraordinarily windy, and since our place lies high and open, we were not very safe in our huts on account of the trees standing around us. Many fled and took refuge in the open. For the same reason there could be no meeting. Jeremy's brother visited Br. David and talked with him for the first time about his heart, asking his advice, what he should do to be saved. He got the answer: "Thou canst and shallst do nothing except give thyself up to the Saviour, bad and sinful as thou art, as a lost man, and believe that he can and will help thee, for his mercy's sake." The Saviour favored the plan that Br. John Weigand should go back to the church.

Friday, June 1. Luke, who, before we came here, had already gone to Sandusky, and was utterly against our remaining here, came yesterday after midnight to frighten the brethren that they might the more readily believe him. He said to some of the sisters that he came to get us, for there was danger at hand, and he saw that their teachers were in danger, whom he wished to rescue. When he was asked where the danger was from, he answered that thirty canoes with Chippewas were come over the lake to Sandusky and Cuyahoga, who would eat us up and kill the teachers. They told him that if he had any thing to say, and was sent, it was not usual to disclose it to women and children, but he should call the brethren together and tell it them. This, however, he would not do, for he said they would not believe him, but he was willing to go to Br. David, and this could not be done till the next day. Meanwhile came Chippewas and Wyandots from Sandusky, also two of our Indians from hunting, who had been in Cuyahoga, but had neither seen nor heard any thing like this. Br. David thereupon spoke with him, led him to his heart, admonished him earnestly and heartily, sternly but kindly, and this had the effect wished for, that he came yet a little to himself, was conscious, acknowledged his failings and backslidings, and begged for forgiveness. Br. David thereupon gave him an opportunity to talk the matter out with the assistant brethren, whom hitherto he had not liked, and to be reconciled with them, of whom also he asked forgiveness, and when all was done he got permission to come to us again, which he desired and promised to do. We were very glad and thankful to the Saviour that he had found himself again. We have indeed trouble with him and must bear with him, but it is better than to have him for an enemy, who can bring upon us vexation and trouble, and has already so done.

Sunday, 3. Br. Michael preached about the work of the Holy Trinity, which has worked out and brought to pass eternal reconciliation for the human race through our Lord, Jesus Christ, whose blood we have cost. Br. David held the congregation meeting from the Scripture-verse, that we, through our Lord, Jesus Christ, have come to the knowledge of his and our dear heavenly Father, who so loved us that he gave his only beloved Son for us. There were present some strange Indians from the neighborhood here on this river.

Monday, 4. William went to Sandusky to get corn. The white brothers had a love-feast for the wedding-day of Br. Zeisberger and his wife six years ago.

Wednesday, 6. Our meeting-hall was finished, where in the evening we had the first service from the text: Whosoever transgresseth and abideth not in the doctrine of Christ, hath not God; at this were present two white people from Detroit on their way to Pittsburg, who remained here several days. As since Easter we have had and could have no communion, this was announced to the brethren for next Saturday.

Friday, 8. Yesterday and to-day the brethren were spoken to with reference to the communion. Edwards held early service. Since now we have a chapel, we begin again to have our morning service as is our custom.

Saturday, 9. The whole church had a love-feast, for which the brethren in Bethlehem had sent us flour; to this came several Indians from the neighborhood, three miles from us down the river, among whom was one baptized by us. They came this spring from Tschinque, and, like us, must plant here, but they are not in the least troublesome, but are very friendly with us. At the love-feast we showed the brethren our thankfulness and recognition of their good will and the industry they had shown in building, and told them the Saviour would richly reward their labor, and this they could every day certainly expect from him, for as often as we came together here to hear his word, he would bless us, and thus they would be, in many ways and richly, repaid, and they would not regret their labor.

Thereupon a letter was read them from Br. John (de Watteville) to the Indian church, to every word of which they gave heed, and which they took to heart, of which we heard afterwards much that was pleasant to hear from the brethren. At the end of the day the communicants enjoyed his body and blood in the holy sacrament, in which one participated for the first time, Lewis, and told of the near presence of the Saviour.

Sunday, 10. After the communion liturgy Br. Michael preached about God's love for us, that he gave his only born Son up to death for us, to reunite us through his blood. A Wyandot, from Detroit, was also present, who, two days before, had come out of the bush from hunting, with a couple of others. His comrades were already away, but he still remained here. He, who is the son of the chief, Astechretschi, over the lake, himself a chief, had spoken nearly all last night with Thomas, whom he knew over the lake, about his condition, telling him he had already long felt in his heart a call to come to us, and something said within him that here was the place where he could be happy, or, at least, where he could hear how he would come thereto. He said to Thomas that he would like to talk with the old brothers, and asked if they must all come together if he wished to say any thing, and if he wished to speak his heart and mind, whether he must talk through wampum, and show his condition in a formal speech.

Thomas answered that all this was unnecessary, that if he
spoke with one or several assistants that would be enough;
they would give him an opportunity to bring to light his
heart, his longing, and his thoughts, and this occurred to-
day, for he spoke with the assistants, telling them his call,
that for two years already he had been restless in heart and
sought the best; that in Detroit he had gone into the
church with the French, but he was not better there, but
worse; that he had spoken with his mother and brothers
about it, that if they went to Montreal they would find something good there, where also there are Indians who have a
minister, but that he had secretly an impulse and inclina-
nation for us, but that he had spoken to no one. After he
had had his talk, he said to the brethren: " Now, my
cousins, hear me; I shall not give you up if ye do not wish
to receive me. My whole mind is to abide with you and
to live as ye do. Tell me now your mind right out, what
ye think." They answered, he must first carefully consider, for many had already come, asked to live with us,
and when they had permission they had gone away, and
had come not again. He answered that who had so done
had not been truly in earnest, but he had no such thoughts;
he wanted still to say to them that he thought first to go to
his friends over the lake, to tell them his intention, whether
they or some of them, perhaps, might not be of his mind,
and if not, he would come back. They answered him, he
would not so find that all would be of his mind, there
would be at least one against him; they would try to dissuade him, and would say so much that he would give up
coming again, but he thought they would not persuade him
to abandon his resolution. Since now he wanted much to
have an answer, we told him he might go; if he came back
again, we would not reject him, but be glad if he were content with us and happy. Afterwards, however, he be-
thought himself, and wished neither to go back over the
lake nor to Sandusky, where he learned his brother was
come from Detroit to look for him, but to him Br. David
had to write a letter in his behalf, wherein he told him that
he was here, and intended to remain; if then any one of his

friends wanted to see him, they would find him here on the Huron River among the believing Indians. William came from Sandusky, where he had spoken with Kuhn, telling him among other things that the place appointed for us was by no means suitable. He answered we must select in the neighborhood a place that did please us.

[Thus far to Bethlehem.]

Monday, 11. A number of sisters went by water to Sandusky to get corn, which a short time ago could be had for a dollar a bushel, but now already costs three dollars a bushel, and goes even higher, for it is very scarce. The brethren were compelled to make fences for some distance around the fields.

Wednesday, 13. From Sandusky came Isaac Williams, his brother, and several others, to get Duncan's flour here, brought from Cuyahoga. As he is well known to the Wyandots and acquainted with them, for his brother-in-law, a white man and a chief among them, tells him every thing and takes advice from him, he was able to give us much information to our comfort. We learned thus that the Wyandots were inclined to let us stay here, that they will not force us against our will to move to Sandusky, if we make representations and lay our desire before the chiefs. It is now always becoming plainer that Titawach-kam and Luke have spun the plot, incited the chiefs thereto, and so urged them that they have given their consent, and then have got a weapon in their hands to come upon us with power and to torment us. These went away on the 15th to Sandusky, after first being present at the early service. Through our Wyandot we learn that the Six Nations are secretly at work and labor to have war begun with the Delaware nation, for which the war-belts already lie prepared in Sandusky. The Wyandots, however, namely, the chiefs, of whom there are only two who know about it, make endeavors that nothing may come of this, and for this they already know means and ways. This was yet wanting to make our misery complete, for our brethren would not be safe a step from town, but we hope the Saviour will hinder this and turn it aside.

Saturday, 16. Accompanied by our heartfelt blessings, Br. John Weigand set out this afternoon for the church (Bethlehem) with an escort of several Indian brethren. At the same time went the two white people from Detroit to Pittsburg, one of whom was a prisoner from Kentucky.

Sunday, 17. Br. David preached and Br. Edwards held the congregation meeting.

Monday, 18. Most of the brethren went out hunting, and there remain at home for the most part only the sisters.

Tuesday, 19. Two canoes, with the sisters, came back from Sandusky, where they got corn. Luke also came from there with his family to remain. He came so humble and so like a sinner, saying he was unworthy to be taken into the church again. What pleased us most was that the assistants, who always had trouble with him when he was here before, had now right hearty compassion with him, wept with him, and held him as dear as ever before. This will be to him an abiding blessing his life-long, and we cannot enough thank the Saviour, who has changed our sorrow over him into joy.

Wednesday, 20. Yesterday and to-day Br. David held the early service in Indian. The brethren hoed our corn to-day.

Saturday, 23. Through the whole week the brethren have been busy hoeing corn, for which there was fine, dry weather.

Sunday, 24. Br. David preached from Isaiah, 40: Comfort ye, comfort ye my people, saith your God, in Indian, no interpreter being present. There were also strangers visiting here.

Monday, 25. The brethren who were still at home went also out for a few days' hunting.

Tuesday, 26. Some sisters went to the lake along the shore to seek some necessities for their labor, as also turtles' eggs, of which they have often brought home many hundreds and thousands, which for them is good food.[1]

---

[1] "We therefore hugged the shore of Lake Erie and landed whenever we required refreshment. To this we were in great degree induced by

Wednesday, 27. The French trader came here, who yesterday got back from Detroit, bringing us a letter from Mr. Askin to Br. David. From there we hear that all is quiet and nothing of consequence to be expected; that the wicked rumors among the Indians about war are pure lies, but that the nations are constantly exhorted and encouraged to peace with the States by the English; that to the Indians in Gigeyunk, on the Miami, whither many are fled and where they waste away with hunger, corn and flour had been sent from Detroit for their maintenance; that business is so bad there that nearly all the merchants become bankrupt.

Saturday, 30. Some brethren, for instance, Thomas, Adam, and Adolphus, who were up the creek hunting, came home. They had seen the country along the creek, but had found no place better than we have here. They brought honey and meat home.

Sunday, July 1. At the sermon, which Br. David preached in Indian, several strangers were present from the neighborhood. Both yesterday and to-day we had many thunder-storms.

Wednesday, 4. A sick Indian, Abraham's son, who several days ago came here with his family from Sandusky, and encamped near by where he became ill, allowed himself to hear something about the Saviour, to whom Abraham preached the Saviour. Not much dependence, however, is to be placed upon the conversion of such people, for we have often seen by experience that as soon as they are well again they go their way and forget all they have promised. He and his whole family, early on the 5th, were present at the morning service, for he was somewhat better. Lea, a great girl, who a short time ago went away from us and married a Chippewa Indian, came here again,

---

the multitude of turtles' eggs with which the beach abounded, and which we easily procured in plenty. . . . We fried them in bear's oil, and found them very delicious food."—Johnston's Narrative in 1790, Harpers, 1827.

23

but we sent her away to-day, for she is wanton and causes mischief among our girls.

From the neighborhood here a canoe-load of Indians came visiting, likewise some Wyandots, who offered to sell our Indians horses they had stolen in the settlements, and they had taken one white man prisoner, but no one would trade with them. Thus they do, each one as he pleases; they give no heed to orders of their chiefs, who are yet busy about making peace.

Friday, 6. David held early service. The Indian brethren hilled our corn. Since we live here upon the creek so near the lake, we see very plainly that there is a sort of ebb and flow in the lake, as we observed last year also upon the islands, so that at times a strong current sets to the west, and the sailors told us that always a strong current starts up before the wind comes from any quarter. We often notice here that a strong current comes up the creek and that the water rises two feet and then falls again. It is not probable, however, that this has any connection with the moon, but the air and wind cause the movement and the rise and fall of the water.

Saturday, 7. Abraham preached the Saviour to his son in his hut, and this two Ottawa Indians heard, who had come here visiting, and with curiosity they went in to hear what was said. When Abraham had finished his discourse, they asked his son what he had said, for he understands the Ottawa, Chippewa, and Wyandot tongues. He interpreted it to them, preached to them, and was not afraid, a rare thing for a savage to do, who usually would not translate nor speak any such thing. Abraham then preached a long time to the Tawas, his son interpreting. They came,

Sunday, 8, to the sermon, which Br. David gave in Indian, about the story of Peter's draught of fishes, especially the words: Depart from me for I am a sinful man, O Lord, and at this several strangers from the neighborhood were present. Abraham's son came to-day to Br. David, talked with him about his heart, and said to him, among other things, that he was now disposed to become a believer, but that at times such fear and anxiety fell upon him that he knew not what to do; it was as if some one said to him: "Thou fool, think not that thou canst be converted; thou canst not so live, it is impossible, and in vain thou troublest thyself. Thou art too great a sinner and canst not leave thy sins nor be free." He disclosed to Br. David much about Satan's tricks, in the midst of which he had lived, from which it was plain to be seen that he was a true servant and slave of Satan, and with such it is much harder, until they come clear from Satan's hands, than with the greatest murderers. He related also that two days before a child had eaten his god, which, with other sacred things, he had tied up in a silk cloth [this was a face from a bear's bone], over which he was so distressed that he feared some great misfortune would befall him, and it might even cost him his life, since he met this bad luck. Br. David said to him that his fear and anxiety were from the devil, who wished to alarm him, and turn him from his purpose of being converted; there was no need for his fear, the Saviour had redeemed him with his blood; he should only believe this, and if he were really in earnest to become the Saviour's and to be saved, Satan could not hold him against his will; he must free himself altogether from his devices and the works of darkness, and wish to have therewith nothing further to do; that he had lost his idol was well; now he was rid of it he should be glad, and no harm would come to him on this account. If this man should be converted he would be a useful man, for he understands five Indian tongues, and can speak to many a one the words of life.

Monday, 9. Some Wyandots who came here stayed over night. In the afternoon came Br. Samuel, and they who, with him, had accompanied Br. Weigand to Pittsburg, back here, having been gone twenty-three days. On the Cuyahoga they made a canoe, for their horses were weary, and brought their lading from there here by water, which also arrived this evening. They brought with them the blankets, axes, and hoes given them by Congress. The corn, however, lies there and spoils. If we had it here the

brethren would be very glad of it, for they need it, yet it
is cheaper here at two or three dollars a bushel than to get
it there for nothing and use three weeks on the road. For
a wonder our Indians get along thus far much better than
a year ago on the Cuyahoga; for this the Saviour gives
them opportunities. For example, the Indians in the neighborhood, also a woman, Ackerlemann,[1] the Frenchman,
Tawas, etc. Br. Weigand left Pittsburg for the country
the same day they did. They brought us a letter from
Br. Ettwein of May 28th, which was best of all for us.
Butler, to whom I wrote, was not at the Fort.

Monday, 10. Br. Edwards held the early service, a
translator being present. Thus far Br. David alone had to
hold the services in Indian. The brethren divided among
themselves the blankets and the other things which had
been brought. Br. David spoke again with Abraham's
son, who now often visits him. To him Samuel preached,

Wednesday, 11, setting forth to him the way to be saved,
very plainly, telling him also the buffetings and hinderances
which usually meet one who begins to think about this;
but all these things he should not regard nor care for,
since they were from Satan, who wished to turn him from
his thought and design of conversion and bring him elsewhere. Br. Jung held morning service.

Saturday, 14. One of our unbaptized boys, whose father
perished in Gnadenhütten, who had heard of us, and is
now in his eighteenth year, a young man, came here and
asked of Br. David that we might again receive him. He
said he had not yet forgotten what he had heard, he still
knew some verses by heart, and liked not to be among the
savages; he would like to be in the church where his
parents, brothers, and sisters had gone from time. He
asked among the brethren if we still had meetings, and
when he was answered yes, he said if he only dared go to
them, for so many years he had heard nothing more. Br.
David said to him that he was now grown and could
already consider how he wished to live in the world and

---

[1] See under May 5, 1788.

to use his time, whether he wished here to live for the Saviour or to be a slave to sin; it was therefore well for him to think about this, and if his wish were to be saved and he therefore wanted to be in the church, he would be welcomed by us; his parents were with the Saviour, he should seek to follow them.

Sunday, 18. Br. Edwards preached, thereupon Br. David conducted the communion quarter-hour and the congregation meeting. In the meantime, in the town, the Saviour was preached to the strangers here visiting, and to them who have lately come to stay. Abraham's son came and told how his heart felt. He had ears to hear, the Saviour opened his heart so that he began to understand. He said: "Now first I see what a wretched and corrupt man I am; never yet have I so known myself, I was blind. I must go to destruction unless the Saviour have mercy upon me." He came the morning after quite early, and said he had not slept the whole night from the unrest of his heart; that he longed to be washed with the blood of Jesus from his sins. He cried out: "I believe that he poured out his blood upon the cross for my sins, died, was buried, and rose again. I believe that nothing in the whole world can help me save him alone. To him I give myself entirely, wretched and sinful as I am."

Monday, 16. Br. Michael held morning service. Three young unmarried men, two of them from those here in our neighborhood, who this spring, on their march, have planted here, got permission to live with us, whose father, also here, is not opposed, but pleased that they wish to abide with us. Abraham's son came and acknowledged his sins, relating his course of life which he had thought over, and brought fifty-eight twigs, the number of sins he had committed, so far as he was conscious of them and could remember, for he said he might well already have forgotten many; all this he wished to give up for the Saviour, and seek forgiveness from him. To-day our Indian brethren came home from hunting in Tuscarawas, where they have had very good luck.

Tuesday, 17. David held morning service. Strangers came visiting here, remaining over night, among whom was Abraham's son's wife and her mother, who came to take away her daughter, but the same night she became very sick, so that she could not be up.

Thursday, 19. Edwards held morning service. Abraham's son came to Samuel, told him how Satan fell upon him and insinuated that Br. David, with whom he had spoken, wished to deceive him and lead him astray, as he had already deceived all those who were here with us. Samuel answered him: "I thought thou wouldst become a believer, therefore have I, for an hour at a time, spoken with thee, telling thee much, and laying out to thee plainly the way for salvation, but now I see that thou wilt only quickly know all, speculatest about all manner of things, and goest to work with thy reason. Thus can I say to thee, all this will help not at all, thou willst remain in darkness, and learn to understand nothing of all that has been told thee about the Saviour. Thou art afraid thou wilt be deceived and caught. Thou hast many reasons to be afraid about Satan's witchery and the power of darkness, wherein thou hast hitherto lived, and which thou hast urged on. Thou hast had no fear of this, though thou wast walking on the straight road to hell. No man has called thee here, no one will retain thee if thou goest again, and if thou fearest to be deceived and bewitched, and thou hast nothing farther to do than to hear something new and to know many things, it is better thou goest soon whence thou hast come." He broke into loud weeping, and said it was still his heart's intention to be converted, and he did not wish to give it up. If this happens it will not be too easy. Satan will hold him as long as he can, for it is much harder with such people than with the greatest fornicators or murderers, who are not so entangled with Satan as is he. An old man, whose two sons have permission to stay here, with which their father was at first well pleased, wished to take them away, and told them so. They answered their father that he could indeed go and live how and where he pleased, and if he loved the life with savages he could remain with them, but they would not go with him. He thereupon ceased urging them, and much more encouraged them to be believers with their whole hearts, so that they could sometime tell him with truth what they had experienced and knew. The same man met Renatus in the bush, and asked him much. The people would much like to come behind our mysteries.

Friday, 20. David held morning services. A large party of strange Indians came here from Sandusky, where the small-pox prevails, and remained over night. They went to boil salt. The brethren cease not to extol to them the salvation of their souls in the blood of Jesus.

Saturday, 21. Michael held morning service. The strangers set forth on their way. A Wyandot chief with several Indians came here for news and to learn how the matter is, for they had heard that Indians are said to be in this neighborhood, they know not who they are, nor of what nation; they have also shot at Indians hereabouts, so that one from fright let his musket fall, and was driven away, and when afterward he went with a party of Indians to get it, it was gone and not to be found, of which we also have already heard. Tawas had gone to the French trader, who wanted to accuse our Indians of it, but he told him our Indians were good people, this he knew, and they did no man harm; that they should have no malicious thoughts towards them. Br. David spoke very earnestly with Abraham's son, whereto he gave him opportunity by relation of his satanic witchcraft, and·told him once for all that if he would not break loose from this and be converted by the Saviour [for he was Satan's bond-servant and slave]. it were better he went away as soon as possible, for such a man as he could not be in the church; he should not think that he could deceive the Saviour and the brethren, he would only deceive himself and suffer the greatest harm. He answered thereupon that it was impossible for him to go again from us, and if we should bid him go, he could not, for he should go straightway to the devil in hell.

In the evening, after the brethren had been spoken with the preceding days, we had the Lord's supper, accompanied by his near presence. Anna Johanna and John Leeth were readmitted. Samuel, who has hurt his foot, received the sick-bed communion.

Sunday, 22. Early was the communion liturgy, and then the sermon by Br. David, at which were present many strangers also from the neighborhood, besides those already here. A woman, who last year on our journey to the lake attended our meetings, which pleased her so well that since then she has often thought of them, came here several days ago, was absent from no meeting, and was only sorry that she had planted so far from us this spring, namely, on the Miami, and said, if this were not so she would at once remain here with us. She is a widow, having a son with her, already quite well grown, who very gladly hears about the Saviour.

Wednesday, 25. Several brethren went to Sandusky Island to buy corn, etc., others went out hunting. After a long drouth, we got a pleasant rain to-day, that held on two days. To mention about the ebb and flow.[1]

Thursday, 26. Br. David held morning service. Three Tawa Indians came here. They had been in the settlements around Wilünk (Wheeling), either to steal horses or to murder. There had been nine of them, who were attacked by the whites, and after the loss of three, who fell fighting, they took flight.

Friday, 27. Some brethren went out elk-hunting. Edwards held morning service.

Saturday, 26. Michael held early service. This week several houses were blocked out. There will be here a considerable town.

Sunday, 29. Mr. Robbins from Sandusky, with another white man, went through here on his way to Pittsburg, with a captured boy, whom the Shawanese this spring had taken on the Kanawha. By this opportunity we wrote to Bethlehem. Michael preached from the words: The poor have

---

[1] Which he did under July 6th last. p. 354.

the Gospel preached to them, and David held the congregation meeting.

Tuesday, 31. By Tackenos, one of our baptized Indians, who came from the Miami to Gigeyunk, where the Delawares and Shawanese have been coming together all this spring, we learned that our erring Indians were also in that neighborhood, that many have died there of hunger, and that all live in perfect fear of being fallen upon by the white people, and on this account send out scouts in all directions. To come to or get at our Indians we see for the time being no way during such disturbances.

Through our Indians there to open a way for us, we see no means; they may and will do nothing in the matter, nor undertake any thing. Should we seek to go thither, we must ourselves work our way through, and by our own means accomplish it, doing something new, so that whoever of them wishes to come to us may have opportunity there, for here, where we now are, we learn, none have a mind to come; they would rather remain far enough away from the white people, but now to try any thing in such times were vain; we must await our time. We learn farther that we have done well in coming here. In Cuyahoga we should not have been left in quiet, and among all the Indians it had been pretty well resolved that if we went to the Muskingum they would come to take us away by force, and then they would have brought us to Gigeyunk into wretchedness. Now that we are here, however, they are well enough contented with us. The more remote nations look upon the Wyandots, Pipe, and his following, and the Indians in Sandusky, as if they held pretty closely with the Americans, as is also true; they would like to have peace with them, and since we are now here, we have from them protection in a manner, for we are not alone. The Delawares in Gigeyunk, as we hear, are considering about going far away from this country, and to this end have treated with the Spaniards and Tuckashaws, and have asked them for land there to live on. The Spaniards have also permitted them

to live there, giving them land, with the condition that
they wish to live in peace and in an orderly manner,
making no disturbance and mischief, but if, according to
their custom, they wish to steal, rob, and murder, they
shall remain away. They have made good promises, however, and matters are so arranged that they will quite
likely move thither.

Wednesday, Aug. 1. From Sandusky, where there is
small-pox, from which some have already died, William
came back. On account of the disease, he stayed there
hardly a half-hour. Furthermore, we let none other of
our number go there, that the disease may not be brought
here.

Friday, 3. Yesterday and to-day Br. David's house
was built and brought under roof.

Sunday, 5. Br. Edwards preached and David conducted the children's service and the congregation meeting.

Tuesday, 7. Edwards held morning service about love
and unity among the brethren. Moreover they were busy
building houses. We learn from Sandusky that six Indians there got the small-pox and four died; that they
have sent for a doctor from Detroit to come there to attend them. The Indians are all very much afraid of it
and on their guard against going thither.

Wednesday, 8. A blind Indian, with his wife, came
here from the Miami, where a treaty had been held with
the Indians. He related about this that ammunition
would be given for them to defend themselves with, if they
should be attacked. by the States, which is always their
fear; that they therefore should keep good watch, and if
they observed any thing should let them know, but we
could not believe all he said.

Thursday, 9. Michael held early service from the text:
Wherefore comfort yourselves together and edify one
another—not from desire of power, but from love one for
another. The blind man, who arrived here yesterday,
came with the intention of hearing the believing Indians
and also of saying somewhat to them or of discussing
with them, that the Gospel was not for Indians, but for

white people. He brought his principia to bear, but could find no success with our Indian brethren nor maintain his ideas, but had to give in and be silent. He remained here three days, going to the meetings, and when he went away said that henceforth he would think about this, how to be saved.

A girl, eleven year's old, Mary Magdalene, Johannette's daughter, whose parents died in the church, came a long way hither from the Miami and Gigeyunk. She had there heard about us, set out on the way to us, found from one place to another among the Indians opportunity to get on to us, and has had good luck. She said she had much longed to come again to us, for she could not be among savages, but desired to be with the brethren. Here again we have an example. Children who wish it can find the way to us alone and the old adults can not come. Who only will, he is helped; who will not, finds many a hinderance.

Friday, 10, and Saturday, 11. There was speaking with regard to the communion. Many strangers go through here and remain over night, who at the service hear words about the Saviour. An old Indian, whose two sons are here, sought to persuade some of ours to leave the church, promising one of our Indians he should become chief, but he could effect nothing, and it appears as if he had only wished to try how steadfast they stood, for he left his children in the church, and a daughter, now with the savages, he will also bring here, but others he wishes to seduce from the church. How does this hang together?

Sunday, 12. David preached from the text: Jesus wept over Jerusalem, and Br. Michael held the congregation meeting. Susanna lay down sick after having been indisposed already for several days.

Monday, 13. After the history of the Brother's Church, which comes from the apostles, had been related to the brethren in a service, and the event[1] of sixty years before laid before them, the communicants had the Lord's sup-

---

[1] At Herrnhut. See p. 199.

per, whereat the Saviour showed himself gracious to us, and also made us feel his near presence.

Tuesday, 14. Br. David read the communion liturgy early, and Br. Michael held the common early service about brotherly love towards one another. Two of our former girls, Susanna and Lucy, came here visiting.

Wednesday, 15. Br. David held morning service from the Scripture-verse: O come, let us worship and bow down: let us kneel before the Lord, our Maker, for the wonder above all wonders, that God, our Creator, became man, and made atonement for us with God by his blood, and gained us eternal redemption. The brethren went together hunting, and brought home meat enough for the whole town. Some sisters, who yesterday wanted to go to the Monsey town, came back to-day, before they got there. They heard on their way that the small-pox had gone there also, wherefore they turned about.

Thursday, 16. The brethren again went together hunting, and brought meat home.

Saturday, 18. From Sandusky came Zachary, who wished to bring here his sick brother, who longed to be with us, but he was so bad he could not bring him. He can neither live nor die.

In Lower Sandusky the small-pox still continues, and many have died from it. He heard that in Tuscarawas and neighborhood three Indians or more are said to have been killed by white people; probably they had stolen horses. In Gigeyunk they are still waiting for war.

Sunday, 19. Edwards preached. David held the quarter-hour of the baptized. Jeremy went into others' towns for bad company, whom we told two days afterwards to leave our place, since he gave not up his disorderly life, after having been admonished at different times, both by Br. David and by the assistants.

Tuesday, 21. Yesterday and to-day the brethren made Br. David's house ready. From Sandusky we heard that already twenty men had died of the small-pox, without counting women and children. Praise be to God, thus far we have been spared this; we let no one go thither, also we suffer no one to come here without examining where he comes from.

Thursday, 23. From Gigeyunk we heard that they await there an American army, which has announced it will make them a visit; that on this account the Indians are again fleeing from there.

Friday, 24. Many strange Indians came here out of the bush from their hunting in the Tuscarawas and the Muskingum, where every thing is safe and quiet; that Indians have been killed there, is entirely false. Also there came with them here some who have been baptized, Susanna and Louisa, who, however, are shy of us, and come not near, being worse than the savages, who yet come to the meetings, but these never. Samuel interpreted again as before.

Sunday, 26. Br. Edwards preached, and David held the congregation meeting. In the evening came Helena, Sam Moor's wife, with her two children, visiting from Sandusky, where she had planted, in the hope we should go there. With her came also two baptized women, Paulina and Elizabeth, who have been many years out of the church.

Monday, 27. Mr. Robbins came back from Pittsburg, who went through here on his way thither, by whom we sent letters to Bethlehem, which also he had properly forwarded, though he himself, on account of the small-pox, did not go there. We heard, to our comfort, that every thing there seems peaceful and good, that the Indians indeed, in Wilünk (Wheeling), and thereabout, are always stealing horses, and from Duncan have stolen many, but that no plans are forming against the Indians.

We moved to-day into the house the brothers and sisters have made for us; hitherto we have been living in a bark[1]-hut. This evening were buried the remains of the little Augustus, who went home yesterday, and our graveyard was consecrated. He was a year and seven days old. Susanna, who has also been attacked by the sickness prevailing among our brethren, and lay sick over a week,

---

[1] Conjectured.

grew better again, but others are severely ill therewith, as Christiana and Renatus.

Wednesday, 29. Yesterday and to-day nearly all our brethren went out gathering ginseng-roots, for which there is great demand; some went even to our island in the lake, where we were so long in camp last year, and where there is as much as if it had been cultivated. For, by hunting, they can earn little or nothing, the skins being worthless.

Thursday, 30. Helena spoke with Br. David, asking permission to live again in the church, which we gave her. From Pittsburg came the former wife of White Eyes, with some others. Not far from the Fort they had been taken prisoners by the militia, who took away from them their horses, pelts, and whatever they had, but had let them go again.

From Pittsburg came a couple of white people, messengers to the chiefs, to invite them to a council. Near Wilünk above sixteen white people have been killed this summer, where also six Indians died, besides the damage done in other places.

Sunday, Sept. 2. Br. David preached about the greatest commandment and held the children's service. Mr. Robbins, who returned from Sandusky day before yesterday, set forth on his way to Pittsburg. For two weeks now we have in town a large number sick with burning fevers. Among the Wyandots eighteen have already died of small-pox, and twenty are sick with it, very few recover. Thus far we have been spared this. Br. Michael held the congregation meeting.

Wednesday, 5. From Sandusky came back again the white man and messenger from Pittsburg, bringing us a letter from Pomoacan, who asked us to send with him a part of the way one or two Indians, as escort, until he is out of danger, for on account of the pestilence they are able to send no one with him, and this we did.

Thursday, 6. Br. David held morning service from the text: There is, therefore, now no condemnation to them which are in Christ Jesus. From Sandusky came a mes-

senger to invite some one of our Indians to a council, to
hear what would be treated of. We heard that the Indians were much afraid that the white people would advance, for which fear a letter from Pittsburg gave them
cause, which the messenger brought out, and they speak
already of flight. May God give peace in this land ! Yesterday and to-day the Indian brethren blocked out the
house for the two unmarried brothers, Edwards and Jung.

Friday, 7. The married brethren celebrated their festival with grace and blessing, in the near presence of our
dear Lord. At morning prayer we begged for his bloody
blessing and nearness for the day; then was the festival
service of the married brethren, from the text of the day :
But if we walk in the light as he is in the light, we have
fellowship one with another, and the blood of Jesus Christ,
his Son, cleanses us from all sin, about this, that in our marriage we can and should lead a life blessed and well-pleas-
ing to God, but for this it is required that connection with
sin shall be broken, and that we, through Jesus' wounds,
shall be cured and healed ; then we can walk in light, and
without fear live for his glory. Whilst the love-feast was
celebrating, Christiana Schebosh, after a sickness of nine
days, departed and ended her course at this time quite
blessedly. In the afternoon was a love-feast for all the inhabitants, and in conclusion the Scripture-verse for the day
was pondered : And take not the word of truth utterly out
of my mouth.

Saturday, 8. Her remains were brought to rest. She
came to the church in Shekomeko, in New York, and
when the Indians there were driven away, to Bethlehem,
with others, where she was baptized, in the year 1748, by
Br. Martin Mack; in the same year she was joined in
wedlock with our Schebosh, with whom she lived in Gnadenhütten, on the Mahony, and when that was laid waste
by the savages, she went to Nain, near Bethlehem and
Weehquetank,[1] and thereafter went with the Indian
church to Philadelphia into the barracks; then, in the

---

[1] Polk Township, Monroe Co., Pa.

year '65, to Friedenshütten, on the Susquehanna [she was a national-assistant], and in the year 1772, with the same to the Ohio, where she was on the Muskingum, first in Schönbrunn and then in Gnadenhütten, until, in the year '81, all was destroyed by savage warriors, and the Indian church carried off to Sandusky. When, in the spring of '82, the brothers, their teachers, were taken from them and carried to Detroit, she went with her daughter, and the latter's husband, with the rest of our Indians, to the Shawanese towns. Her son died at the massacre in Gnadenhütten. Her husband, Br. Schebosh, had already, in the autumn, been taken captive in Schönbrunn by the militia, and carried to Philadelphia, from which place he went to Bethlehem. When she heard that the brethren were in Detroit, she came to them in the spring of '83, on the Huron (Clinton) River, where her husband, the same summer, to her great joy, came back again to her from Bethlehem, with whom she then lived quite pleasantly, and went steadily hand in hand with him, more than ever before. Last year, in Cuyahoga, she had a severe illness. Thus she passed through all changes and tribulations with the Indian church, enduring much misery and trouble, which was not easy for her, and at times this was too hard for her. Especially was she inclined from fear to live too much alone, if it seemed to be dangerous, and too willingly to believe the lies and frightful stories, whereby she made life hard, not for herself alone, but she was of no use to others, but rather a harm; this often grieved us, that she wasted her time therewith so uselessly. Even then, however, she knew how to find comfort and advice nowhere else than with the Saviour, for she always came to herself again, and clang to him, who always gave her aid, and it never occurred to her that she would anywhere be better and safer than in the church. The Saviour has never made her ashamed, has upheld her, and in good time let her depart in his arms and bosom. She is now in safety there, where evil is no more to be met, the Lord be praised; she left behind a daughter and two grandchildren in the church. She was over sixty years old. In the evening we laborers, together with Br. Schebosh, had a blessed Lord's supper, in reference to the late choir festivals.

Sunday, Sept. 9. Brother Michael preached. Many strangers, Delawares and Chippewas, were here. Edwards held the congregation meeting.

Monday, 10. David held early service. Helena set out home again, and will return to us as soon as may be.

Tuesday, 11. David held early service. Yesterday and to-day most of the brethren went to the lake in different places and some to the islands, to dig ginseng, that they may get clothing from its sale, for by hunting they can earn little, the pelts being worth little. They get for a bushel three or four dollars; if, then, they come to a place where there is a good deal of it, it repays their trouble. Sicknesses lessen now among us, wherewith many have been afflicted, for instance, yellow fever, which attacks the head, and they who have it lie for many days speechless.

Wednesday, 12. A Shawano came here from Gigeyunk, who tracked an Indian, and here overtook him, who had stolen his horse and twice run away. The Shawano came only to get the Indian, and said if he came home he would be killed, for he was the greatest thief among the Indians, and had already stolen much.

Friday, 14. We learned from the Shawano that things are said not to be so bad in the Indian land as we have always heard, that the chiefs are for peace, and that the Shawanese let their prisoners go, and have already surrendered many; that, to be sure, there are wretched creatures who go to war and say there would be war, but he knew there would be no war, for he was present in the council and knew what the chiefs had resolved. This was comforting news for us.

Sunday, 16. David preached from the Gospel: No man can serve two masters, and Edwards held the congregation meeting. Few of the brethren were at home. There came two Mingoes here from Sandusky, where some dwell. From them we heard that the chiefs have not been invited

24

to a council at Pittsburg, but that a message with a piece
of tobacco had been sent them, and it was said they should
smoke this in their pipes, and earnestly look at the road to
Pittsburg, they would soon see some one coming; they
should hold themselves ready to receive the messenger.
Also they got an admonition because they let horse-thieves
go in and out among them.

Wednesday, 19.   Joseph, who, a short time ago, had
sent us word by a savage, and begged us to have compassion with him, and permit him again to come to us, for
he had been sick and was hardly yet recovered, came, upon
getting leave, with his wife, an unbaptized woman, to remain.

Thursday, 20.   To-day and the following days the brethren got home from the lake. Some canoes which had
gone to the islands were much hindered by windy weather
and kept there a long time, so that they could not get away,
and as they were not provisioned for such a length of time
they suffered generally great hunger, until by good weather
they got away.   While they were there ships came from
Detroit and Niagara and anchored, from which they wished
to buy some provisions, but got little.   On one ship was
Joseph Brant, with seventy Indians, on his way to Detroit.   They all came home, however, with good ladings.

Saturday, 22.   At noon ten white people arrived with a
herd of cattle from Pittsburg for Detroit.   We are not
pleased that they now begin to make their journey through
the place where we live, but we have no help for it, for
wherever we are, white people and Indians at once find
their way to us, even if it be a hundred miles out of their
road.   They did not stay in town, but went a little further
on beyond the river and encamped, but we were yet
anxious they might here come to harm from the Chippewas and Tawas, who live on the lake.   Our fear also
was not vain, for,

Sunday, 23, while we were in our chapel at the sermon,
a party of Chippewas and Tawas came, who had already
heard about them, opened the doors of the chapel and
peered about, seeing us assembled.   Some Indian brethren

went out to them, and they made no further disturbance. When we separated, we learned that they had come with no good intention, but wanted to fall upon the cattle-drivers. We gave them food, talked with them, and admonished them to do no such thing, telling them there was no war, and if they used hostilities it would be nothing else than declaring war. They promised to do no harm, but only to speak with them and hear how they were. Some of our Indians ran to the camp of the white people, and when they no longer found them there, for they had already broken up, they followed after them and gave them warning thereof, and brought them back again. When now the Chippewas came, they talked with the white people, saying they should not go farther, but turn about, giving as a reason that they could not get through, but would lose every thing, and even be themselves killed. In the evening they came into the town together, and the Chippewa head-man asked for one of the cattle from them, which they promised and gave, also one for us, which, however, we did not take. It did not stop here, but they had to exchange muskets and horses, for which they gave wretched and good-for-nothing wares, and so at last they got rid of them after promising to turn about. They still remained here the 24th, and some of our Indians bought a few cows,

Tuesday, 25, but the French trader came, who told the white people to set out on their way to Detroit, and not to regard that liar, the Chippewa, there was no such danger as he told them. This they did, and crossed over the creek again to-day into their camp, and,

Wednesday, 26, continued their way. Michael held early service. We had heard that another party of drovers had lost their way near the lake, and were near Sandusky Bay. Quite early we sent an Indian to them, who lead them here, for we feared they might fall into the hands of the Chippewas.

Thursday, 27. Now and for some time afterwards there was daily much visiting from strangers. A big boy with his friends came here, and did not at all wish to go away,

but remained here, saying he wished to live like the believing Indians, that he was old enough to think for himself how he wanted to live, and told his friends they
should let him go. Another, the friend of Adolphus, from
the Monsey town, came here visiting, expressly to hear
something good; with him Adolphus spoke almost the
whole night, answering all his questions. When he went
away he said he should soon come again.

Saturday, 29. We had the Lord's supper, the brethren
having been spoken with the preceding days.

Sunday, 30. Communion liturgy. Michael preached
and David held the quarter-hour for the baptized and the
congregation meeting from the day's Scripture-verse.
There was a conference with the assistants about matters.

Monday, Oct. 1. Edwards held early service. Br. David
wrote to Bethlehem by Joshua, who escorted the two
white people to the fort. A woman from the Monsey
town on the Sandusky came here out of the bush from
hunting and begged the brethren to tell her something
about the Saviour. She remained here over night and it
happened. Our Jeremy, who has been for a time apart from
us, although nearly every day he has been here for a visit,
came to-day with his wife to remain, upon his earnest
wish and prayer, after getting permission from the assistants' conference. He has lately taken this wife, and she
will also gladly be the Saviour's.

Tuesday, 2. On the other hand, we saw ourselves compelled to send A. Regina from the church [David held
early service], which had the good and blessed effect that
it was for her a blessing, and we took her again anew.

Thursday, 4. To-day and lately different houses have
been built. Our town grows, and we increase in numbers.
All the Indians who come here cannot enough wonder
that in so short a time so many houses have been built,
and so much work done. Edwards held morning service.

Saturday, 6. Michael held morning service. Two women, who several days ago came to visit us here from the
Monsey town to hear something good, and have omitted
no service, went home again, but left their things here,

saying they should come back after gathering their harvest.

Sunday, 7. David preached. Edwards addressed the children, and David held the congregation meeting.

Wednesday, 10. Many went for some weeks' hunting to Cuyahoga. We got a message from Pomoacan to send some one to the treaty at Tawa (Ottawa) River, but no one of our Indians went. Pomoacan does not yet know that our Indians have nothing to do with treaties. Br. David's additional building was blocked out and made ready.

Friday, 12. Helen's daughter [Scapp] came here with her husband, and rejoiced to see us again. Her parents were in the church and now are both dead. The smallpox makes great havoc among the Wyandots both sides of the lake. It is noteworthy that it afflicts just these and no other nations; even those who have fled far away into the bush have yet had it. Many houses in Sandusky have lost all their dwellers, stand empty, and there are said to be hardly so many alive and well as have died. In Sandusky about sixty, and over the lake also above thirty have died.

Saturday, 13. This week the brethren began to get in their corn. Even that which was planted late and which we thought would not mature, has ripened, and thus far, the middle of the month, we have had no harmful frost. Lewis and others came back from harvesting.

Sunday, 12. Br. Edwards preached. David held the congregation meeting.

Tuesday, 16. The brethren harvested the fields of Br. Zeisberger and his wife.

Thursday, 18. The brethren went together hunting. Michael held early service.

From Gigeyunk a couple of Indians came to Thomas, to give him news of the circumstances in which they are, for one of them is a great friend of his. They complained that the Delaware nation was in grievous condition, they knew not whither to go nor where to settle; where they now are they cannot remain, since the nations will not suffer them there; they have made entreaty the whole summer, sending message after message to the Spaniards to make arrangements with them, and to move thither; some indeed have already gone there, who now send them back word to let no one follow, for they are there in very narrow straits, and would gladly come back were it in their power; they were not sure of their lives, the nations there having resolved to root them out; they were hemmed in and could not come free; they would have to be helped; since now the Delawares saw that they had no steadfast place, they first turned to the Six Nations and asked them for land; they answered them they could not help them, for they had themselves not a foot of land they could call their own; they addressed the Wyandots, who told them they had given them leave to dwell on their land, had also told them how far the bounds of their land extended, but that they, the Delawares, had disregarded their request, and had gone over their boundaries to other nations, therefore they would make them no more offers. The Twightwees, whom they then addressed, had pointed out to them a place where they could settle, but where they were surrounded by swamps, and also, as it were, closed in. They suffered hunger, too, all the time, for their corn did not thrive, and was frosted. So it is with the Delaware nation, which a few years ago greatly flourished, but since the old chiefs, Netawatwes and White Eyes, are dead, it goes with hasty steps to ruin.

Saturday, 20. The brethren harvested the fields of the single brothers. The Lord has blessed all our fields, and the brethren have all a rich harvest to gather, a great kindness for us.

Sunday, 21. Michael preached about the wedding-garment, Christ's blood and righteousness, which we have given us for nothing, wherein to appear before God. David held the congregation meeting.

Tuesday, 23. We learn that the Delawares in Gigeyunk have again murdered six white people over the river. From Pittsburg Indians came with rum, who, without our knowledge, before we were aware of it, for they came not

into town, encamped here in our neighborhood, and caused
us two disorderly days and nights by the drunkenness they
brought about among strange Indians, who came into town;
they also shot our swine, so that, from their drunkenness,
we had for once to omit our service. The Indian, Amochol,
came here with his wife and stayed several days, who always, as long as we were upon the Ohio, showed himself a
friend of the brothers. He said that he and his wife were
of one mind about coming here into the church, but he
would like to bring his sons also, and will seek therefore
to bring them around to be of his mind.

Friday, 26. Inasmuch as we have several times since we
have been here, heard a wicked report that the Chippewas
cherish hostility against us, and indeed for this reason,
since they say we sold their land over the lake to white
people, although we ourselves have not yet heard it from
them, and yet they often come, and we have also asked
them about it, our Indian brethren were uneasy about the
matter, having lately even heard it from Delawares, and
wished something to be done. So for their satisfaction we
sent Br. Edwards with some Indian brethren to Detroit,
and Br. David wrote about the matter to Capt. McKee and
Mr. Askin, to learn how much there was in the thing, and
also that it might be put out of the way. These brethren
started on the 28th with a good wind over the lake for
Detroit. Matthew, who came to us in the spring, went to
Gigeyunk to get his things there, to be back again in two
weeks. By him we sent word to our Indians that we
longed very much to see some one of them.

Sunday, 28. Br. David preached about the strength we
have in the Lord, our Saviour, and find in his merits, if
only we always live thereon, to overcome, uninjured, Satan's temptations. Michael held the congregation meeting.

Monday, 29. By Luke's son, who came from Sandusky,
we heard that the treaty on the Miami had been concluded,
the young people released, and told each one could go to his
hunting, and that nothing had happened. At the same
time we heard that most of our Indians were also present at the treaty, and this made us wonder so much the

more, because they were already so near us, and yet none of them had come to visit us.

Wednesday, 31. After most of the brethren were done with harvesting, they went out for chestnuts and some, hunting. Moreover we have had several cold days and very windy weather, with snow and rain, in turn.

Sunday, Nov. 4. Br. Michael preached about this, that we should forgive one another's faults as the Saviour also daily freely forgives our faults. Br. David held the communion quarter-hour about the commandment we have from God to love one another, and not to cherish any ill-will, much less hate, one towards another. which does away with all the benefit of the holy communion, so that we have no advantage therefrom, which we should and can have. By the Scripture-verse: Lord, thou hast been favorable unto thy land : Thou hast brought back the captivity of Jacob, the brethren were reminded not to forget the kindness the Saviour had hitherto shown us, to recall the Saviour to mind therefor, which would lead us to thankfulness towards him, that we should put our confidence in him alone, and pray that he go farther with us, and send peace to the land. From Detroit came the drovers on their way back to Pittsburg. They had been on the Miami, where three thousand Indians were said to be assembled; when they came there they lost by the Indians over eighty head of cattle [and thus over £200], which they shot down, and there was no defence nor check. They had letters from McKee and Brant for Congress, and brought a letter from the chiefs in Sandusky to Br. David, wherein they recommended to us, in the name of all nations, to convoy their people safely to Pittsburg, that no harm might befall them, for they were express messengers. They did not speak very favorably in regard to the intentions of the Indian nations, and believed a war was intended, and preparation therefor was made. They yet gave four months' time. They were accompanied to the Fort by four Indian brethren. From Pittsburg came the Indian brethren, Joshua and Michael, with a white man. They left Mr. Robbins, who wished to be gone, on the

Mahoning, and believe he is back again; since they were attacked by warriors at Salt Lick, whom, however, they drove off, so by this way it is no longer safe to travel. We had hoped for letters from the church, but they brought nothing.

Tuesday, 6. Strange Indians were here visiting who attended our meetings.

Friday, 9. There came from Detroit a boat-load of people, among them two families, who, ten years before, had moved there from the States, and now went back again, among them was a family from Hebron (near Lebanon, Pa.), who were acquainted with the Brothers Langgard and Zahm, for the man had gone to school there.

Saturday, 10. After the brethren had been spoken to, we had the holy communion, with the near presence of our dear Lord. To-day Br. Edwards came back from Detroit with the three brethren, Stephen, Peter, and Tobias, after twelve days from home. He had spoken with the commandant there, Maj. Matthews, who was upon the point of going down to Canada, as also with McKee and Mr. Askin, about the reports we had heard of the discontent of the Chippewas. The commandant took with him Br. David's letter to McKee, to ask further about it from Johnson and others. Otherwise McKee could not much advise him in the matter, but yet he had learned that the Chippewas inhabit our houses in our town, and have planted there. On the other hand, Mr. Askin had nothing further to say in the matter, so that is to be hoped that we have nothing to fear from the Chippewas, since they have our towns and fields in their own possession. Moreover, in Detroit, he had found things quite otherwise, and met with fewer strangers than when we were there.

Sunday, 11. In the afternoon the people from Detroit set forth again towards Pittsburg. We had to let them hire an Indian brother, Thomas, as pilot. They had with them two women and many children, Br. Edwards preached and David held the congregation meeting.

Monday, 12. From Pittsburg came Mr. Robbins, with

some goods. One of his people was wounded by wicked Indians and mortally.

Tuesday, 13. We had a day of blessing in the near presence, of our great Elder of his churches, who made himself known to us in a wonderful way and overwhelmed us with blessing from his bloody fulness, so that our hearts were melted to tears before him. Early in the morning there was a common service for the sake of strangers. Aftewards all the baptized (had a service), in which, after a discourse from the text^of the day, Luke, amid many tears, received absolution from the church, and was again taken into it. The congregation then fell upon their knees, asked gracious absolution for all their failings and shortcomings, gave ourselves anew to him, and asked him further to continue his blessed rule among us, to be graciously pleased to walk among us and after his heart to do with us, and we vowed to him anew obedience and fealty.

Wednesday, 14. Mr.'Robbins turned back to Pittsburg. Michael held early service.

Thursday, 15. Yesterday, to-day, and the following days our Indian brethren went off to their autumn hunt, some to Cuyahoga, others elsewhither, and were scattered in the bush. From Gigeyunk there came a boy, Michael's son, who has not been baptized. Gideon, as we hear, who was in Sandusky this summer, but came not here, is dead.

Friday, 16. Delawares came from Gigeyunk here visiting. Of Helena, Samuel's former wife, we heard she was in Sandusky and would come here as soon as she could.

Sunday, 18. David preached, Michael conducted the children's service, and Edwards held the congregation meeting.

Tuesday, 20. A white man, a Quaker, who lives in Chester, below Philadelphia, his father being named Isaac Pile, and who this summer was taken prisoner on the Wabash by the Biankeshaw [1] Indians, who brought him

---

[1] "Piankashaws on the Wabash: In 1780 but 950; since driven west." Drake's Book of the Indians, p. x. They are mentioned in many Indian treaties.

to the Miami towns, where he got away, came here without having been seen by Indians on his way, and begged us with tears to help him to Pittsburg, but this was
hard, for our Indians were all off hunting, or a part in
Pittsburg.   At last our Samuel had pity for him, and
though he was lame, took him away on Thursday, the 22d,
for which he was glad and thankful, for we could not have
kept him here long, through fear of strange Indians.

Thursday, 22.   Helena, Sam. Moor's former wife, came
here from Sandusky, with her two children, daughter and
grandchild, to remain, for whom we vacated a hut to live
in.   Also Cornelius' son, Matthew, came back again from
Sandusky, but did not come to the Miami town, as he
had intended and thought, since the Indians there were
not yet come back from the treaty.

Friday, 23.   Aaron also came here with his wife from
the Miami.   We heard the comforting news that the nations at the treaty were yet more inclined for peace than
for war, and that the Indians who in the spring had fled
in crowds to the Miami towns, in order to be able to prepare for war there, less disturbed, have now nearly all
come back again, which is a good token of their disposition for peace.   There were also different strange Indians
visiting here.   By Aaron, Welandawecken sent us word
that he had not yet forgotten what his uncle, Israel, had
said to him and impressed upon him, when he made over
to him his office of chief, when we were in Sandusky,
namely: He should love the believing Indians; be helpful to them and aid them, and, so far as lay in his
power, protect them from the wicked Indians and love
goodness, which Israel himself had also told us when we
made objections to him and reproached him that he had
put him in his place, for we knew him well.   Now, says
this Welandawecken, he has not forgotten that, but has
yet done nothing, since we are under the sway of Pipe
and Pomoacan; the time would yet come, however,
when he would tell us something, and we should hear
something from him, if again he once had a firm place, for
now he was disturbed and a fugitive.   We will not throw

aside this word, but retain it till the right hour; who knows, a door may yet thereby be opened to us to go farther with the Gospel. If now we consider his words, it cannot be that he means only the believing Indians, for he has many of our Indians around him, who, so to speak, stand under him. Why then should he fish for the handful with us so earnestly, and if he had them all, what good would that be to him? He means then not so much the believing Indians as the missionaries, and thinks: If I have them, who are the queen-bees, the believing Indians will come together about them. Whether his affair comes from an upright heart, be that as it may, we will leave it unexamined, if only something can thereby be won for the Saviour and his affair. May the Saviour give us peace in the land!

Sunday, 25. David preached in Indian, no interpreter being present; strangers were present, as, also,

Monday, 26. Strangers frequent the services much more eagerly than the baptized who wander in error. They come but seldom, if they are here. They are ashamed, for their conscience pricks them.

Thursday, 29. Christina bore a son, and,

Friday, 30, the wife of Abraham's son, Gegaschamind, also bore a son.

Saturday, Dec. 1. Two Frenchmen came here and remained over night.

Sunday, 2. 1st Advent. David held all the Sunday services in Indian.

Monday, 3. All the sisters went for nuts, others got meat.

Thursday, 6. Also winter weather and snow came on, the first this autumn.

Sunday, 9. David preached, baptizing the little son of Ignatius and Christina, born on the 29th of last month, with the name Philip, into the death of Jesus. He came back yesterday home from hunting. Late in the evening young Joachim came from the Miami towns here for a visit, with his wife and three children. His father, old Joachim, is in Detroit, where he passes the winter.

Wednesday, 12. Thomas came back from Pittsburg.

Thursday, 13, Samuel, and Saturday, 15, Adam, with their company (arrived), who are the last, all having escorted white people to the Fort. A letter from Ettwein, dated at Philadelphia, Sept. 8, '87. Thomas and his company used nineteen days in getting to the Fort, for there were nine children with them. Had not Thomas been with them, they would have starved in the bush, for, when they got from here to Cuyahoga, their provisions were all gone, and Thomas kept the whole party of seventeen in meat all the way. He was so lucky as to shoot twelve deer along the way, for he dared not go away from the company. On Saturday, the 15th, all our hunters came home. Gen'l St. Clair, now the agent, asked Samuel what we would do if there should be war, and where we thought of going, but this he would not answer him. We saw from the circumstances that we had something to expect. Should there be war, we are in a bad way. Where should we turn? Among the savages we are less secure, and to the white people we cannot bring the Indians, for we cannot trust them either, on account of the dangerous militia. We can take no forethought, much less come to any resolution, and we should only burden our lives. Therefore we commend ourselves to our dear Father to guard and protect us.

Sunday, 16. Br. Michael preached. In the following service for all baptized, Helena, who came here to remain on the 22nd of last month, was absolved and again admitted to the church. In the communion quarter-hour the Lord's supper was announced to the brethren for next Saturday.

Monday, 17. We brethren made more benches for our chapel. Although it is much larger than the one in Cuyahoga was, yet it is already too small, and if we should remain here longer, we must enlarge it.

Thursday, 20. Speaking for the Lord's supper, as, also,

Friday, 21, it was continued. The young man who came to us on the 15th of last month from Gigeyunk,

Michael's son, who had lived with us in Thuppeküuk, when a boy, having now become a man, got leave from the assistants, upon his request, to live here.

Saturday, 22. We had the holy communion in the near presence of our dear Lord. Strange Indians from Sandusky, among others, Moses, also, with his family, came here visiting. Aaron, who made a long visit here, and certainly did not go away with a quiet heart, was, as we hear, almost killed in a drunken brawl.

Sunday, 23. Br. Edwards preached from to-day's text: Christ hath abolished death and hath brought life and immortality to light through the Gospel. It snowed hard all day, and a deep snow fell.

Monday, 24. We had a very blessed Christmas-watch, begun with a love-feast. At consideration of the incarnation and birth of our Saviour countless tears were shed. We laid our thanks before him and our gratitude for his holy incarnation, passion, and death. At the end candles were distributed and all went joyfully home.

Tuesday, 25. Br. Michael preached, and then the children had a service and sang: The Infant in his manger lay, with joyful hearts and mouths. In a service after this, Gegaschamind, Abraham's son, his wife and the child born here on the 30th of last month, which is the whole family, were baptized into the death of Jesus amid many tears, both of those baptized and of those present, the first with the name Boaz, his wife with the name Abigail, and the child Gottlieb. This was a heart-moving affair, and accompanied with the near presence of the Holy Trinity. This is again a clear proof of the extraordinary mercy of the Saviour, for Br. David, to whom he told the whole story of his life, certified that we never yet had had to do with a servant and slave of Satan of a kind like him. May the Saviour protect him and them, and let them prosper to his glory and honor. The brethren who have their baptismal day on this day, came with the assistants to a love-feast together, whereby was singing and exhortation. Several begged for the bath of baptism. Strangers were here during the holidays visiting, were present at all services, and looked on at the baptism.

Wednesday, 26. Br. Edwards held the early service. The assistants met with the brethren to attend to all sorts of circumstances and necessities. We have been for some time speaking with the assistants about building a school-house, so that the assistants also may have a place where they can meet in an orderly manner. This they now themselves brought about without our aid. We should not have suggested it to them now in the winter and during the deep snow. We have also always waited until we should certainly know whether we should be here longer than this winter, but since all the brethren were so for it and willing, we said nothing, and let it go on. Thus they went,

Thursday, 27, to work, earnest and comforted, and made the beginning. The strangers who were here visiting during the holidays, and had heard, publicly and privately, the word about the incarnation and birth of the Saviour, and had also been present at the baptism, went back home, promising to come again soon.

Sunday, 30. David preached from the text: When the fulness of the time was come, God sent forth his son, and Edwards held the congregation meeting. Several came and expressed their longing, both for baptism and for reception into the church.

Monday, 31. They were done with blocking out the school-house. The assistants spoke with Jeremy and his wife and made peace between them.

At the accustomed time we assembled for the close of this year, beginning with a love-feast. We thanked the Saviour for all the goodness, grace, and kindness he had imparted to us, bodily and spiritually, having blessed us in every way, so much the more our hearts were aroused to praise him and to be thankful to him therefor, for we had expected a hard year, at least during the summer, but he has overwhelmed us, doing more than we hoped. We begged gracious absolution for all our faults and short-comings, for if we regard our Indians as a whole, we are

always moved to thank him for the grace he shows in
them, but in individuals much is wanting; we wish they
were better, and we are aware of their deficiencies. From
this we learn the great patience and mercy of our Lord
and Saviour, Jesus Christ. We commended ourselves to
the protection of our dear Father, and to the guidance and
fostering care of the Holy Ghost. Thus comforted, we
entered upon the new year, and with the assurance that
he, through this new year also, will show himself among
us our good and gracious Saviour, and will bring us
through all our anxious and difficult circumstances.

About this year the following is yet to be observed : We
had arranged for this, had prepared for it, and made the
necessary dispositions for it, to break up in the spring
from Cuyahoga for the Muskingum. When the time
came, however, to carry out our plans, we found so many
hinderances and troubles, whereby we were much perplexed and distressed, that for our Indians' sake, whom we
did not wish to bring into danger and want, we did not
have the satisfaction of conducting and ending the affair.
After we had received directions from the Saviour to leave
Cuyahoga and to settle between Pettquotting and where
we were, we broke up April 19th, and on the 24th arrived
there. But even then we were not allowed to rest, for we
had hardly all got there when we received a message from
the chiefs that we could not stay there, but must come to
Sandusky. Then we had to set forth upon a longer way,
until, on the 8th and 10th of May, we all came to Pettquotting and saw that our time was gone and we must
necessarily look about to see where we could plant, that
we might not fall into too great need of food. We resolved to remain there, let the result be what it might. And
now Satan ceased to rage, we obtained rest, which we have
enjoyed since we have been here. We learn here, however, that the Indians had already agreed that they would
come with an army and take us away, provided we had
gone to the Muskingum, and that would infallibly have
followed, for they spoke together decidedly about this, not
only about taking the teachers captive, but killing them.

We had our chief cause of anxiety, where we should get the means of life. We were in no condition, on account of the great distance, to get the five hundred bushels of corn, granted us by Congress, which lay at McIntosh, but herein also the Saviour has wonderfully cared for us, for after we came here and were already busy planting, there came a party of Indians from the east, who wished to go to the Miami, but finding us here they remained in our neighborhood and planted. They had much corn, from whom our Indians were able to buy much at a cheap rate. Another Indian, a woman, who had planted here the year before, and buried her corn [over fifty bushels], came here and did likewise; thus were we helped, and our Indians fared better than the Indians in Sandusky, and we had always comforted ourselves with the thought that there we should find relief.

Brs. Michael Jung, and John Weigand came, the first April 30th, and the other May 2d, to us on our march, whom Heckewelder had accompanied as far as Pittsburg, and they also had their share in our pilgrimage, especially upon the stormy lake; they rejoiced us with letters from the church, wherewith we were refreshed. The last went back to the church June 16th, after having first done us good service, so that we came somewhat into order. The small-pox.

We acknowledge it as an especial kindness and thank our dear Lord for the quiet and peace he has let us enjoy. Also in regard to the savages it is as if Satan's wrath and scorn against us were allayed, for formerly we had to bear so many wicked threats, which did not cease while we were in Cuyahoga and in other places. There is now indeed in the Indian land no peace, nor do we know what we have to expect, we leave that to our dear Lord, we have our best trust in him. If we wished to have much care and to vex ourselves hereover, it would help us not, and we should only make ourselves trouble, therefore the more pray we: God give peace in this land.

25

The nations are indeed before him as a drop of a bucket. (Is., xl, 15.)

The Scripture-verses and texts, which we received in March by way of Pittsburg, were our daily food and nourishment for our hearts. The preaching of the Gospel was a blessing to many strangers, and has found reception with many.

There have come to us eighteen persons without reckoning Luke's family, which also has come back to the church. One baptized girl, Lea, has left us, who married a Chippewa.

Nine adults have been baptized this year, five children, and three have been taken into the church.

We have had the holy communion nine times, to which five brethren have been admitted.

One couple married, Lewis and Esther.

Christina Schebosh and the little boy, Augustus, have died.

At present with us—

20 married couples	40
6 single men	6
7 single women	7
3 widowers	3
8 widows	8
10 big boys	10
10 big girls	10
19 boys	19
20 girls	20
Total	123

[Of whom 40 are communicants.] ·28 more than at the close of last year.

CHAPTER VIII.

1788.

NEW SALEM, ON THE HURON, OHIO (PETTQUOTTING).

Tuesday, Jan. 1. Br. Michael preached about Jesus, who redeems his people from their sins, as the angel, Gabriel, foretold. The baptized brethren renewed their covenant with the Saviour, to give him obedience and faithfulness; we gave ourselves anew to him, asking for his blessing and help thereto. A sister, Elizabeth, received absolution, and Louisa, a grown girl, was taken into the church. From the neighborhood we had strangers visiting, who were present at the services and heard the Gospel.

Thursday, 3. David held early service from the Scripture-verse: I am thine, save me. From the bush Indians came here from hunting, and remained several days, among them one, Amochol, with his family, who before, in the autumn, was here for a while visiting, and his daughter's husband; both these are not dead in their hearts, but are uneasy about themselves, and seek what is good. Another was from the the family of the departed White Eyes, his brother's son, with his family; these heard the Gospel not without blessing for their hearts. Moreover, during the holidays the brethren have worked industriously to get the school-house ready, but now for over a week it has snowed nearly every day, and yet the snow is not deep, always melting from below as more falls.

Sunday, 6. In the morning service, which Br. Edwards held, we asked in particular for the Saviour's presence and blessing for the day, and commended ourselves to him, and with us all heathen churches to his grace. In the second service Jeremy's brother was baptized into the death of Jesus by Michael Jung, with the name Mark, at which service many strangers were present. There was a love-feast, and in the congregation meeting the grown girl, Pauline, was taken into the church. It was a day of grace as well for strangers as for brethren; the first were moved and there was great feeling among them. Samuel preached to Amochol and his daughter's husband, Amelia's brother, half the night, and both were so convinced of the truth, especially when he described to them the Saviour upon the cross, how his hands and feet were pierced with nails and his side transfixed, that they broke into floods of tears. The Saviour be praised that the Gospel of his incarnation, passion, and death is not preached and heard in vain.

Monday, 7. Edwards held early service. Among the strangers went on the work of the Holy Ghost. The brethren told them they should take with them what they had heard here as provision for the way, and industriously think it over while hunting. To-day they went away. On the other hand, Weskochk during the holidays was ready to leave the church, and could not be held back, for she loved the world, and went to-day back whence she had come.

Tuesday, 8. Michael held early service. Our schoolhouse was roofed and the floor laid, but since for several days it has been intensely cold, they had to let it rest without finishing it. Mr. Wilson came from Sandusky on his way to Pittsburg, and stayed here several days.

Thursday, 10. David held early service from the text: And grieve not the Holy Spirit of God. A Chippewa sent us a lying message with a piece of tobacco, which we sent back again whence it came.

Saturday, 12. Edwards held early service. For two weeks now it has been very cold, snowing nearly every day, and the snow is now two feet deep, and as our town is very high on a hill, it is a cold place.

Sunday, 13. Br. Edwards preached. The large boys had for their day a service from last year's text: Yet I would have you wise unto that which is good but simple concerning evil. There were snow-squalls all day. We wrote to Bethlehem.

Monday, 14. David held morning service. We left to

the assistants to arrange some/matters concerning the brethren. What concerns outward circumstances among the brethren, for instance, a business or affair where the right is to be seen to and matters arranged, where it concerns common work and so forth, we let the assistants attend to and bring things into order, only we look to it that right and justice are maintained, and nothing is decided by regard to persons. Weskochk returned to her husband.

Tuesday, 15. Michael held early service. Mr. Wilson, who came here from Sandusky, went away to Pittsburg, Joshua, the Indian, accompanying him as far as Cuyahoga. By him we sent letters to Bethlehem. He gave us hope that peace would soon be made with the nations, since this, he said, was now treated of with them on quite another footing. The Indian brethren went away, partly bear-hunting, partly to seek places for sugar-making, but these are not to be found less than ten or twelve miles from here, but from deep snow they could not go far, on which account they are thinking about snow-shoes.

Saturday, 19. Edwards held early service. Since Christmas we have cold, winter weather, and quite deep snow. When now two days ago we had a little warm, rainy weather, we hoped the snow would go off, but it changed soon, and to-day and to-night so deep a snow fell from the north-east as we have not yet had the whole winter. We had to break out the roads in town, also the approaches to them.

Sunday, 20. David preached about the laborers in the vineyard, which parable he applied to the brethren, that in the church it often happens that the first become last, the last first, if brethren use their time badly in the church. In the evening, conference with the assistants, about increasing their number, especially of female assistants. Heard their thoughts.

Tuesday, 22. All the brethren came home. They could do nothing on account of deep snow. The brethren met in the evening, the men and women separately, and sang.

Wednesday, 23. Michael held early service about this, that we, of ourselves, were unable to think any thing good, much less to do, that we have need of the Saviour for every thing, and without him can do nothing. Amelia's brother came here from the bush, and straightway expressed his disposition to live here, and said that Amochol was on his way hither. He told Samuel his life for many years.

Joshua, who went with Wilson to Cuyahoga, came back. The snow there does not go over the shoe, while here it is knee-deep.

Thursday, 24. Amochol with his family came here from hunting, of whom mention was made under the 6th of this month. They could not stay away long.

Friday, 25. It snowed again and the snow was now three feet deep, so that it was hard to get wood. Amelia's brother got leave to live here, after he made himself acquainted with our rules.

Saturday, 26. Br. Edwards held early service about a holy walk, and one well pleasing to God, for which we should strive through the Saviour's grace, who gives us the power thereto. The brethren got wood ready for us. The snow was now three and a half feet deep, so that there was no hunting.

Sunday, 27. Michael preached about the sower. Preaching was farther made to the strangers, for which they longed. We see that they have ears to hear; some find themselves moved, and say: "I have heard how it looks in my heart." David held the communion quarter-hour and the congregation meeting.

Monday, 28. Amochol with his family of five persons was received to live with us. He had given us to understand his longing therefor already before, when he was here in the autumn, and now he stands steadfast thereby. He said that he had already once resolved to come to us, when we were still living on the Muskingum, but had not then arranged his matters properly, for he had taken his friends and the chiefs into counsel, since he had always been a fellow-counsellor; they had held him back,

telling him he should wait awhile and not be the first,
they would yet all become believers, and thus nothing
came of his resolution. For this reason he had separated
himself from the Indians for ten years, had not gone into
their towns, but had supported himself in the bush alone
hunting, so that he might come to us without temptation
as soon as we were again established; he had let neither
his friends nor the chiefs know any thing about it, that
he wished to come to us, for if he had done so, they
would have known how to answer him much; they would
still learn it, but have no opportunity to say any thing to
him about it. Already he is quite advanced in years, an
honorable man, only it is a pity he is baptized, of which
he knows very little, only thus much, that his mother, the
well-known French Cathrine,[1] brought him to a French
priest in Canada, when he was a little boy, and he baptized him. While the assistants were together and talked
with them all, his son, a large, fine looking man, said to
him in Mingo [for he thought there was no one there
who understood this language] : "But thou hast already
elsewhere been baptized, what will now farther be done
with thee?" When the old man told the brothers he
was baptized, his son asked, and said : "Must he then
be baptized again, now that he is with you?" The brethren answered him : "No, he will not again be baptized,
but taken into the church." They showed them a like
instance in our old Cornelius. This, his son, asked the
brothers about many things, telling them also he did not
do it to dispute with them, but wishing to know how it was
with us in this thing or in that. Among other things,
he said also that he had again forgotten how it was with
the seed, of which he heard yesterday, which fell upon
the field. Samuel answered him : "The seed, which is
the word of God, comes many times to a heart as hard as
a stone, but it falls thereon, often starts up, but such a one
makes his heart hard, so that it cannot take root, and
thus must perish. Thou canst then observe in thyself

[1] See note under Jan. 4, 1791.

that thy heart is hard. All thy friends, thy father, mother, brothers, have spoken from their hearts and brought to light their longings, but thou, on the contrary, hast been silent the whole time, and this is a token that thy heart is yet too hard. The seed of God's word cannot enter nor take root." He replied : " Yes, certainly, so it is with me."

Friday, February 1. Yesterday and to-day was speaking with the brethren in reference to the Lord's supper.

Saturday, 2. We had a very blessed communion, of which Renatus now first partook, the Mohican, who, on account of his trial in Easton,[1] is known in the church. He wandered about also many years in the wilderness, and came to us at Gnadenhütten, on Huron River (Michigan). Luke and Peter were readmitted. A grown girl, Johannette, was candidate. A mighty grace prevailed thereby ; the brethren were all together covered with blessing from above. Many brethren usually came from the chapel after communion to our house to kiss us, and this they did of their own accord, not bidden, but to-day the whole body of communicants came, kissed and greeted ; even went farther and exchanged among themselves the kiss of love and peace. The Lord's supper is to our brethren a blessed thing and sacrament, which they value high and dear; it is more than all to them and is always a great blessing for them. If they had it not they could not stand.

Sunday, 3. Early in the morning was read the communion liturgy; afterwards the sermon by Br. Edwards, and David held the congregation meeting.

Monday, 4, was a windy day, with snow, so that from this we had to give up early service.

Tuesday, 5. The cold was the severest we have had the whole winter, and lasted also two or three days.

· Friday, 8. In the morning service from the text: Jesus is able to save them to the uttermost, that come unto God

---

[1] He had been accused of taking part with savage Indians in the murder of a settler, Stinton, in October, 1763. He was arrested, put in prison in Philadelphia, tried in Easton, Pa., and acquitted.

by him, seeing he ever liveth to make intercession for
them, etc. Ah, Lord Jesus if I had not thee, etc. The
discourse was about the boundless mercy of the Saviour towards the greatest sinners, if only they wished to be
blessed and helped; but further it was shown that he who
not only does not wish to receive grace, but treads it
under foot, causes vexation and harm in the church. This
comes to pass because he has again opened his heart to
Satan. In the Scriptures we were advised and commanded
to cast out from among us such wicked opponents. Thus
it was told the brethren that Mamasu, on account of his
wicked conduct, which he had been guilty of, should be
shut out of the church till he acknowledged his sin and
repented from his heart.

Saturday, 9. Edwards held early service. By a Chippewa, who came here from Cuyahoga, we heard that the
snow there is above a man's hips; that the Chippewas suffered greatly from hunger, having no snow-shoes, and had
already eaten their dogs, until they could make snow-
shoes.

Sunday, 10. David preached on this subject, that the
Saviour had been tempted, even as we are, but yet without
sin; that therefore he now has compassion with our weak-
ness and is mighty with the weak to help them; that
Satan cannot harm them. Michael held the congregation
meeting. We have a right prophetic word.

Monday, 11. Edwards held early service. Matthew,
Cornelius' son, also Joachim, with his family, went back
to the Miami, the latter promising to come again if there
should be peace. The former has now been with us nearly
a year. We and the Indian brethren have spoken much
and often with him, exhorting him to think of his soul's
salvation and to reflect farther. All, however, seems to
be in vain. He cannot resolve to be wholly the Saviour's.
Achguachter, who has been here so many days, when she
saw Boaz, said there came utter scoundrels to us, seeking
protection, since they were not safe among the Indians, on
account of their misdeeds. If we were to regard this we
should receive none.

Wednesday, 13. Yesterday and to-day many went out to seek sugar-places, Samuel, William, and others, for there is a thaw and the snow is become less by half. Edwards held morning service.

. Friday, 15. Chippewas came begging for corn, for they have seldom any thing to eat except meat, while hunting. Michael held early service. Samuel and others who sought sugar-places came home.

Sunday, 17. Michael preached about the Canaanite woman. Two white people from Detroit came here on their way to Pittsburg, who remained here several days, the snow was so deep. Br. David conducted the quarter-hour for the baptized. The brethren were directed to knowledge of their misery, to learn to know their hearts, since then they would always find reason from need and from love to look to him.

In the evening, in the congregation meeting, Jeremy was freed from his great trouble, who had been openly put out of the church, for which reason more than a week he endured great need and anxiety, so that he could neither sleep nor eat, and could find no rest day or night, and seemed more like a corpse and an object worthy of pity. Upon his repeated woeful request, he was again compassionately received, to his great comfort and confusion.

Late in the evening the especial watchfulness of the Saviour for us was shown, for while the single brothers, with some Indians also, were with Br. Zeisberger and his wife, their house took fire, and this had gone so far that if it had been unobserved a few minutes longer, it could not have been put out, for the house inside was altogether in flames. But the Indian brethren ran at once into the burning house and extinguished the fire before the roof caught, so that the damage was but slight and to be disregarded, and this fell mostly upon Br. Edwards.

Monday, 18. Br. Edwards held morning service. He asked the brethren with himself to thank the Saviour for his gracious protection in the calamity of fire. Jeremy came quite early to express his thankfulness for the mercy shown him. It was as if he were come from death to life, and we can believe that this will bring about his perfect cure and everlasting salvation. We have indeed many times more trouble, yea, perplexity, with an intelligent soul than with twenty others, but if it then be won for the Saviour our trouble is richly rewarded. We are for this purpose here, to save souls for the Saviour, and we cannot pride ourselves upon this, that we have done what we could. Then we must stand back, and the Saviour has only to make good our faults.

Tuesday, 19. Michael held early service upon the sacrifice of Jesus upon the cross for our sins. Many brethren went to their sugar-places.

Friday, 22. Michael held early service. Old Beata came and told her heart, that she could not see wherein she had fallen short; this was shown her, and therefore she perceived it. She said: "I am already so old [she is perhaps a hundred, or not far from it] that I can retain little of God's word. I forget straightway what I hear, but I yet believe it is all the truth." She was told it was not necessary for her salvation to know much and to retain much, only this little, that the Saviour had died and shed his blood for her, that her sins were forgiven her for his blood's sake, and for his blood's sake she would be saved. A white man from Detroit came, who on the lake, where his horse broke through the ice, lost it and every thing. He went to Pittsburg.

Sunday, 24. David preached from the Epistle: Be ye therefore followers of God. Michael held the children's service and Edwards held the congregation meeting. The rest of the time was used in speaking to the brethren, hearing and advising them, who came home from the bush, and will again go to their sugar-huts.

Monday, 25. David held early service about praising and thanking the Lord, for which we always find cause; if we come to the Saviour with our poverty and misery, we are comforted and made content therewith; this always gives matter for bringing praise and thanks to the Saviour. The brethren went away, nearly all the brothers to their sugar-places. Abraham remained as watchman.

Tuesday, 26.   The three white people set out for Pittsburg, Jeremy going with them as far as Cuyahoga.

Wednesday, 27.   From Sandusky, whence Helena came
back, we learned that many Indians were come there from
the Miami towns, and many more were expected, since
there is a great famine there, and that many too wish to
come to us here, among them some who have been baptized, such as Gertrude and others.   On the contrary,
there are others who refuse, and say they shall not come
here; that David now attracts the Indians to himself that
they may be killed by the Virginians.   Others again say
that we yet live too far away; if we were nearer them they
too would be converted.

Saturday, March 1.   Many of our brethren came home
to the Sunday services, and Br. Edwards delivered,

Sunday, 2, the sermon from the Gospel from the words:
Gather up the fragments that remain, that nothing be lost.
The brethren were admonished to take good care of the
gifts they received from the Saviour's hand, to squander
nothing, and to make no needless waste, but to enjoy them
with thanksgiving, and make good use of them, in order
that the Saviour might not withdraw his gifts from them,
and force them, after suffering want, to acknowledgment
and gratitude.   Cold weather still continued.   The creek
has been frozen since Christmas.

Tuesday, 4.   Early at break of day Esther was delivered
of a son.   Br. Edwards held early service.

Thursday, 6.   At the early service the little son of
Lewis and Esther, born day before yesterday, the 4th, was
baptized with the name Nathaniel.   From Pittsburg came
Mr. Wilson, with a company of several white people and
Indians on their way to Sandusky and the Shawanese
towns, as ambassadors to invite the nations to a convention to be held at the Falls of the Muskingum.   By this occasion, though they were over three weeks in getting here, to
our exceptionally hearty joy, comfort, and refreshment, we
had letters of October and November of last year, likewise
the Scripture-verses and texts for this year.   To-day's,
with which we began them, was very impressive and note-

worthy. It read : Again in this place, which is desolate, without man and without beast, and in all the cities thereof, shall be an habitation of shepherds, causing their flocks to lie down. Who knows in what waste and rough region of the world, which now is looked upon with horror for flesh and blood, in a short time, thy tents shall stand! Ah! may the Saviour bring this to a perfect fulfilment!

Friday, 7. Michael held early service. Leonard Nath. Davis' son, came, with his wife, visiting here. Mr. Wilson with his company set out for Sandusky.

Saturday, 8. A good number of brethren was at home for the Sunday services. Edwards held early service. Abigail, who emptied her heart to us, said, among other things : " Now, since I have been washed with the Saviour's blood, I feel that I am much worse than before, there come to me so many wicked thoughts ; this often puts me in despair, for I think I should be yet better than I was. When I was still among the savages I had no reason to complain about this ; further I had not thought of it, in this way I had rest, but now, when I am aware of these things, my heart is not well, I would like to be rid of them." This was explained to her, and she was told she should not be anxious and puzzled about this, for when she was yet a heathen she was blind and dead in sin, had no consciousness what sin was, nor what a Saviour was; she had certainly not been better, but much worse; now, however, that she had feeling in her heart, she felt her misery and depravity, since in her heart nothing good dwelt; therewith she should always go to the Saviour, tell it, and complain of it to him, seek forgiveness from him, for then she would always anew be comforted and kindly regarded by him.

An unbaptized woman, who with her children was here visiting, asked her son, a grown and married man, why he did not go to the meetings. He answered : " It is not needful for me to go to the meetings ; I have done nothing bad in my whole life ; they who have committed many sins, they alone need it, they may go and hear."

Sunday, 9. Br. David preached about the sacrifice of

Jesus for our sins, that avails perfectly and eternally, so that since the great atonement-sacrifice of Jesus on the cross all offerings end and cease. Many strangers were present. Br. David spoke with Leonard, reminding him of his baptism and what the Saviour had done for him, and exhorting him to turn again to the Saviour. At first he was very timid, but afterwards he said he was very glad Br. David had spoken with him, he would now think about it. Jeremy's second brother, who came here to visit for a few days, and at first used to say he was going off hunting and only wished to see his brothers first, plainly spoke out his mind and desire to live here and be converted, for which he got leave. Thomas, who is a friend of his, had spoken with him one evening and preached the Saviour to him, whereafter he could not sleep the whole night. His brother asked him what was the matter that he could not sleep. He answered he was thinking much about what he had now heard, that he was very restless, would like to remain here, for he could not possibly go away. His brother replied to him: "Go and state thy condition and desire to the teachers or to an assistant, thus wilt thou be rid of this and get repose." He ran now at midnight about the town, but since everybody was asleep he could find nobody but Boaz, who was just baptized and could not tell him much, yet he spoke him comfort and gave him courage, so that in some manner he became quiet until he could speak out his whole heart. This is usually the first step and period with a savage heathen who is coming to the church. He is aware of something extraordinary about him, he is convinced and moved by a mighty grace, which indeed he understands not, and cannot name, and knows not how it happens to him, and whence it comes. He becomes restless, he runs about seeking repose, and would willingly be rid of the thing. This lasts until he is received, when for a time he has rest and is glad and thankful. When thus he comes farther to baptism, he has to go through the second period of a similar kind, likewise accompanied with a mighty grace. With baptism the ice is broken, the worst is over, and from that time he comes quietly to an evangelical, blessed way, and knows not exactly how he comes thereto.

Sunday, 10. Edwards held the early service. From the Miami towns came David with his family, by way of Sandusky, and with them, from the latter place, a whole drove of Indians for a visit.

Thursday, 13. By a Wyandot, who came here yesterday, on his own business, we learned that the chiefs there are still always of the mind to take us away from here, and that we have soon to expect an embassy from there. We well understood what induces them to this, namely, that already last autumn many Indians wanted to come to us, they prevented them, and would not let them come. Now they see again that they are coming hither in stronger number, and they cannot prevent them. They think: " It is better we take them amongst us, so that we may keep the people with us, and we shall make them useful if there be tributes, for instance, to contribute wampum, if strangers come hungry, to furnish corn, and so farther; then we have help in them." Thus their reasons are not so stupid. On the other hand, we are ruined if we live near them or among them. We could raise no cattle or they would be killed, and what is the worst, is their drunkenness—for the sake of a single reason—were our stay to be thought of for other reasons, since it now seems that many Indians wish to be converted, Satan and his servants seek to put a stop to it, to hinder it, and ruin it. May the Lord see to it, and do what is right! It is his affair. He will not suffer to be cut from his hands his inheritance, won bitterly and with blood.

Sunday, 16. Most of the brethren were present at the Sunday services. Br. Michael preached about the Saviour's entrance into Jerusalem for his passion. Then were the communion quarter-hour and the congregation meeting, which Br. David held. Among some strangers was observed the work of the Holy Spirit; to them their sinful depravity was disclosed.

Tuesday, 18. Yesterday and to-day was speaking to the brethren. Some strangers went home, who wished to

persuade others, who were still here, to go with them, but
these said they wished to remain, for they liked to hear
the word of God; among them was a daughter of Boaz,
and her husband, both unbaptized.

Wednesday, 19. Michael held early service. Among
several strangers and the unbaptized was to be seen the
work of true grace in their hearts. Jeremy's brother,
about whom mention was made under the 9th Inst., kept
up his longing for rest and peace in his heart continually.
We thought he would, at least for a time, enjoy peace and
contentment after he was received, but no, he could not
be content with that alone, but he wanted much to have
a consecrated heart. He had come every day since to pour
out his heart, and to-day he said that he knew not how
to help himself, nor anywhere to find advice and aid on
earth; he wished to give himself to the Saviour and the
brothers, wretched and full of sin and shame as he was,
whether he would not, perhaps, be gracious and merciful to
him, if not, he should be lost. He said he wanted to say
this to us, and thereby he wept bitterly. If now men
who do not believe, and call all this enthusiasm, saw a
blind, aroused heathen, perhaps they could by him be convinced that this is God's work, and not man's doing or even
boasting. No man with all his eloquence and shrewdness
could convince a heathen of his sinful and depraved condition; but this the simple story of Jesus' dying upon the
cross can do, and hearts are bruised so that they know no
rest and no counsel. In the evening the communicants
had the washing of feet, after reading the story. We
asked absolution from our dear Lord, and gave ourselves
up to him for washing and cleansing from all our faults
and transgressions.

Thursday, 20. Towards evening was read the story of
our Saviour's agony and bloody sweat on the Mount of
Olives, which was listened to with great attention and excited hearts. Then the communicants had the Lord's
supper on the night when he was betrayed. Johannette
was, for the first time, a partaker. Elizabeth and Tobias
were candidates.

Friday, 21. The communion liturgy was early read. Then was begun the reading of this day's history, which was continued during the day, in four parts, with chorals intermingled. By consideration of all the sufferings, the scoffing and ignominy, reproach, bonds, and scourging, and his whole tortures from head to foot, hearts were mightily moved and many tears shed, and among the new people there was much commotion, so that there was none who was not mightily affected, and some were quite melted. Of this we heard the evening afterward cheering proof. Of the new people came one after the other, for a long time, and till late in the night, complaining of their misery and wretched condition, with many tears, and gave us to understand their longing for the bath of holy baptism and cleansing away of their sins. Among them was old John Cook, who came in tears, and laid before us his perplexity about his wretched state, for which we were no little delighted, for with such Indians, baptized in religion, it is always harder to come to acknowledgment of their misery than for a savage heathen. The assistants also made good use of the time after all services, assembling together baptized and unbaptized, so that they had no room in the house, but most had to stand outside the house and listen, and the assistants spoke with great earnestness, from the fulness of their hearts, about the great love of the Saviour for poor sinners, whom he has brought to light through his bitter passion and countless sufferings, so that the whole town was aroused.

Saturday, 22, was Quiet Sabbath, and in the afternoon there was a love-feast. At the Scripture-verse and text it was mentioned that the Saviour has sanctified and blessed both our night-rest and our rest in the grave, so that we live equally with him, sleeping or awake.

Sunday, 23. We assembled early at daybreak, and after greeting the church with the words: the Lord is arisen, we read a part of the Easter liturgy in the chapel, and went then to our grave-yard, and, at the usual place, asked for eternal communion with those who had this year

26

departed, Sister Christina and our brother, the child
Augustus. Thereupon the story of the resurrection was
read, to which the new people especially listened very at-
tentively. Br. Edwards preached, and in the afternoon,
towards evening, after consideration of the Scripture-
verse: Ah! Lord God, behold thou hast made the heaven
and the earth, etc., amid the many tears both of the baptized and of the spectators, by the bath of holy baptism,
three were buried in Jesus' death, namely, the brother of
Jeremy and Mark, by the name of John Martin, Wassa-
pahk, Anthony, and Michael's son, who came here this
winter from the Miami, John Thomas. At this service a
mighty grace and the near presence of the Holy Trinity
were to be observed.

[So far this diary sent to Bethlehem.]

Monday, 24. David held early service. At the Scripture-verse: And seek the peace of the city whither I have
caused you to be carried away captive, etc., and the text:
Remember that Jesus Christ was raised from the dead, the
brethren were admonished to abide by the word of Jesus'
death and passion, and to hold fast thereby, then also to
seek the good of their fellow-men, and to try to make
known to them the word of life on every occasion.

Leonard, who, since the 7th of this month and during
the holidays, has been here, and was touched anew, went
back again to speak with his aged parents, whom he
wanted much to bring here with him, and will come for
good at planting-time. He was told to behave well, for
which he had the demand in his heart; he was told to seek
the church again and rescue his soul while there was yet
time.

Tuesday, 25. David held early service. At the text:
For as much then as the children are partakers of flesh
and blood, he also himself likewise took part of the same,
etc., the brethren were brought to remember to-day as a
mighty day (Annunciation), wherein young and old of
either sex have great share, since his incarnation, his whole
life and walk in the world, even to the cross, the grave,
and the resurrection, are for us, of which we should make .

good use, to become sharers in that which he thereby has
acquired for us. Finally we thanked him upon our knees
for his incarnation, passion, and death, and asked him to
make that always plainer to us through his spirit. The
brethren were then dismissed, since for a week now they
have been interrupted in their sugar-making, and have left
much undone, the brothers to their spring hunt and the
sisters to sugar-boiling.

Friday, 28. John Cook, who wishes to find his son
somewhere near the Fort and to bring him here, on which
account he planned a journey, came and begged us to think
of him, that the Saviour might watch over him and bring
him successfully here again, which we promised him, but
bade him also not forget the Saviour and to call upon him,
who would again help him hither. Both yesterday and to-
day came some of the new people to tell their hearts, to
complain of their unholy state, and they showed their
longing for the forgiveness of their sins. Thomas' brother-
in-law and sister, who have been here visiting for several
days, went home. They both said they wanted to come
again soon, they liked to hear about the Saviour. They
went hunting, and said they would straightway come here
and not to the savage towns.

Sunday, 30. Michael gave the sermon, to which only a
very few came from the bush, on account of their necessary labor in sugar-making, which must be attended to,
for they have to arrange according to the weather and
observe the time. In the second service we thought of
those baptized during the year, seven brethren, commend-
ing them to the care of the Saviour and of God, the
worthy Holy Ghost, to let them grow and thrive in the
church, and to increase in love and gratitude, to his honor
and joy.

Tuesday, April 1. Almost all went off hunting, so that
only some old people were at home.

Thursday, 3. John Martin, who, with his brother, Mark,
went hunting a few days ago, came home. The former
said he could not remain away so long as he had thought,
for he was anxious, fearing he should lose the blessed feel-

ing and his joy in the Saviour, but was heartily thankful
that he had kept him blessed. Two Mingoes came here
from Sandusky, with a white man yet to come, on their way
to Pittsburg.

Friday, 4. Mr. Wilson came here from Sandusky with
John Nicholas; he went,

Saturday, 5, away to Pittsburg, by whom we sent letters
and diaries; the other went back to Sandusky to await the
resolution of the nations about the treaty. We had the
first thunder, with heavy rain. Phœbe and her husband
came here.

Sunday, 6. Some brethren came to the sermon, which
Br. David delivered. Br. Edwards held the congregation
meeting.

Tuesday, 8. David held morning service in Indian.

Wednesday, 9. David held morning service in Indian.
From Sandusky came Boaz's brother and sister for a visit.
He said he, too, would like to be converted and live like
the believers. One of his sisters was born in the church
in Languntouteniink, but not baptized, her mother not
being baptized. The people are now always dissuaded and
forbidden to come to us, and the more eager they are to
come hither to see and hear; the more they forbid, the
worse it becomes. What then drives these people to us?
Certainly not men, for they seek to hinder it. This is the
work of God and of the Holy Ghost, to bring to the Saviour
the souls that have cost him so much, and to make them
partakers of the blessedness he has won for them.

Saturday, 12. Michael held early service. Our people
all came home from their sugar-huts and from hunting.
Boaz's brother went away, saying if he came home again
from hunting he wished to come here to stay. A Mingo
Mohawk, who has a sister, also wishes to live here.

Sunday, 13. Br. Edwards preached. In the afternoon
the little son of Renatus and A. Regina was baptized with
the name Augustus.

Tuesday, 15. Edwards held early service. A party of
Indians, which has encamped here two days and also visited our meetings, went upon their hunt. Some thought

and suspected they were going to war. With the party went Mary Magdalene, a grown girl, secretly away.

Wednesday, 16. David held early service. The Indian, David, who some time ago came here from the Miami, expressed his wish now again to stay in the church with his family of six persons, and was received. Phœbe, formerly a single woman in the church, brought here on the 5th Inst. her husband, a savage, who begged permission with his wife to live here with us, and was also received. The Indian brethren set about fence-making. On account of the new-comers we must fence in two new fields.

Friday, 18. The brethren were done with making fences about the lowest field on the creek. It became necessary from the lay of the land that we should include within the fence two Chippewa fields which our brethren planted last year and wished to plant again this year, for otherwise it would have doubled the work, and since also we wished to have friendship with them we were glad to include their fields in our fence; also on account of our cattle, which might do them damage, for which they were glad and thankful, and considered this as an act of friendship.

Saturday, 19. David held morning service. The Indian brethren went in common hunting, and brought home four deer, woodcock, and other game, for their work of fencing.

Sunday, 20. David preached about the promise of the Saviour to send to us the Comforter, who punished the people of the world for their unbelief that they did not let themselves be sharers in righteousness through Jesus' blood, and that they wished to remain yet longer under the power of the princes of this world, whose power the Saviour has destroyed, redeeming us with his blood. In the afternoon the little daughter of David and Salome, born on the Miami, was baptized, receiving the name Augustine in holy baptism. We learn, to our joy, that we shall win for the Saviour still more of the Indians who settled below us last year after our arrival and planted. A family, our Abigail's sister, who, since we have been here, has wished to hear nothing about the Saviour, nor has she come to our meetings, said that she did not wish to go with the devil into everlasting fire, as she had heard all unbelievers would do. She has already twice come to hear about the Saviour, and wishes now to be converted.

Monday, 21. Edwards held early service. The brethren resumed fence-making; some sisters went to Sandusky.

Tuesday, 22. During a service for the baptized brethren, the widower, Andrew, and A. Salome, a single person, were married. On this occasion information was given to both old and young how they were to conduct and behave themselves in the church, if they live for the Saviour and wish to show themselves children of God. Many new people being with us, such an exhortation was needful.

Wednesday, 23. The brethren were done with fencing. They have fenced in four fields. There is also a good piece of land left for strangers who may, perhaps, yet come here this spring. White people from Detroit, Connolly's[1] son, came here on their way to Pittsburg. His father is commandant there.

Friday, 25. Michael held early service. Sisters came back from Sandusky, where they got corn. We heard that some of our Indians, Nathaniel, Lydia, and others, were on their way hither.

Sunday, 27. Michael preached and Edwards held the afternoon service. In the service for the baptized, Anthony, a single man, and the single woman, Esther Amelia, Cornelius' daughter, were married.

Monday, 28. David held early service. Samuel went to Sandusky to speak with his brother, of whom for a long time he had always been hearing that he wished to come to us, but had trouble and opposition from the chiefs, who did not want to let him go. He had been with us over the lake, and wished even then to stay with us, but could not effect it for the same reason. Several other brethren went there to get corn, among them Boaz, whom the spirit of bearing witness forces to preach the Saviour to his

---

[1] The well-known Dr. John Connolly, Lord Dunmore's agent. He had been in command at Pittsburg in 1774.

friends, especially to his mother, and to the Indians. He becomes very sad upon seeing that they do not receive his words, but whenever he meets a strange Indian, to him he announces the Saviour and the blessedness he has won. Though he does not always hit the mark, and is not practical, yet it is much better and more pleasing to us than if he listened to the foolish chattering of the savages or even applauded them.

Wednesday, 30. Samuel returned from Sandusky, where he spoke his mind to his brother and friends, especially to the former, who, already over the lake wished to be with us, but it is the same with him now as it was then, namely, he cannot get free. He is a counsellor, much looked up to and depended on. Samuel spoke his mind to them that he should live and die in the church; he wished to see them and speak with them once more, since they were so near, but now that they were moving farther away he would perhaps not see them for a long time, possibly never again, and if any one of them wanted to see him he must come to him; he remained by the words of everlasting life and blessedness until he should depart from this world; he would be glad, indeed, if they would share therein to be eternally blessed, but if they wished it not he must let them go their own way, but he had wished to tell them this. His brother answered that he had nothing to say in reply; he believed that to be the right thing and the way to be saved, but for the time being he could not; he should hold him dear, and let him know if any thing dangerous were afoot which concerned us; we could plant quietly this spring; before the year was over matters would be clear and circumstances would have come to some determination.

We learned now the true state of the nations, how they are disposed. All nations at the last conference upon the Miami agreed upon peace with the States, except a part of the Wyandots in Lower Sandusky, of whom fifteen men survive the small-pox sickness. They are ill-disposed, and wish to have revenge upon the white people for having lost so many people by the small-pox. Then a part of the Shawanese do not wish to acquiesce, of whom there are said to be twenty odd. They made the proviso, however, that if all did not wish for peace, those who did wish for peace should all go over the lake, but those who wished to have war should remain there and fight out the matter alone, and not come among the others, for they wished to tell the States to consider all Indians this side the lake as foes, with whom they should now settle their affairs. They wished to come together again this spring and speak farther of this.

Thursday, May 1. Br. Edwards preached. In a separate service it was impressed upon the hearts of the baptized brethren that the daily and constant walk with the Saviour, whom we cannot indeed see, but in whom we believe and whom we love, disposed us in faith to believe in him, to cling to him, the Vine, even to beholding what we have believed. We adored him, and asked from him our steady abiding with him from need and from love.

Saturday, 3. There came two Mingo families here, and remained over night, with wives and children, and when they heard that to-morrow would be Sunday, they resolved to stay here over Sunday, and wished to hear a sermon; from their talk we gathered they had been baptized by a French priest. By occasion of their saying that a certain time every year they had to scourge themselves to atone for their sins, our Indians said that was a hard service to have to torture themselves in vain. Among them was one, Joseph Brant's Longus, from whom we learned also that the Six Nations were much inclined to peace, and were laboring to bring it about.

Sunday, 4. David preached and then held the communion quarter-hour. From the Miami towns came Lea, Susanna's sister, and Lydia, Gabriel's wife, both sick, the latter with two children, by way of the Sandusky, also Jacobina, with her present husband, a savage, all to remain. Several of our baptized and some savage Indians will also come here, but are waiting to see if there will be peace. It is well, however, that something always occurs to hold them back, that the concourse may not be too great, and we can remain in good order.

Monday, 5. Michael held early service. Boaz' mother, Ackerlemann, who came here yesterday from Sandusky, and asked reception, received permission therefor. She came here a year ago with her son and wished for his conversion, he was such a bad man. He remained here, but she did not yet deem it needful, and went away, but yet had no peace, and was scoffed at by the savages as a Sunday-Indian, since her son was here. They said she would also yet come to us. When now her son, Boaz, went there, a few days ago, she resolved to come with him to us, and said: "The Indians named me from sport a Sunday-Indian, though I was not one, but now I will make it true, and become a believer." Also Lydia with her two children was received.

Wednesday, 7. Many strangers came here visiting, among whom was one Packanke's[1] son, who called our Indians happy, saying they had a pleasant life together; this was not elsewhere to be found, only with us. On the other hand, at times some come here, who seek to cause trouble.

Friday, 9. David came from Sandusky, where he got corn. He met there his two brothers from the Miami, one of whom came here with him, who did not wish to go back to his mother, a baptized woman. She sent word to David he should hasten back to her, and not go to the believers, for they would all be killed by the Virginians, which is the common saying everywhere among the Indians, and yet they all come here to us and have no fear. Thereupon he sent word to her that if he had heard she was in trouble and wanted to come to the brothers and knew not how to proceed, he should have arisen at once and have brought her with horses, but since he heard this other from her, he could not go, he would go sometime to get his things when it should be convenient. Gertrude

---

[1] Packanke was head-chief of the Monsey tribe of Delawares, at first very friendly to the missionaries. He was probably never converted, but recommended his children to receive the Gospel. Drake's Book of Indians, V. 25.

and several Indians in Sandusky would also like to come
to us, to whom the Monsey captain, Titawachkam, says
they shall not, and prevents them, saying he wishes soon
to invite one of our teachers thither, to preach to them,
when they will all become believers. This is the old story,
which we know and have long understood. When the
chiefs and head people see that the preaching of the Gospel
finds too great acceptance, and that they cannot hinder it and
hold back the Indians with the lies they invent, then they
wish themselves to invite a teacher, saying they also desire
to become believers, that the Indians may not run away
from them. Yesterday and to-day there was speaking
with the brethren. We had then,

Saturday, 10, the holy communion, to which were readmitted old Beata, A. Paulina, the white Helen, and Renatus. Tscholens, Luke's daughter's husband, and Lea,
Susanna's sister, got leave to live here.

Sunday, 11. The communion liturgy was early read,
and then Br. Michael preached about the office and labor
of God, the Holy Ghost, among mankind, especially in
bringing them to Jesus Christ, their Redeemer and Saviour.
About this subject in the service for the baptized yet more
was said to them, and plainly. They were told it had especially to them been given to understand the work and
care of the Holy Spirit in the hearts of believers, for they
had received him and he dwelt in them; to them it had
also been given to hear his voice; now it was required of
them to show obedience and fealty, thus would he maintain them in Jesus Christ in the right and only faith to the
end, always giving them the assurance that they were the
children of God and the possession of Jesus, that he and
his Father loved them, for they had cost him his blood.
We thanked him with humble hearts for all the grace and
truth he had shown us, begged him further to stand by us;
we asked also absolution for our negligence and omissions,
and that often we had not regarded his voice and admonitions, and vowed to him anew fealty and obedience. We
got from him the comfort and the assurance in our hearts
that he will do this in us.

In the concluding service young Abraham was taken into the church, and one was baptized with the name, Moses.

Tuesday, 13. Different brothers went out hunting and the sisters planting.

Thursday, 15. Mr. Wilson came here from Sandusky, bringing us letters of December, February, and March from Bethlehem and Litiz. We learned at the same time that in a few days the nations would hold a convention near Stony Point (Monroe Co., Mich.), to which also Mr. Wilson was going, from which place they would at once break up and go to the treaty on the Muskingum.

Saturday, 17. Michael held early service. From Detroit two white people came, whom William,

Sunday, 18, accompanied to Cuyahoga, for as yet there is no regular road, but our Indians steer from here through the bush. Br. David preached from the Gospel about Nicodemus and the Holy Trinity, that all three Persons have contributed to the redemption of the human race, and through our Helper and Saviour, Jesus Christ, have brought it about and accomplished it.

A savage, proud Indian, more than a week ago, came here from his hunting lodge, more than two days' journey away, and had remained several days, in which time he came also to Br. David, who asked him whence he was and came. This he told, and said he would like to hear something about the Saviour, for he had once already heard something. Br. David talked with him, and told him it was well and needful that he thought about being happy here in time and there eternally; if this was his mind and wish, the Saviour would help him thereto and give him power, who had won it for us by his blood, which he had poured out for our sins, dying for us, and so on. He listened thoughtfully, and went back again to his hunting-lodge quite still. Two days ago he came again with all he had gained hunting, omitted no service, and it could be seen that he was not without reflection, but he said nothing, and was on his guard, and wished to drive away his unrest. To-day he came to Br. David in full heathenish state, hung with silver and wampum, sat by him, placing his storm-cap, which was decked with all sorts of feathers and ribbons, straightway at his feet, which is not usual with a savage, and sat awhile quite still. He then said he came not only for thus much, but wishing to tell him he should also like to live with us, if he should be allowed, giving at the same time the reasons why, namely, he found no place where he could be well, let him think of any part of the world he would, but here with us he believed he had found it; he wished to conceal nothing, but to say outright that he was a bad man, had led a sinful, wicked life, had been nine times in war, had killed also five white people, and so farther; since he had been here before, however, in his hunting-lodge he had thought over what he had heard here, and had felt a strong impulse to come hither. Br. David asked him whether he had already conversed with any one of our assistants about this; he said, no. Then he said they would call him, and he could tell them his desire and longing. "Indeed," said he, "I do not know how or what I shall speak," for many think it must be done in a formal speech, upon which the answer follows. Br. David said to him we did not require many words from him, but this alone, whether he wanted to live here for this reason, that he wished to be saved and live for the Saviour, renouncing his heathenish life and being. He went away, but was full of restlessness, came again, and had no peace until it happened, and thus, the evening after, he was received, to his great comfort. The next morning at the early service he appeared like another man, for he had cast aside all his heathenish state.

Tuesday, 20. Edwards held early service. The brethren planted our field to-day.

Wednesday, 21. Four white people came here from Pittsburg, on their way to Detroit, and stayed here a couple of days, and towards evening one, Hamilton, from the same place, with flour and salt.

Thursday, 22. An Indian came from the Fort with strong drink, and encamped near by. We tried in vain to get him into town and to take care of his strong drink, yet he promised to give no one any of it; meantime we kept good watch, for it made us uneasy and concerned, and one had to be bound.

Friday, 23. White people came through here from Pittsburg with cattle for Detroit, from whom our Indians bought a few head. On the 24th they went on farther, for Sandusky.

Sunday, 25. David preached. Some white people, among them two officers, came in and went to Detroit.

Wednesday, 28. Hamilton went back to the Fort. David held early service. In the evening Wittiger came from Sandusky with a prisoner who had been condemned by the Shawanese to be burnt, but whom the traders had ransomed, and now he was on his way to the Fort.

Thursday, 29. Edwards held early service. An Indian with his wife, John Martin and Mark Longus, who a few days before had come out of the bush, at their request got leave to live here. Now there are four from this family with us. Jeremy having made the beginning. Our people were very busy planting, since for several days the weather has been dry. This year the spring is late on account of much rain, and therefore they have been much hindered in planting. We learn that the Indians begin to assemble over the lake for the convention.

Saturday, 31. Jacob and his company came home from hunting, after being gone more than two months, but they had little or no success.

Sunday, June 1. Br. David preached about the great feast. A young man, Gischikelema, who lately came here to live, and who promised to behave according to our rules, and kept not his promise, was informed by the assistants he must leave our place.

Monday, 2. Michael held early service. Then the assistants had to speak with Jeremy and Weskochk. We had for some time been thinking of increasing the number of assistants, and had considered together about it, but our plans then came to nothing, Some days ago we spoke with our assistants also about it, and found them of the same mind with ourselves, proposing the same per-

sons. Two days since, the Saviour approved the two brethren, Luke and Stephen, to be chosen as assistants. The
former had before, in Schönbrunn, been among the number. Among the sisters, however, we found none, and yet
we need them much, having only two, namely, Bathsheba
and Sara Nanticoke. We hold this evening a pleasant
love-feast with them, seven brothers and two sisters, at
which they were told what their office and business were
in the church, namely, to be watchers, to prevent trouble
where they could, thereby to follow a good course, and to
go before the brethren with a good example, to love one
another, and to agree in mind and heart, which would be
their force that they would accomplish great things.

Tuesday, 3. David held early service from the Scripture-verse: For I, saith the Lord, will be unto her a wall of
fire round about. Since we heard that our cattle had
done much damage in the fields of the Chippewas in our
neighborhood, and we saw that through the whole summer
we should have trouble in this way, for among Indians the
rule is that if cattle do harm in their fields, the damage
must be made good or they shoot the cattle dead—quite
without reason, for there is no fence about their fields—we
wanted to have peace, so we had to give them seed-corn to
plant again and make them a good fence, which was done
to-day and the following days. An Indian with his wife,
who are mentioned under May 29th, were advised to go
away from us, for since they have been here they have quar-
relled together, and the woman left him.   ·

Wednesday, 4. Edwards held early service. We proposed to the assistants a formal speech at the treaty on
the Muskingum, to be delivered to the chiefs, which we
gave into their hands and explained the matter; this
had their approval and was better received than we expected, since our Indians for several years have been so
disposed towards the Indian chiefs as not to wish to have
any thing to do with them. They have done, however,
according to our wish, and perhaps we shall again come to
friendly intercourse with them, if we remind them of the

old friendship and renew it, for many of the former chiefs are still alive.

Thursday, 5. David held early service. Thereupon A. Salome, on account of her extraordinarily wicked conduct and adultery committed, the like of which was never before in the church, was put out of the church, who went away also to-day, for she should stay here not a night longer.

Saturday, 7. Two French traders came here by water with corn and flour, all of which our Indians bought, and went away again. Susanna (Zeisberger) went to bed again sick.

Sunday, 8. Br. Michael preached from the Gospel about the lost sheep, and then was the service for the baptized brethren. The congregation meeting had to be omitted on account of heavy rain and thunder. Then came through here again drovers with a great herd. Two Mingoes came from Pittsburg with rum. We lodged them and took their rum for safe-keeping until they went away, and we accompanied them beyond our bounds with a guard. Notwithstanding all our care, it did not get off untouched, for Chippewas watched for it, followed after them when they were gone, and also two from here, who afterwards came to town drunk.

Monday, 9. Edwards held early service. Some went to Sandusky to get corn, and,

Tuesday, 10, Adolphus went with his family to Sandusky to get corn, and he took A. Salome there to her mother, for she could not be here. By Sabina's brother we learn that six Delawares who went to war died in it. Br. Michael Jung, with three Indian brethren, Adam, Tobias, and John Martin, went to the Fort to get some necessities for us. We have had for some days now trouble and vexation with Gischikelema, who is here only to corrupt our young people. We had him sent away, but he went not, and we were obliged to keep a watch in the night to oppose the evil. If we receive new people we have trouble and labor to expect. They come and force themselves upon the church, and as we do not know the people, we do not like to reject them, but make trial of them. They promise also to behave according to all our rules, but when they have become established, then some begin to live their heathenish life in the church, make us anxiety and vexation, and we cannot get rid of them, so that we have enough to do to oppose the wicked spirit that is in them.

Wednesday, 11. There came again white people, mostly Germans, with cattle, on their way to Detroit. Our people again bought some from them, so that our Indians have this summer easily and cheaply acquired cattle, of which there is now a great herd.

Friday, 13. The assistants' conference reconciled Jeremy and Weskochk.

Saturday, 14. Boaz' Andrew went to Sandusky. Edwards held early service. John Thomas, who went with Br. Michael to the Fort, turned about not far from Cuyahoga with a cow the drovers had left behind, and given to whoever of our Indians should find her, and brought her here. Helena came from Sandusky. We learn that a young Mingo, Jonathan, baptized by us, died there. About a week ago his mother sent us word we should get him here. He said to a sister that he was not to blame for having to die among the savages; a year ago he wished to come to us, but his mother had not permitted him.

Sunday, 15. David preached and held the quarter-hour for the baptized. McKee's brother came back from Detroit. No Indians had gone to the treaty upon the Miami.

Monday, 16. John Cook came from the Fort with a white man and Chippewa Indians. He came not as he had gone, and has indeed lost his belief, for he brought liquor with him, but this he left behind. Also, Helena's son, Francis, came, with his family, from the winter and spring hunting. David held early service.

Wednesday, 18. Many strangers came here, who attend the meetings, but both among them and also among those who are already come to us, little earnestness is to be seen for conversion, and it is as if they were not the right people; meanwhile we have patience with them and wait.

Thursday, 19. Edwards held early service. A conference with the assistants about Moses and Paulina, Luke's daughter [these were united in marriage by the assistants], and especially about our young women, who are quite generally in a very bad way. By Indians from Sandusky we learn that the council on the Miami is broken up, for the Six Nations and others are not come. It is now said they will come together in thirty days. It now comes to light that the Six Nations have instigated the Chippewas to declare war against the Delaware nation, of which last year we already secretly had heard. No other reason can be found for this than a severe speech which the departed White Eyes made in Pittsburg to the Mingoes, which is said to have given rise to this. For several years they have been working that all nations should unite and hold together, but it appears they will at last be discordant among themselves. Eight Delawares and Mingoes lately went to Wilünk (Wheeling) on the Ohio to murder and steal, of whom only three came back, the others perished. The leaf begins to turn, and the Indians almost always pay the penalty. We learned that this spring three of our Indians who went to war died, Thomas, George, and one who was not baptized.

Friday, 20. White people came from Detroit, young Farsithe, Capt. Thorne, and others, with the prisoners, on their way to Pittsburg, one of whom was Col. Mitchel, who in the year '77 was stationed in Bethlehem with the baggage, and knew the brothers. This spring, on the Ohio, he was captured by the Shawanese, and ransomed by the merchants in Detroit for two hundred dollars. They were conducted on the 21st by the Indian, Thomas, to Pittsburg. We heard that in Detroit they were still planting, on account of the late high water. From Pittsburg came one Wittiger, who six days before had spoken with Br. Michael Jung and his company on the Mahoning; all well, but from high water had been much hindered on their journey.

Sunday, 22. Edwards preached. David had an earnest

27

hour with the children on account of bad conduct, and held the congregation meeting. We had a conference with the assistants, who spoke with John Cook till late in the night, reminding him of his promises to behave according to our rules and exhorting him to keep order in his house, and they impressed it upon him. A Frenchman from Sandusky Bay, with his wife, made us a friendly visit and went back.

Monday, 23. The brethren hoed our plantation. Br. Edwards held early service from the Scripture-verse: I will be as the dew unto Israel. Joseph, in whom it can be seen that his end draws near, was, at his request, absolved on his sick-bed in the presence of several brethren.

Tuesday, 24. The brethren built a house for John Cook, who has thus far lived in one lent him, who has again made clear that he will be the Saviour's and hold to his first resolution, made when he came here. If people come to us about whom we have hesitation and doubt, whether they will remain and thrive in the church, we have the foresight to build them a house ourselves, so that in case they do not get along well in the church, if things change with them and we have to send them away, they cannot plague us and say: "It is my house, from which no one can drive me," as we have already had instances.

Thursday, 26. Lea went from time, who,

Friday, 27, was buried. She came here the 4th of last May from the Miami towns, having sent word from Sandusky, where she became ill, that we should bring her here. She came to us with her mother, over the lake, but when the latter died she went away, came again and went. Since now we knew her, we did not wish to bring her here without first knowing why she would come to the church, but yet let it happen upon hearing she would probably not recover, and her sister went for her. · She promised also not to leave the church if she should be well again, but this was not true, as results showed, for after she was here, she was not at all concerned about herself, indeed joyful that she was with her sister, who took care of her, but she longed for nothing else. The sisters often talked with her

to be concerned about her salvation and to seek forgiveness from the Saviour, but she took it not to heart and
heard it not willingly.   Br. David visited her and talked
with her, but she remained stubborn.   We heard afterwards from Lydia, with whom she came, and who took
care of her here for several days, that she had said she
was not going to die, and when she was well again she
wished to go away; she had not come here to remain, but
only to have better care bodily.   The text of the day of
her death read: In whom the God of this world hath
blinded the minds of them which believe not, lest the
light of the glorious Gospel, etc.   And thus it was with
her.   It was a sad and mournful instance, the like of
which we have hardly yet had in the church.   She was
buried in especial quiet, and thus we began a grave-yard
for the unbaptized.

Sunday, 29. David preached from 'the text: Know ye
not that so many of us as were baptized into Jesus Christ
were baptized into his death, and Edwards held the congregation meeting.

Monday, 30. David held early service. To-day finally
came Gelelemend, already in the third year of his journey
from the Fort hither, with his whole family, and encamped
in sight of our town, where many of our Indian brethren
visited him.

Tuesday, July 1. At the early service, which Br. Edwards held, Gelelemend,[1] above mentioned, was present,
with three sons, one already grown. We heard once again
frightful stories about a war party of Chippewas, who were
come from Michilimackinac to the mouth of this creek
and wanted to go the Pittsburg road to war, which made
us much concerned about our Br. Michael Jung with his
company, whom we were now every day expecting back from
there, and we thought of sending some Indian brethren

---

[1] A grandson of Netawatwes, friend of the Americans and opponent
of Capt. Pipe. He was obnoxious to the Monseys, and for a long time
lived in concealment in Pittsburg. Much of his subsequent history is
given in this diary. He died in January, 1811, about eighty years old.
See Drake's Book of the Indians, V. 95.

to meet them and escort them hither. Since the Chippewas and Indians in our neighborhood could not persuade
them to turn about, they at last brought the matter to this
point, that they went another way down to the Ohio, for
they did not wish to have this way closed, where many
Chippewas, Tawas, and other Indians encamp hunting, so
that in some measure we were quieted. They marched by,

Wednesday, 2, in sight of our town. At the outset, when they came here, they said that thousands of
their nation would follow them, but when at their departure they were carefully questioned, they said they did not
know whether more would come, so that we thus saw they
had told only lies. We heard, by way of Sandusky, that
Brant and the Mingoes held a council in Detroit, of which
in a short time we should hear something.

Thursday, 3. Br. Edwards held early service. David
then spoke with Gelelemend, who expressed to him his desire and longing to be with the church again, for he had
twice been expelled on the Muskingum, when we were
there, for he was then very much involved in the affairs
of chief, and at last became chief in Goschachgünk. Now,
however, that he is free and has nothing more to do with
affairs, although last year the Delaware chiefs visited him
and proposed to him to come again and be chief, but he
had declined, we could not refuse him for the third
time, but received him, after the assistants had first spoken
with him and his wife. He came very meek and outwardly very poor, so that we all had great pity for him,
and sought to help him what we could. He said to Br.
David, whom he had not seen for seven years, that he had
countless times wished himself with us, for in Pittsburg,
where he retired during the war, he was often no day sure
of his life, on account of the militia; when then he
thought of going to us over the lake, he knew not how to
come because of the Indians, who likewise wished his life.
He was quite revived and cheerful when he got permission
to be one of our inhabitants, for he was much cast down
and in fear he might be again rejected. If the chiefs in
such condition come to us, we will receive them heartily

and cheerfully, show them love and kindness, and the greater is our joy if they thrive for the Saviour in the church and become eternally happy. In the evening the assistant, Samuel, delivered a discourse to all the brothers and sisters, very effectively, in the school-house. The assistants have reasonably much to do.

Friday, 4. All the brethren helped plant one piece more of corn. Although it should not ripen, yet it will be good to eat, so that they have yet something to hope for.

. Saturday, 5. By way of Sandusky, from which place daily this week Indians have come here, we learned that Pomoacan, the Half-King, died in Detroit, whither he was gone to a council. According to appearances, he was again our friend since we have been here, for he called us hither, though it may not have been without a purpose, for such people do nothing without a purpose. From Detroit came two white people, Loveless, with a woman, on their way to Pittsburg, who were brought there in the war as prisoners and had known us there. They were accompanied to the Fort by Frank.

Sunday, 6. Edwards preached about the great miracle, above all the Saviour did, that the Creator of all things became man, suffered bitter death for his fallen human creation, and thereby brought about eternal redemption. David held the children's service and the congregation meeting, the latter from the Scripture-verse, with reference to the words of the Saviour: Ye are the salt of the earth and ye are the light of the world, that the Saviour's people shall be a blessing for the world and bear fruit. A young unmarried man, Levi by name, who, a grown boy, had been baptized on the Muskingum, and came here last evening, came to-day quite early to Br. David, made himself known, and begged leave again to come to the church. He said he could no longer be among the savages, for since he heard we were here he had no rest, his heart told him he belonged to us; he had come for no other reason than to ask permission to be allowed to come to the church. Here is seen the wide difference between a savage and one who has been baptized. Here was found a field that, plainly to be seen, had been worked before, for when Br. David told him he did well in again seeking the Saviour and the church, and reminded him of his baptism, the tears ran down his cheeks. He was told that the assistants would call him and speak with him, to whom he should disclose his heart and wish, who would then speak farther with him; this thus happened, and he got leave to come here. He was so pleased with this that he said he had told his grandmother, Gertrude, two days before, upon leaving her, that he would come back again in eight days, but since now he received such good words and comforting answer he wanted to go back to Sandusky to-morrow morning and bring her here with him. An unbaptized maiden, or woman, whose mother died in the church, came here some days ago to remain, and wished not again to go away. She was also received after she had been brought into a family and cared for.

Monday, 7. Edwards held early service. We heard that five of the thirteen warriors who went by five days ago, came back last evening without accomplishing any thing, very hungry.

Tuesday, 8. David held early service. A sickly, unbaptized woman came here a few days ago and wanted much to stay here. As a child she had been in the church, and after the death of her mother, who was baptized and blessed, she was taken by her father among the savages. Last winter she came here visiting with her husband and omitted no meeting, as also now. To her an Indian doctor had said she was not sick in body, nothing was the matter with her, but she was sick in heart and in mind; she might well have been at the meetings of the believing Indians and thought much about what she heard there; no doctor could help her, she must go to the believers, there she would soon be well. Her husband went through here not long ago on his way hunting, and had said that when he came back he wanted to come straight here and stay. As we could not support the wife, since at times we are badly supplied with food, we advised her to go back again home and wait for her husband, until he came and expressed his wish to live here, and this she did, though not very willingly.

In the evening quite late Br. Michael Jung came back from the Fort, having been much delayed by heavy rains and high water, after being gone just four weeks. We thanked the Saviour that they had made the journey without opposition from warriors, having been troubled about them, for if nothing had happened to endanger his life, he might have been robbed. He brought us a letter from Br. Ettwein, dated June 10th and 14th, from which we saw that other letters, written in May, were still delayed. A letter from Br. Abraham Reinke,[1] from Yorktown, (Pa.), of Aug. 28th, last year, only got here at the same time.

Wednesday, 9. Br. Michael Jung held early service. Afterwards the Lord's supper was announced to the communicants for next Saturday. At noon a Chippewa war-party came in with drumming and singing, after their fashion, to dance and beg from house to house. Abraham, the assistant, went at once to them, stopped them and addressed them, saying we knew why they were come, namely, to get something to eat, being hungry; they should sit down and be quite quiet, we did not wish their dancing and drumming here, they should then have plenty to eat. This they did, sat down, and they were fed their fill. The chief reason why they came here was that they wanted tobacco, and also a hog, which we gave them, and they drew off again. They admitted themselves that they were sent to war, not by the English, but by their own chiefs, and this was not only true, but the English were opposed to their going, and we heard afterwards that they stole out of Detroit.

Thursday, 10. Thomas came back, who had accompanied white people to the Fort. Col. Joseph Mitchel, who had been a prisoner, wrote back by him, praising the good conduct of Thomas, their pilot, both on the journey thither and at the Fort, and thanking our Indians for the friendship and love he had met here.

---

[1] Born June 15, 1752, and died Feb. 16, 1833; pastor of various churches in Pennsylvania and at Hope, N. J.

Friday, 11. David held early service. In the afternoon the war-party came back again, in a quiet and orderly way, and announced they had something to say. We gave them to eat, and then they said they were stopped in Detroit, but had secretly stolen away; they said then that, perhaps, grandfather did not like to see the way to the Fort made insecure, and gave us to understand that if he did not like to see it, they would rather turn about. Our Indians made a speech with a string of wampum, advising them to turn back again, and this they promissd to do, but this is a reproach for warriors, they will be ridiculed if they turn back and have nothing to show that they have been stopped. We got together some provisions for their homeward march. They wanted to remain over night here and have a dance, but we told them we did not allow dancing here; in other towns they might dance, but not here, and so they went away.

Saturday, 12. After the brethren had been spoken to on previous days, we had the most blessed enjoyment of the body and blood of our Lord in the holy communion, which we have not had for five weeks from want of wine.

Sunday, 13. The communion liturgy was read early, and then Br. Michael preached. Afterwards was the quarter-hour for the baptized. By a wild Indian we had a letter from Br. Ettwein in Bethlehem, of May 5th. After he had gone, we heard that he was one of several horse-thieves, who did not come into town, having stolen horses in Pittsburg, and he came in only to deliver the letter.

Tuesday, 15. The Indian, of whom mention is made under March 8th, who did not hold it needful to go to the meetings, having done nothing wrong in his life, came here again some time ago, and for a week had longed to live here, with whom the assistants spoke, and to whom they listened. He said that when he was here before he believed he needed nothing, but since then he had thought about himself, and found that all his doing and behaviour was sin, and that there was nothing good in him, wherefore he would like to be in the church, in hope that

the Saviour would pity him, forgive his sins, and bless
him. The brethren asked him also about his outward circumstances and gave him advice, since he wanted to live
here, which he received.

Wednesday, 16. Edwards held early service. Thereupon was a conference of assistants, especially concerning
our young people, for instance, Pauline, Cornelius' daughter. We considered how to correct disorderly living, and
where we could help. Many went hunting, as did Jacob,
and many with him. Br. Michael Jung grew sick again
since he has been at home, especially with toothache, as
also Susanna.

Thursday, 17. David held early service about bringing
our requests and prayers before the Saviour with thanksgiving. The assistants met with the brothers to regulate
matters in business and behaviour. In the afternoon the
Chippewa warriors came back, who had gone by here
fourteen days ago, with five scalps and one prisoner, the
Quaker, who last autumn, in the Miami towns, had escaped
and come here, and was taken to the Fort. He was now
again made prisoner, on the Muskingum, at the place
where preparations were making for the treaty, where
these warriors made an attack. They had strict orders to
fall upon no Indians, and were not prepared for an attack
until the warriors had accomplished their object, yet the
Chippewa head-man perished there. There is a very bad
prospect of peace, it is turned aside, and no one knows
whether or when they will come together, for all prelimi-
naries thereto come lamely forward. The French in Sandusky Bay gave the prisoner advice to escape when he was
over the lake in the settlements. William came back from
Sandusky.

Sunday, 20. David preached from the Epistle that all
we find in Holy Writ about the people of God is given us
for example and exhortation, that we should not let ourselves lust after wickedness, that all the works of darkness, though they happen secretly, will come to light, and
that nothing will remain concealed before him who has
eyes like flames of fire; therefore we should seek a recon-

ciled heart and to have peace with God, that our transgressions may here be done away with and blotted out by
Jesus' blood, so that we, clad in the righteousness of his
blood, may appear before God. Br. Edwards held the
congregation meeting from the text: As every man has
received the gift, even so minister the same one to another,
etc., that we have to look one upon another as members of
one body, whose head is Christ, and that each member
should be useful, helpful, and a blessing to the others, so
that none can think it needs no other.

Monday, 21. Michael held early service from the Scripture-verse: I will get them praise and fame in every land
where they have been put to shame, that the Saviour will
be glorified through believers in him; therefore he will
place them for a blessing, and let them shine as a light
which shall not be hid; what he does in them shall be seen
for the glory of his name.

By our Indians who came from Sandusky, we heard
again unpleasant stories that the Chippewas in great number were coming over from Detroit, wishing to plunder us
for having sold their land, which news made much stir
among our brethren, and was thoroughly talked over.

Tuesday, 22. We considered again about the thing,
after having already considered it two days ago, but then
we had not to ask the Saviour. To make our Indian
brethren content, however, we asked the Saviour again,
whether we had to do any thing in the matter, and he let
us know that we should send some Indian brethren over
the lake to get information and speak with the Chippewas.
We proposed this to the assistants, and it was not to their
mind, but they declined, and we must so let it be for the
present, but we found afterwards that all was nothing but
lies, there being nothing in the thing.

Wednesday, 23. Br. Edwards held early service from
the Scripture-verse: And I will give you pastors according to mine heart, etc., and said that the brethren should
carefully obey their teachers according to the words of the
Apostle Paul, for they watched over their souls, but it happened at times that they wished to be wiser and shrewder,

thinking they understood better, and thereby they came to need and confusion, so that in the end they knew not what to do, and made things hard for themselves and also for their teachers.

From Sandusky a Wyandot counsellor came, who understood Delaware, and brought us news that a messenger from Detroit was come, where the nations were assembled for a conference, with a message to the Indians of this purport: They should not go away from home a short mile, nor go to the Fort; it would not last long, and we should hear how circumstances turned out. Some of our Indians were just ready to go to Pittsburg; they were also delayed. We saw from this that they were upon the point of going to the treaty. He was charged to speak farther with our Indians, and to find out what our mind was in regard to remaining here, and he said, since they had heard lies on every hand, this had given him occasion to ask, which now he did. The assistants replied to him and laid our condition before him, how it then was with us; that in Cuyahoga we got a message from Pipe with a belt, who called us to Pettquotting to live, saying that his uncles, the Wyandots, had given it him; that he had vacated it so that we should occupy it. We departed last year from Cuyahoga and had wished to settle on the deep creek (perhaps Vermillion River), where a messenger came, who told us we could not live there, we should come to Sandusky, there a place was set apart for us, but he mentioned nothing about the former message we had received; finally we had come here to Pettquotting, and as it was already time to plant, we remained here, but had let our uncles know that we were forced to remain here and plant, that we might have something for our wives and children to live on. The uncles were well content with this, and said to us that no one would or should molest us, and if the times continued good and peaceful, perhaps we could remain here longer, but should any danger come they would let us know. Since then they had said nothing to us, and we remained and had again planted here; thus our affairs stood, and so we held to what the Wyandots had said. It

appears, however, that they will not leave us here, and
think indeed of making us come to Sandusky, for it
arouses much attention among them that all are running
to us, and they are not capable of hindering it. Why
have they compelled us to settle here? We had not so intended; they have themselves to blame, and should have
no thanks for it.

Friday, 25. Sisters came back from Sandusky with
corn, which they had bought. Among our brethren hunger and want of food grow stronger. Corn is hard to get
and very dear, three dollars the cheapest. N.B.—The many
strangers cause us want.

Sunday, 27. Edwards preached about this, that the
Saviour is sad, yea weeps, over men who are indifferent in
regard to their salvation and wish not to accept what he
has earned and won for them. Br. David conducted the
children's hour and Michael held the congregation meeting. In the afternoon came Nathaniel Davis, with his
wife and children, six persons, to remain here. He said
at once that he came here for good and had left nothing
behind except his plantation. They were still all full of
the death of their son Leonard, who made a long visit
here this spring, and they said that after he came home he
was quite another man, had then no longer pleasure nor
rest, and was always urging them to go to the church, and
when he became ill [his illness lasted but two days] he
prayed to the Saviour all the time and also exhorted his
parents to call upon the Saviour with him, that he would
be merciful to him. till his breath ceased. He had also
begged them, when he was gone, not to delay, but to
hasten to the church, and this is indeed the motive for
their coming here at the time of the greatest need. It is
true that in this way we are always adding to our trouble
and care and much labor, but yet it gives us joy when the
erring sheep are again assembled in the fold, at the same
time that we do not compel them, and if we tried to do it,
not only would it be of no use, but rather a hinderance,
but the Saviour brings it about himself, for we call no one
to the church. so that if they thrive not they have not to

reproach us as if we had overpersuaded them. Who will
only wait until the Saviour acts, he can speak of success,
for if he begins to work, certainly the work goes bravely on.

So also day before yesterday a young man, named Christian came here, who as a child was baptized in the church,
and ceased to live here; he came to Br. David and spoke
with him. The assistants talked with him about his circumstances in detail, for there was much in him to cause
hesitation, for last winter in a drunken brawl he had killed
a Cherokee Indian.

Monday, 25. We have good, comforting news from the
council over the lake, from which we see there is a better
prospect for peace than ever before, and that they are now
upon a good path. The news was related and made known
in full to our Indian brethren, to their sympathy and pleasure, for hardly anywhere will there be greater joy, if peace
be concluded, than with us, since we see with our own eyes
the misery and want if a new Indian war should break
out, and we should feel them most. From the Delawares
in Gigeyunk we likewise hear good news, that their
chief has very strictly forbidden their young men stealing
or doing further damage. The Twightwees, Tawas, and
others have this spring given the Delawares land from the
Miami to the Wabash, so that now again they have their
own land to live on. Now we hear that the Delaware
chief, who became chief in Israel's place, has always an
eye upon the believing Indians, for once already he has
sent us word that since we are here this side of the lake
he still thinks upon what his uncle, Israel, told him, when
he gave over to him his chieftainship, namely, to love the
believing Indians and their teachers, to do them good and
protect them from wild, hostile Indians, so far as he could;
but he had been so far distant from us, having himself no
certain and abiding place, that hitherto he could not be
very serviceable to us in any thing, but the time would
come when he would be in condition to carry out his suggestions, when first again he had a sure abode. We had
shortly before heard that one of his counsellors, whom we
well knew, will come express to us and speak with us. The

chief Welandawecken is now reported to have said that if there should be war, and this still hangs in the balance, he would take from here far enough out of the way the believing Indians, with the missionaries, over whom he claims a right in virtue of his orders; but if there should be peace, he would let us stay here. Thus, should there be war, we are already provided for, and our care is in vain. Things will go again as we have already experienced them. We must go whither we are taken; we may wish it or not, and shall have no choice in the matter. Nathaniel Davis spoke with us about his coming to us; that his whole thought was of giving himself anew to the Saviour and living for him. He said he had lost much by staying away from us so long; that the Saviour was not content with his tarrying among the savages, for he had planted two years and harvested nothing. His crops had either been destroyed by frost or by bad weather. Want had forced him last autumn to pass the whole winter hunting, having nothing to eat, and what they planted this year was frostbitten in the middle of summer, and thus they had little or nothing to eat.

Thursday, 31. To-day, and for many days, we have had many visits from strangers, yes, not a day is the town free from them. As our Indians have little to eat, they go industriously to the whortleberries, which are a great help for them; some take their children there for food, where they can eat their fill and have much pleasure too.

Friday, Aug. 1. David held early service from the text: Therefore, my beloved brethren, be ye steadfast, unmoveable, always abounding in the works of the Lord, for as much as ye know that your labor is not in vain in the Lord, to this effect, that our labor here should be to become so minded as was Jesus Christ, also to learn from him who was meek and of humble heart. Thereto belongs that we should stand fast by him; then will the Holy Ghost make us recognize our corrupt hearts, wherewith we go to the Saviour and let them be purified by his blood. The end of this our labor would be to be established with him, and to live eternally with him. At noon Joseph was

released from this vale of tears, dying peacefully. David
had been with him shortly before, and had encouraged him
to pray to the Saviour, soon to take him to himself, and
this he did.

Saturday, 2. After the early service from the text: Examine yourselves whether ye be in the faith; prove your
own selves, of which application was made, the remains of
the Indian Joseph were buried. He was baptized Jan. 1, '74,
in Gnadenhütten, on the Muskingum, by Br. Schmick,[1] but
as long as he was in the church he went a bad way, and
would never come right. When he was talked with, it was
his regular complaint about himself that he was a bad, utterly corrupt man, but thereby it was ever the same thing,
for he loved sin, and therefore could not be free therefrom,
and yet he could not remain away from the church. He
came to us again on the Huron River (Michigan). We had
indeed great doubt about receiving him, for he was one of
those who had tortured Col. Crawford to death in Sandusky, and he had himself scalped him while yet alive.
When he was told that on account of white people, who
would learn what he had done, he could not be with us, he
was yet unwilling to be refused, and begged us only the
more pressingly to have compassion with him, for he must
be lost eternally, and he said he would rather himself go
to Detroit to the commandant and beg for pardon. For a
time all seemed well, and it appeared as if he were perfectly in earnest in being converted anew with his whole
heart. At his request he was absolved, but it did not last
long, and he came little by little into his old bad way, yes,
it went so far that we were forced to send him away again.
In Cuyahoga he sought us out again, wishing to be with
us, but we took little notice of what he said. Last autumn,
when he lay sick in Sandusky, he begged us again and
again to let him come to the church and end there his remaining days. Hearing that he would not recover, we
permitted him, in hope that his soul might be rescued,

---

[1] John Jacob Schmick, 1714–1778. He came to America in 1751; was
busy in Pennsylvania and Ohio missions till the year before his death.

and our hope was not in vain. He found his heart, that he had never been just and upright, and had always kept back something that he did not wish to give up and let go. Now he saw where the trouble had been, that he had never succeeded in being quite blessed. This he said to the brethren, who visited him, and warned them not to do as he had done, for he was alone to blame that he led in the church a bad, unholy life, and had used his time so vilely. At his request and longing he was absolved upon his sick-bed, whereupon he passed happily his few remaining days. In him it could be seen that the Saviour had forgiven him his transgressions, and he wished that the Saviour would soon free him from this vale of tears and take him to himself. Thus he died, a repentant sinner, and so we were not sorry for the pains and trouble we had with him, for he was afflicted with a contagious disease, but we thanked the Saviour for the mercy he had shown him. Moreover, to-day, by the assistant, Abraham, who came from Sandusky, we got letters, by way of Pittsburg, from Bethlehem and Litiz, of May and June, to our no common joy. From these, and also from a letter expressly about the matter from Geo. Wallace, Esq., from Pittsburg, we learned the arrival of our things from Bethlehem.

Sunday, 3. Michael preached from the Epistle about this, what it had cost the Saviour to redeem us by his great sufferings and bitter death. Many strangers were present, to whom Samuel preached the Saviour meanwhile with great earnestness; in particular he described to Suckachsun his dead and unreceptive heart, and told him he had no more reflection and consideration than a cow. David held the congregation meeting from the Scripture-verse and text, that the Saviour had left his throne and magnificence with the Father, had come into the world, putting on our poor flesh and blood to seek the lost and to save sinners.

Monday, 4. Edwards held early service.

Tuesday, 5. Michael Schebosh came with A. Johanna and Joseph from the island in Sandusky Bay. In Detroit little produce, no wares, not a shirt to be had.

Wednesday, 6. All the brethren who were at home went hunting in common, and the sisters for whortle-berries, with which they now get much help until the corn is to be eaten, and that is very soon.

Levi, mention of whom is made under July 6th, who had leave to live here, came now, but had left his grand-mother behind, who did not want to come yet. Also still more strangers came here, among them Philippina. In our neighborhood the savages who dwell there made this evening a sacrifice and dance, to which strange Indians went also, who had come here. They have never done the like since they have been here, but we will be thought-ful about this at a good and suitable time, to get them away, for this gives a hold for Satan. We thought at first that, perhaps, many of them would wish to be converted, but usually it is worse with neighbors who are so near us; they live just by, and yet never come to the meetings; on the other hand, those who are far distant come.

Thursday, 7. Edwards held early service from the Scripture-verse : That whoever trusts in him will not come to harm. Many came here from the elk-hunt with meat; thus also our heavenly Father gives something, that they can live.

Sunday, 10. Br. David preached and then held the com-munion quarter-hour, for to the communicants the impor-tant, great day and the Lord's supper were announced. The assistants came together and spoke with our brethren, Joshua, John Cook's son, and his wife. David spoke with Gelelemend, who visited him,

Monday, 11, and showed his longing for the bath of holy baptism. It was first pointed out to him and told what it particularly depended upon, not upon our own running and racing and our own works, but upon God's mercy and the entire surrender of the heart.

Wednesday, 13. At the text: For as the body is one and hath many members, and all the members of that one body, etc., something was said to the communicants about

28

the importance of the day,[1] and they were thereby reminded that through the grace of Jesus Christ they are
also members of his body, of which he is the head, that the
Holy Ghost has called and assembled them by means of
the brothers, for no other end than to make them members
of his body, to show himself mighty in them, that his name
may be glorified through them; therefore the church
should be to each one great and indispensable. After begging absolution, we enjoyed his body and blood in the
holy sacrament, to which A. Charity was readmitted the
first time since she came from Cuyahoga, after receiving
absolution.

Thursday, 14. Four Chippewas came visiting here, remaining a couple of days. One of them was from Huron
River, and told us, for he spoke very good Delaware,
that he lived in Br. Zeisberger's house, that the houses
were all occupied by Chippewas, and no white people
lived there except Conner, to whom they had given leave.
It was very pleasant for us and our Indian brethren to hear
true news from there, after already having heard so many
lies, for now we saw there was nothing in the thing. The
Indian brethren also spoke to them about the Saviour, the
Redeemer of all men, that we through faith have forgiveness of our sins and life eternal, and that he is lost who
does not believe. They visited, too, the meetings, and
otherwise were well entertained, as things now are, when
everywhere there is little to eat. They went back again
on the 16th, and we gave them some food for the way. He,
from Huron River, whose brother is chief there, said he was
much pleased here, he wished in the autumn to come again
and live also as we did. We told him then he should also
bring his wife with him. After they were gone some Chippewas from Sandusky Bay, who had heard that some of
their people had been taken prisoners by the whites, came
here to learn about this. They were told that this was
true, that the war-party which had been murdering
there was the cause of it, for after the massacre occur-

[1] See p. 199.

red, the white people had surrounded and captured a Chippewa party out hunting. They had not touched the women, but only the men, but as those did not wish to leave their husbands, they had gone with them; no harm had befallen them; they were well kept and guarded till the treaty. With this they were content.

Sunday, 17. Br. Edwards preached from the Gospel about the good Samaritan, and Br. David held the quarter-hour for the baptized from the text: For as many of you as have been baptized into Christ have put on Christ. Michael held the congregation meeting.

Tuesday, 19. Br. Edwards held the early service from the text: For whatsoever is born of God overcometh the world; and this is the victory that overcometh the world, even our faith. The[1] spirit of the Lamb, which rules us, his blood, which binds us together, his grace, which sits at the helm, bring about the victory everywhere. He said that if the brethren simply let themselves be ruled by the Spirit of God, were obedient, held together in one heart and mind about the word of the blood and death of Jesus, and stood fast by him in faith, they would have perfect victory to boast of, even in the worst and most dangerous circumstances, for in them they had nothing farther to do than to be still and look to the Saviour, how he conducts his own with a mother's hands, according to the collect in to-day's Scripture-verse, and to praise him therefor. Here we cannot go on, since Scripture-verse and text are so appropriate, without describing in detail a circumstance which has occurred to us, since now we see things together in their connection, and have to-day awaited their fortunate conclusion, wherefor the Saviour must receive abundant praise and thanksgiving, for he alone has done it without our help. It is known that when two years ago we came away from Huron River and Detroit, the commandant, Maj. William Ancrum, and Mr. Askin prepared two ships to take us to Cuyahoga, and likewise gave us for our houses

---

[1] Collect.

and the labor we had there done, a bill of credit for two
hundred dollars, for which in Cuyahoga we got flour, which
was a real and substantial help in our extremest need, when
we were in the wilderness, remote from Indian and white
settlements, so that thereby, though it was not quite suf-
cient, we were put in position to be able to plant somewhat
and outwardly to get along. When we came here a year
ago from Cuyahoga, we were always hearing from Sandusky that the Chippewas were discontented with us and
blamed us for having sold their land to white people. To
quiet our Indians, for they cannot well bear such talk, we
sent Br. Edwards with some Indian brethren to Detroit, to
find out about the affair, and Br. David wrote about this
both to Mr. Askin and to the agent, Capt. McKee, whose
advice we begged, but nothing farther was done in the
matter; we saw that in Detroit little account was made of
this. Moreover, Chippewas lived in our towns, which we had
left, so we let the whole matter alone, for we saw not what
we could farther do in the thing, thinking that if we stirred
therein, we might make the evil worse, perhaps, and arouse
the Chippewas, and thereby get ourselves into trouble.
Our comfort was that we had acted openly before the eyes
of all men, and uprightly; we had done nothing secretly,
nor in the dark, but we have learned thereby not to do the
like again, and in the future to save ourselves such trouble;
it shall be to us a Nota Bene hereafter. This spring and
summer the affair was warmed up again, and served up to
our Indians, as often as they went to Sandusky, for from
that place in particular it came here through wicked, ill-
disposed Indians; they had sold the Chippewas' land [they
said]; they would come over therefore and plunder us,
and thus get their pay. And to make it quite probable, lies
upon lies were invented and piled together, yes, the news
once came that two thousand Chippewas were already near
the lake here. We asked the Saviour once whether in the
affair we were to ask him, and nothing was to be done.
We were then at rest in the thing, believing what we had
heard to be lies, but yet could not reassure and quiet our
Indians. Therefore upon a new alarm we again turned to

the Saviour and inquired if we had any thing to ask, and he said, yes. We made then the following questions: Whether Br. David with some Indian brothers should go to Detroit to see what was to be done? Answer: Whether Br. David should go? no. Whether Indian brothers should go, was approved. They, however, did not want to go unless some one of us went too, and so the matter remained, and though nothing was done, yet we laborers were really helped, that we were not so overrun by our Indians, for on our part we considered it all a lie, but yet could not make our Indians so believe. Now the French trader, whom Samuel had verbally charged to get information, two months ago, from the Tawa chief in Detroit, to whose hands every thing must go, brought us the following speech, accompanied by a string of wampum: "Grandfather, ye believing Indians on Huron River, it has been brought to my ears that ye are accused of all sorts of evil, and burdened with the charge that ye have sold the Chippewas' land on Huron River (Michigan), that the Chippewas were angry about this, and would therefore come and take away all ye have, of which I had never heard. After I received the news, I assembled the Chippewa chiefs and head-men, and in open council asked them whence this accusation came, and whether any one had let such talk go out of his mouth, and expressed it, but we have found no such person among us, and know nothing thereof. This we can say of you on the Muskingum and on the Huron River here, where ye lived, that ye neither troubled yourselves about land nor war, nor any thing else, except to attend to your worship of God; that is your chief business, this we know. I will hereby let you know that all ye have heard are lies. Whether they have come from wretched busy-bodies, Delawares, Wyandots, or Chippewas, or from white people and Indians together, we cannot determine, and must so let it be. I will say to you, however, believe not the lies; the like has never come into our thoughts, as ye have heard, and comes not from us. Take this string of wampum for a token, and if any one farther comes to unload his lies to you, show him this, and

if he, or they, do not want to credit it, let me know, I will
myself come and punish them for this. Grandfather, here
on Huron River thou hast lived on our land; it is pleasant to me that thou now livest on my land, the other side
of the lake, also on Huron River. Thou art still in my
arms and in my bosom." This Tawa chief is also the
head-chief of the Chippewas, and can call them together
as often as he finds it needful, for all first comes to him,
and then he communicates it to the others. He lives opposite Detroit, on the east side of the river.

¹Although the Delawares and Wyandots always described to us the Chippewas and Tawas as the wildest
people, and strove to paint them frightful to us, we have
always found the opposite. They did not do us the least
harm over the lake, neither in our cattle nor our fields, and
placed nothing in our way. Here, likewise, we find them
the same; we have no reproach to make them, and we see
now that their chiefs are our friends, and better friends than
the Delawares and their chiefs, and whence comes this?
Perhaps we can find out, if we seek a little. It cannot
come from this that the Chippewas are better and more .
virtuous than other Indians, or that they love goodness
more than the Delawares; yes, if we went to another
strange nation, with whom we yet have no acquaintance,
we should find the same, that they would be more kindly
towards us than they who have known us for so many
years and have had intercourse with us. The Chippewas
and Tawas are quite wild, raw heathen, have yet heard no
word of God, no Gospel, none of them have yet been converted, have yet no knowledge. They love the believing
Indians, not because they believe in Christ, for of this they
know nothing and think nothing of it, but because they
are an upright, orderly, and peaceful folk, liking friendship with every one. They have and know no reason why
they should hate us. On the other hand, the Delawares
and Monseys have for many years heard the Gospel, are
not so ignorant and blind as not to know better, many of

---

¹All this to the 20th is crossed out in the original.

them having already become believers. Those now who do not wish to be converted are opponents, though they are convinced that the Gospel of Christ is the truth, for they wish to remain in sin, they become the foes of it and of the believers also, if not openly, yet secretly, since hatred lies in their hearts. If they come to us, they are our best friends, but behind our backs, in their own towns, they speak nothing but ill of us.

Wednesday, 20. Chippewas again came here and remained over night, among them two who had been prisoners at the mouth of the Muskingum, in Fort Harmar, and in irons wherewith they were bound, but they got free. They gave as a reason that they had heard they would all be hanged. All the prisoners, of whom there are yet four there, with their wives, lived on Sandusky Bay, and are well known to us.

Thursday, 21. There came here together Chippewas and Tawas from Sandusky Bay. An old man made a formal speech to our Indians, of the following import, in short: "Grandfather, I come to thee troubled and distressed, in hope of getting from thee some comfort and advice, for a short time ago, when we were undisturbed and quiet, and were only thoughtful for our wives and children, to get them something to eat, it happened one morning unexpectedly that a war-party from over the lake came to us on its way to the settlements of the white people. This pleased us not, and disturbed us in our pleasant repose. We asked them who had sent them at a time when the leading men of all nations were assembled in Detroit, and were working hard to bring about a stable peace. They answered that their father over the lake [the English] knew about the thing, but we did not believe this, and though we did every thing to persuade them to turn back again, representing to them also that they would bring into danger many of our young people who were out hunting and knew nothing of this, yet they set out on their way. Some of our people out hunting, having heard that the States were peacefully disposed towards all Indians and received them as friends, went near the Fort hunting. Just as they

came there it happened that the war-party mentioned made
an attack upon the place where preparation was made for the
treaty, and killed several white people. This was the cause
that our people, who were out hunting and feared nothing, were captured and taken into the Fort, where four of
them still are, but two have escaped. We take refuge in
thee, grandfather, and believe thou wilt not refuse to forward this, our speech, to our elder brother in Pittsburg, for
I have the greatest confidence in thee, and thou art known
there also, namely, the following words: Brothers, I beg
thee have compassion with me, and let my young people,
who are prisoners, again go free. They have done thee no
harm, have not even thought it, but were out hunting. If
thou will grant me this, my prayer, I and all my people
will hold fast to the chain of friendship which our old, wise
men, now assembled in the great council in Detroit, are
making, and· with this string of wampum will bind fast
our hands thereto."

Friday, 22. The Chippewas went back home again,
and two of our Indians, Stephen and Boaz, went with
their speech to the fort. Meanwhile many Delawares from
Sandusky came here. Our Wyandot also came for a visit,
mention of whom is made in last year's diary. When he
then went away from here to Sandusky, the small-pox
broke out there, by which nearly the whole town died out
and only two families survived. This year they have
built on another site and have burnt the old town. He
took care of his brother in his sickness, who died of the
small-pox, and then he took the disease himself, but recovered. He said he came here once more to see us and to
tell us he had not forgotten what he told us last year,
that he remained thereby; he wished to and must yet live
with us, and in this purpose had not changed; he waited
for his mother from Detroit; when she came he could tell
his mind to her, but not persuade her to come to the
church unless she were so disposed.

Sunday, 24. Br. Michael preached, and David held the
congregation meeting. Two white people came from Pitts-

burg with a woman. They went on again to Detroit by water on the 26th.

Monday, 25. Helen returned from Sandusky, by whom we heard that the nations in a few days would come together on the Miami, so as to go from there to the Muskingum for the treaty, but no one yet knew precisely what they had determined. The Indians are every where in anxiety, that where the march of so many men is made, their fields will be eaten up, as if locusts came there and devoured every thing.

Wednesday, 27. David held early service. From Detroit a boat came with thirteen white people, who went on to Pittsburg, Thursday, the 28th, for whom we must get seven horses ready, for some of them were sick. Thus all come to us, Indians and whites, seeking help. Joseph Brant, with two hundred Mingoes, is on the Miami, and now they will soon go on to the treaty, for they cannot stay there long, there being but little food. Our Chippewa also arrived, who passed the winter with us in Cuyahoga, with his wife from hunting. He stayed several days with us, for they were pleased here, and our Abraham spoke to them the words of life.

Friday, 29. We had a pleasant love-feast with the two single brothers on their birth-day, wishing them the Saviour's blessing from his bloody fulness for their day.

Sunday, 31. Br. David preached from Gal., vi., 7: Whatsoever a man soweth, that also shall he reap. Then the widows, seven in number, all communion sisters, had a blessed service from their text: Nevertheless I live; yet not I, but Christ liveth in me, and then we had with them a love-feast. The Saviour showed himself very gracious to them, and one could observe a blessed feeling. Edwards held the congregation meeting.

Monday, Sept. 1. Michael held early service. Gelelemend expressed again his longing wish for baptism. He said: "I am one of the greatest sinners, and must be eternally lost, if the Saviour does not pity me and with his blood cleanse me from my sins. In him alone I put my trust, for I believe he has died for sinners and has

shed his blood for me also, therefore I await with longing to be a sharer in grace." Ah, how has this man, the
great chief of Goschachgünk, changed ! How now is
he become so meek, that he comes like any other sinner,
weeps and begs for grace at the Saviour's feet! If we are
glad and have compassion, how must his loving heart be
disposed towards such a poor sinner!

We learned by way of Sandusky the comforting and
joyful tidings that nineteen nations have united in a
grand council for peace, and have sent off an express to
Pittsburg to make known there that they will soon set
out for the treaty, where they could be expected ; that
the nations have given a sharp rebuke to those warriors
who, contrary to all orders, have been disobedient and
have murdered, and they have taken their prisoners from
them, whom they will bring to the treaty. We heard also
that there is again small-pox in Sandusky, and now also
in the Monsey town.

Thursday, 4. A sick child of a widow was baptized by
David before its death with the name Ephraim. His
mother came here some time ago. Likewise, some time
ago, a woman came here with her husband, with the view
of lying-in here; for she feared she would die, being already
somewhat old and this her first child. She had a hard but
fortunate delivery. This is already become evident that
Indians in dangerous, doubtful circumstances take refuge
with the believers, thinking that if they are with us there
will be no danger, or at least that they will find it more
tolerable than if they were with the savages. Generally
they come not to grief in this belief. We see from this
how the brethren are aroused, like hawks for birds, to win
a soul for the Saviour, and incorporate it in the church.
This evening also our dear brother, Schebosh, died in peace,
after a nervous sickness of two weeks.   •

Friday, 5. In the early service the little son of Adam
and Sabina, born yesterday, was baptized into Jesus' death
with the name of John Renatus. Towards evening the
remains of our brother, Schebosh, who yesterday departed
in peace, were buried, and at the same time with him the

little boy, Ephraim, two months old, who was baptized yesterday. Since we find nothing written about the former, we will tell of him as much as we know and can remember. He was born May 27, 1721, in Skippac (Montgomery Co., Pa.), in this country, came about the year '42 to the church in Bethlehem, where he was baptized by Br. Jos. Spang(enberg),[1] and soon came to the Lord's supper. He was shortly afterward brought among the Indians in Meniolagomekak (Monroe Co., Pa.), where a small number of Indians was served by the brothers, and in Gnadenhütten, on the Mahony, where he remained until it was destroyed by the savages. In the year 1746 he was joined in wedlock with Christiana, with whom he lived in marriage forty-one years, and she died just a year ago less three days. Of his children one daughter is still here in the church, and two granddaughters. His son was among the number of martyrs in Gnadenhütten. He was besides with the Indian church in Nain, near Bethlehem, afterwards with a part in Wechquetank,[2] until they also, owing to the troubles of war, had to flee to the barracks in Philadelphia. From there he went in '65 to Friedenshütten, on the Susquehanna, in the year '72 to the Ohio, where he lived first in Schönbrunn, and last in Gnadenhütten on the Muskingum, until Sept. 3, '81, he went with the Indian church in captivity to Sandusky, from which place, however, the same autumn he went back to Schönbrunn to get corn, but was there taken by the militia, with. his daughter, her husband, and others, and brought to Pittsburg, where, however, they were soon set free, so that they could go to their friends, but he went from there to Bethlehem, bringing to the brothers the first trustworthy news of the whole occurrence, and he refreshed himself in the church from the fatalities he had endured. In the year 1783 he

---

[1] Augustus Gottlieb Spangenburg, 1704–1792. He was a professor in the University at Halle, a position which he lost when he became a Moravian in 1733. He was in America eighteen years, presiding over the church. He was known as Br. Joseph.—De Schweinitz' Life of Zeisberger, p. 15.

[2] Polk Township, Monroe Co., Pa.

undertook a journey to Detroit and Huron River, where
he came to us again with Br. Weigand at the beginning
of July, meeting there his wife and daughter, and this was
to us no common joy. There he remained until in the
year '86, in the spring, April, we, with the Indian church,
there assembled, went back over the lake to Cuyahoga,
and in '87 came here to Pettquotting. For a year now,
and especially this spring, he failed noticeably in strength;
it could be seen he was nearing the end. After twice having the palsy, he was asked if he thought he should die.
He answered with composure and resignation: Yes, he
should indeed depart, saying also to his daughter that he
should not recover from this illness. He had no pain, but
spoke always of his weariness. He was serviceable to every
man, without distinction, white or Indian, at all times
ready to help where he could. He bore his cross with patience, for in this life he seldom had things easy and good,
but he was never heard to complain or fret, even if things
were hard with him, and he had not even enough to eat.
He loved and was loved; this could be seen especially in
his sickness. The Indian brethren all found it a pleasure
to watch by him, a number of brothers and sisters remaining with him half the night and longer. We shall long
miss him among us. His stay here below will remain to
us and to the Indian brethren in blessed remembrance. He
is now at home in peace, and all is forever well with him;
of this we are glad with our whole heart, and thank the
Saviour for his election, but still send tears after him. His
mortal life lasted sixty-seven years, three months, and eight
days.

Stephen came back from the Fort with an answer to the
message of the Chippewas about their captured people on
the Muskingum. In the answer they were referred to
their chiefs and the assembled council of the nations, who
had already been enjoined to deliver up the murderers,
which would bring about the release of their people, who
are held till the treaty; the heads of the nations should
give the decision.

Sunday, 7. At morning prayer we asked for the near

presence and blessing of our dear Lord for our married brethren on this day. Then they had a service from their text. Br. Edwards preached. In the afternoon was a love-feast for all inhabitants. In the congregation meeting an end was made by the blessing of the church. It was a day of blessing and encouragement for the brethren. The Saviour made himself known to us and let us feel his presence and nearness. In conclusion, we laborers had the most holy enjoyment, and strengthened ourselves with the body and blood of our Lord in the holy sacrament.

Monday, 8. Jacob and his company came from the Fort and from hunting and with them three white people, one a woman, on their way to Detroit. They wished to have Indians as escort, which we could not give, but we advised them against going by land, as being dangerous for them, as they had cattle and must meet a great number of Indians, who from hunger would take every thing away from them. We had much vexation, care, and trouble with them, and were much concerned lest they should come to harm here from the Chippewas, for they are not very well disposed towards white people, since their people are in captivity. Thus have we always with the white people more trouble and plague than with the Indians; they are such a stupid folk, more stupid than Indians. At last we found a way out, since by land they could go neither forwards nor backwards, to get them to Detroit by water, and that finally happened. They set out on Wednesday, the 10th, Andrew with them.

Friday, 12. An Indian from the neighborhood, who has already been here many days and said he wanted to remain here, but knew not why, we bade go home. Michael held early service.

Saturday, 13. David held early service. Boaz and Michael came from the Fort, and in the evening Thomas and William with our things from Bethlehem.

Sunday, 14. Michael preached, David conducted the children's service, and Edwards the congregation meeting. David discoursed to the children about their text this week. Children, obey your parents in the Lord, for this is right.

Monday, 15. David held early service from the Scripture-verse: But the just shall live by his faith. We had news from Sandusky that five hundred Chippewas and Tawas would go through our town on their way to the treaty. Should this occur, we could not depend upon our fields, for they would eat up every thing they found. We thought: If the Saviour permits it, he has good reasons for it. Perhaps we shall become known among nations yet strange, and herewith we comforted ourselves. If only something comes to the Saviour from this, all we have shall stand at his service.

Wednesday, 17. Weschnasch came here from hunting and visited us. He holds us dear and has always so shown himself towards us, that to him the door to the church is yet open, also on his part, for if people have once sinned towards the church, usually they have no longer a heart for us, but get out of our way.

Friday, 19. Suckachsiin came here from the Fort with liquor. We indeed ordered it to be taken care of, but it was not guarded and watched, and so it happened that we had this night and,

Saturday, 20, a drunken bout in town, which caused us much uneasiness and vexation till evening, when the storm abated. This is a matter against which we must oppose ourselves with earnestness and all our strength, for if there shall be times of peace this business will be actively carried on by the savages, for they bring nothing more willingly here, and are thus a plague to us, and this already begins, which cannot be.

Sunday, 21. Instead of the sermon Br. David delivered an earnest discourse and exhortation to all inhabitants, reminding those who love the Saviour and wish to live for him in one spirit and mind, to oppose the disorder and sinful things that wish to come among us. Then was the communion quarter-hour, when this matter was again touched upon, and the brethren were told that it was sad and distressing if from this company brethren let themselves be seduced to drunkenness, thereby giving a bad example. They were told at the same time that none of those could or should come to the Lord's supper. Michael held the congregation meeting from the text: Take heed unto thyself. We read the church-journal.

Monday, 22. The assistants had labor nearly the whole day in speaking with some brethren and new people, who had taken part in the drunkenness, and this was not without use and blessing. Edwards held early service. A woman died in the neighborhood, who lay sick for a long time, always longing and begging to be brought to the believers, among whom she wished to die. No one, however, would bring her. Even yesterday, her last day, she wished to come here to us, and some brethren had to go there to make her coffin and help bury her.

Thursday, 25. Edwards held early service from the Scripture-verse, which was noteworthy (Hab. ii., 14).

Friday, 26. Yesterday and to-day there was speaking with the brethren, for there was much to clear up, and some had to abstain from the Lord's supper.

Saturday, 27. We had a happy and blessed communion, though conscious of our sins.

Sunday, 28. At the sermon, which Br. Edwards delivered, was a Chippewa, who understood Delaware and Shawano, and had already before once or twice been at our meetings. He came afterwards to us and gave us to understand that he would like to hear something about the Saviour, he would willingly listen, believing we knew, more than he, what pertains to man's welfare, for he knew not otherwise how to express it. We soon gave him an opportunity, calling the brothers, Samuel, Abraham, and Boaz, the first understanding Shawano a little, the latter, Chippewa. They spoke with him, and he told them he was sorry he could not understand all, and talk with them plainly, for he believed they knew what makes a man good and happy; that knew he not, but would gladly hear. He asked the brethren what they thought about dreams, upon which Indians build so much. He said he would not forget what his father, who died four years ago, said

to him, namely, that the Indians were not upon the right
way to eternal life, they would find it hard after this life,
and had nothing good to hope; that there were Indians
who knew something better, how man could attain thereto,
to have eternal life, and he who believed it would live
forever, although he died.   His father had also told him
that after his death he should not go away from here, for
the time would come when the believing Indians would
come here to Pettquotting to live, to them should he hold,
and from them he would hear that which he should receive
and believe.   The Indian could not then have known we
should come back over the lake, this being in the year
'84, when we ourselves yet knew nothing thereof.   Since
that time he had thought much about it, when he had
been hunting alone in the bush, and could not forget it,
much less now, when he saw that had happened which
his father had told him, and we were now dwelling here.
He said that when he came among his people and refused
to dance, they called him a Sunday Indian, saying he
looked down upon them and would yet come to us.   Samuel now began and said to him: "What we now say to
thee, thou canst be sure is the truth.   Neither dreams, nor
sacrifices, nor any thing wherein the Indians put their
trust, thinking thereby to get happiness and eternal life,
is of any help or use, it is all in vain, and brings no comfort nor hope, but God, the Maker of all things, himself
came down from heaven to the world, became a man, like
ourselves. lived thirty years in the world, then for our sins
was nailed to the cross, with nails through his hands and
feet, and his side was pierced through with a spear, for he
poured out all his blood.   He died upon the cross, was
buried, and on the third day rose again.   His disciples,
and those who believed in him, saw him, and after his
resurrection, he tarried forty days here below, and yet
spoke much with believers in him, telling them what we
all must know in order to be saved.   Thus has he won
life eternal and salvation for us and for all mankind, in
laying down his life for us and pouring out his blood.
Who now believes this, him all his sins are forgiven, and

God receives him as his child, he is blessed here and forever. This alone it is that makes us blessed, the blood of Jesus Christ, the Son of God, and upon the whole earth there is nothing else, or better, to be found to help us, and even if a man came into heaven, knowing nothing of this, nor of the Saviour with wounds in his hands and feet, and in his side, heaven itself would to him be a hell." The Chippewa listened devoutly, and sat awhile deep in thought, until he heard it said, " He went towards heaven and his disciples looked after him," then he asked if he would come again, and was answered: " Yes, he will certainly come again and all men will see him, believers and unbelievers, the former will be glad and live with him forever, but the others will weep and groan, that were such unbelievers and now see themselves deceived." Dear brethren, this is the first one of the great, numerous, and strong Chippewa nation to ask about God, in whom can be observed an anxiety and longing to be saved, and who would like to know how to attain thereto. He is also the Chippewas' Saviour. He will also yet be known of them and prayed to, and his name will be glorified by them and in their tongue in spite of all hinderance and opposition of Satan. May he let their time come and their hour soon strike! Amen. We read the church-journal.

Monday, 29. In the early service consideration was had of the holy angels, and there was mention of what we enjoy through their service for protection and care on the part of our dear Lord, many a misfortune and danger being prevented by them, of which we are not in the least aware, for which we are bound to thank him and to praise him. In the service a couple of verses about the holy angels were translated. We thank the Saviour and his atonement that his angels so cheerfully serve us, and that they come down from their heights to aid in our redemption.

Tuesday, 30, and Wednesday, Oct. 1. The brethren harvested our plantation, at which strangers also helped, who were come here, which always occurs with the great-

29

est pleasure, and if one, from sickness or some other reason, must omit it, to him it is a source of sadness.

Friday, 3. Indians came from the Fort with cattle
which they had bought.

Saturday, 4. This whole week the brethren were busy
in their harvest, in which our dear heavenly Father has
richly blessed us. They were exhorted to enjoy it with
thanksgiving, and to make careful use of it.

Sunday, 5. Michael preached about the wedding-garment. David held the children's service. Edwards held
the congregation meeting.

Monday, 6. Many houses again built this autumn.

Thursday, 9. After early service, held by Br. Edwards,
from the Scripture-verse, a sick child, three years old,
John Cook's grandchild, was baptized with the name
Anna Johanna, for which they had begged. His oldest
son, who came here some time ago with his wife and child,
came to-day and announced his intention to live here,
about which he had spoken with the assistants, and was
received.

Friday, 10. After the early service by David, the brethren were told to stop their labors upon their fields at
night, since a disorderly life arises from it and sicknesses
are caused.

Saturday, 11. Two white people from Detroit went
through on their way to Pittsburg. A thousand Indians
on the Miami at the treaty.

Sunday, 12. David preached, Edwards held the service
for the baptized, and Michael the congregation meeting.

Tuesday, 14. The brethren industrious in their fields.
Edwards held early service.

Thursday, 16. David held early service. Yesterday
and to-day we had trouble again with Indians who came
with liquor from the Fort, so we had to keep good watch.
We took their casks for safe-keeping, as soon as they got
here, from all who came drunk; they gave us trouble, but
all went off without much disturbance.

Friday, 17. We learned from Benjamin, Nathaniel
Davis' son, who came from the Fort, that Br. John Hecke-

welder was come there, wishing to get to us, but afterwards he had heard he was gone to the Muskingum, but as we had no letters or any thing in writing, we could do nothing. He said he had delivered letters there, which a white man had taken with him to Sandusky.

[Thus far sent to Bethlehem.]

Sunday, 19. Br. Edwards preached, and David held the congregation meeting.

Monday 20. Edwards held early service. We had a conference with the assistants about sending brothers to the treaty, and four brothers were appointed to go. Gelelemend, who is summoned there, as it were, by the commissioners, has no real desire to go, and we do not wish to encourage him thereto, for he will get nothing there for his heart. Yesterday again he gave us to understand his disposition and longing for baptism, waiting with eagerness forgiveness and cleansing from his sins. We considered, moreover, about a dwelling for John Cook's son, to whom Samuel has lent his new house, also about Christian's affair.

Tuesday, 21. Michael held early service. By John Leeth, who went to the Fort, we sent away to Bethlehem a packet of letters and the diary.

Wednesday, 22. At the early service the brethren were reminded to get the school-house ready before they went away hunting, so that school might begin, whereupon they went to work at once. David held early service.

Friday, 24. Michael held early service about the good Shepherd who laid down his life for his sheep and fed them from his wounds. Four white people came from Detroit, among them a woman who had been a prisoner, whom a boy and a girl were to follow by water, who were prisoners, who afterwards also came here.

Sunday, 26. David preached and Edwards held the congregation meeting. From Detroit we had a letter from Mr. Askin, who offered to buy corn of our Indians for goods, since there this year was a failure of crops, and corn is scarce.

Monday, 27. Michael held early service. The white

people set out for Detroit who were prisoners from New River,[1] and as they said, were not over eighty miles from the Wachau (in N. Carolina), of which they had heard, but where they had never been. One of them came back again the next day, sick and unable to go farther. From the Delaware chief in Gigeyunk, Welandawecken, a messenger came, bringing us a speech of this import: "My friends, ye believing Indians in Pettquotting, it looks as if we should have bad times, for it is still uncertain whether we shall have peace or war, the nations having been able to reach no conclusion, and while they have been together they have only exchanged words among themselves and wrangled, one with another, so that it does not seem that peace can be brought about. I therefore let you know hereby that it is resolved that I and my people shall settle at the fork of the Miami, which land the Wyandot chiefs have appointed us to live on, whither also I invite you believing Indians to dwell with us. Ye will therefore prepare for this as soon as your circumstances shall permit." We received this, his speech, and considered his words, but found therein nothing judicious, for, in the first place, there is no mention made when the affair was concluded and who the chiefs and persons were, who were present; secondly, he gives no reason for his pretension to the right of taking us away and moving us from here; nothing is said of the speeches we made to the old Netawatwes; also he does not mention the messages we have received since we are this side of the lake, and so we can think nothing else than that he has acted for himself quite alone, without taking the advice of any one; thirdly, it is not a peaceful message, but a bad one. Thus we could not accept the message; he must send us a better one if we are to give heed to it. We sent back the messenger with the answer, that we thanked him for the news contained in his speech; we had hoped, indeed, when they had consulted so many months and labored for peace, to hear something better and more cheerful, but we thanked him for his trouble in

---

[1] A tributary of the Great Kanawha, in the western part of Virginia.

sending us a messenger to give us information, and yet that we hoped and comforted ourselves with the thought that we should hear still better news. We exchanged strings. The brethren then let him know that we had in our hands messages from Pipe, from the Wyandots, and from the Tawa chief, which in part called us here and in part expressed their satisfaction at our living here, which we did not value slightly nor place aside as bad, but held to them and would abide by them. The messenger was at the same time come here to call away Gelelemend, Jacob, and his two sisters [but no one gave heed to him], and Thomas, all friends of the chief. If they already thus come forward it is a sign that they have nothing good in their thoughts, but intend war.

Thursday, 30. Our Chippewa who, with his people, had passed the winter near us in Cuyahoga, and since then had for us love and friendship, who often also visits us here, whose brother is chief on Huron River, over the lake, came here, remained two days, and went away with his people to the treaty on the Muskingum. He said, while it was so uncertain in regard to peace, if we wished to go again to our town over the lake, and would only say the word to him, that he would accomplish with his brother at the treaty that we could move back there. We had always heard that five hundred Chippewas and Tawas would come through here, but things have changed, and these are all that come this way, and they go in company with our brethren. We were sorry the Tawa chief did not come here, as he had intended. He has fallen out with McKee, and from vexation will not go to the treaty.

Saturday, Nov. 1. The brothers, Samuel, Stephen, Thomas, and Tobias, set out for the treaty, on having heard that the Indians were already gone from Sandusky. Br. David wrote to the Commissioners that though it was not usual for our Indians, for good reasons, to be present at treaties, and Sir William Johnson[1] never summoned

---

[1] Sir William Johnson was born in Ireland, 1715. He came to America in 1738 to manage the property of his uncle, Sir Peter Warren, in

them, but told the Indians that the believing Indians
made him no trouble, being taught to lead a spiritual life,
but that the others cost him pains to keep them orderly
and peaceful, yet we made use of the occasion to speak
with the Indians and nations, and to say somewhat to
them. He made known to him the chief thing we wished
to say to them, and wished them good success and the
blessing of God for all their plans and deliberations in
their council. We had this summer often heard good,
favorable reports about peace with the Indian nations,
until at last they assembled on the Miami, where, however, they had done nothing but wrangle among themselves, and the nearer the time came for going to the
treaty, the worse had been the outlook. What they had
now done in the Wyandot towns, where they were assembled, of this we had no information. Our comfort and
hope were that the Saviour is yet President in council, and
can bring their wicked plans to nought.

Sunday, 2. Michael preached. David held the congregation meeting.

Monday, 3, was a communion quarter-hour, and the
Lord's supper was announced to the brethren for next
Saturday.

Wednesday, 5. Messrs. Isaac Williams and Parke came
here from Sandusky, the latter, a Detroit merchant, who
would like to buy a couple hundred bushels of corn, of
which there is great want there, since last summer there
was a failure of the crops, and wheat and corn came to
nothing; but we can not advise our brethren to sell their
corn, for afterwards they will themselves come to want,
for among the Indians especially in Gigeyunk there is already want all the time.

Friday, 7. From Sandusky we learn by Benjamin, Nathaniel's son, that Br. John Heckewelder had been seen in

---

the Mohawk valley. Here he acquired wonderful influence among
the Indians by learning their language, and especially by the justice
of his conduct towards them. He took part in the various expeditions
of the English against the French in Canada, and in 1759 became commander-in-chief. In 1765 he was made a baronet. He died, 1774.

Fort Harmar on the Muskingum, and awaited brothers from here. From Detroit a couple of white people came here on their way to Pittsburg and remained two days.

Saturday, 8. The brethren having been spoken to on previous days, we had the most blessed enjoyment of his body and blood in the holy sacrament; at this were candidates, John Thomas, young Abraham, and Abigail.

Sunday, 9. Edwards preached, David held the children's service, and Michael the congregation meeting. Andrew was earnestly and plainly talked with for his disorderly conduct, and he was advised to go elsewhere, since he had no disposition to live for the Saviour, whereupon he began to weep. We wished he might be thoughtful, and become concerned for himself.

Monday, 10. Br. David held the early service about love for the Saviour, which makes life blessed; then he told the brethren they could now be gone to their autumn hunt until Christmas.

Tuesday, 11, and the following days, the brothers went off for the autumn hunt, the sisters for chestnuts and other nuts. We had a hard day. Andrew was told to leave our place, and the day after A. Paulina, and this was told the brethren at morning prayer.

Thursday, 13. Edwards held early service. Nicholas Smaan, who has been four years from the church, came with his wife, Johanna, and three children, John, Beata, and one unbaptized boy, with the view of remaining here. Lately came here also young Joachim's wife, whose family, also on the way hither, are encamped not far off, for the sake of hunting a little. With the children school was again begun, which causes much joy and a new pleasure among them. Indeed, single and married people, who have already had schooling, come to practice reading, having now time for it.

Sunday, 16. At the services many brethren were present, who are hunting in the neighborhood or out for chestnuts and other nuts. Michael preached about the advent of Christ. There was a service for the baptized in

reference to the 13th,[1] which we put off till to-day, so few
brethren were at home. We begged him to acknowledge
us as his people, to make himself known to us, to oppose Satan and all temptations, to interest himself faith-
fully for his flock and to feed us daily on his merits and
sufferings, and to make us people of his own heart, so that
his name might be glorified among the heathen. We
thought also of our absent brethren. We begged forgiveness of all our faults and shortcomings, gave ourselves
anew to his blessed rule, vowed and swore to him fealty
and obedience. In the following service for the married
brethren, the single brother, John Thomas, and the widow,
Cathrine, were married. Meanwhile we made use of the
assistants, since during the week they are not at home,
but off hunting, to speak with some people, and those
baptized, in particular with strangers, who are already a
long time here to no purpose. They were requested to
go farther, so as to make no trouble.

Monday, 17. Edwards held early service. Late in the
evening young Joachim came here with his wife and children, to remain. The next day quarters were found for
them, as likewise for Nicholas Smaan's family; with him
the assistants spoke yesterday, and having heard he was
an Indian captain, and so he must go to the treaty as part
of his duty, the brothers told him he should go, and if he
remained of this mind and persisted in living with the
church, he should give up his office, so that he might not
be burdened in the church with Indian affairs, and have
an unblessed, unsatisfactory life, and this he promised to
do. He then went away with Gelelemend to the treaty, but
both left their wives and children here. This Smaan was
a captain under the chief, Welandawecken, so that we cannot wonder that he sent us an invitation to settle at the
Fork of the Miami, for he sees that the Indians will come
to us. This very message the counsellor, called the Big
Cat, was to bring here, but as they got news that we had

---

[1] When "The Brethren's Church calls to mind the important truth
that the Lord Jesus is the Chief Shepherd and Head of the Church."

a message from the Tawa chief, who has established us
here, he refused to be the messenger, saying it would be
in vain and to no purpose, that we would not accept it,
whereupon the chief got another messenger, who knew
nothing about the thing; he brought us the message and
got the proper answer.

Wednesday, 19. A Frenchman, accustomed to go about
among the Indians, came here, bag and baggage, and
wanted to quarter himself upon us unasked and unan-
nounced, for he saw a large town here, and gave out he
wished to work for pay for the Indians, and as he was unwilling to be persuaded to go away, we were forced to put
him with all his effects into a canoe and take him away.

Thursday, 20. From Sandusky came old Maria Elizabeth and Sophia, Jacob Gendaskund's[1] only surviving
daughter, for the first time, who is married, and they constantly attended the services. Several strangers have lately
been here visiting, among whom is found at times bad ma-
terial, who give us trouble and have to be well watched,
that they may do no harm, for freedom in the Indian land
has often bad results and makes it hard. An unbaptized,
large boy, Cook's step-son, came to Br. David weeping,
and upon being asked what ailed him, he replied that his
step-brother, a savage, had burnt his a b c board, and said
that if he gave himself up to this he would be a good-
for-nothing man, a worthless fellow, and had scolded him;
he had complained about this among the brethren, and yesterday cried the whole evening about it. He said that if
his step-father went from the church he would not stay
with him, he would not leave the church. Br. David con-
soled him and promised to give him a book in lieu of the
a b c board, for he had perfectly learned his alphabet in
three or four days, and was already beginning to spell, for
if Indian children desire any thing they apply themselves
to it day and night, and become not weary.

Sunday, 23. Br. David preached about the wise and the

---

[1] He had been baptized in 1770.

foolish virgins, and Edwards held the congregation meeting. Several brethren came from their hunting-camp.

Tuesday, 25. Edwards held early service. Yesterday the brethren were all away for the autumn hunt.

Wednesday, 26. The first touch of snow fell.

Sunday, 30. Edwards preached about the coming of the Saviour into the flesh, and David held the children's service upon the same subject, exhorting the children to joy over the Saviour's birth, who thereby brought both them and us much good.

Monday, Dec. 1. Strangers came here for a visit, among them A. Salome. Old Maria Elizabeth came, and in tears spoke out her heart and longing for comfort from the Saviour.

Thursday, 4. The people, especially the sisters, for hardly any brothers were at home, got wood for us. In the afternoon, toward evening, the brothers, Samuel, Stephen, Thomas, and Tobias, came back from the Muskingum, but could not await the treaty, for the nations, encamped sixty miles from the Fort, will not come, and the affair may yet be long protracted. They came back thus without accomplishing any thing, but meanwhile had met there Br. Heckewelder and Matthias Blickensderfer, (a surveyor), and spoken with them. We now got by them the letters and journals from Bethlehem.

Tuesday, 5. In the morning service the greetings from the church were given to the brethren.

Sunday, 7. David preached about the promise made to the brethren in olden times by the prophets. Some brethren had come from their hunting-camp. Br. Edwards held the congregation meeting.

Tuesday, 9. Indians came from Sandusky here. A large boy, who has lost his parents, came to Br. David and begged to live here. Upon being asked why, he replied that he was pleased here, and did not like to be among the savages. When he was told how he would have to conduct himself here, and that we must first know where he could live, which had already been said to him,

he answered he would like to go to school, which meanwhile Br. David permitted, till he should be received.

Thursday, 11. Ignatius came with two white people, on
their way from Pittsburg to Detroit. They came to him,
where he was encamped, hunting, and were four weeks on
their journey. A family was still behind from want of
horses, for they had lost theirs, and they went the day
after to bring them in. We heard, at the same time, that
the Chippewa, who is mentioned under Sept. 28th, and
had consulted the brethren about his salvation, had been
burnt while hunting by an explosion of powder, so that
he will hardly recover.

Saturday, 13. In the assistants' conference we considered about old Maria Elizabeth and the boy who had announced his wish to live here. The former was received
and provided with shelter, but about the latter, we found
trouble, for we did not know where he would be under
oversight. On this occasion the assistants were plainly
told what our plan is in regard to the reception of strange
Indians. In the first place, but chiefly, if any of our
baptized return to us, who belong to us, but for various
reasons have been separated from us, we were bound to
take them, to establish them again, and help them to the
right way; secondly, if savages or children came, asking
for reception, we were bound in duty to help all, and to
seek to bring them to the Saviour, for his blood bought
souls. Thereby now we are always getting more labor,
many times want, also, care and trouble, but to make it
more easy and comfortable for ourselves, we must not refuse people without sufficient grounds and send them
away, even though they were seducers, who did harm in
the church. This admonition was needful, for it has happened that people have been received whom we either had
to send away, as they did not behave according to our
rules, or they have themselves gone away, and now some
had come to the disposition to receive none, or only such
of whom we had proof that they would thrive. Over
this matter the assistants afterwards talked with one

another by themselves, and discussed it, and it was well
approved.

Sunday, 14. Br. Michael preached. In the communion
quarter-hour Br. David announced the Lord's supper for
next Saturday, and held the congregation meeting.

Wednesday, 17. John Leeth came back from the Fort
with his wife, having visited her friends twenty-five miles
from Pittsburg. Her own sister, who yet knew her, for
they had both been captured by Indians, knew her still,
but had not known whether she was still living, the greater
therefore was her joy when she saw Elizabeth,[1] so that for
a quarter of an hour she could speak not a word. She
and her husband had yet something to pass through, for
they were strongly urged by their friends to remain there,
but this they refused to do. They were both very glad to
be with us again, as if something had been given them,
they knew not what. David held early service.

Thursday, 18. Edwards held early service. A Mingo
came here at night from the Muskingum, from whom we
learned that the nations were at last gone to the treaty,
and that we should soon hear something thence. Several of our Indians also came home from the autumn
hunt.

Saturday, 20. After the brethren had been spoken to
the preceding days, whereto the Saviour gave especial
grace, so that all trouble, which had arisen, was allayed,
and only one person remained away, the communicants
enjoyed his body and blood in the holy sacrament in the
most blessed way. A sister, Betsy Leeth, was a partaker
for the first time, and Boaz was a candidate. Two brothers, Thomas and Ignatius, were readmitted after receiving
absolution.

Sunday, 21. After the communion liturgy, Br. Edwards preached from the Epistle: Rejoice in the Lord alway, and David held the congregation meeting from the

[1] Butterfield, in his edition of Leeth's Narrative, Robert Clarke &
Co., 1883, p. 42, says: "From the descendents of Leith, I learn that
this young woman's name was Sally Lowrey." See note, p. 299. Under
Dec. 20, following. Zeisberger names her "Betsy Leeth."

Scripture-verse and text, whereby he laid before the brethren the example with Thomas, and said that if a heart begins to see and recognize the boundless love of the Saviour, it is aroused to call out with wonder and astonishment: My Lord and my God.

Monday, 22. Much was discoursed to the children, the large boys and girls, about putting aside what was unbecoming, for many new people come here, who do not yet rightly understand—for example, finger-rings—and they are hung with silver bells, coral, and wampum, which is indeed usual among savages, but is unsuitable for our children, being not savages at all, but belonging to the church of believers.

Tuesday, 23. The great boys and girls got wood ready for the school-house, in which the brethren helped them and went with them, for it is a pleasure to them that their children so industriously learn, most of those who began their a b c's now beginning to spell.

Wednesday, 24. Christmas Eve began with a love-feast. We were joyful and thankful for the Saviour's holy birth and incarnation, which we considered, and to the Infant in his stall and manger we brought our thank-offerings and we sang, at which all present were much affected, for the little Jesus [our heart's delight] made himself known to his little band here, gathered from the heathen, very graciously, of which the tears on many a cheek bore witness. At last we kneeled before the manger and brought him our hearty thanks for his astonishingly great love, which he showed for us, and also especially for this, that he had it made known and assured to us by his blood, and had given us understanding and also enlightened our hearts by his Holy Spirit. At the end candles were distributed to the children, and they were told how the wise virgins went to the Saviour with trimmed and burning hearts, whereupon they all went joyfully home. At this strangers were present and also a Mingo, who had asked to be present at the Christmas Eve services, and was very attentive, to whom the brethren had already made the Saviour known, what he had done for us and for all nations, and now it only depended upon this, that they should receive and believe it, if they wished to be saved.

Thursday, 25. Michael preached from the Gospel, Luke, ii. Then the children had a service, singing joyfully and humbly the Infant Jesus in the manger. In the following service, after a discourse upon the day's text: He is not ashamed to call them brethren, Gustit, a single woman, was baptized into Jesus' death with the name Rahel, which not only made great excitement among our unbaptized, but also among the strangers, who, to have a good view, stood up on the benches, for they sat in the back part of the room. Hereby we made to ourselves the remark that all sorts of people and nations listen here to the Gospel, that nowhere is it less preached in vain than here, for it is worth the trouble, that to the poor, blind Indians, who know not that they have a Saviour, this should be preached, and if we do not at once see the fruits thereof and harvest them, we can certainly reckon upon this, that the fruit will not be wanting.

Saturday, 27. David spoke plainly with J. Cook's son, who has sold his wife to the French trader for goods received, and had to keep away during the holidays, whose father induced him thereto.

Sunday, 28. David preached from Gal. iv, 4: But when the fulness of time was come, God sent forth his son, etc., and Edwards held the congregation meeting from the day's Scripture-verse.

Monday, 29. Michael held early service. When hitherto we had heard nothing about the treaty [1] with the Indians, to-day we had the unplesant news by an Indian from Sandusky that they were all gone back home, having done nothing, since the Mingoes, during their stay there, were all the time murdering, and thus no peace could be. Of this we heard,

Tuesday, 30, yet more by a white man from Sandusky, that some of the Wyandots and others besides, such as Brant and the Mingoes, were come back; that the Indians

_____
[1] This treaty was made early the next year.

generally are very anxious, and the chiefs say that if many perish not now by the sword, many must die of hunger, for they have nothing to live on and would not be able to plant; that.Pipe, with Wyandots, Delawares, some Tawas and Chippewas, also Mingoes, had gone to Fort Harmar, about a hundred, and they were not yet come back.

Wednesday, 31. We assembled about eleven o'clock for the close of the year, having first a love-feast. We called to mind the great kindness and mercy enjoyed from our dear Lord this year, and encouraged one another to give him praise and thanksgiving therefor. We find also at the end of this year manifold causes to be grateful and thankful, for he always does better and more blessedly in all cases than we can hope or expect. We asked his forgiveness of all our faults and shortcomings and for his acknowledgment of us, his poor and wretched creatures. We thanked him in particular for the outward quiet he had lent us this year during our course here below, and we commended ourselves farther to the protection and oversight of our dear Father in Heaven, especially as we again find ourselves in uncertain circumstances, not knowing whether we must soon again take the pilgrim's staff in our hands and wander away, where the Saviour, our only refuge, conducts us, not after one or another particular way and manner, and guides us for our good, and should it happen, as appears probable, we know not at all whither we shall retire to find for ourselves a place of refuge.

In outward affairs our heavenly Father has blessed us, has given us bread and maintenance, by richly blessing our fields, though in spring and summer there was much want and hunger among our brethren, and though hunting was bad, and they could get little thereby, yet we must wonder how they got clothing, so that they always have it in their need, and go about better clad than the savages, who have some silver hanging in their ears, their noses, and about their necks [which is their grand array], but otherwise are almost naked and quite poor. All the Indians who come to us are then in perfect poverty, have neither food nor clothing, and in their hearts nothing to make them contented and happy, and are thus equally poor in body and in soul.

The chief thing which gives us joy and courage is this, that the Gospel of Jesus, our Saviour, his incarnation, passion, and death for us and for all the world, is not preached in vain; we see that it always finds hearts and ears. It opens the hearts and ears of the dead and blind heathen, and brings to them life and feeling. Ah, may he still give us peace! This would contribute to him and his affair, for if there be war, the Indians have no time to think about them, the yearning for murder leaves them no time for them. The festivals, Easter, Whitsunday, Christmas, etc., were noticeable and always accompanied with great blessing.

Baptized, six adults and six children. Received into the church, eight. The holy communion we had eight times, whereto came two. Married, were three couples. Came to the church, forty-six persons. Died, four, namely, Schebosh, Joseph, Lea, and a child, Ephraim.

There live here—

31 married couples	62
Single men	11
Single women	7
Widowers	9
Widows	1
Big boys	11
Big girls	14
Little boys	27
Little girls	22
Total	164

Among them one hundred and thirty-two baptized [and of these forty-nine are communion brethren], forty-one more than at the close of last year. We have been forced to send away five, namely, A. Salome, Andrew, Anna Pauline, Jeremy; John Martin went away of his own accord

END OF VOL. I.